THE ADVENTURES OF
LAZARUS GRAY ™

BY BARRY REESE

To Chris:
Happy Reading!

Barry Reese

THE ADVENTURES OF LAZARUS GRAY
A Pro Se Press Publication

Front Cover Illustration by Anthony Castrillo
Back Cover and Interior Illustrations by George Sellas.
Titles, Logos, Supplimental Graphics, and Production Design by Sean E. Ali

Edited by Tommy Hancock

Pro Se Productions, LLC
133 1/2 Broad Street
Batesville, AR, 72501
870-834-4022
proseproductions@earthlink.net
http://www.proseproductions.com

THE ADVENTURES OF
LAZARUS
GRAY ™

THE ADVENTURES OF LAZARUS GRAY™

TABLE OF CONTENTS

THE SOVEREIGN
CITY PROJECT ™

MYTHS, MYSTERIES, MONSTERS, AND MEN
HOW BARRY REESE SET THE CORNERSTONE FOR SOVEREIGN CITY
By Tommy Hancock

Everyone knows you can't build a city in a day, right? No need to dust off the tired adage and discuss Rome is there? Good.
Even though construction takes some time, a city and all that goes with it can actually be birthed in a lot less than a day. In the space of three or four emails, to be precise.

The Sovereign City Project, the first collected volume of which you now hold in your hands, was a simple concept in its complexity. I have the honor of planting the seed in the fertile minds of two of the best New Pulp Authors I know, of having a shared city where each of us wrote a character that was the central part of our individual stories while that character resided in Sovereign with whatever the other two also created. As already stated, these weren't just any two authors. Barry Reese and Derrick Ferguson brought not only mad creative and writing skills to the Project, but also decidedly different viewpoints on where their characters would come from and most definitely where they and Sovereign City itself would go. I was more than glad to be the third conspirator in this plot to create a fantastic world of New Pulp fiction.

With authors in place, Sovereign itself had to come into some sort of existence, even if it was in the abstract initially. That came rather quickly as well, the name and the origin of the city all tied together, as it should be. The founders of this settlement (Both the actual three authors that created it and the fictional fathers we decided founded it) wanted it to be the ideal

American city. To have everything every other city had all in one place, so it would have a waterfront and there would be mountains nearby as well as flat farmland on the other side of town, etc. and so forth. Essentially, Sovereign City sprouted up in the most perfect place in the United States for an all purpose City. Our imaginations.

Obviously the next step in the process of breathing the life of words and images into Sovereign City would be populating the world with its good and bad, its movers and shakers, the characters that would be the axis the entire Project turned on. I came to the idea with a character already conceived, Doc Daye-The 24 Hour Hero. Derrick stepped up and had his own Fortune McCall sail into Sovereign's harbor for action and adventure. And although adventures of each of these stalwart Sovereignites are forthcoming very soon from Pro Se Press, the hero that shines brightest as the most prolific and first to fight for all that is right in the City is a man who wakes up in his first story with no idea who he actually is.

Lazarus Gray is yet another New Pulp character destined to be a classic from the mind and pen of Barry Reese. Known for his 'Rook' universe as well as dabbling in other characters, Barry brings every skill and talent in storytelling, every trick of the trade, every bit of Pulp he has ever exhibited and mixes it wildly together in the form of Lazarus Gray.

Shrouded in a mystery and cloaked in questions, Gray steps off the beach he awakens on and jumps head first into adventure, wrapping himself in the enigmatic aides that make up his Assistance Unlimited. Morgan, Eun, and Samantha, all solid New Pulp creations in their own right, add a depth of emotion to the stoic enigmatic figure that Gray casts in each and every story. Another prominent character that Barry builds a brick and puddle at a time is the City itself. Cast in a veil of crime and corruption, Gray's Sovereign is one that will not survive without a man like him looking out for it. Lastly villains as vile and colorful as any yet to grace a page populate each and every tale, each one more evil and harder to beat than the rest.

What Barry does in this series of stories is truly set the tone for the Sovereign City Project. Quoted often already as saying this character is sort of his homage to the Avenger, Barry goes beyond that, I believe. These seven stories, including one that guest stars Barry's Rook, are more than simple tales of daring do, dying devils, and distressed dames, although they are definitely all that in spades. THE ADVENTURES OF LAZARUS GRAY is a study in evolution, both of character and concept. Barry very carefully lays out a blueprint for Gray and those around him and then just as judiciously adds what is necessary to build on it a bit at a time. The people you meet in the first story are changed and different by the time you finish the last page. They grow, they mature, they succeed, and they fail. And Sovereign City, again a character all its own, goes through exactly the same pains and processes.

Characterization. Evolution. True city and world building. And all the creatures, mad scientists, gun toting thugs, mystical malevolence, and witty banter that anybody could handle. It's all here, providing Sovereign City with just the right building blocks for it to grow even farther. Thanks, Barry.

Really, really cool stuff.

Tommy Hancock
Pro Se Editor in Chief
9/17/11

THE GIRL WITH THE PHANTOM EYES

An Adventure Starring Lazurus Gray
Written by Barry Reese

———— ∞∞ ————

Chapter I
Man on the Beach

Sovereign City, Summer 1933

Lightning tore across the sky, briefly illuminating the gloomy scene below. Sovereign City Harbor was home to more derelict vessels than the average man could count and a pitiful stretch of shoreline did little to improve the look of the place. It was covered with washed-up debris, the dried bones of fish and several dozen broken bottles.

A well-built man lay facedown on the shore, his face turned to the side. A long streak of blood ran from his temple down his cheek and his eyes twitched continuously beneath their lids. He wore black trousers, a ripped white shirt and black loafers. His hair was more gray than brown, making him look older than he was, though a close examination of his features revealed that he was in his late twenties.

Again lightning brightened the beach and a loud crash of thunder seemed to permeate the haze surrounding the man's brain. His eyes opened and he slowly pushed himself to his knees, looking slowly around himself. His breathing was measured and regular, though his jaw was clenched as if he felt some inner pain. With a grunt, he rose to his feet and staggered toward the city, one hand pressed tightly against his side. At least one rib, possibly two, had been broken, though he couldn't remember how it had happened. In fact, he couldn't remember anything at all – he didn't know his own name or how he came to be here. He cast one quick glance back at the choppy waters but saw no nearby boats or ships from which he could have come. The vessels moored in the harbor were surely too far away, he mused.

Another rumble of thunder seemed to rock the ground upon which he walked. He momentarily lost his footing and slipped back to the moist earth. His fingers closed tightly around something as he sought to catch himself, something cold and metallic buried in the dirt. He brought it close to his face, peering through the darkness at it. A rain began to fall then, large drops that cooled his burning flesh.

He was holding a small medallion. A notch on the top indicated that it normally had a cord of some kind that ran through it, allowing its owner to wear it. It depicted a nude human man with an erect penis, bearing a sword in his right hand. His head was that of a roaring lion. On the back of the medallion were two words, a name that had been scratched into the surface with some sharp object: *Lazarus Gray*.

"You okay, pal?"

A policeman was approaching, pointing a flashlight directly at him. "I think so," he answered hoarsely.

"Looks like you took a spill."

"I hit my head while swimming to shore." He wasn't sure why he was lying, why he wasn't telling the policeman that he didn't know who he was or how he'd gotten there... but the lies came easily enough.

The policeman stopped a few feet away him, trailing the flashlight up and down the man's body. "I don't think so, pal."

"What makes you say that?"

"Your clothes ain't wet."

He looked down, cursing himself for not having noticed something so obvious. He slipped the medallion into his pocket and forced a smile. "Would you believe I've been on the beach long enough to have dried out?'

"How about you tell me your name?"

After pausing for a brief second, he uttered another lie and by doing so he unknowingly set himself down a dangerous path. "My name's Lazarus Gray."

The officer's eyes narrowed and he quickly threw a punch at the man who was now calling himself Lazarus. To his own surprise, Lazarus moved aside with practiced ease and threw up his hand to catch the policeman under the chin with a karate chop. He then gripped the man by the shoulder and pulled him close, driving a knee into the officer's stomach. He finished him off with a backhand that sent one of the man's teeth flying from his mouth.

Lazarus stood over the fallen man and realized that he wasn't panting at all. He had reacted automatically, fluidly calling upon skills he hadn't even known he'd possessed. He knelt down and searched the officer's pockets, finding a black leather wallet that contained three dollars in cash, a driver's license in the name of Arthur Redwood and a small photograph of a handsome man with gray-tinged hair, dressed in a tuxedo. Lazarus knew that this was a photo of himself, even though he couldn't recall ever having seen his own face. He pocketed the photograph and stood up, having come to the conclusion that this man was not a police officer at all. Up close, his badge looked fake and there was nothing in his wallet to verify his position with law enforcement. Though he couldn't recall how he would have known this, Lazarus also recognized that the gun in the man's holster was not regulation issue.

Lazarus looked back toward the city and made his decision. He had to get away from here. Answers would come later but for now he had to keep moving. This man had intended to harm him, possibly even kill him. He couldn't take the chance that this man was operating on his own: in fact, something told him that wasn't the case at all. Lazarus stripped the man of his weapon, pushing the barrel of the gun into the front of his slacks. He pulled the tails of his button-down shirt out of his pants and let them hang, obscuring anyone's view of the gun.

Moving with the grace of a jungle cat, Lazarus Gray began to move through the shadows, heading into the bright lights and squalid streets of Sovereign City.

 LAZARUS GRAY
MYSTERIOUS LEADER OF ASSISTANCE UNLIMITED

Chapter II
A Hero For Hire

February 2, 1935

Robeson Avenue had become one of the more famous streets in Sovereign City. The transformation from an unassuming, mostly abandoned locale to one where gossip columnists routinely camped out was the direct result of Lazarus Gray choosing it for his home base. In the months since he had awoken on the beach, he had slowly built a reputation as a man with skills that could prove useful to those in need. He had parlayed incredible knowledge about the workings of the stock market, taking the small amounts of money he earned and transforming it into enough capital to open his own business. Dubbed Assistance Unlimited, this business existed for the sole purpose of helping those in need. Gray charged nothing up front for his services, preferring to be paid when the job was complete. He asked only what the client could afford and not a penny more. With the city reeling under the twin terrors of a stagnant economy and rampant corruption, the papers had seized upon Lazarus Gray as a figure of great interest and one capable of inspiring hope.

Gray had purchased all three of the buildings that lay on Robeson Avenue. The heart of his complex was a three-story structure that had once been a hotel. Gray's three associates used the first floor, while the second had been gutted and converted into one large room that was used for meetings, briefings and research. The third floor was off-limits to everyone but Gray himself and was his private domicile.

Across the street were several storefronts, all of which had closed down at the dawn of the Great Depression. Lazarus had purchased these, ensuring that no one would operate any businesses next to his own set of offices. He had continued to use the name Lazarus Gray for two reasons: the first was that he had no other name to use and the second was that he hoped it would draw out those who might know the truth about him. So far, it had failed to accomplish the latter.

Lazarus Gray had found a measure of peace in helping others, even though his own past was lost to him. Though he was notoriously tight-lipped and rarely showed strong emotion, his aides had come to love him. All of them had come into his employ after themselves being helped by Gray.

Morgan Watts was forty-two years old and pencil-thin. He favored black suits and fedora hats and not even his closest friends had ever seen him without a necktie. He kept his dark hair slicked back and his moustache waxed. Morgan was Gray's liaison with the underworld for he himself had once been a part of the city's mafia. Though he was nominally a free man now, the tentacles of organized crime ran deep and a part of him would always be loyal to his old 'Family.' Those ties paled beside only one thing: his allegiance to Lazarus Gray, who had helped him out of a tight jam that could have cost him his life.

Samantha Grace was the only female in Gray's employ. A stunning blonde whose parents were wealthy philanthropists, Samantha had grown up with every opportunity possible. She could speak five languages fluently, was a champion swimmer and was a veritable encyclopedia on topics as varied as fashion, European history and the socio-political climate of the Orient. Samantha had come into Gray's employ after her father had fallen prey to a blackmail scheme. Lazarus had managed to apprehend the criminal behind the plot, managing to destroy the photographs that could have compromised her family's good name. Admiration for the work that Lazarus performed had led the twenty-year-old into seeking a position with Assistance Unlimited.

The final member of Assistance Unlimited was a Korean named Eun Jiwon. After moving to America with his parents over a decade before, Eun had found his family's fortunes in disarray. His father had opened a small grocery store but when local crooks began to demand protection money, Eun started a covert series of attacks on the criminals. He had been mildly successful for a time, vandalizing their operations and becoming a general nuisance, before they'd finally figured out who was behind it all. Eun's family store had been burned to the ground and his parents murdered. The young man would have thrown away his own life in a vain attempt at revenge had Lazarus Gray not intervened, helping him channel his aggression into a healthier direction. Eun was in his mid-twenties and extremely handsome, though his angry demeanor kept almost everyone at arm's length from him.

As intriguing as those three were, the real attraction at Assistance Unlimited was Lazarus Gray himself. Dressed in gray slacks and a matching shirt that was somewhat reminiscent of a hospital orderly's uniform, the strangely detached man kept a close eye on everything that went on in the city. Those in authority at City Hall alternately feared or welcomed him, depending on how corrupt they had become.

Lazarus was standing in front of the window, scanning the articles on the front page of The Sovereign Gazette. He was in the expansive room that spanned the entire second floor of his headquarters and the sun that shone in through the glass left a tiny rainbow across his cheek. It was just a few minutes past nine in the morning and it was expected to be another wet day in the city. It had rained off and on for nearly six days in a row and the weathermen were predicting a lot more of the wet stuff before the city could dry itself off.

Lazarus was reading about a series of brutal slayings that took place in the downtown area, several of which had been attributed to men working in the service to The Monster. The so-called Monster was someone that had yet to cross paths with Lazarus but from all that he'd heard, The Monster was an increasingly powerful figure in the Sovereign underworld.

"Good morning, Samantha. Is there trouble?" Lazarus said these things without looking up from his paper and he stopped the pretty young Miss Grace in her tracks.

Regaining her composure, Samantha smoothed out her skirt and stepped up close to her employer. "It always throws me for a loop how you do that. I was trying to be quiet that time."

"You would have successfully snuck up on almost anyone on earth," Lazarus said, folding up the newspaper and tossing it onto a nearby tabletop.

"But not you."

A faint ghost of a smile appeared on Gray's lips but it vanished so quickly that Samantha wasn't sure it had really been there at all. "You were coming to tell me about the gentleman in the rain slicker."

Samantha crossed her arms and tilted her head slightly. "How in the world did you know that?"

"The window. I was standing in front of it and saw a man approaching our building before I started reading the paper. He looked appropriately dressed for the weather."

"His name is Peter Scanlon and he says it's urgent. Something about a missing girl."

"Has he tried the police?"

"Yes. But they think he should be sent to the loony bin, apparently."

"And why is that?"

"The girl he's looking for – she has glowing eyes."

Peter Scanlon was on the first floor, in a small room set aside for potential clients. Its walls were painted a soothing shade of blue and a fresh arrangement of flowers was in a vase by the door. Morgan Watts was keeping

Scanlon company, leaning against one of the walls and watching the little man fidget nervously. Scanlon had refused to give up his rain slicker upon entering, preferring to keep it on. He was slightly paunchy in the way that middle-aged men tend to get and his head was covered by a few thin wisps of hair, combed over in a vain attempt at maintaining the semblance of youth. He wore thick glasses and was constantly pushing them up the bridge of his nose.

"Sure you don't want some coffee, buddy?"

Scanlon frowned and shook his head. "I told you I didn't. Why do you keep asking me that?"

"You're acting more nervous than a bride on her wedding night. If the coffee won't settle you, I have some stronger stuff in the back."

Scanlon seemed to be considering the offer when the door opened and Gray stepped in. Samantha was right behind him and she glanced quickly at Morgan, shaking her head. Morgan smirked, knowing what it meant: she'd bet him three dollars that she'd be able to sneak up on Gray this time.

Gray pulled up a chair and sat down across from Scanlon, ignoring the slightly fearful look that he received. Gray's eyes were mismatched: one was emerald green, the other dusky brown. They seemed to burn with some sort of awful inner fire, as if there was a bottomless well of fury lurking within his placid expression. "Tell me why you're here, Mr. Scanlon."

"Didn't the girl tell you?"

"Miss Grace told me some of it but I'd like to hear it from you, in your own words."

"I have money," Scanlon began but he stopped when Gray's eyes narrowed ever so slightly.

"We can discuss my fee at a later time. Right now, I'm concerned only with the reasons behind your visit."

Scanlon nodded, looking away. Without having the full force of Gray's stare on him, he seemed to relax. After taking a deep breath, he pushed his glasses up the bridge of his nose and began speaking in low and somewhat embarrassed tones. "I don't have a particularly glamorous life, Mr. Gray. Nothing like yours, to be sure. I repair typewriters for a living. I work for a Mr. Steinberg, down on 42nd street. He's a good man and he pays well for the work. I like it but it's awful lonely sometimes. It's just me at home, you see. I've never married and haven't really come very close." Scanlon looked up quickly and his cheeks reddened when he realized that Samantha was still in the room. She gave him a reassuring smile that seemed to say that she wasn't judging him, nor did she pity his state. "A week ago I stopped by O'Malley's Pub for a drink after work. It was a Tuesday night and the place was mostly empty, except for a few regulars."

"Are you a regular, Mr. Scanlon?" Morgan asked, taking a pipe out from the inside of his jacket. He lit it with a match and had just begun puffing away when Scanlon answered in the affirmative.

"I don't go every night but often enough, I suppose. Well, there was one person there who most definitely wasn't a regular. It was a girl, about twenty-five I'd say and so lovely that my heart broke just looking at her. She was wearing a white dress that ended just above her knees, white high-heeled pumps and she had a flower in her raven-black hair." Scanlon's voice had acquired a dreamy air to it and Morgan was barely able to stifle a snort. Samantha motioned for him to stop, but it was obvious that she was amused as well. "Anyway, I took my usual seat and didn't approach her. She was out of my league and I knew it. So you can imagine my surprise when I heard her angel's voice from next to my shoulder, asking if she could sit with me. I stammered a yes and tried not to look too eager. She sat down next to me and I could smell her perfume. It was like fresh rose petals."

Morgan cleared his throat. "I think I can sense where this might be going. This dame of yours… was she a working girl?"

Scanlon's mouth fell open and he looked like he might rise up and walk out. "Heavens no! Where on Earth did you get that idea? She wasn't like that. Not at all, sir!"

"Please continue." Gray spoke softly but the tone was so commanding that Scanlon at once gave a nod and resumed his story.

"I could tell right away that she was sad about something. She looked like she'd been crying. I tried to make small talk with her but she was obviously too upset. She said she just wanted to be near me, that I made her feel safe. I bought her a couple of drinks but she barely touched either one. When I realized it was getting late, I told her I had to go and she asked me if I'd walk with her to get a cab."

"And she never told you her name?" Samantha asked.

"No. I didn't ask, though. I didn't even realize I hadn't until… well, later." Scanlon cleared his throat and brushed his glasses back up over the bridge of his nose. "It was raining outside so I took off my jacket and held it over her head. She said it was gallant of me and I felt her touch my chest, kind of pulling me to her. I was just a little taller than her and so I was looking down at her. It was obvious she wanted me to kiss her. I was going to do it, too, but that's when I saw her eyes." He reached out suddenly and gripped Lazarus by the sleeve. "They were glowing. It was kind of an ice blue color and her pupils seemed to vanish as I was looking at them. Her eyes were just empty, with that strange glow. It was the most beautiful and terrifying thing I've ever seen in my life. Is that possible? To be attracted and repulsed by something simultaneously?"

"I see it all the time," Morgan whispered.

"Yeah. In the mirror every morning." Samantha winked as she said the words, continuing the teasing that was part and parcel of their friendship.

Scanlon licked his lips. "I'll take that drink now, if you don't mind. Water will do."

Morgan sprang into action, leaving the room and returning a moment later with a glass full of tap water. "There you go," he said with a grin.

Scanlon downed the drink in two quick sips. He waved away Morgan when the thin man reached for the glass to offer a refill. "I was going to kiss her anyway. Even with the glowing eyes. I mean, I know it sounds awful, but the chance to hold a girl like that overwhelmed any fears I had about her eyes."

"And what happened?" Gray prompted.

"I don't know. I blacked out or something. The next thing I knew, I was lying on my back, with a tingling in my forehead. Two men in suits were dragging the girl away from me. They were shoving her into the backseat of a sedan. A third man was behind the wheel. She was screaming for me to help her but I couldn't think straight. By the time I was on my feet, they were gone, the car turning the corner at the end of the street."

Morgan looked at Gray. "One of those boys must have clocked him from behind. That's why he can't remember anything. And his head was buzzing from a concussion."

Lazarus stroked his chin but said nothing.

Scanlon rapped his knuckles on the table. "I do remember something else, though. I memorized the license plate number of that car. It was 30-T46."

"That could prove most useful," Gray said. He didn't bother writing the number down and his aides weren't surprised. His mind was like a steel trap, capable of storing even the most trivial of data. "Did you receive medical treatment after this event?"

"I did. The docs at the hospital said I was fine. No trace of a concussion," he added, looking directly at Morgan. "But they did say something really strange. They said I was in a dangerous state of dehydration. I think they thought I was nuts when I told them that was impossible. Of course, the looks I got from the cops were even worse. I told them everything, thinking some of it might be important, but as soon I got to those phantom eyes of hers, they tuned me out."

"Phantom eyes," Gray repeated. "An interesting turn of phrase." He stood up and made for the door, speaking over his shoulder. "I'll look into this. Please leave your address and a phone number where you can be reached with my associates."

Scanlon rose, looking surprised but pleased. "I really hope he can find her," he said to Samantha. "She was so pretty and she said I made her feel safe. I can't stop feeling guilty over letting those brutes take her away."

Samantha took him by the elbow. "If there's anyone in Sovereign City who can find her, it's Mr. Gray. You can count on that."

Morgan watched the pretty young girl lead the man from the room, soothing him with her confidence. He was glad she felt so positive about this one because he was anything but. The whole story sounded crazy, from the part where a pretty girl would put the moves on a guy like Scanlon to the part where her eyes turned into glowing spotlights. Still, if the boss thought there was something to it, Morgan would jump in with both feet. Lazarus Gray had earned that level of trust and then some.

———∞∞∞———

The leader of Assistance Unlimited rode the elevator to the third floor. Only one lift in the entire building had access to his private quarters and that one required a key to operate. Once he was alone in his quarters, Gray stepped into his bathroom and stared at himself in the mirror. As always, the face that stared back at him was virtually a stranger's. He recognized the contours of the features from having lived with him the past eighteen months but he still lacked a connection to them. It was like he was living in someone else's body.

Phantom eyes, Scanlon had said. Something about those words seemed to trigger a residual memory in Gray, sparking things that he had forgotten until this day. They were images from another life, from before he'd woken on the beach.

He was in a temple in Tibet, hiding in the shadows. A nude young girl was bound to an altar, her screams stifled by a strip of cloth jammed into her mouth. Standing in a semicircle around her were six men, dressed in dark robes. One of them wore a ram's skull over his head, its horns curling to the sky. Two burning braziers were the only illumination in the room and the light danced off the curved blade the man in the horned helm held over the girl. The blade was raised and in that moment, Lazarus thought that the man's eyes had taken on a strange cast, as if they were glowing from within. It was like some dread phantasm had entered the man's body and the only sign of it was through those eyes, the portals to his soul.

Why had he been there? Was he taking part in this awful ceremony? Or was he there to stop it? He didn't remember what became of the girl but he felt certain she was dead now.

Lazarus shook away the memory, suddenly feeling damp with sweat. "Who am I?" he asked aloud.

As always, there was no answer.

———∞∞∞———

Chapter III
A Trail of Blood

"I'll be damned if I know why a man like Gray would hire a chink."

"Keep your voice down. He might hear you."

Eun Jiwon maintained a forced look of placidity but he was quite aware of every word that was being said. The two female file clerks were in an adjoining room, looking up the information he'd requested. He was dressed smartly in a dark suit, white shirt and tie. With some people, it helped to appear as Western as possible. For others, though, it only accentuated the fact that he was a foreigner.

The woman who had called him by the racial slur returned with a slip of paper in her hand. She gazed at him from over her horn-rimmed glasses and the set of her lips made it appear she had just taken a bite of a sour apple. "I was able to find out who that license plate belongs to," she began. "But I'm afraid I'm going to have to ask for verification that you're getting this for Mr. Gray. We don't give this sort of thing out to just anyone."

Eun's eyes must have betrayed his irritation because the woman drew back slightly. "I gave you the signed request from Lazarus. If that's not good enough for you, perhaps you should pick up the phone and call him? I'm sure he's not doing anything more important right now than talking to a filing clerk."

The stinging rebuke had the intended effect and the woman simply shoved the paper at Eun, quickly turning away with a harrumph. Eun looked at the words printed on the sheet, identifying the owner of the car as a Jonathan Nero. He tapped the name quickly. "Are you sure about this?"

The woman looked back at him, disdain pouring from her. "Quite. I may only be a filing clerk, but I know how to look things up. Or do you need me to read it for you? I know some of you boys have trouble with English."

Eun bit back the reply that threatened to erupt from him. He could speak and write fluently, almost undoubtedly much more impressively than this woman. But he knew that Mr. Gray would be upset with him if he made a scene. He simply wrote down all the information that was on the paper and left the original on the counter. He hurried from city hall, offering a few brief nods of his head to the people he recognized in passing. Working for Lazarus Gray meant that Eun often came into contact with the people of power in Sovereign City. This was both good and bad. For every one honest cop or upstanding city councilman, there were three more that were crooked.

Eun walked to a black roadster parked outside and slid easily into the passenger side seat. Gray was behind the wheel, looking as still and quiet as a statue. "The car belongs to Jonathan Nero."

If Eun had been expecting his employer to show surprise, he was disappointed. Gray simply nodded, his eyes narrowing only slightly. Nero was a very wealthy man, owning a large number of tenement buildings in the city. By all rights, he should have had most of his real estate condemned. But being one of the chief contributors to the mayor's coffers never hurt.

"We should go and talk to him," Gray said, shifting the car into drive. He pulled out onto the streets and began directing his vehicle smoothly through the traffic. It was midday, just a few hours since Scanlon had visited Assistance Unlimited. The streets were glistening with wetness, evidence of a shower that had just passed through. Thick clouds of pollution hung over the city, combining with the rain to evoke memories of London in Gray's mind. He didn't recall when he'd visited the city but he was certain that he had. A vague ache in his heart made him think that he had lost someone there.

"Chief?"

Gray realized that Eun had been waiting for him to respond to something. "Sorry. My mind was wandering."

"Thinking about the case?"

"Yes," Gray said, thinking once again how easily lies sometimes came to him. "What were you saying?"

"I'm not sure it's wise to just drop in on a man like Nero. There are already folks who think you're given too much freedom to move about. If Nero thinks you're pressuring him, he could go to the mayor and have the screws tightened on you."

"I'm not afraid of that."

Eun looked out his window and waited a moment before speaking again. "What does scare you, Chief?"

"What do you mean?"

"We've all heard you cry out at night, like you're having the worst kind of nightmares. Samantha and Morgan both say we shouldn't mention it, that you're entitled to your privacy. But I think we're family now, whether we want to admit it or not. And if something's eating away at you, we should know about it. So we can help make it better."

Gray slowed the car to a stop in front of a house that could only be described as a mansion. A large stone privacy fence surrounded the property with wrought iron gates preventing unwanted access. "Eun, I appreciate what you're saying. But there are reasons why I keep certain things to myself."

"Like anything to do with your past? None of us know where you come from or what you did before you opened up Assistance Unlimited. It's strange sometimes, realizing how little we know about you."

"Do you trust me?"

Eun turned to stare at Gray. "Of course I do. With my life."

"Then allow me this. When I feel I can tell you more, I will. I'm not deliberately keeping things from you. To be honest, you know almost as much about me as I do. Lazarus Gray is probably not my name."

"I don't understand."

"I'm an amnesiac. I woke up here in Sovereign City back in '33."

"Why didn't you tell us?"

"I'm not sure. I seem to instinctively try to limit how much others know about me. One reason for my attempts at staying in the public eye was to draw out anyone who might know something about me." Gray hesitated. "Let's keep this between us for now."

"You don't want me to mention it to the others?"

"I'd prefer you didn't. It's not a matter of trust. It's... I'm not sure what it is. But I feel it's better to keep the truth about me as quiet as possible."

Eun frowned, not liking the idea of keeping secrets from his friends. But he felt honored that Gray had shared this with him and so he simply nodded, agreeing to the request.

Together, the two men exited the vehicle and approached the gate. Before they reached it, a broad-shouldered man in a dark suit appeared on the other side. A bulge in his jacket made it clear that he was armed and something about his manner indicated he wouldn't hesitate to use his weapon.

"Can I help you gentlemen?" he asked, in a voice that was a little higher than would have been expected.

"My name's Lazarus Gray. I need to speak to Mr. Nero."

"About what?"

"That's private business between he and I."

"Mr. Nero's not seeing anybody today." The man adjusted his coat and seemed disturbed by something. "You can leave your card if you want."

Gray's eyes narrowed, watching the man closely. He was an expert at analyzing body language and he was picking up telltale signs that this brute was not only hiding something, he was afraid. The rapid blinking, the slight hint of perspiration on the upper lip and the fidgeting with his coat all added together as evidence. "Mr. Nero is here, isn't he?"

"Yeah but like I said, he's not seeing anyone." The front door of the house opened then and a second man emerged. He was slender and sported a blond moustache. In his left hand, he was clutching a black medical bag.

"Louie!" the doctor yelled. "We need to talk."

"Wait here," Louie said, turning his back on Gray so he could find out what the second man wanted.

Lazarus sprang into action. He took one step back and then flung himself at the gate, latching on with a steely grip. He pulled himself up and over quickly, dropping to his feet before the men on the other side of the gate had even realized what was happening. Louie spun about and muttered a curse, raising a fist. Gray caught it in midair and, in an amazing display of strength, applied so much pressure that the big man fell to one knee, groaning.

"I'm going to let you go," Gray said. "And you're going to open the gate so my friend can come. And then," he added, looking up at the doctor, who was watching him with mouth agape, "We're all going to talk."

The doctor nodded. "Louie, do as he says. We don't have time for this nonsense."

Louie glared at Grey as he got back to his feet, muttering under his breath as he went to open the gate for Eun.

The doctor stepped forward and offered a hand. "Doc Barrington. I recognize you from the papers, Mr. Gray."

"Is something wrong with Mr. Nero?"

Barrington looked over at Louie and obviously made a decision to share information with Gray. "He's sick, deathly so. There's nothing I can do for him here. He has to be taken to a hospital or he won't last through the day."

"May I see him?"

Barrington consented, knowing the many stories that swirled around Lazarus Gray. It was said the man had once performed delicate heart surgery in the middle of a filthy alleyway, using only a pocketknife. Louie followed right on their heels, glaring at Eun the whole way.

"What's the problem, big fella?" Eun chided. "Jealous that I'm better dressed than you?"

"Shaddup," Louie muttered. "None of you guys are supposed to be in here. Mr. Nero's gonna get my goat for this."

"I'm afraid your employer isn't in the position to terrorize anyone right now," Barrington said. The doctor led them through an impressive home, furnished so expensively that it crossed the line from opulence to garishness. As they neared the room where Nero was resting, an unpleasant odor filled the air. It was reminiscent of spoiled meat and Eun had to raise a hand over his face to keep from gagging. He noticed that Louie came to a halt, well away from the door. If the smell bothered Barrington or Gray, neither man gave any sign of it.

Nero was sitting up in a chair, a blanket covering his legs. A window near him was opened, letting in what passed for fresh air in Sovereign. Gray had seen numerous pictures of Nero and the man before him only bore a passing resemblance to him. Nero looked thin and emaciated, the skin drawn taut against his skeleton. He wore a robe that hung loosely from him, evidence of how much weight he had lost.

"How long has he been like this?" Gray asked.

"He came in for an appointment two weeks ago and was perfectly fine. But yesterday I got the call that he was sick. I found him like this. Both he and Louie assure me that he's been eating and drinking but he continues to waste away. He's lost seven pounds since last night. It's like he's just drying up before my eyes."

Lazarus noticed that Eun straightened at the doctor's words. Scanlon had reported similar symptoms after his encounter with the phantom-eyed girl. Given the fact that a car registered to Nero had been seen with the girl in tow, this seemed confirmation that Nero had come into contact with her.

Gray approached Nero and pulled up a chair so that he could examine him. Nero's eyes were sunken orbs and there was a general air of malaise about him. Gray suspected that not even a state-of-the-art hospital would be able to save the man at this point. Soon, organ failure would be setting in. "Mr. Nero. I need to ask you about a girl."

Barrington looked confused but Eun placed a hand on his arm and gestured for silence. Louie was still outside the room, as if being near his employer in this state was too much for him.

"A week ago," Gray continued, "a young woman was kidnapped outside a tavern here. The man who had been with her says that she was quite beautiful but that her eyes possessed unusual properties: he described them as phantom eyes. The car she was bundled into belongs to you. Do you know her?"

Nero took a deep, rattling breath and slowly nodded his head. "They took her. I was trying to help her but they won't let her go. Not after all the money they spent on her eyes."

"Who are they?"

Nero licked his lips and his eyes fixed on something past Gray's shoulder. His voice sounded paper-thin. "She was such a lovely thing growing up. I loved her with all my heart but I put such pressure on her. I'd wanted a son, you see. And nothing she did was ever quite going to make up for the lack of a son."

Gray turned his head, his eyes finding the object that was holding Nero's attention. There was a photograph on the wall of a gorgeous young woman, wearing a white skirt and a violet blouse. She was hanging on the arm of Jonathan Nero, a bright smile on her face. "She's your daughter?"

"Yes. Her name is Wilma."

Gray reached out and squeezed Nero's hand, feeling the bones under the shifting flesh. "Tell me who has your daughter."

"She's with Doc Pemberley and his gang."

Eun gasped. Pemberley was a discredited scientist who had been busted for conducting experiments on vagrants and runaways. The man sometimes sold his services to various mob bosses as well, creating gases and weapons that aided them in their nefarious exploits. Gray had finally brought the man to justice about six months ago but Pemberley had gotten off on a technicality. He'd fled the city in the aftermath and, until now, Eun hadn't known he'd returned. The young Korean looked over at his employer but, as usual, Gray had his poker face on and was revealing nothing of his own thoughts.

"Please tell me more," Gray pressed.

Nero groaned, prompting Barrington to say, "I don't think this is wise. He's far too weak. He needs to be in a hospital."

He's going to die," Gray said firmly. He saw no surprise in Nero's eyes at that proclamation. The poor man knew this to be fact. He could feel it, after all. "Before he passes, let him help me save his daughter."

"She fell in love with Pemberley's son," Nero whispered, losing strength. "I forbade her to see him but you know how young people are. All of that only made her want to be with him more. Eventually, the boy died after volunteering to help his father with his experiments. Then the bastard turned his attentions to my daughter. He did something to her eyes, turned her into a host for something awful. And when she escaped, she was too afraid to come home to me. People who are around her... they suffer. The thing inside her needs to feed." Nero coughed and tiny flecks of red and white dotted his lips. "Somebody at that bar recognized her, though, and gave me a call. I sent my boys to bring her home."

"How did she end up with Pemberley again?"

"It made her go back to him."

"What did? This thing you said is inside her? What is it?"

Nero's body began to shudder and a rattling sound emanated from his throat. Barrington rushed forward and tried his best but there was nothing to be done. Jonathon Nero, as powerful a figure as any in Sovereign, was dead.

Lazarus stood, leaving the room while Barrington was checking for any last signs of life. He and Eun hurried past Louie in the hallway, exiting the house before the big man could ask what was wrong.

"What now, Chief?" Eun asked. "We gonna stop in and see Doc Pemberley?"

"We need to check in on Morgan and Samantha immediately."

Eun slid into the passenger seat of the car, suddenly realizing that he wasn't sure what the duo had been assigned to do. "Where are they?"

The strong line of Gray's jaw tightened. "They're supposed to be visiting Doc Pemberley right now."

"What in the world are you talking about, Chief?"

Gray kept his eyes on the road but he was able to recount for Eun the reasons behind their associates' current mission. As usual, it involved the fact that Lazarus kept his cards close to the vest and rarely shared all the facts with anyone, including his employees.

"After speaking to Mr. Scanlon, I was struck by what he said about the young woman's eyes. He called them Phantom Eyes."

"So?"

"When I helped bring Doc Pemberley to justice, I took it upon myself to go through his files. I found several references to some kind of surgery that he had dubbed The Phantom Eyes Project. It involved grafting some sort of parasite behind the eyes. It would derive its nutrition from the moisture found in living beings. If a victim could be found, the creature was able to absorb moisture through physical contact, a process that would lead to the host's eyes glowing. In the absence of a victim, the parasite would begin feasting upon the moisture found in its host body until they were drained dry. Sometime last month, I heard unconfirmed rumors that Pemberley had returned to this city. I managed to trace him to a brownstone on Maxwell Street."

Eun tapped his chin thoughtfully. "But what kind of creature could do that, though? I've never heard of anything that could do those things."

Gray glanced at him and the look on his face chilled Eun to the very core of his being. "That's because it's not a creature of this world."

Chapter IV
The Eyes of Doom

Melvin Pemberley was fifty years old, though he could pass for a man in his mid-thirties. He was handsome in an Aryan sort of way, with short-cut blond hair, blue eyes that resembled chipped polar ice and a coolly efficient manner of conducting himself. He tended to wear the type of white lab coats so often associated with scientists and was rarely found without a pair of surgical gloves on his hands.

Doc Pemberley's appearance generally caused people to believe he was a hard-working man dedicated to science. The truth was a good bit more sinister. Pemberley was completely amoral. Where the average person would cringe, Pemberley stared unabashed. When a normal man would rush in to save those in need, Pemberley was more apt to pick up a sheet of paper and begin recording the events occurring before him.

And then there was the peculiar interest in the macabre.

Doc Pemberley was not only a world-class authority on scientific matters, he was also an amateur occultist, with a collection of books that would be the envy of almost any parapsychologist in the world. Even the good men and women at Miskatonic University would have been impressed by his holdings. He had one of several books that had been personally bound by the infamous Felix Cole, whose skills in handling the works of the damned were impeccable.

The combination of good looks, remarkable intelligence and a total lack of morals made Doc Pemberley a very, very dangerous man.

He was presently living in a rented brownstone located not more than three blocks from the harbor. He had a gang who worked for him, dangerous enforcers who didn't mind breaking the necks of those who bothered their boss. His activities were funded through a wide variety of jobs he took for the various crime lords in the city. He worked for them all, creating weapons of hideous damage for each. The fact that he sold to their enemies as well didn't deter any underworld boss from doing business with him. He was simply that good at killing people.

Doc Pemberley walked up the stairs to the second story of his home, moving so quietly that the two men assigned to guard a certain door didn't hear him. Their names were Vince and Coley and they were little more than vicious dogs on two legs. They would have worked for Pemberley for free as long as he kept providing violent entertainment.

Vince's voice carried a bit more and his words were what had led to Pemberley's decision to use stealth. "That girl needs to be put down. Did you see what she did to Jake? The guy looked like a prune when he died. It was like every bit of water in the guy had been drained out!"

Coley shifted his weight from foot to foot. He was a good bit shorter than Vince and a lot stockier. "The Doc says she can't really control it so it ain't her fault."

"A rabid animal attacks and attacks 'cause it's sick in the brain," Vince retorted. "It ain't really its fault, right? But you still gotta kill it or it's just gonna hurt more people. Same with this dame."

"The Doc says-- "

"I know what Pemberley says! But the man's got a screw loose and everybody knows it! I like the guy 'cause he keeps us busy, you know? But maybe this is one time he ain't thinking straight."

"Gentlemen."

Vince and Coley both froze in place, their heads turning in unison toward Pemberley. He stood very close to Vince, his hands pushed deep into the pockets of his lab coat.

"Boss," Vince said, sounding a bit shaky. Though he was far larger than Pemberley, there was no denying the fear that shone in his eyes. "I want to explain."

"There's no need," Pemberley replied. "I understand completely."

Vince sighed, looking relieved. "You do? That's great. I was just saying that I thought maybe you were wrong on this one. Nobody's perfect, right?"

"Certainly. I obviously made a mistake when I hired you." Pemberley's right hand slid from his pocket, a scalpel held in his palm. The hallway light flashed off its polished surface. Doc Pemberley swung the weapon with practiced ease, expertly slicing through Vince's throat in such a way that there would be no hope of saving him. He was going to bleed out right there in the hallway.

Vince's eyes widened and he reached up with both hands to clutch at his throat. He staggered away, bumping into Coley, who was watching him with a face bleached of all color. Vince tumbled into the railing, his momentum causing him to flip right over it. He fell to the first floor, landing with a sickening thud.

Pemberley reached out and cleaned his scalpel on Coley's lapel. "Is there anything you'd like to say to me, Mr. Coley?"

Coley blinked, swallowing hard. "I'm sorry?"

"Good enough for now. I don't brook insubordination. It makes me feel like I can't trust you. And we should all trust one another, shouldn't we?"

"You bet, boss."

"Good. Now go clean up the mess downstairs while I check in on Miss Nero."

Coley hurried away, grateful that he wasn't sharing his partner's fate. Not today, at least.

Samantha Grace walked slowly toward the brownstone, her heels clicking on the cobblestones. Morgan Watts was right behind her, his eyes glued to the swaying motion of her hips. Though they engaged in constant bantering, there was nothing particularly romantic about their relationship. Morgan would certainly have been open to such a thing but Samantha kept herself at a distance from most men and Morgan wondered if she wasn't secretly carrying a torch for Lazarus. He hoped not, because he had a feeling that it would only lead to heartache for the pretty girl.

The Chief had dispatched the two of them out here for reasons mostly unknown to Morgan. Gray had simply said that he needed them to check in on the place and that he had reason to suspect that Doc Pemberley or his associates might be making use of the residence. Morgan was familiar with the doctor, having bumped into him on many occasions back in his criminal days. Pemberley had been a strange sort and Morgan had made sure to never spend too much time alone with the man.

"Should we just give a knock?" Samantha asked, standing outside the front door.

"How about you let me do that and you look around the back?"

Samantha gave a pixyish grin. "Don't you think they'll be more relaxed if they see me standing here than you? Or are you just worried that little old me is going to get hurt?"

Morgan frowned. "Quit kidding around, would you? Pemberley's a nasty one. If he's hanging around this place, we both have to be on our toes."

"Fine, Morgan. You don't have to be surly about it." Pouting, Samantha began moving around the side of the house, not sparing another glance at her companion. Morgan felt like calling after her but he held his tongue. She was right about him not wanting her to get hurt but he didn't want to admit it. Besides, he reasoned, Pemberley might remember him. If he did, then Morgan might be able to come up with some explanation for what he was doing there. What would Samantha say? That she was going door-to-door selling cookies?

Morgan was about to knock on the door when he heard a loud thud come from inside the house. It sounded like something very heavy had been tossed from one floor to the next. He tried the door but found it locked and some sixth sense told him that now would not be a good time to alert anyone to his presence. Whatever had happened in there couldn't have been a good thing.

Taking a step back, Morgan noticed a vine-covered trellis that led to an open second floor window. Quickly glancing around, Morgan made a quick decision. He tested the trellis to see if it could hold his weight and, after deciding that it could, he threw himself into the act of climbing up to the exposed window.

<hr />

Around back, Samantha heard the noise as well. She froze in place, expecting to hear a scream or shout but when none came, she slowly slid up against the rear door. To her pleasure, she found that it opened easily at her touch and she stepped into the kitchen area. The place was filthy and completely lacking a woman's touch. The sink was piled high with dirty dishes and flies buzzed about, landing repeatedly on a couple of half-eaten sandwiches left on the counter.

Samantha was made of stern stuff but she had to shove a hand over her mouth when she found the dead body in the foyer. The man was lying face down with a rapidly spreading pool of blood beneath him. He was quite obviously dead but she still bent down to check for a pulse. Finding none, she looked up and saw no signs of anyone else. Had he fallen by accident? She tilted his head to the side and saw that wasn't the case. His throat had been slashed.

It was then that Coley entered the room, a large carpet under one arm. He'd meant to roll up his friend's body and dump it into the trunk of his car but he forgot all about that when he came face-to-face with the pretty girl kneeling on the floor.

Samantha stood up quickly, forcing a pleasant smile on her face. "Hello. The back door was open."

Coley grimaced. He didn't like hurting dames but he knew that Pemberley wouldn't be pleased if he let the girl go. "You shouldn't be here," he said as he dropped the carpet to the floor and took a heavy step toward her. "I don't know who you are but today's a very unlucky day, girlie."

The big man towered over the pretty young blonde but there was no fear in her eyes as he approached. He lunged for her with two meaty hands extended but she calmly grabbed hold of his wrist and twisted, using his momentum to send him flying head over heels. He landed on his back, the air momentarily knocked from his lungs.

Samantha pushed her advantage, jumping into the air and landing hard on the side of his head, the heel of her shoe connecting with his skull. He cried out and swatted a hand toward her, making contact with the back of her leg. His strength was enough to knock her off-balance and she had just regained her footing when he scrambled to his feet. The spot where she'd kicked his head was a bright crimson in color, matching the fury that was rising in his eyes.

He snarled out a few colorful insults but Samantha had heard worse. When he came at her again, she noted that he was a bit more careful this time. He threw a ham-sized fist at her head but she ducked under the blow and threw a karate chop into his neck. She'd aimed it directly at his windpipe and the sudden wheezing of his breath told her she'd accomplished her goal. She then straightened and drove her knee directly into his genitalia. The blow made him whimper and as he doubled over, she grabbed him by the hair and shoved him toward a marble countertop nearby. The cracking sound of skull meeting marble was sickening and he slid to the ground, not moving.

Samantha smoothed out her skirt and adjusted her hair before looking up the stairs. She knew she should check out the rest of the house but given the fact that there was now two dead men in the foyer, it seemed prudent to allow Morgan to accompany her. She opened the front door and was surprised to see that her friend was absent. With a concerned look on her face, she shut the door and contemplated what she should do next. The sensible thing would be to exit the building and look for Morgan.

But sensibility wasn't really what defined Samantha Grace.

After closing the door again, but leaving it unlocked in case Morgan returned, she spun about and began treading carefully up the stairs.

———

Wilma Nero sat on the edge of her bed, feeling a mixture of satisfaction and shame. There was a dead girl on the floor, a streetwalker that Pemberley had procured for the purpose of feeding the creature lurking behind Wilma's eyes. As always, Wilma had tried to stop it from happening but it was impossible. Her eyes had begun to glow and the girl's moisture had been drained right out of her. She now lay on the floor, as leathery as an Egyptian mummy. Wilma felt a deep sense of wholeness within her, as the monster began to slumber with its full belly, but she also felt revulsion at what she had become.

Pemberley had entered her room, though she hadn't noticed at first. When she finally looked up at him through red-rimmed eyes, he was standing at the foot of her bed, looking at her expectantly.

"How do you feel, my dear?"

"Like a monster. How else should I feel?"

"You're not a monster. You're part of something beautiful and wonderful. Utterly unique in all the world."

Wilma stood up and the sudden motion made the thing behind her eyes begin to stir. It felt like a troublesome tickle, she thought, and shivered at the realization that she was getting used to its presence. "Would you think it so wonderful if I let it feed on you, I wonder?"

"You couldn't stop it if you wanted to," Pemberley answered with a sneer. "It's the one in control, not you. You're nothing more than a very pretty traveling case. That thing in your head knows that I'm the one who gave you to it and I'm the one who can help it and its children flourish."

Wilma looked down at her feet. "How is my father?"

"Dead most likely."

The callous way he said those words hurt Wilma more than anything. It reminded her of how he'd dealt with the death of his son. He'd been more upset at the loss of his experiment than anything. "I'm going to kill myself," she whispered. "I'm going to throw myself out that open window."

"You and I both know that's not true. You can't. It won't let you."

"What is this thing?" she asked, reaching up to gently touch the corner of her eye.

"I've explained it to you before," Pemberley said, reaching out to take her by the shoulders. He steered her back toward the bed and gently pushed her down until she was seated on the mattress. "It's a creature called an aquaas. It's actually a very ancient life form that was birthed out amongst the stars. A few dozen of them fell to earth during the 19th century, scattering all across North America. They were encased in hard shells that resembled meteorites but it was really just another stage of their development. They encase themselves in those rocky exteriors to survive the rigors of space. I first learned of them a few years ago when a man sold me several of the creatures, still in their capsules. I cracked one open and imagine my surprise at what I found: a tiny little monster with an insatiable desire for the kind of moisture found only in living things. After I witnessed its habit of burrowing behind the eyes of its still-living victims, I came up with the idea of surgically implanting them, making them far stronger."

"And to what purpose? Just to show how sick human beings can be?"

Pemberley knelt in front of her, holding her hands in his. "You're the prototype to not only a new form of life – a melding of human and aquaas – but also the first of an entirely new type of soldier. Imagine a whole army of men and women who can kill without guns or knives. All they'll need is their eyes."

"I think I've heard enough."

Pemberley stood up quickly and whirled about. Morgan Watts was pulling himself in through the window, a pistol clutched tightly in his right hand. "Morgan Watts?" Pemberley asked in shock.

"I'm flattered you remember me, Doc."

"I remember everyone. I'm a genius."

"And a modest one, to boot." Morgan waved the gun at Pemberley, indicating he should step away from Wilma. He did so and the girl looked at Morgan in confusion. "Don't worry, doll, I'm getting you out of here. I work for Lazarus Gray and if there's any man alive who can get that thing out of your head, he's the one."

"It seems like you have the upper hand," Pemberley admitted. "I should warn you that I have an armed guard outside who is twice your size and three times as deadly."

Morgan was about to reply when he heard a series of thumps from downstairs, followed by a gasp that sounded disturbingly familiar. In a split-second he realized what was happening: Samantha had managed to find her way inside and come toe-to-toe with the guard that Pemberley had just described.

In that moment when Morgan's attention was divided, Pemberley sprang toward him. The crazed doctor batted aside the hand holding the pistol and he then proceeded to throw a haymaker punch that caused Morgan's entire body to snap around. Pemberley then slammed Morgan's head into the wall hard enough to chip the paint.

As Morgan fell to the floor, groaning in pain, Pemberley snatched up Wilma by the wrist, holding it so tightly that the girl whimpered in pain. "We have to get out of here," he hissed. "I have plans for you and I can't afford any of Gray's minions getting in the way."

"Please," Wilma cried, "just kill me! I can't go on like this!"

Pemberley laughed then, a maniacal sound that so frightened the girl that she fainted in his arms. "No death for you," he hissed through grinning lips. "You won't be so lucky, my dear."

<hr />

Morgan Watts felt something cool and wet press against his forehead and he winced in pain. He opened his eyes to find himself on a couch, Samantha perched beside him, looking concerned. "Where's Pemberley?" he asked, trying to sit up but quickly laying back down when his head throbbed in agony.

"He's gone," Lazarus Gray answered, stepping into view. Eun was right behind him, the young man looking troubled and more than a little angry. "We arrived a few moments ago and Samantha filled us in as much as she could. You ran into the doctor himself, I presume?"

"I did. He had the girl with him, too. The one with the Phantom Eyes. I heard him talking to her. She's got some sort of monster in her head and--"

"We know all about that," Eun said, smirking a bit. He always liked knowing more than Morgan – it was a competition between the two. "Do you know where he's taken her?"

"No. I know he said he had some kind of plans but that's all I could hear before I blacked out."

Lazarus turned away, having already examined Morgan. He knew that the man was going to be hurting and unsteady for a bit more but there wouldn't be any permanent damage. "I may have an idea where he's gone," Gray murmured and instantly his three aides grew quiet, giving him their full attention. Gray reached out and picked up a small writing tablet from a nearby table. The top sheet had been ripped away but his keen eyes detected the imprint of pencil marks on the next page. He used the pencil that had been sitting next to the tablet to gently reveal what those imprints had been, rubbing the side of the graphite over the writing. An address came into view and Gray's keen memory told him that 1935 Monk Avenue was an old warehouse, abandoned when the owning company went belly-up a few years before he'd arrived in Sovereign. There was also a time listed next to it, one that was less than an hour away. "Eun, please take Morgan back to base. He needs time to recover. Samantha, you're to come with me."

"Chief!" both Eun and Morgan exclaimed in unison. The two men looked at one another and it was Morgan who continued on. "Chief, I'll be fine. And you can't go into a showdown with Pemberley with just Samantha! You need Eun and I!"

Samantha crossed her arms over her chest and glared at Morgan, obviously not liking his implications. "Are you saying I'm dead weight?"

"No!" Morgan answered. "I just mean… C'mon, Chief. You know we want to be in on this one."

Gray looked at them with steady eyes, the mismatched pair narrowing. His emerald eye seemed to shine just as brightly as the brown one darkened. "I appreciate your desire to help but you're in no condition for a fight, nor can you drive at the present. Eun will take you back and he'll make sure you stay there."

Eun nodded, his respect for Gray overriding his own desire to argue. Morgan, too, slumped in defeat.

"Don't worry, boys," Samantha said with a triumphant grin. "I'll give Pemberley a swift kick in your honor."

Chapter V
The Man From Berlin

The German was dressed like an undertaker and he leaned heavily on a walking stick that was topped by a roaring lion's head. His eyes were narrow slits that radiated such anger that Pemberley was surprised they weren't smoking. Walther Lunt had once been a handsome man but a beaker of acid thrown in his face had ruined his good looks. Now one half of his face was twisted into a horrific visage that frightened even the prostitutes who were paid to spend their nights in his bed.

"I expected better accommodations than this, Herr Pemberley," Lunt said with obvious disdain. His eyes raked across the rat-infested warehouse. There were boxes stacked here and there but for the most part the cavernous facility was empty. The squeaks of its current inhabitants sometimes filled the air, as if the rodents were protesting the intrusion of the humans into their domicile.

"We make do with what we have," Pemberley said. His iron grip on Wilma's arm never wavered. "I brought her here so you could see first hand what I've done. And you can tell your leader that I can do this for his army, if he funds my research."

"I work with Hitler, not for him."

Pemberley inclined his head. They'd been over this before. "I apologize. But soon enough, everyone will answer to him, won't they?" Pemberley laughed. "I do admire the man, not only for his ability to resurrect the slumbering giant that is Germany but also for his private views on race and science. I've heard much about his desires to--"

"Enough." Lunt stepped forward and removed Pemberley's hand from Wilma's arm. "I would like to look at her myself."

"Be careful. The aquaas recognizes me as its master but it may strike you."

"I do not think it will," Lunt responded. He was looking at Wilma's eyes intently, ignoring the revulsion that was marring her beauty. The girl was unable to tear her gaze away from his ruined face.

Pemberley stood nearby, his heart hammering in his chest as Wilma's eyes began to glow. The blue light seemed to shimmer before becoming an almost blinding glare. Pemberley wanted to warn Lunt again about the danger but the German would have simply ignored him again. The man had the air about him of someone who considered all others to be inferior. He was an occultist, one whose knowledge of the hidden worlds dwarfed even Pemberley's. The group he headed had no name, or at least it was one that hadn't been shared with Pemberley, but it was pervasive, with members spread throughout the world.

"You're quite potent, aren't you? And always so hungry." Lunt was speaking not to Wilma but to the aquaas that lurked behind her eyes. He pushed her away so hard that she tripped over her own feet and fell to the dusty floor. She screamed as she landed in the pervasive rat droppings. "You have more of these things? Or are you waiting for this one to lay eggs so you can harvest them?"

Pemberley gestured to one of the boxes nearby. "I've collected nearly ten of them. Three were damaged when I got them and one of the aquaas died when my son perished. But that stills five in addition to the one that Wilma is carrying."

"May I see them?"

"Of course." Pemberley moved away from Lunt, grabbing the lid of the box. He yanked on it, pulling it loose. "I'm hoping you'll let me accompany you back to Germany. Things are getting far too tense around here. A local meddler sent some of his men to my house today. They're on to me again."

"You're saying the police know you're back in Sovereign?"

"Not the police." Pemberley tossed the box lid to the floor, where it landed and sent up a cloud of polluted dust. "There's a group in town called Assistance Unlimited. They make a living out of sticking their noses where they don't belong. Their leader's some mystery man named Lazarus Gray."

Lunt gripped Pemberley hard about the shoulders and spun him about. "What did you say?"

"His name's Lazarus Gray. What's wrong? Haven't you heard of him before? The guy's famous!"

"Why would I keep up with your local politics?" Lunt said with annoyance. He looked past Pemberley into the box, where the rest of the alien creatures lay in their immobile states. "Lazarus Gray," he repeated. "How long has he been active in this city?"

"Less than two years. But they've been busy ones. He's responsible for the troubles that got me banished from the city for awhile."

"Intriguing." Lunt smiled then but it was cold and reptilian. "I'm impressed with you. You've kept your word to the letter. You've successfully grafted one of these creatures to a human being and kept them both alive. And you have more to spare."

"Then I'll get my funding?"

"You're going to be a very important man in the days to come, Melvin." Lunt turned back to Wilma, who was back on her feet now, her eyes downcast. She looked broken and tired. "Did the aquaas make her like that? Or was she always so weak-willed?"

"A little of both," Pemberley said.

The door to the warehouse opened suddenly and two figures stepped in, pistols held in hand. Pemberley growled, recognizing Lazarus Gray immediately. The stoic-faced man was virtually impossible to forget, even if Pemberley hadn't possessed a mind like a steel trap. Lunt also reacted with recognition, his eyes widening in shock.

Gray noted both men's reactions but it was the man with the scarred face who most disturbed him. Not only did he seem strangely familiar but the lion's head on his walking stick looked eerily like the half-man's head on the back of Gray's medallion.

Samantha noticed Gray's hesitation and stepped up. "Both of you need to back away from the girl and put your hands up."

Lunt noticed that Pemberley did so, though he was muttering under his breath. The German, however, did something far more surprising. He slammed the butt of his walking stick down hard on the floor and then tossed the stick away from him, throwing it with all his might toward Samantha and Lazarus.

Gray somehow sensed what was about to occur. He shoved Samantha behind him and moved to protect her. The stick seemed to shimmer in midair and when it landed, it was not a piece of wood at all… it was a fully grown African lion, its mouth open in a roar that shook the walls. The beast's jaws were slavering and it looked like it was half-starved and mad with hunger.

"Chief, what the hell?" Samantha whispered.

Lazarus raised his pistol and fired as the creature rushed toward him. Two bullets sank deep in the mighty beast's chest but it continued on, leaping upon him. His weight sent Gray to his back and only Gray's tremendous strength managed to hold the snapping jaws away from his face. Gray let his gun drop so he'd have all his fingers free for the herculean task.

Samantha was momentarily taken aback but she quickly realized the deadly predicament her employer was in. She took a step toward the lion and directed her gun at the side of the beast's head. It whirled toward her but this only meant that her shot hit home directly between its eyes. The lion let out a roar of surprised pain and fell forward onto Gray. A lion's dead weight would be enough to leave most men unable to move, but Gray was wriggling free before Samantha even realized he was doing it.

Pemberley slammed into the girl, knocking her hard into the door. A cry of pain erupted from her lips and Pemberley drove a fist into her pretty face, knocking her out. Samantha was a wildcat in battle, with the ability to deal with men three and four times her size… but when taken by surprise, she was helpless as anyone else would be.

Gray saw Samantha fall and though his face did not show it, a burning ember of rage flared into an inferno in his heart. He gripped Pemberley by the collar and drew him toward him. One powerful punch later and the vile scientist was lying on the ground, blood and mucus streaming from his shattered nose.

A cry of pain drew Gray's attention back to Lunt, who was holding a struggling Wilma by her hair. The girl's eyes were glowing blue, indicating that the aquaas was feeling threatened.

"Seeing you here, like this, is a revelation," Lunt said.

"Who are you? How do you know me?" Gray's voice was filled with emotion, which would have shocked his employees. He normally kept a tight lid on his private concerns but he was unable to do so now. This man before him might know the truth about who he really was, or at least know how Gray could find out more.

"You're a hero to these people, aren't you?" Lunt said. "I wonder if any of them know how much blood is on your hands? And the audacity of calling yourself Lazarus Gray!" Lunt shook his head. "The others will think me mad when I tell them that you're alive… and that this is what you've become."

"Please help me," Wilma whined, straining her head so she could see Gray. "Please help me… or kill me." Her eyes flashed brighter with every painful word.

Lazarus realized that while he desperately wanted answers, he had to free Wilma. That was his first priority and everything else would have to take a backseat. He reached into one of his pockets and pulled out a small dagger. "Let her go."

"No." Lunt cackled and the scarring on his face reddened, making it look like the veins between were about to burst out into the light. "If you want the bitch so badly, then take her!" Lunt yanked her back so her neck was stretched taut. With his free hand, he pulled out a knife of his own, one that gleamed in the warehouse lighting. "But if I were you, Mr. Lazarus Gray, I would drop your weapon and step away from the door. Otherwise, I'll slit her throat from ear-to-ear."

Gray was calculating the odds of throwing his dagger and hitting the German. He was a crack shot with both throwing knives and handguns but it was still an awful risk. The girl had begged for her death but Gray wasn't about to take that route. He would protect her until his own dying breath. She was an innocent victim in all of this, despite the crimes of her father.

Before Gray could make his move, Lunt began to cry out. The skin of his face and hands began to wither, as if something was sucking the moisture right out of him. He dropped his hold on Wilma but it was too late. The aquaas had sensed the threat to its host and was now responding, using all of its power to remove this dangerous creature. Lunt opened his mouth and he tried to scream something at Lazarus but Gray couldn't make it out. The man's mouth was too dry and his tongue was beginning to break apart, turning to dust that ran down Lunt's chin. He fell to the floor, a horrible hitching sound coming from his chest. He ended up posed just above the floor, looking like a strange sculpture made of leather and bone.

Wilma fainted again, her will no longer enough to keep her going. Gray hurried toward her and had just knelt beside her when he heard the door to the warehouse slam shut. He looked up in alarm, his eyes scanning over the still form of Samantha. It was Pemberley, making a break for it.

Let him go, Gray decided. Justice will find him soon enough.

***

Wilma Nero smiled gratefully. "Thank you so much, Mr. Gray. I don't know how I can repay you."

The girl looked so bright and cheerful, it was almost impossible to think that until a few days ago she'd been the host to an alien parasite. She sat with Peter Scanlon in the meeting room of Assistance Unlimited, facing Lazarus and his aides. She was holding Peter's hand and the man looked ecstatic. Once Gray had told her that it had been Scanlon's chivalric desire to help her that had led Gray on to the case, she'd warmed to the man considerably.

"No payment is necessary," Gray replied. "Your case has given me more than you know and monetary recompense would only taint that."

Wilma looked confused but she nodded. After she and Scanlon had been shown out, Gray turned to face his staff, all of which were looking at him with interest.

A faint smile touched Gray's lips and vanished just as rapidly. "Ask away."

The three of them exchanged glances and it was Morgan who spoke up first. "The moisture-eating worm?"

"I removed it myself and threw it into the fireplace. I also disposed of the others that were in the warehouse."

"Pemberley?" Eun asked.

"Still on the loose. We'll have to keep an eye out for him. He's dangerous and growing more unstable by the day."

It was now Samantha's turn and she realized that the boys had left it to her to broach the most difficult subject. "What did you mean about this case giving you so much?"

"Is that really what you want to ask?"

Samantha swallowed hard. "When I was on the floor, I heard some of what was going on. Between you and that German. It didn't make much sense."

Gray sighed, looking quickly at Eun and then back to Samantha. "My name isn't Lazarus Gray. I don't know what my name is. I woke up in the harbor during the summer of 1933. All I know about myself are a few scattered memories… and this." He pulled out the medallion from his pocket, holding it up for the others to see. "A lion-headed man and the words Lazarus Gray scrawled on the back."

"You've checked your face and prints against the FBI files?" Morgan asked.

"Of course. No one recognizes me and I have no record that can be traced. But that man knew me. He's a piece from my past."

"And the lion?" Samantha asked. "How did that man do that? Was he a magician?"

"A literal one, perhaps. There are strange things in this world, things that defy rational explanations. Some of my memories are related to human sacrifice and occult gatherings." Gray clasped his hands behind his back and looked at each of them, his eyes slowly shifting from one to the other. "I have a feeling that things will never be the same for us. I cannot promise you that we will continue to face gangsters and rapists. If any of you want to walk away now, I will understand."

Morgan grunted. "Are you kidding, Chief? We all owe you our lives. Whatever happens from here on out, you've got Assistance Unlimited at your side."

Gray saw the determination in their eyes and nodded grimly. Though he would never say it aloud, he loved his aides. That was why he was both pleased to hear that they would stay with him and also more than a bit frightened. In the nocturnal war that was looming ever larger in Sovereign City, one that was threatening to involve forces beyond explanation, there was no guarantee that any of them would live to see the dawn.

THE DEVIL'S BIBLE

An Adventure of Lazarus Gray
Written by Barry Reese

———— ∞∞ ————

Chapter I
Eight Pages

Harry Nance held the envelope to his lips with trembling fingers. His tongue dragged heavily across the strip of glue that would seal away the eight parchment leaves. When he was done, he checked the addressed he'd hurriedly scrawled, verifying that it was correct: 6196 Robeson Avenue, Sovereign City. Satisfied that it would reach its intended audience, Harry dropped the envelope into the mailbox and pulled his long overcoat tighter around his body. A harsh wind was blowing, carrying with it the salty scent of the harbor and the acrid odor of a heavily polluted city. Sovereign was a harsh place to grow up and Harry liked to think that if he'd been born in another place and time, he could have been something great.

The truth was that Harry was like so many men in the world: he was willing to trade his soul for easy money. He was a lazy soul, one who wanted the trappings of success but who wasn't willing to put in the hard work required to achieve it honestly.

And now the devil was coming to collect his due.

Harry looked up at the nighttime sky, his heart hammering in his chest. He'd

MORGAN WATTS
FORMER MAFIA SOLDIER - NOW ONE OF LAZARUS
GRAY'S TRUSTED AIDES IN ASSISTANCE UNLIMITED

made a terrible mistake and wished desperately that he could undo it… but it was too late for apologies. Besides, what was on those eight pages was so terrible that not even a man like Harry could leave them in the wrong hands. That's why he'd packaged them up and sent them on their way, intending for them to end up someplace safe.

Two men stepped around a corner up ahead, blocking Harry's path. Both of them wore dark clothing, the sort that had once been associated with those Oriental assassins dubbed Ninja. Each of the men held a three-pronged blade that Harry knew was called a sai.

Harry whirled around, intending to retreat in the opposite direction but he came to an abrupt stop. There were three more men standing behind him, two of them ninja. The third was all the more frightening: for he was leader of these men, who collectively were known as Black Heart. Black Heart served Malcolm Goodwill, one of the most ironically named human beings on the planet. Goodwill had no love for any person other than himself. Standing six feet, six inches tall, he looked down on virtually everyone. Goodwill had silver blond hair and arched eyebrows. He dressed like a European aristocrat and had cultivated a pseudo-British accent, despite the fact that he had been born in Philadelphia.

"Harry," Goodwill said with a shake of his head. "I've treated you well, have I not? Didn't I give you a bonus last Christmas? And when your mother needed eye surgery, who paid for it?"

"It's wrong what you're doing," Harry stated but his words lacked conviction. The fear made his voice shake too much to carry moral authority.

Goodwill gestured for his ninja to move closer to Harry. They encircled him but held off from making any attacks. "That's not really for you to decide, now is it?"

Harry looked around but the streets were deathly silent. No cars could be seen and if there were any beat cops about, they were staying to the shadows. A few drops of rain began to fall and Harry was glad of it. They would help hide the tears that were threatening to come. "I don't have the pages anymore. They're gone."

"Where are they?"

Harry swallowed hard and summoned every bit of courage he possessed. He tried to pretend he was a movie star, someone like William Powell. "I'm not gonna talk. You might as well kill me, Malcolm. Sometimes a man has to do what's right and for the first time in my life, I'm gonna do that."

Goodwill stared hard at him and then slowly reached into his jacket and retrieved a cigar. He took his time in lighting a match and touching it to the tip of the cigar. After puffing on it several times, he smiled at Harry. "Good for you, Harry. I admire you for this." He looked at his men, who stood at the ready. "Well? You heard the man? Let's not ruin the moment by giving him the chance to beg. Kill him."

Harry's eyes opened wide and he immediately regretted his earlier bravado.

He started to beg for another chance but the men surrounding him struck too quickly. Their blades fell upon him, carving him up like a Thanksgiving turkey.

Goodwill puffed away on his cigar, anger blazing in his evil heart. He couldn't believe that a petty numbers runner like Harry Nance was undoing all of his carefully laid plans. He tried to think of where a man like Harry would have hidden the papers and finally came to the conclusion that Harry had never been the sharpest tool in the shed. The papers were probably hidden away somewhere in his apartment.

The dark-clad members of Black Heart returned to their master, leaving Harry's corpse in the middle of the sidewalk. "Let's go, gentlemen. We have places to be."

The headquarters of Assistance Unlimited was located at 6196 Robeson Avenue. Lazarus Gray had purchased all three of the buildings that lay on this city block, transforming what had once been an unassuming neighborhood into the beating heart of his enterprise. The centerpiece of his holdings was a three-story structure that had once been a hotel. Gray's three associates used the first floor, while the second had been gutted and converted into one large room that was used for meetings, briefings and research. The third floor was off-limits to everyone but Gray himself and was his private domicile.

Across the street were several storefronts owned by Lazarus, all of which had closed down at the dawn of the Great Depression.

Samantha Grace, the pretty blonde who was the only distaff member of Assistance Unlimited, was sorting through the mail while gazing out the window. A typical drizzly morning had greeted her upon waking and the distant rumble of thunder suggested that the worst was yet to come.

The majority of letters the group received consisted of interview requests. The press, it seemed, could not get enough of the mysterious Lazarus Gray. All of these were dropped into the trash. Lazarus wasn't in this racket for publicity and neither were his aides. All of them had suffered because of the criminal elements and each had sworn the same oath as their leader: to stop at nothing until the innocent people of Sovereign City were able to walk their streets without fear for their safety.

An unmarked envelope caught Samantha's attention and she slid a stainless steel letter opener under its side. The envelope opened easily, spilling a handful of papers onto the floor. Samantha knelt to retrieve them, muttering a bit under her breath. Her scarlet colored skirt rustled about long legs as she rose to her feet and she became aware that someone was watching her. Looking over her shoulders she saw Morgan Watts gazing with admiration. "Something I can help you with, Morgan?" she asked.

"Not at all. You're just a welcome ray of sunshine, that's all."

Samantha rolled her eyes but silently welcomed the attention. Morgan was a handsome man but he was a good bit older than her and had a checkered background. A former gangster himself, Morgan was the Chief's eyes and ears on the street. Samantha, who came from a high-class background, found Morgan's past exploits somewhat exotic but she would never think to ruin their friendship by pursuing romantic interests. She believed Morgan felt the same but he was a man, after all. He was bound to look upon occasion. "Look at these," she said, flipping through the pages. "Strangest things I've ever seen."

Morgan took one of the pages from her and studied it. That it was quite old was undeniable. It felt like calfskin and the page was crammed with writing, all in Latin. Each sheet was extremely long, measuring nearly three feet in length. "Who sent these?"

"There's no return address."

"Too bad my Latin's so rusty."

Samantha smirked, knowing that Morgan knew as much about Latin as he did about ladies' fashion. In other words, virtually nothing. "I'll take them to the Chief."

"Sounds like a plan." Morgan handed over the sheet he'd been holding and cleared his throat. "Listen, doll, you doing anything Saturday night?"

Samantha blinked, wondering if she'd heard correctly. "Just the usual: hanging around headquarters and waiting for something to happen."

"Well, I have these tickets for the movie house. It's nothing fancy, mind you – one of those Evelyn Gould adventure flicks – but I was thinking that since I have two tickets and there's only one of me that I should take somebody with me."

"Are you asking me on a date?"

"No!" Morgan guffawed and Samantha wasn't certain if she should feel relieved or insulted. "It's just two friends, doll. Nothing more than that. Believe me!"

Samantha fought to keep a frown off her face. "That's fine. We can do that, Morgan. But I can't promise anything, really. I mean, anything might come up between now and then."

"Of course. Same here."

"Good." Samantha turned away and headed toward the stairs. She didn't look back at Morgan but if she had, she would have seen him wincing. Their conversation hadn't gone anywhere along the lines of what he'd intended and he was beginning to wonder if there was something about Miss Grace that would always leave him tripping over his feet.

Lazarus Gray was not a particularly large man but there was something about him that made men pause when they saw him. It might have been the mismatched eyes, one a sparkling emerald and the other a brooding brown. Or it might have been the stern, almost emotionless cast of his features. But most likely it was the way he moved, with the elegant grace of a dancer and the dangerous tread of a panther.

Eun Jiwon normally considered himself a very dangerous individual. Quick and athletic, the young Korean had proven himself capable of dealing with two or three grown men in combat but against Gray, he found himself simply outclassed. The two men were sparring now, throwing punches and kicks so quickly that they were little more than blurs to the naked eye. But Eun knew that Gray was holding back, a supposition that proved correct when Samantha entered the training area, an envelope in hand. Gray ducked another one of Eun's fists and delivered two quick chops to the younger man's midsection, knocking the breath from his lungs. Gray then finished him with a kick to the knee that left Eun temporarily hobbled.

Gray straightened and gave his opponent a polite bow. "Excellent work, Eun."

The Korean stared at him in disbelief. Though he was far younger than Gray, he was panting and covered in sweat while the older man looked fresh as a daisy. Eun gingerly walked over to pluck up a towel and was using it to wipe off his brow when Samantha handed over the papers to Gray.

"This came in the mail this morning, Chief. No return address. I took Latin in school but I can't really make heads or tails of this."

Lazarus studied the pages very carefully, his eyes raking over the words. "Everyone needs to come together in the briefing room. Immediately."

The tone in his voice brooked no further discussion. Samantha whirled at once, heading off to fetch Morgan. Eun, meanwhile, set the automatic recording devices that answered the phones when the team was busy. Within moments, all four members of Assistance Unlimited were gathered around a sturdy oak table.

Gray sat at the head of the table, the papers arranged in two rows of four in front of him. He was dressed in black slacks and a white shirt today, the sleeves of which were rolled up to the midpoint of his forearms. It was a fairly casual look for Gray but even so his ever-present tie was in place. "We have an interesting case before us," Gray said at last. "These pages are extracted from a tome known as the Codex Gigas."

Morgan leaned forward. "How do you know that?"

"The content of the pages leads me to that conclusion but it's borne out by the size of the sheets themselves. The Codex Gigas is the largest extant medieval manuscript in the world. It weighs over 160 pounds and has measurements of 36 inches in height, nearly 20 inches in width and over 8 inches in thickness."

Morgan glanced over at Eun, who gave a shrug of his shoulders. None of them were surprised that their leader would be able to quote such figures off the top of his head, but it was impressive nonetheless. Despite the fact that his own past was a mystery to him, Gray's head was filled with data about subjects both famous and obscure. "Okay. So it's an old book. What's it about?"

Gray picked up on one of the pages and studied it. "The tome contains the Vulgate Bible, as well as many historical documents. The entire thing is written in Latin and legend has it that Herman the Recluse compiled it in the Benedictine monastery of Podlazice near Chrudim. It's drifted from hand to hand since then but was seized in 1648 as plunder by the Swedish army. The rest of the book is currently part of the National Library of Sweden. People have known for years that there were eight missing pages and these appear to be them."

"Are we going to contact the Swedes, then?" Eun asked.

"No. Not yet. You see, there is a bit more to the story. There is a legend attached to it and these pages may shed some further illumination upon that. I daresay the secrets contained here are worth dying for."

Morgan sat back and grinned. "Well don't keep us in suspense, Chief. Spin the yarn for us."

Gray stood up, clasping his hands behind his back as he began to pace slowly back and forth. His voice remained low and even but all of his aides found themselves leaning forward as he talked, drawn in by the tale he was weaving. "The story goes that Herman the Recluse broke his monastic vows and was sentenced to be walled up alive in the monastery."

"Must have been some nasty business he took part in," Morgan muttered, drawing a stern frown from Samantha.

Gray continued as if he hadn't heard Morgan's interruption. "In order to avoid this fate, the monk promised that he would create a book that would contain all the knowledge of man. The other monks, hungry to see his fall from grace, demanded that he do this in a single night. Having no other choice, he agreed and began to work. At some point in the night, he gave in to despair, knowing that he would never have a hope of succeeding. And so he turned to the one being who might help him: the Devil himself. Satan claimed the monk's soul and completed the book for him, going so far as to insert a self-portrait on page 577. The image is a horrific depiction of the Devil and all those who gaze upon it feel a shiver go down their spines. It's like staring into the abyss. Modern scholars who have studied the manuscript are adamant that a single hand wrote it all, with no discrepancy due to age, sickness or simply the passage of time. It's estimated that it would have taken twenty years or more for a single person to create such a work."

"So the work isn't cursed?" Samantha asked. "I can't believe Satan would create something like that and not have it be something incredibly evil."

Gray looked at her. "In addition to all the histories included in the tome, there are also magical spells. These are mostly exorcisms but it's been rumored for centuries that the missing eight pages contained spells of summoning, rituals that would allow mortal men to summon entities of great power and bind them."

"And do they? Eun wondered aloud. He reached for one of the pages and held it up before his eyes. The writing looked like gibberish to him but he couldn't deny that there was a tingling sensation in his fingertips whenever they made contact with the paper.

"Yes. They do."

Morgan exhaled loudly and when everyone turned to look at him, he shrugged. "I just don't see what the big deal is. So we found some old papers that have magic spells written on them. So what? We're not actually going to act like we believe in this stuff, are we?"

"What about the Scanlon case?" Samantha reminded him. "Mr. Scanlon comes to us and hires us to track down Wilma Nero, who happens to have an alien creature living behind her eyes? And I run into a man who turns his walking stick into a lion, right in front of me? Who's to say what's real and what's not? Besides, it's obvious the Chief believes in it and that's good enough for me."

"Thank you, Samantha." Gray took back the page that Eun had been holding. He took all eight pages and put them back into order. "I have every reason to believe that these pages have been used to summon a demonic entity. Unfortunately, without these pages, whomever has done so is in a world of trouble. The spells that are used to bind the demon must be performed on a regular basis or else the hold begins to weaken. Likewise, the demon cannot be banished without the words on these pages."

Morgan tapped his chin thoughtfully. "So somebody sent us these pages to screw somebody else over?"

"Possibly. Or they may have wanted us to use the spells contained on these pages to banish the demon in question."

"But where do we go from here? We don't know who sent the pages or who might have summoned these things, assuming that they have." Morgan stood up. "Looks to me like we're at a dead end."

"Not necessarily. There are actually two clues here and they both bear investigating. Firstly, the envelope itself is oversized to accommodate the size of the papers." Gray lifted up the envelope and turned it so that the backside of it was facing his aides. "Look closely at the bottom here. You'll note that someone recently wrote some numbers down. The imprint went through the paper that was used and onto the envelope. It's a local phone number. I took the liberty of checking with the operator before this meeting began. It's the phone number of an importer named Malcolm Goodwill. I'd like for Samantha and Eun to pay him a visit."

"Will do, Chief," Eun piped up. "Should we tell him why we're there?"

"No. Go under the pretense of wanting to buy some something that would remind you of home. Given your ethnic background, it won't surprise him that you'd be looking for hard-to-find items that the usual stores here wouldn't stock. He runs his business from his home so you may also get the opportunity to learn about his personal life."

Morgan began to grin. "And what about you and me, Chief? What angle are we taking?"

"We're going to visit a man named Harry Nance."

"Nance? I know him. Small-time numbers runner. A real small fish in the big Sovereign pond."

"He might be a bigger fish than you think." Gray tapped the papers. "Because he's the man who sent us this envelope."

Chapter II
The Black Heart of Malcolm Goodwill

Harry Nance's apartment was never particularly well kept but now it looked like a tornado had descended upon it. The mattress had been ripped off the bed and sliced apart while every drawer and cabinet had been opened and rifled through.

The black-clad ninja had finally admitted defeat and Goodwill had banished them back to his home. He remained behind, however, sitting on Harry's couch, in the middle of the mess. He'd hoped that something would occur to him, some clue as to where Harry might have stashed the pages.

A chill took hold of the room as the temperature dropped some twenty degrees in the space of mere seconds. Goodwill glanced down to see that his breath was now visible, emerging from his mouth in tiny clouds of carbon dioxide. Goodwill took out a cigar and lit it, using the expensive smoke as a calming influence.

A humanoid figure took shape beside him. The smell of cinnamon filled Goodwill's nostrils, overwhelming even the acrid odor of his cigar. He kept his eyes straight ahead, however, refusing to turn and look at her.

"Do you have something for me to do?" a feminine voice said and Goodwill felt his resolve weakening. When he'd summoned this demon, he'd expected almost anything besides what he'd gotten. A female with a seductive voice and a body to kill for… but a face that was so horrid that even one glance meant that you'd forever see it when you closed your eyes at night. Her name was Sazar and she was a blood demon, one who relished sex and death in equal amounts. "I grow tired of walking invisibly at your side."

"It's what I want of you. If people see you, it's going to cause problems."

A soft foot began to rub against his leg. "Don't you like me, Malcolm?"

"Of course I do. But now isn't the time." Goodwill stood up, taking a long drag on his cigar.

"I need to eat," the demon said petulantly. "I haven't killed in days. Why didn't you let me sup on Harry Nance? You wasted all that blood."

Goodwill didn't answer at first. He had kept her at bay because he'd sensed his hold on her was slipping. He needed the stolen pages from the Codex Gigas to renew his power. Without it, she could easily slip her bonds and turn on him. He wondered if she could tell that her leash was growing ever longer. "I'll let you feast this evening," he said. "Now be gone!"

Sazar rose from the couch and rubbed his shoulders. He could smell her soft skin and a part of him yearned to take her. But the thought of her face was too much for him and slowed the rush of blood that she always brought on. "There are other things I hunger for as well. Can you promise to satisfy those desires as well?" she teased.

"Of course. With relish." Goodwill reached up to squeeze her hand. A knock at the door made him pause and he quietly hissed. "Vanish. Now."

Sazar withdrew her hands but he could hear the challenge in her voice. "One of these days you'll recognize my power, Malcolm. I'm not your toy."

Goodwill ignored her, walking toward the door and peering through the peephole. A skinny young brunette was standing there, wearing a threadbare green dress. Her hair was soaked from the morning rain.

"Harry? You in there?" she asked. She knocked again. "Let me in if you are. I'm drenched to the bone."

A girlfriend, Goodwill mused. There was always the chance she might know something. He'd have to silence her afterward, though. He couldn't run the risk of her talking to the cops or telling anyone about the things he'd be quizzing her over. He cast one glance over his shouler to make sure that Sazar was invisible and then he opened the door, reaching out quickly to grab the girl and yank her inside. "Come in, my dear."

"Who are you?" she asked, staring at the ruined apartment in shock.

"I could ask the same of you."

"My name's Doris. I'm Harry's girlfriend."

"Then I'm sorry for your loss."

"What are you talking about? Where's Harry?"

"My name is Malcolm Goodwill. Harry might have mentioned me. I'm his employer. Or was, to be precise."

"Why do you keep talking like that?" Doris suddenly put a hand over her mouth. "Has something happened to Harry?"

"He's dead. I'd imagine if it were not already in the papers, it will be soon. He was cut up last night. Had more holes in him than a hunk of Swiss cheese."

"Oh my god." Doris looked as if she was about to cry but Goodwill tossed her onto the couch and her head seemed to clear. She looked around at the apartment, noticing how it had been rifled through. "What's going on here?" she asked.

"Your boyfriend stole something from me. Eight pages from a very old book.

I want them back. Do you know anything about them?"

"Harry wasn't much for reading," Doris said, shaking he head. "I don't know anything about... Oh." A strange expression passed over the girl's face and Goodwill knew that she had just remembered something.

"Tell me!" he demanded, raising a hand as if to strike her.

Doris flinched and began to speak rapidly. "He said something about having seen somethin' that he shouldn't have. Said that he was gonna do somethin' about it! That it was time to be a man. But he didn't tell me any details! I swear it!"

"But you knew enough to know it had to do with my papers."

"Yeah. When he was telling me about it, I saw some old papers on his table. He'd bought a big envelope to put them in."

Goodwill narrowed his eyes. "Was he going to mail them to someone?"

"I don't know. Honest!"

Goodwill turned away, seething internally. Had he misjudged Harry? Had the man not been so stupid as to hold onto the papers himself? He glanced back at Doris, catching her as she stared longingly at the door. She was going to either make a break for it or begin screaming soon. "Sazar," he said and Doris looked at him in confusion. "Feed."

The spectral form of a nude woman became visible at his side. Even Doris, as heterosexual as any girl could be, was forced to silently acknowledge the loveliness of Sazar's form. But then Doris let her eyes travel up the long neck and settle on the horrific visage that was Sazar's face. A scream died in her throat and Doris drew back as Sazar lunged for her.

Goodwill watched for a moment or two before looking out the window. The sounds of Sazar lapping at the girl's spilling blood were nauseating.

Down below, he saw a black sedan pull to a halt in front of the building and two men emerge. One of them was very familiar to Goodwill, as he was to almost any citizen of Sovereign: Lazarus Gray, whose grim features were regularly depicted in newspaper photographs. As leader of Assistance Unlimited, Gray was a constant thorn in the side of the underworld.

Goodwill waited until Gray and Morgan had entered the building and then he yanked opened the window. The fire escape lay below and he nimbly swung his legs down onto it. The metal structure was slick from the morning rain but Goodwill held his balance well. Looking back into Harry's apartment, he said, "Sazar, there's two men coming up. When they get here, please take care of them and then come back to the house. Understood?"

Sazar looked up at him and grinned. Blood dripped from her chin in copious amounts and she allowed one hand to paw at the dead girl's breast. Feeding always stirred her passions to dangerous levels. "I'll devour their hearts," she swore.

Goodwill said nothing, descending the fire escape in silence. The arrival of Gray might be nothing more than coincidence but he didn't really believe in chance. If Gray was here... and Harry had planned to send the pages to someone... then it all added together that he might have sent them to Assistance Unlimited.

Everybody knew the group was housed on Robeson Avenue and Goodwill suddenly realized that if Gray were here, then the place might be abandoned for the moment.

Grinning, Goodwill moved to his car and slid behind the wheel. Perhaps, he mused, things might work out after all.

— ◦◦◦ —

"**S**o tell me again how you know it was Harry who sent us the papers?" Lazarus Gray took the steps two at a time, forcing Morgan to hurry in his attempt to keep up. Morgan was a slender and fairly athletic man but he was in his forties and had enjoyed life to the fullest. His words were punctuated by gasps between nearly every word.

"I took the liberty of calling Sovereign Office Supply. Envelopes of that size aren't particularly common. They remembered a man coming in a few days ago, wanting to purchase a single envelope. Most of the time, buyers purchase them in packs of 5-10. The man's name was Harry Nance. The manager of Sovereign Office Supply knew him because Nance's girlfriend worked at the diner next door."

"And now we're gonna see if we can get him to talk?"

"I'm afraid it won't be that easy." Gray reached into one of his pants pockets and pulled out the morning paper, which was rolled up. "I grabbed this on the way out of the office. Notice anything on the front page?"

Morgan slowed to a stop, grateful to have the opportunity to catch his breath. He saw only a few items of interest: The Monster, one of the leaders in the Sovereign underworld scene, was still Public Enemy Number One according to the police chief and an unidentified man was found hacked to death in the early hours of the morning. "I don't get it," he admitted at last.

"I'm fairly certain that the dead man is Harry Nance." Morgan looked at his employer expectantly and Gray continued, "The murder took place down the block from a mail box. The postal stamp on the envelope shows that it was picked up at mail box # 5, which coincides with that street. I reason that he was murdered immediately after placing the envelope in the mail chute."

The two men resumed their trek upstairs, not taking much interest in the dingy surroundings. Harry had lived in one of the more squalid areas of town and the building stank of mildew and rat droppings. It was a far cry from the relative opulence of the Assistance Unlimited headquarters and reminded Morgan that it wasn't so long ago that he was much like Harry Nance: a man down on his luck with no obvious prospects. A chance encounter with Lazarus Gray had caused him to reevaluate his position in life and he'd soon traded a life of crime for one of decency and hard work.

Gray stopped outside Harry Nance's apartment, a strange look on his face.

He held up a hand, indicating that he wanted silence from Morgan. He pointed to the dusty floor, where nearly a dozen footprints could be seen. One set, the most recent from the looks of them, belonged to a woman in heels.

Lazarus knelt in front of the keyhole and placed his eye up close. At first all he could see was a room in ruins, with papers and cushions overturned. But then he saw a red pool on the floor, along with the legs belonging to Doris. He stood up quickly and took a step back. He then threw his shoulder against the door, which popped open with a crash. Morgan had drawn his pistol as soon as he'd sensed Gray's intentions and he followed his employer into the apartment, scanning for any signs of threat. He was the first to lay eyes upon Sazar. The demon was stepping toward him from his left, her arms outstretched. Her nude body immediately caught his gaze and held it but his eyes inevitably traveled up and his breath seized in his chest.

"Chief? We've got trouble," Morgan wheezed.

Gray, who had been moving to check on Doris, whirled about. His eyes widened at the sight before him and he immediately sprang into action. Sazar was hissing like a cat, one that was hungry for blood. Gray slammed into her, the impact crashing them both into the wall, shattering the plaster. Sazar craned her neck, trying to bury her fangs in his throat but he was able to hold her at bay with his mighty strength.

Morgan raised his gun but was too afraid of hitting Gray to pull the trigger. He moved closer, ready to take any opening that presented itself.

Sazar strained against Gray, her arms wrapping tightly around his torso. She squeezed with inhuman strength and even Gray, whose tolerance for pain bordered on the uncanny, was forced to grunt. "Let me taste you," she whispered. "It will only hurt for the first moment or two. And then you will shiver in pleasure. You will beg me to continue."

"I doubt that," Gray retorted, gritting his teeth as his ribs began to grind together. He brought his head back and then slammed his forehead into her face. Blood spurted from her nose and she howled in pain, clutching all the tighter. Gray was unaffected by the horrors of her face – though he remembered virtually nothing of his past before arriving in Sovereign, he was somehow sure that he'd seen worse than this in the past.

"I'm going to tear your heart out and rip it into chunks," the demon screamed.

Gray realized that she was unused to pain, having grown accustomed to inflicting it and not receiving. He took a chance by releasing his hold on her shoulders and instead grabbing her by the head. He drove his thumbs into her eyes and she howled like a banshee, tossing him away.

That gave Morgan his opportunity. He raised his gun and fired, sending all of his available shells into the demon's body. She jerked repeatedly, thrashing about as blood flowed from her wounds. She raked the air with her claws and vanished, screaming inhuman obscenities at them both.

Morgan blinked. "Is she dead?"

"No. Something like her can't be killed, only driven from this plane. She'll slink away to heal her wounds." Gray examined Doris and frowned. "Dead."

Morgan knew there were few things in the world that his employer hated more than failing to save an innocent life. It didn't matter that he'd had no inkling that this girl was in danger. Gray would still beat himself up over her demise.

Gray looked about them, his expression returning to its neutral state. "It looks like someone was hoping to find those papers here. That's a good sign. Means they're unaware that we have them."

"So now what?"

"We notify the authorities and have them pick up this poor girl's remains. Then we head back to headquarters and plan our next move. With luck, Samantha and Eun will be returning at the same time."

Morgan placed his gun back into its holster and lowered his voice. "Chief, what was that thing?"

"A blood demon. They exist just outside our range of vision. There are only a dozen or so in existence but they're old, far older than Man." Gray's expression darkened. Morgan was certain he was mulling over the fact that he would be able to recall such information while simultaneously being unable to remember things about his own life.

"Life just gets stranger, doesn't it?" Morgan whispered. Gray's lips twisted in an almost-grin but it vanished so quickly that Morgan wasn't sure if he had imagined seeing it.

"That it does," was all Lazarus said in reply.

Chapter III
Houses of Death

Eun crouched on a tree limb overlooking Goodwill's fenced property and he didn't like what he saw. He climbed down to where Samantha was waiting for him and she could tell from the look on his face that something wasn't right.

"Is Goodwill at home?" she asked.

"Didn't see him. But there are men walking around in the yard, guarding the estate. And I saw several that were dressed as ninja."

"I don't have the foggiest idea what that means," Samantha admitted.

"No reason why you should. Ninja were mercenaries back in feudal Japan. They specialized in assassination, espionage and sabotage. I didn't know anyone still practiced their dark arts but with how strange Sovereign's becoming, nothing should surprise me."

Samantha put her hands on her hips and thought things over. They were in an expensive neighborhood but in Sovereign that just meant the trash wore more expensive clothing. Even so, it was a heavily patrolled area by the police and despite the fact that all members of Assistance Unlimited held special privileges with law enforcement, she was in no hurry to attract any attention. "These ninja are deadly, I take it?"

"Assuming they've really undergone ninja training? Yes. Quite."

Samantha looked back at the fence. It was about ten feet high and cobblestone, which actually made climbing a bit easier. There were plenty of places for hands and feet to find purchase. "I say we go inside," she said at length.

Eun grinned, admiring her spirit. They were the two youngest members of Assistance Unlimited but they rarely spent much time together. Eun was a private man with a lot of anger in his heart. As such, he actually found it easier to work along Lazarus, who rarely pushed or prodded him on an emotional level. But that didn't mean that he didn't love Samantha and Morgan. They were all part of the Assistance Unlimited family, despite their differences in methods. "Last one over is a rotten egg."

Samantha arched an eyebrow. "Are you challenging me?"

"Are you afraid of losing?"

"Oh!" Samantha stifled a laugh. "You're on." The slender girl kicked off her high heels and stuffed them into the small handbag she was carrying. She slipped the leather bag straps over her left arm and threw herself against the fence. She scrambled up like a monkey and threw herself over with abandon. She landed in a crouch, her skirt billowing about. She looked up triumphantly to see that Eun was already there, leaning against the fence.

"Sorry," he said with a shrug and a cocky grin. "I do believe you're the rotten egg."

Samantha stood up and quickly put her shoes back on. "Scoundrel," she said teasingly.

The two of them grew quiet as one of the ninja rounded the corner. The black-garbed man didn't see them and he stopped so that he was standing with his back to the house. He pulled away the cloth covering his face and Eun saw clearly that he was Japanese. As they watched in silence, they saw him take out a cigarette and light it. He had just begun to smoke it in earnest when Eun crept up next to him and put the barrel of his gun against the ninja's head.

"Make a sound and I'll kill you," Eun promised. It was something of a hollow threat since none of Assistance Unlimited killed unless it was absolutely necessary to save either his or her own life or someone else's.

The ninja's eyes widened as Samantha came into view. "The two of you are making a mistake," the ninja said with only the faintest hint of an accent. "Turn and leave now and you might get out of here alive."

Eun tapped a symbol on the black cloth. There was a circle surrounding a heart, with blood dripping below. "What does this mean?"

"We are Black Heart," the ninja said, obviously thinking that would be explanation enough.

"I've heard of them," Samantha said. "I didn't know they were... ninjas or whatever you called them. They're killers for the mob."

"We perform a needed function," the ninja retorted. He flicked his cigarette to the ground. "We do jobs for the mob but that doesn't mean we work for them."

"Then whom do you work for?" Eun asked, pressing the gun harder against the man's head. "Mr. Goodwill?"

The ninja struck quickly, driving an elbow up against Eun's arm, knocking his gun hand toward the sky. The ninja kicked Eun in the stomach before turning on Samantha. From the look in his eyes, he obviously expected to make quick work of the girl.

Unfortunately for him, Samantha Grace was far more than she appeared. Raised by philanthropic parents who were willing to pay for any tutelage she desired, Samantha was a mistress of several forms of martial arts. She nimbly stepped aside when the ninja lunged for her, delivering a powerful chop to the back of his neck as he passed. She then finished him off, kicking him hard in the rump, knocking him headfirst into the tree where Eun had been perched only moments before.

Samantha held out a hand and helped Eun get back to his feet. "Hope you don't mind that you were saved by a rotten egg."

Eun brushed himself off. "Not at all. Thank you."

The two of them peered around the corner and saw that they were momentarily in the clear. They sprinted across the yard and ducked inside a side door on the house. Once inside, they paused in a hallway, keeping their voices barely above a whisper.

"Now what?" Eun asked.

Samantha shrugged. Originally, they were supposed to nose around and look for clues about how Goodwill tied in to those papers. But given the number of Black Heart ninjas running around, it seemed that the man was involved in something dirty no matter what. She was about to say as much when they heard voices from a nearby room. She crept over and placed her ear against the door, confusion making her eyes widen. She recognized one of those voices but the impossibility made her doubt what she was hearing. She looked over at Eun and saw that he was watching her closely.

The first of the voices, which was unfamiliar to both of them, was speaking in hurried tones. "He'll be back soon. If you'd just wait, I'm certain he'd want to speak to you."

"I don't have time for that," the other man responded. It was this person that had evoked the frightened response in Samantha. He spoke with a German accent but he was quite fluent nonetheless. "Tell Mr. Goodwill that I want those papers and am willing to pay for them. This is not open to negotiation. If he tries to withhold them from me, I'll kill him and everyone who stands at his side. Do you understand?"

"Yes, I'm quite clear on that."

"Good. Tell him I look forward to hearing from him soon."

Eun and Samantha flattened themselves against the wall, hiding as the door opened and the German emerged. He was dressed like an undertaker and he leaned heavily on a walking stick that was topped by a roaring lion's head. His progress carried him away from the Assistance Unlimited agents but Samantha was certain that this was Walther Lunt, the cultist who had tried to work with the vile Doc Pemberley during the group's most recent case. The right side of Lunt's face was a ruined mass of flesh, scarred by an acid attack years before.

"That's him," Samantha whispered when he'd vanished down the hall. "That's the man who turned his cane into a lion. He tried to kill me!"

Eun frowned. "That doesn't make sense. That cane's back at headquarters. Besides, you said he was dead."

Samantha swallowed hard. "He is. I saw him die. Heck, I went with the Chief to drop his body off at the morgue. That's how we found out his name. He's a big muckity-muck in Berlin." Eun started to suggest that maybe the man had a twin but he fell into silence when Samantha grabbed him by the sleeve. "C'mon," she said, "Let's follow him."

"What about Goodwill?"

"Forget him. This is far more important!" She locked eyes with Eun and leaned in close. "Remember, Lunt said he knew who the Chief was. If there's any way we can help Lazarus find out about his past, we have to do it."

Eun considered it briefly and then nodded, following her in pursuit of Lunt. He'd been the first of the group to find out the truth about Gray's amnesia and he knew how much it ate away at their employer. She was right: nothing was more important than finding out the truth.

Malcolm Goodwill stood outside 6196 Robeson Avenue and stared at the imposing black doors, adorned with only a single metal placard. The words "Assistance Unlimited" were embossed on its surface. A small buzzer was located beneath the sign and Goodwill considered it for only a second before he pressed it with one gloved hand.

A mechanical-sounding voice responded at once. "I'm sorry but all agents of Assistance Unlimited are currently away on missions. If you would like to leave a card with your name and number, you may slip it beneath the door and someone will get back to you as soon as possible. If this is a matter of life and death, please press the buzzer twice more: one long and one short."

Goodwill paused, both amused and perplexed. He'd spent a good twenty minutes wandering around the building and had no obvious means of entry. All the windows were barred and shuttered and the doors had a strange kind of lock on them that he'd never encountered before. The somewhat strange method of breaking in by ringing the doorbell had finally presented itself as the only possible thing to do. Now a mechanized voice was walking him through the process of getting inside? It was bizarre, indeed.

After pressing the buzzer twice, with one long and one short, Goodwill took a step back. The twin obsidian doors slid open quickly and the voice returned. Was it his imagination that it now contained a note of urgency?

"Please enter immediately. The doors will close behind you so make sure you have all companions and belongings with you."

Goodwill hesitated a moment, uncertain what he should do. Would he be trapped inside? In the end, he jumped inside, hoping that he'd be able to find his way back out when the time came.

He found himself in the large foyer that greeted all guests of Assistance

Unlimited. As the doors hissed shut behind him, the locking mechanisms sliding into place with a loud clang, Goodwill approached the small receptionist desk that lay straight ahead. The building had once been a hotel and there were still a set of boxes behind what had once been the front clerk's area, though there were no longer keys for each room. The mechanized voice returned, startling Goodwill. The man jumped and then immediately felt stupid for having done so.

"To your right you will find a small sitting area. Please wait there for someone to assist you. If you need medical assistance, please pick up the courtesy phone on the counter. It will dial a doctor who is on call 24 hours a day and they will be here within fifteen minutes."

Goodwill glanced about but was unable to pinpoint where the voice was emanating from. He tapped his fingers on the desk and frowned. This whole thing seemed absurd. What kind of security system allowed anyone inside, when all they had to do was lie about it being an emergency? And now he was being asked to sit still, when he had the freedom to wander through the entire complex? It certainly seemed that Lazarus Gray wasn't the genius the papers made him out to be.

Goodwill spotted an elevator as well as a set of stairs. He took several steps toward them but came to a halt when he bumped into something hard and unyielding. He rubbed his nose while reaching out carefully, tracing it with his fingers. There appeared to be nothing there but upon close examination he found there were virtually invisible barriers all around, blocking access to anywhere but the foyer and the sitting room. Evidently, they had slid down from the ceiling when he'd entered the building.

Cursing, Goodwill reconsidered his earlier impression about Gray and his security. He drew out his handgun and pointed it toward one of the barriers. He pulled the trigger and immediately regretted the decision. The bullet ricocheted off of the barrier and narrowly missed embedding itself in Goodwill's shoulder. It struck the wall behind him and flew back again and Goodwill fell to the floor, covering his head with his hands. The bullet continued whizzing back and forth for what seemed like an eternity before the room finally fell into silence.

Slowly rising back to his feet, Goodwill forced himself to take several deep breaths. He strode toward the front doors and pushed on them, only to find that his worst fears were confirmed: the doors were locked and no matter how hard he pushed, they refused to budge. The building was in sort of lock-down mode, triggered by his foolhardy decision to claim he was in the middle of an emergency.

For a moment, Goodwill gave over to his rising anger. He kicked and screamed like a petulant child, so caught up in the moment that he dropped the false British accent he usually used. In those moments, he spoke once again like the Pennsylvania boy that he truly was.

When he was done venting, Goodwill found himself thinking back to how this affair got started. The infamous Doc Pemberley had fearfully come calling at Goodwill's front door a few weeks back, claiming that he'd narrowly escaped capture. He needed quick money, he'd said, and had offered Goodwill a number of interesting items in exchange for enough cash to get him into a new safe house. Goodwill had grown bored with the entire affair until Pemberley had brought out several ancient pieces of paper, claiming that they had been written by the devil himself. How Pemberley had acquired them had never been explained but Goodwill had felt something rush through him when he'd held those papers. He only had the barest familiarity with Latin but he could understand enough to know that these pages were priceless. Even if he wasn't able to make them do the things that Pemberley claimed, he could sell them to collectors and make a fortune.

It was only after he'd summoned Sazar that he'd realized why Pemberley hadn't used the spells for himself. There was a price to pay for magic like this: Sazar could kill him easily and would have no qualms about doing so. The only thing holding her in check was the words that bound her to his will.

Goodwill realized that he was in a very bad situation. If Gray or his aides caught him now, all his plans would fall apart. He'd planned to use Sazar to extort money from many of the most powerful men in the city. It had seemed like a good plan but all it had taken was one two-bit hood growing a conscience to upset everything.

"I'm hurting, Malcolm."

Goodwill spun about, eyes wide. It was Sazar. Her gorgeous body looked almost as bad as her face: she had bullet wounds all over her flesh and she was leaking buckets of blood. "What the hell happened to you? Gray did this?"

"Yes. I'm so weak." Sazar reached out for him, using his shoulders to steady herself. "I could barely find you, I'm so dizzy."

"Can you get us out of here? Take us back to my home?"

Sazar looked at him with blood-rimmed eyes. "I'm not sure. Traveling is hard for me. With you along, too…."

"Take me there and I'll get you as many people to feed upon as you desire."

"I might need to feed before then."

Goodwill caught her meaning, noting the way her eyes lingered over the pulsing vein in his neck. He raised his voice commandingly, hoping she wouldn't push the issue. If she did, he was done for. He didn't remember the proper words to control her. "Sazar! I am ordering you to do this. Take us both home. Now."

Sazar mumbled ancient words under her breath. He didn't understand them but their meaning was clear enough. She was growing tired of following his orders. She gripped him tightly against her naked bloody flesh. "I will do what I can," she hissed. "But in return, I want six strong men and three healthy women. Do you understand?"

Goodwill blinked. She'd always been sated after only one or two kills. Either she was as weak as she claimed or she was simply trying to see what she could get away with. "I'll do it," he promised. "Just get me out of here."

Sazar closed her eyes and Goodwill immediately wished he had as well. They vanished from the Assistance Unlimited headquarters and momentarily entered Sazar's home realm. Everything was made of dripping, shifting blood. There were mountains of the stuff, fountains of red running down rocky passages until they mingled in a flowing river of gore. There were things swimming in that stream, horrible things that made Sazar's terrifying visage look beautiful in comparison. Goodwill tried to look away but found that he couldn't. He could only stare and hope that his sanity wouldn't give way.

As suddenly as it had begun, it was over. Sazar loosed her grip on him and fell to the carpeted floor of Goodwill's study. Malcolm leaned heavily against the edge of his desk, trying to keep from vomiting. He kept attempting to banish the things he'd seen from his mind.

"I need to feed," Sazar whispered.

Goodwill thought about letting her starve but he quickly realized how foolish a thought that was. She'd rip him to shreds before that happened. "Martin! I need you!"

Goodwill's butler rushed into the room, shock on his portly features. "Sir? How did you get inside?"

"No time for that now. She needs to feed. Six men and three women. Round them up, however you have to."

"So many?"

"Yes, damn it!"

Martin nodded and backed away from Sazar, who was looking at him with altogether too much interest. "Sir, a man came by, seeking the papers. He offered to pay for them but said he'd kill you if you refused. And one of our guards was attacked by an Oriental man and a blonde woman."

Goodwill guessed those two were agents of Gray. But the other... "Who was the man who wanted to buy the papers?"

"He said his name was Walther Lunt."

Goodwill shrugged, not recognizing the name. "If he comes back, we'll let Sazar deal with him. Now go and get her something to eat."

Martin hurried from the room, leaving Goodwill to sit down heavily in his desk chair. He had no idea who this Lunt was – did he work with Gray? Or was he someone new? If it was the latter, how did he know about the papers?

"Pemberley," he hissed. The doctor must have told this Lunt about the papers. Probably they didn't even belong to Pemberley in the first place. He might have stolen them from this German. "If I see you again, Pemberley, I'm going to cut your heart out."

Chapter IV
A Ticket to Hell!

Lazarus and Morgan were the first to return to their headquarters and it only took a cursory look at the front entrance to know that something was very wrong. The building was in full lockdown mode and could only be opened by a series of verbal commands known only to Gray and his aides.

The two men entered cautiously, expecting to find someone in near hysterics. That was the typical way they found people who used the life-or-death request to open the doors. When they found no one at all, Morgan stood in the middle of the foyer and scratched his head.

"What the heck? Where could they be?"

Gray knelt down and picked up a small bullet from the floor. From the way the tip was mangled, it was obvious that it had bounced off the semi-invisible walls several times. "Remember that we are dealing with the supernatural."

"You think they just walked through the walls?"

"The blood demon vanished right in front of our eyes, remember? It's conceivable our guest may have done the same. We should check the camera footage."

Morgan followed his employer behind the old clerk's desk. The room behind had a large television screen mounted on a table with several cables and tubes projecting out from the device. Gray had modified this particular television technology so that it could record the features of anyone who came to the front door. This footage was then archived, allowing Assistance Unlimited to build a detailed record of all their cases.

Gray was looking through the recorded data when Samantha and Eun burst into the room, both looking slightly out of breath. Morgan, who had been nursing a small glass of bourbon, stood up quickly.

"You two okay?"

Samantha looked at Gray, who remained intent on the screen. "Chief, we saw Walther Lunt. He's alive. He was at Goodwill's place and he said he was going to kill Goodwill unless he sold him those papers."

Gray nodded but said nothing.

"Didn't you hear me?" Samantha asked, her voice raising an octave. "He's supposed to be dead!"

Gray turned his mismatched eyes on her and sighed. "His body vanished from the morgue less than 48 hours after we left it there. I had assumed that members of his cult had taken it for their own purposes. They may have revived him."

"You're talking about resurrecting the dead," Eun whispered.

Samantha crossed her arms over her chest, anger flashing in her eyes. "I've had enough of this."

Morgan raised his eyebrows, amazed that Samantha would speak to the Chief like that. Nobody was brave enough to use that tone with him. Nobody aside from a pretty young blonde who couldn't have weighed more than a hundred pounds, it seemed.

Gray's entire body was oriented toward her now. "Please explain."

"That German tried to kill me. He **threw** a **lion** at me!" She emphasized those words to such an extent that they seemed like a verbal slap in the small room. "You're telling me that you knew he might still be alive, or resurrected, or whatever. And you never mentioned it to us? Did I ever tell you how much it hurt to find out that you'd been keeping it from us that you were an amnesiac? I thought we were more than just your employees – I thought we were friends and maybe even some kind of family. But that's obviously not the case if you're going to continue keeping secrets from us. Well, I'm not putting up with it anymore. You either start treating us with some actual respect or I'm leaving."

The silence that descended upon the room after that pronouncement was shocking in its totality. No one was even breathing, it seemed.

Gray's face remained impassive but there was a flicker of emotion in his eyes that weakened Samantha's anger somewhat. Though he often came across as a stoic and somewhat robotic individual, Samantha had always sensed a well of sadness within her employer. Now she felt regret for her harsh tone. "You're right, Samantha. I apologize."

Morgan blinked in surprise. "You do?"

"Of course. She's absolutely correct. I trust all of you with my life; I should trust you with all my information as well. I don't keep secrets from you out of maliciousness. It's second nature to me, I'm afraid. Whatever life I led before arriving here in Sovereign, it was one in which duplicity was quite common. I find myself lying all too easily and keeping information close to the vest is a part of that."

Samantha relaxed her body. "I'm sorry, Chief. I didn't mean to--"

"No, you don't have to apologize. Like I said, I'm the one at fault. I'll try to do better in the future but I ask that all of you be understanding that being open and sharing doesn't come naturally to me."

"We've all got trust issues," Morgan said. "Heck, for most of my life, I could have been killed for spilling the beans when I wasn't supposed to so I understand where you're coming from. It's hard to get away from that."

Gray nodded, considering Morgan's words. To Samantha, he asked, "So you're going to stay?"

"Of course. I wouldn't really have left."

"Good." Gray turned and pointed at the screen. A crisp black-and-white image showed the man who had entered the building. He was well dressed and very tall. "That, my friends, is Mr. Malcolm Goodwill."

Eun grunted in annoyance. "There goes any lingering doubt about his involvement in all this."

"I guess you were right, Chief," Morgan muttered. "He must have had that demon come and rescue him."

Gray nodded, staring at the image on the screen. "He came here to get those papers back, which meant he was taking an incredible risk. I think it's safe to say that a man so desperate to have something wouldn't be able to turn down an invitation to get them back."

"What are you thinking?" Eun asked.

Gray said nothing, instead choosing to walk over to a nearby phone. He picked it up and quickly dialed Goodwill's number. Behind his back, his three aides exchanged smirks. Despite his best intentions, Gray simply couldn't keep from milking the dramatics from any moment.

"Mr. Goodwill, please. Tell him it's Lazarus Gray holding for him." Gray faced his aides and placed a hand over the mouthpiece of the phone. "If he wants the papers so badly, we'll simply give them to him." Samantha let out a little gasp but all three of his aides fell silent as Gray resumed speaking into the phone. "I'm impressed that you were able to escape the Assistance Unlimited Headquarters. It definitely shows that you're a man of great power. So great that we would like to bring about a truce of sorts. We have the papers that once belonged to your man but we have no interest in retaining them. We're willing to pass them on to you in return for a small fee reimbursing us for our trouble. Whatever you think they're worth. We can meet at the old Trembley Coal Plant on Skiver Way. Within the hour, yes." Gray hung up the phone and nodded smartly to his aides. "Everyone get ready. I'd anticipate Mr. Goodwill being quite treacherous so we should respond in kind."

<hr />

Walther Lunt sat in front of the fireplace, stirring the embers with a poker. The ruined side of his face ached today, as it always did when rain was on the way. It was an odd affliction. He'd heard of men and women whose arthritis worsened when storms were looming but ravaged acid burns? It had to be a first. "We should leave soon. We're supposed to be on the other side of town in half an hour."

The woman seated near him crossed her stocking-encased legs, knowing that the movement would catch his interest. Lunt was a lecherous sort and Miya Shimada was attractive enough to keep him in perpetual arousal. A Japanese-American, Miya had shoulder-length black hair that shimmered in the sunlight. Her body was the perfect mixture of the two races that made up her ethnic background: the slim features of the Japanese melded with the hips and breasts of a Western woman. "We can leave when you've finished your drink. I have to say, you're looking much better than you did when I first saw you," Miya said teasingly.

Walther grunted in acceptance of that. "I owe you my life. Or, rather, my second life."

"Our masters aren't done with you," Miya pointed out. "That's why they dispatched me to resurrect you. In the end, all of us are but pieces on their grand chess board."

Walther picked up a glass of cognac from the table in front of him and he sipped it in silence. When he finally spoke again, his words were so low that Miya had to strain to hear them. "Have you found out anything useful?"

Miya looked around their shared hotel room and pursed her ruby red lips. Walther had been hopeful that they'd become lovers but Miya hadn't allowed that to happen. They were living here under the pretext of being husband and wife to throw off any who might be looking for them but she harbored no romantic feelings toward him. It wasn't just because of his face, either. There was only one man who had ever tasted the pleasures of her flesh. He had been the first in her entire life that had seemed to be her intellectual and sexual equal. "Nothing that you didn't already know. He arrived out of the blue in 1933 and immediately made a name for himself. He first came to the attention of the press when he involved himself in the kidnapping of Arthur Lingold's baby. The entire country was riveted by the case since Lingold's exploits as a pilot had won him so much acclaim. And now his infant son was missing, with only a bizarre ransom note left at the scene. Lazarus Gray managed to find the child and bring those responsible to justice. From there, it's been one success after another. His agency, Assistance Unlimited, is considered the last hope for those who have nowhere else to turn. He's considered quite the hero."

Miya realized that Lunt was staring at her over the rim of his glass. "The way you speak of him," the German said. "It's clear you still harbor feelings for the man."

"He's hard to forget," Miya admitted.

"Sad that he can't say the same for you. Apparently, he remembers virtually nothing."

"That can be a blessing in some ways," Miya countered. "How is he to know the difference between the true past and a fiction?"

"What are you planning?"

Miya stood up, her body moving enticingly beneath her dress. "I seduced him once before. Why shouldn't I be able to do it again?"

"What if seeing you again sparks his memory? The last thing we need is for him to remember who he really is. Or who we really are, for that matter."

Something dark and malevolent flashed in Miya's eyes. "If he doesn't accept the way things have to be, then I'll just have to kill him. Again."

———— ⚬≈⚬ ————

"**I**t's suicide."

Goodwill looked over at the Black Heart ninja who had spoken. The man was one of the group's leaders but it was still rare for him to openly challenge Goodwill's decisions. After looking around at the other ninja who stood watching, Goodwill asked, "Would you care to explain that?"

"You want us to lie in wait while you approach Assistance Unlimited with only that... thing... at your side? You could be cut down long before we could respond. Take us with you."

"I'm not looking for a fight. Not right now. I need those papers." Goodwill glanced over at Sazar, who was watching them with all the disinterest of a bored cat. She was toying with her nakedness, raking her fingernails over her flat belly and across her nipples, making them stand up in sharp little points. She was successfully distracting many of the ninja, but not their leader, nor Goodwill.

"But surely you don't expect them to hand them over. That is not the way of Lazarus Gray or his men."

"Yes. That's why I'll have Sazar with me. She'll be invisible and ready to strike at a moment's notice. Assistance Unlimited may be capable of handling normal men like yours but they won't be able to handle her."

The ninja's eyes were the only part of his face left visible but they flashed with anger. "They nearly killed her the last time, didn't they?"

Sazar hissed and moved forward but Goodwill held up a hand and she stepped back, though she looked like she might ignore him at a moment's notice. "I appreciate the fact that you believe in your men so much," Goodwill said. "That confidence makes you one of my best assets. But the discussion is over. Do you understand?"

The man nodded and bowed. "As you say."

Goodwill waited until all the ninja had left the room, heading toward the vehicles that would transport them to the old coal factory. There they'd take up positions all around the property, hidden out of sight.

"Why didn't you tell them about Walther Lunt?" Sazar asked.

Goodwill turned toward her, keeping his eyes on her breasts. They were so much nicer to look at than her face. He had called Walther Lunt and asked him to meet him at the coal factory immediately after getting off the phone with Gray. Sazar had been with him when he'd made the call but he'd deliberately made sure that none of the Black Heart knew about it. "Because I think the time's come for me to abandon Sovereign City and I'm going to need a lot of cover to make that happen. When Lunt arrives, I'm expecting all hell to break loose. That's when you and I take off. We'll leave my ninja to fight both Assistance Unlimited and Lunt's men."

"After you've gotten the papers back," she whispered.

"Yes."

Sazar slid around in front of him, undulating her hips like a serpent. "You don't remember the spells, do you? That's why you're so desperate to get the papers."

Goodwill tried to retain his bravado but some of his willpower began to wilt. She knew he was helpless now. "I remember enough to bind you," he bluffed.

Sazar laughed throatily. "You amuse me, Malcolm. For that reason – and because I've fed recently – I won't kill you. But don't think that you're my master any longer. I can come and go as I please."

Goodwill cleared his throat and moved around her. "Let's get going, shall we?"

———

azarus Gray and his people were the first to arrive. He had chosen this site for several reasons: first and foremost, it had been abandoned for years, meaning it was unlikely that any innocents would be hurt. Second, Gray owned it, meaning any collateral damage that occurred would only cost him and not anyone else. Finally, he had set up the old factory as an emergency base for Assistance Unlimited, meaning that it had a stash of weapons and equipment hidden around the property.

Gray had Samantha stand with him in the large parking area, which had a gravel surface. It was here that he planned to make the proposed exchange. Morgan was perched on the second floor of the nearby factory building, where he was waiting with a high-powered rifle. Eun was hiding behind some old mining equipment, ready to explode onto the scene if required.

Five minutes before the agreed-upon meeting time, the Black Heart ninjas arrived. Eun spotted them first, watching with amusement as nearly a dozen of the men spread out, hiding behind any cover they could find. They must have parked their vehicles a mile or so away and come the rest of the distance on foot.

He did nothing, though, remembering the plan. When one of the ninja tried to take his spot for his own, however, he quietly took the man by surprise, snapping his neck with a move so exquisite that few on the planet could have matched it. Of course, one of those men was his employer.

The next to arrive was Goodwill, who drove himself in a small roadster. He parked thirty feet away from Gray, who stood with the papers clasped in his hands. Goodwill emerged from the vehicle and looked around in dramatic fashion. He smiled at Lazarus and took several steps toward him. "I confess, I'm surprised to see you here. I'd thought you were leading me into a trap."

"And yet you still came," Samantha said.

"Yes," Goodwill responded, frowning. He obviously didn't appreciate having one of Gray's underlings answering him. "So, Lazarus. I've brought you enough money to cover the transfer." Goodwill reached into the pocket of his slacks and Morgan tensed above. When Goodwill's hand emerged holding a wad of bills taped together, Morgan's finger relaxed on the trigger but he still remained ready to fire if need be.

Gray caught the money when Goodwill tossed it to him. Without even bothering to count it, he handed the bills to Samantha. "I must warn you, Mr. Goodwill, you're dealing with things best left alone." He held up the pages and his already grim face turned even darker. "You risk not only your life but your immortal soul."

"I appreciate the concern," Goodwill answered, still using his faux British accent. "Now may I have my papers back?"

"Why did you kill the young woman we found in Nance's apartment?"

"Because she knew too much." Goodwill extended his left hand. "The papers, Lazarus. Now."

"Of course." Lazarus took several steps forward and pushed them into Goodwill's hand. Before the transfer was fully complete, he stared into Goodwill's eyes and said a series of words that sounded like gibberish, unless you knew that they were the ancient tongue of the demon world.

Goodwill's eyes opened wide, for he did recognize them. They were the words he'd not been able to remember, the words that bound the demon to whomever spoke them.

Sazar suddenly became visible, standing just to the left of Goodwill. She stared at Gray with mounting interest, wondering what he would order her to do. Now that the spell had been spoken, she was his to command.

"Blood demon," Gray said loudly, "capture him – but do not kill him!"

Goodwill snarled, spinning away from Sazar. He held the papers in his hand – if he could just have the time to read the words on them, he could try to wrest control of her from Gray. Or banish her, if need be. But before he got more than three steps away, Sazar was on, throwing him to the ground and crouching over his chest. Her mouth was open near his neck, close enough that he could feel the heat of her breath and feel the spittle that dripped from her tongue. "No! Please!"

he whispered.

At that moment, the Black Heart ninja sprang into action. They had held off, waiting for a signal from Goodwill, but now it appeared that he was in no position to summon them. They rushed forward, leaping and spinning impressively. Their swords flashed in the murky Sovereign sunlight. Eun moved into view, clashing with several, but it was Morgan who did the most damage. From his vantage point, he was able to pick them off at will, pausing only long enough to reload his rifle. During the bloodshed, Gray remained exactly where he'd started out, though he now had Samantha clinging to him. The girl buried her face in his shoulder, averting her eyes from the mayhem. The Black Heart assassins died in droves, bullets riddling their bodies, save for the few that Eun killed by hand.

When the sounds of gunfire had faded, Gray ordered Sazar to step away. She did so but was obviously hungering for a taste of Goodwill's blood. Now that all remnants of his hold over her had faded, she saw Goodwill as nothing more than food.

Goodwill rose to his knees, looking up at Gray in astonishment. "You're not human, are you? You're just as much of a demon as she is. Nobody human could stand there and be so calm."

"I'm as human as you," Gray responded. "But I've chosen to live my life with meaning. For those who traffic in death, there is only more death. But those who live for others will find a richer meaning."

"How trite," Goodwill said with a laugh. "You don't really believe that, do you?"

"I do. It's a lesson that Harry Nance learned at the end. That's why he risked his life to make sure that someone learned what you were up to."

Goodwill glanced over at Sazar. "Kill me if you want but don't let her do it. Please."

"I don't plan to kill you at all. I'm going to turn you over to the authorities. But before I do, I want answers. What do you know about Walther Lunt?"

"Not much. He wanted to buy these papers. That's it."

Gray looked disappointed and Samantha knew that he was more troubled by Lunt's resurrection than he'd let on. She could sympathize – here was an actual piece of his past and he couldn't make sense of it.

At that moment a crack rang out and Goodwill's body lurched to the side. Blood sprayed from his head and Samantha instinctively looked up at Morgan, thinking he had fired the deadly shot. Gray, however, knew that someone else had been behind the blast. He pushed Samantha behind him and drew his own handgun, looking in the direction of the shot.

There he saw him, standing beside a black sedan. The German held a Mauser in one hand and his walking stick in the other. It was Walther Lunt, who gave a mocking salute before sitting back behind the wheel.

Eun sprinted up beside his employer. "Should I?" he began but Lazarus shook his head.

"You'd never make it in time," Gray muttered as Lunt spun his vehicle away from them, kicking up gravel as he did so. "All you'd do is get yourself shot."

"Why did he kill him?" Samantha wondered. "Goodwill didn't know anything about him."

"Maybe he was angry over not getting the papers," Eun suggested.

Gray said nothing, not even when Sazar lunged on Goodwill's bleeding corpse, lapping it lustily. He knew the real reason why Lunt had done it: because there was something dark and cold inside Lunt's soul and he wanted Gray to know that he could have done that very same thing to Samantha or Eun or Morgan. It was a taunt, the proverbial 'you can't stop me.'

"Chief? You gonna get rid of her?"

Gray glanced at Morgan and then at Sazar. "Yes. You're right." He walked forward and repeated the rest of the spell, this time banishing her from this plane. Unlike Goodwill, his sharp mind allowed him to remember such details. The blood demon howled in disappointment but she vanished in a puff of dark-tinged smoke, leaving the odor of brimstone in her wake.

Gray bent down and plucked up the missing pages from the Codex Gigas. "So much death, all over these." He quickly ripped them to shreds, tossing the remains into the air, where they were quickly snatched up by the wind and carried away.

"Those were priceless," Samantha reminded him. "Shouldn't we have turned them into a museum or something?"

"They were created by the devil," Gray retorted. When he stood up, Samantha shrank away from the fury in his mismatched eyes. It didn't reach his features, which remained unmoved, making it all the worse. "When we find things like that, we have to destroy them. No matter the cost."

"Sure, Chief," Morgan said. "We got it."

Gray nodded, walking away from them. He felt like this case had gone awry. They had accomplished nothing, save for destroying the cursed papers. Lunt was still free, as was Pemberley. Harry Nance and his girlfriend were both dead. It left a sour taste in his mouth but it did solidify his desire to see things through to the end. He would not rest until the monsters of the world were slain and the truth about his past had been laid bare.

No matter the cost.

———— ∞ ————

Miya Shimada sat silently in the passenger seat while Lunt drove back to their rooms. She had hidden out of sight during their confrontation, knowing that it wasn't quite time for her to confront her former lover. She had managed to sneak a peek at him and she was reminded again of all that she'd found so intoxicating about him in the past: his determination, his well-formed physique and his smoldering eyes. They were almost enough to make a corrupted woman believe in redemption.

Almost.

A smile touched her lips and she whispered to herself, "Lazarus Gray." She repeated the name a few more times, as if tasting it. "I wonder what you'll do when you find out about yourself."

She laughed then, startling Lunt, who looked at her as if she were insane. She sat back in her seat and closed her eyes, imagining the days to come. She wasn't sure how it would resolve itself but she knew that it was going to be fascinating to watch.

THE CORPSE SCREAMS AT MIDNIGHT

An Adventure of Lazarus Gray
Written by Barry Reese

———— ∞ ————

Chapter I
The Lady in White

"God is dead."

Samantha Grace shifted uncomfortably, casting a nervous glance at Morgan Watts, who sat beside her. They were the only members of Assistance Unlimited at headquarters, so it had been they who had been tasked with interviewing the young woman who had come to their door, seeking help. No one came to Assistance Unlimited unless they had exhausted all other means of aid, for Lazarus Gray and his followers were as feared as they were loved. This wasn't because any member of Assistance Unlimited cultivated an aura of fear; it was simply a result of Sovereign City's innate nature. The city was as corrupt as any in the United States and even good-hearted people tended to be distrustful of anyone who seemed to operate out of a spirit of altruism, as Gray and his people did. When everyone seemed corrupt, the virtuous were regarded with suspicion.

"Could you repeat that, Ma'am?" Morgan asked, leaning forward. He was forty-two years old and pencil-thin. As always, he was dressed in a black suit and tie, his fedora hat resting on the tabletop next to his right hand. His dark hair was slicked back and his moustache waxed.

SAMANTHA GRACE
BEAUTIFUL, BRAVE, INTELLIGENT AND CAPABLE
MORE THAN A MATCH AGAINST ANY MAN

The young woman in white visibly composed herself before continuing. She looked a few years older than Samantha, which put her somewhere in her mid-twenties. With dark hair, dusky complexion and large, liquid eyes, she was in stark contrast with Samantha, who had golden blonde hair, blue eyes and a peaches-and-cream skin color. The lady in white had the air about her of a woman used to getting her way. She had not been pleased to learn that Lazarus Gray was away on business, meaning that she'd have to reveal her private affairs to his employees. "I told you: God is dead. That's what the corpse said."

"That's what I thought you said," Morgan muttered. "Think you could back up and start over? So far, what you're saying isn't making a whole lot of sense."

The woman sighed loudly and closed her eyes for several seconds, obviously trying to steel herself for what was to come. "I'm sorry. I'm not normally so cross."

Morgan somehow doubted that but he forced a smile. "It's okay. We're used to it. People come to see us in all sorts of states."

"I'm sure," she answered. "My name is Lorraine Mitchell. My husband was President of the Sovereign People's Bank. You probably heard about his death. It was in all the papers two weeks ago. He had a heart attack in his study in the middle of the night. I was sleeping at the time and was awoken by a terrible, blood-curdling scream. I sat bolt upright in my bed and looked at the clock. I distinctly remember that it was exactly midnight."

"It must have been terrible finding your husband's body like that," Samantha said, trying to be comforting.

The withering stare she got in return silenced her immediately. Morgan could sense that Mrs. Mitchell didn't care much for Samantha and he wondered why. Then again, some beautiful women simply had it in for other gorgeous dames, he mused. There could only be so many Queen Bees in some women's lives, after all. "I suppose it was," Lorraine answered. "Though my husband and I had a marriage of convenience. It was based out of mutual need, not love."

"How so?" Samantha asked, dispensing with pleasantries. Her tone was now clipped and much more formal. It was the exact same tone she'd been using with Morgan lately. He'd invited her to see a film with him not long ago, swearing it was simply one friend wanting to spend time with another. But things had gone so well that he'd tried putting the moves on her afterward, leaning in to steal a kiss after the show. He was pretty sure he could still feel the sting of her slap to his face.

"My husband inherited his position at the bank but his father was adamant that he find financial security on his own. As such, my husband was given a job but he wasn't able to touch a penny of his family's fortune. He tried to turn his salary into something more substantial in the stock market but as we all know, that's not nearly as easy now as it was back in the Twenties. Eventually, he came up with an easier route to financial success: he married me. I'm quite wealthy and my husband found my checkbook just as desirable as the swish of my hips."

"And what did you get out of the... partnership?" Samantha inquired.

"I've never been one for romance, Miss Grace. I planned to have children someday and I wanted them to have plenty of opportunities. My husband's family name would have provided those in spades. Unfortunately, he died without giving me a child. It was just like him. He wasn't much of a success at anything, really." Lorraine opened her purse, taking out a cigarette. "Do you mind if I smoke?"

Morgan retrieved a set of matches from the inner pocket of his jacket. He lit her cigarette and she took a few puffs before continuing.

"One of my husband's favorite ways of spending my money was visiting Europe. He cultivated a lot of friendships over there, especially in England. I think it made him feel very Continental." Lorraine chuckled coldly. "When he came back from his last trip, he'd brought back a trophy. He said it was for me but I knew better. What would I want with a moldy old corpse wrapped up in bandages?"

Samantha reached down and smoothed out the folds of her skirt. She was aware of Morgan watching her movements and she tried to ignore it. She was still a bit angry over their evening out together, though most of her anger was actually directed at herself. She shouldn't have put herself in that position, nor should she have laughed so hard at his jokes. She'd encouraged him and even though he was handsome and intelligent, they were coworkers. She couldn't jeopardize her position with Assistance Unlimited over a romantic fling. Clearing her throat, she asked, "Where did he manage to acquire a mummy?"

Lorraine waved her cigarette dismissively. "Oh, owning a mummy was all the rage in England a few decades back. Anyone who was anyone had at least one of the little Egyptians propped against the study room wall. They'd have unwrapping parties, where the owners could show them off to their friends. Ghastly, if you ask me. Anyway, my husband had a friend over there – a Mr. Garmont, I believe – who was in possession of three of the things. They were just stacked up like cordwood in the attic. Well, my husband fell in love upon seeing them. He simply had to have one. So he bought her and brought her back."

"Her?" Morgan asked.

"Yes. Garmont told him some cock and bull story about the mummy having once been a princess of some sort. He insisted we call her Femi around the house. The thing stank like old linen and formaldehyde. He was in the room with it when he died, which wasn't a surprise. He spent most nights in the study with her."

Morgan tapped his fingers on the tabletop thoughtfully. "And at what point did the mummy speak to you?"

"Exactly three days after my husband's death. It was the day of his funeral and I was restless that evening so I couldn't sleep. I wandered around our home nursing a bottle of scotch until I ended up in the study. I happened to glance at the time and noticed it was 11:59. I had just sat down at his old desk when the clock struck twelve... and the mummy began to move. I was terrified, I'll tell you that. The little bitch turned her head and looked right at me and I swear to you that I wasn't drunk enough to have imagined that. She looked right at me and screamed. It was an awful sound, like someone was witnessing something so horrible that they couldn't bear it." Lorraine's fingers began to tremble and her cigarette dropped ash onto her white dress. She brushed it away and licked her lips nervously. "When the screaming was finished, it told me, 'God is dead.'"

"And has this happened to you since?"

"Every three nights, like clockwork. The only differences have been slight. The second time it happened, she raised and arm and pointed at me. The third time, she took two steps in my direction. Every time she screams, she gets closer to being animate again. I think she killed my husband. I don't know if it was intentional or not, but she caused the heart attack that killed him. I'm sure of it."

Morgan looked at their client through narrow eyes. "And the mummy spoke to you in English?"

Lorraine paused, as if the implications of that hadn't occurred to her. "Well, yes."

Samantha nudged her partner. "Doesn't mean anything. If a mummy really can come back to life, that's more amazing than it being able to speak English."

Morgan had to agree with that. They'd both seen things that defied description, which meant you couldn't discount anything.

"When is it supposed to happen again?" Samantha wanted to know.

Lorraine looked very pale. "Tonight. She screams again tonight. That's why I came here. I want to hire Lazarus Gray to be there. To protect me. To tell me I'm not insane. And, maybe, to kill her."

"I'm willing to do that," Lazarus Gray said. All eyes turned toward the man who stood in the doorway. How long he'd been there, no one was sure. He sometimes moved with the stealth of a jungle cat, soundlessly coming and going. He was a well-built man with gray-streaked brown hair, making him look older than he was. His eyes were piercing and mismatched: one eye was a startling emerald, the other a dull brown. He wore a dark suit and tie but there was something primal about him, something that suggested he would be just as much at home in a loincloth. "But before we come over tonight, there are a few things that must be done."

Morgan rose, smiling. "Chief! Boy, am I glad you're here! Did you hear everything?"

"Enough." Gray nodded at Samantha. "Please make a transatlantic call to this Mr. Garmont. Find out the history of this mummy and if anything unusual occurred with it in the past. Morgan, I want you to go upstairs and get Eun. I believe he's about to start filing the papers from the case I was just on. Tell him to set those aside and go with you to the Sovereign People's Bank. Tell him to find out if Mr. Mitchell had a safety deposit box. He needs to get access to it."

"My husband didn't have anything like that. If he had, I'm sure his father would have given me the key at the funeral."

"Perhaps." Gray favored Lorraine with the briefest of smiles but the expression didn't reach his eyes, which remained cold and determined. "I will need you to authorize something for me, Mrs. Mitchell. I'm going to need to see your husband's body and confirm that there was no foul play involved."

Lorraine's lips became a hard, thin line. "My husband's buried in the ground."

"Yes. But if you give permission, I can pull a few strings and have him exhumed immediately."

With a shaky voice, Lorraine whispered, "Whatever you think is needed, Mr. Gray."

"Good. I'll help you with the appropriate paperwork. Morgan, please escort Mrs. Mitchell back to her home. Examine this mummy while you're waiting for us. Make sure that it's what it looks like and that no one is playing a cruel trick on our client." Gray nodded crisply, energized by the mystery before him. "Let's get to work. We only have about twelve hours before the corpse screams again."

Chapter II
Questions With Deadly Answers

Eun Jiwon stepped into the bank, well aware of the stares he received. He was smartly dressed in a black suit and tie but his Korean features made him stand out. He had come here a few times when his parents were alive and he remembered the shame he'd felt when his father had begged for an extension on his loan. The flames of anger never truly died, he realized. They just dimmed to flickering embers, ready to reignite at the proper moment.

"Can I help you?" asked one of the bank's employees. He was an older man with silver hair and thick glasses. He regarded Eun with curiosity but not outright distrust like so many others did. A small nametag placed over his heart indicated that his name was John Mitchell.

"I work with Assistance Unlimited." Eun held out a small business card with the group's address and logo printed on it. The logo showed an open hand, palm up, with the words Assistance Unlimited printed across it. Beneath these were the address 6196 Robeson Avenue and a telephone number. "We're currently investigating a matter concerning Lorraine Mitchell and I'd like to have access to her husband's safety deposit box."

John Mitchell's face fell and his eyes became guarded. "That would be my son you're talking about. What kind of case are you working on regarding my daughter-in-law?"

"That's private, I'm afraid."

"So is my son's safety deposit box."

"So there is one? Mrs. Mitchell indicated that she didn't think there was, since you hadn't given her access to it upon your son's death." Eun held his ground, even as John Mitchell's demeanor became darker.

John glanced around at the other customers and employees, many of whom were watching them. He lowered his voice and took Eun by the elbow, steering him toward the vault. "My son kept a box. All of us do. Sometimes we keep things of personal or business importance in them. A lot of times, it's not things we'd like for our wives to see."

"Is that the kinds of things in his box?"

"I don't know. I have no clue what's in there. But when he died, I couldn't bring myself to look inside. It's still too soon. My son was a disappointment to me in many ways but I loved him. When Lorraine didn't ask about the box, I assumed he hadn't told her about it. And if he hadn't told her about it, then there was some reason as to why."

Eun nodded. "I understand. I promise to use discretion. Unless it's pertinent to our case, I won't share the details of anything I see with Mrs. Mitchell."

"I would appreciate that. Keep in mind that the only reason I'm doing this at all is because of who your employer is. That man's done a lot of good in this town and Lord knows we need more people like him." John gestured for a guard to open up the room containing the safety deposit boxes and he led Eun inside, closing the door behind them. He walked straight toward one of the boxes and placed it on the room's single table. After fishing out a master key from an inside pocket on his jacket, he opened the box and pushed it toward Eun. "I do hope my daughter-in-law isn't in any kind of danger."

"That's what we're trying to find out," Eun admitted. He peered inside the box, finding several envelopes of varying sizes. He peered into several of them, finding handwritten notes and erotic French postcards. From the feminine scent on several of the notes, Eun guessed that Mr. Mitchell had at least one woman on the side, perhaps more. He also found nearly three thousand dollars in cash and a small handgun. All in all, it was rather typical stuff for a man who was living a double life.

But it was the contents of a small manila envelope stuffed at the bottom of the box that caused Eun to pause. There was a necklace of some kind inside, one with a gold chain and a small seven-pointed star pendant. The pendant was lined with tiny diamonds, causing it to glitter brightly in the light. It was very old and Eun knew that it was probably priceless. On the back of the pendant were a series of minuscule hieroglyphics.

John Mitchell stood a few feet away, obviously unwilling to look into the box himself. Perhaps, Eun mused, he was afraid to find out what his son might have been involved in. "Did you find anything?"

Eun held up the necklace. "Have you ever seen this before?"

"No, I haven't." John moved forward, staring at the pendant. "I know he recently purchased a mummy. I wonder if that came with it?"

Eun dropped the necklace into a pocket and pushed the box back toward Mr. Mitchell. "I'll take it with me so Lazarus can look at it. If it turns out that it's not related, I'll see that it's returned here."

"Can't you tell me what's going on?"

Hesitating, Eun considered opening up to the man. It was obvious that despite whatever problems he might have had with his son, he did love him and that extended to his widow as well. Lazarus hadn't specifically told him to hold his cards close to the vest but Eun knew what his employer would do in this situation and he elected to follow suit. "I'm sorry. Rest assured that we're doing all that we can."

Eun spun about and exited the room, aware of the necklace's weight in his pocket. It was far heavier than he would have expected. Somehow, this was tied into the mystery of the mummy and he was willing to bet that Lazarus would be able to figure out how.

Samantha tried to not feel slighted as she waited for the transatlantic call to go through. Every member of the Assistance Unlimited squad was given equal preference when it came to the jobs they performed and this sometimes meant getting stuck with nothing more exciting than talking to someone on the phone. Samantha knew it was an important task but she still ached to be out in the field, where the danger truly lay. It wasn't that she was addicted to the excitement, but she certainly enjoyed the rush that came with surviving a near fatal encounter.

Of all four of them, she was the only one with family still living. Eun's parents had been murdered, Morgan's were long gone and Lazarus... well, poor Lazarus wouldn't have known if he had a wife and kids somewhere. His memory of his life before waking up in Sovereign City was a jumble of confusing images and sounds. It sounded awful to Samantha and she often wondered how lonely he must be.

She sighed, trying to talk herself away from this line of thinking. Lazarus wasn't the most romantic of men but there was something about him that enticed her. She hoped it wasn't simply the pity factor but she couldn't discount that. She did feel the urge to mend his broken heart.

And then there was Morgan. She felt badly for having slapped him but couldn't bring herself to apologize.

She was so lost in thought that it took her a few seconds to realize there was a man on the line now, repeatedly saying hello in a distinctly British voice: "I say, is there anyone there?"

"Is this James Garmont?"

"Yes, it is! And to whom am I speaking, young lady?"

"Samantha Grace of Sovereign City."

"Ah! The little girl of Sheridan and Amanda? I met your parents years ago at a charity get together. Never forgot them. Such a charming, good-humored set of people! What can I do for you, love?"

Samantha paused. Garmont knew her parents? Did Lazarus know that? If so, it explained why he wanted her to handle this call. Sometimes the things he knew bordered on the supernatural. "They speak highly of you as well," she lied. "I'm calling to ask you about Mr. Mitchell. He visited you not long ago and purchased a mummy, didn't he?"

"I believe he did, yes." Samantha fought the urge to stare at the phone. All the good nature had faded abruptly from Garmont's voice. He sounded quite brusque, in fact. "Terrible pity about his death. I heard about it from mutual friends. Give my best to his wife, will you?"

"Please," Samantha said, sensing that he was close to hanging up the phone. "His wife is at her wit's end. She says the mummy is talking to her and moving about. Every third night, it screams at midnight. I know how it must sound but I'm trying to help her. Did anything unusual ever happen with the mummy while you owned it?"

Garmont sighed and it was such a weary sound that Samantha felt a surge of sympathy for him. She could hear him sit down heavily. "That thing has been nothing but a terror. I tried to talk him out of taking it but he wouldn't listen. He was obsessed with her, just like I was." Samantha said nothing, sensing that he would continue in his own time. "I collected the things, mummies I mean. I bought a few and enjoyed showing them off to blokes from the pub. It was good for a laugh now and again. But then a gypsy came knocking on my door one day... I nearly had the help drive her away, she stank so fiercely and you can't trust them, you know? They'll steal you blind if you let them. But she told me she had heard I liked mummies. She said she had one and she was special. So I walked out to her wagon and took a look. Even all dried up and swathed in bandages, she was beautiful. I could feel it in my loins." Garmont's voice trailed away. "I'm sorry, Miss. That's not proper, is it?"

"It's okay. Please go on."

"Well I bought her, of course. And the gypsy told me that she was a princess named Femi. She also told me that what made Femi so special was that she wasn't truly dead. She slept in some sort of awful twilight haze. As long as you kept the seven-starred pendant in the same house, she wouldn't wake up. Move it far enough away, though, and she'd start to revive. It would be slight, at first, but every three days she'd get a little stronger, until at last she was warm and gorgeous again."

"There's a necklace, you say?"

"Yes. I gave it to Mitchell, though I suspect he did the same thing I did. He eventually wanted to see what would happen if she woke up. I had her for nearly three months before I gave in to temptation. There was something about her corpse that made me weak." Garmont's voice became strained and even over the distant phone connection, she knew he was crying. "I buried the pendant out in the garden and then waited. Every three days, she got a little stronger... until finally she came to me and her hips were alabaster white and her breasts were full and ripe. She had raven black hair and almond eyes. She tore at her cloth coverings until all of her sex was exposed and she took me right there on the floor. It was... it was like nothing I'd ever experienced. She was in control the entire time and she took me... like she was claiming me." Garmont grew silent and Samantha almost thought she'd lost the connection when he continued. "When I woke up, I found her in the kitchen. She'd killed the butler and eaten his heart. I ran screaming but they were all dead: the maid, her daughter, even the dogs. All ripped apart by my princess. She came to me again and the Lord knows I'm not sure if she planned to kill me to... or take me back to her bed."

"What did you do?"

"I ran to the garden and dug up the necklace with my bare hands. Once I had it, she returned to her sleep. Her skin went dry and the blood dried up inside her, turning to dust. Any time I felt tempted by her, I'd remember what she did."

"When she was waking up from her sleep... did she scream anything at you?"

"Oh, good heavens, yes. God is dead. Every night. The gypsy told me that the gods of ancient Egypt had punished her. She'd been part of a cult that believed the gods were all dead and gone, that their hold on the people should no longer be enforced. The gods punished her by transforming her into what she is now and the knowledge of that keeps her angry. She shouts her fury at them every chance she gets."

Samantha realized that she should have been writing all of this down. No worries, she thought, there's no way I'm forgetting any of this. "How and why did Mr. Mitchell end up with her?"

"I'd put her and the other mummies in the attic. I'd like to say I'd forgotten all about her but that would be a lie. She haunted me. Even now, I can still feel her lips against mine and the heat of her breath on my neck. When Mitchell came to visit, it was around the time that I was gathering things up for the church rummage sale. I asked him to help me bring down an old box of clothes from the attic and while we were up there, he saw the pile of mummies. I could tell how interested he was and I have to admit that I shared the story quite freely. I didn't hide the danger from him, though. I knew it wouldn't matter if I did. He was smitten, just like I had been. And I wanted her out of my house. So when he asked if he could buy her, I was more than happy to take his money. I shouldn't have done it, I know that. I knew the risks for my friend but I was a bloody coward!"

Samantha pressed on, sensing that Garmont was near his breaking point. "All we have to do is find the necklace and bring it close to her? Then she goes back to sleep?"

"Yes...." Samantha thanked him and hung hurriedly. If she'd waited just a second longer, she might have heard something of vital importance. Garmont continued speaking, not having heard her goodbye. "But you have to watch out for Them. They'll be drawn to her and they'll do whatever they can to make sure you don't interfere with her resurrection. Miss Grace?"

Garmont stared at the phone in horror. He'd been so caught up in recounting his sins that he hadn't told her about Them. How could he have been so stupid?

———— ✻ ————

For a dead woman, she looked pretty good. Morgan stood in front of Princess Femi, his eyes traveling the lines of her body for the umpteenth time. The linen hid her face and there was ripeness to her scent but even in her dried out state, there were hints that in life she had possessed the kind of figure that would have set the hearts and minds of men aflame.

"You look like my husband, the way you stare at her." Lorraine stood behind him in the doorway to the cluttered study. She had two glasses of wine in her hands and she slowly stepped forward to offer one to Morgan. He accepted it with a rakish smile. "What is it about her that holds men in thrall?"

"Can't put my finger on it," Morgan answered. He sipped the wine and his grin widened. This was good stuff, much better than anything he could usually afford. "Thanks for this," he said, holding up the glass.

"You're welcome, Mr. Watts."

"Call me Morgan."

"Only if you call me Lorraine."

Morgan noticed the look in her eyes and he recognized what might be happening here. She'd been trapped in a marriage of convenience and now that she was free, all those pent-up desires were being amped up by the danger she'd found herself in. It was a dangerous cocktail, especially where Morgan was concerned.

Clearing his throat, Morgan took a large gulp of the wine and set the glass aside. "I better start examining her."

Lorraine looked slightly perturbed but said nothing. She sat down on a small couch nearby and watched him approach Femi. She leaned back and her breasts strained against the fabric of her white dress. Morgan tried to ignore her. Not that long ago, he would have gladly accepted her unspoken invitation. But these days, he was a valued member of Assistance Unlimited and he had a job to do.

And there was also the matter of Samantha. Sure, she'd made it clear she wasn't interested in romance but it still felt like cheating to consider going to Lorraine Mitchell's bed.

Morgan ran his hands down the mummy's slim hips and patted her down like he was a cop checking for weapons. He moved the body and examined the wall behind her as well. There was absolutely nothing unusual about her.

"I don't see any signs that anyone's playing any kind of joke on you, Mrs. Mitchell. This here is your ordinary kind of mummy."

"You have a good sense of humor. I like that in a man."

Morgan cleared his throat again, wondering when the others would be arriving. He was about to suggest that they step out into the garden and finish their wine in the sunlight when a prick on the back of his neck caught his attention. His hand flew up and slapped against the skin. He'd thought it was an insect biting him but his palm came against something small and sharp. He yanked it out and stared at in growing horror. It was a tiny blow dart with some kind of amber-colored fluid dripping from the tip.

He whirled about to look at the window, which was open slightly to let in a breeze. A swarthy man's face was there, the blowgun raised to his lips for another attack. Around the man's eyes was thick mascara, making his eyes seem like white orbs in a field of black. "Lorraine!" he hissed but it was too late. His head was swimming so much that he toppled over to the floor, even as the man shot a second dart at Lorraine. She gasped in alarm, the wine glass falling from slack fingers to stain the carpet.

Lazarus Gray stared at the corpse of David Mitchell. He wore a small gauze mask over his mouth and nose but it did virtually nothing to help with the smell. Decomposition was a natural thing but its effects on the human body were not pretty.

Hovering nearby was the city's coroner, a grossly fat man named Sheedy. Sheedy was munching on a cruller doughnut, not disturbed in the least by the grisly scene before him. Death was part of his every day existence and in the crime-riddled streets of Sovereign, he frequently saw things that would churn the stomach of lesser men. "So what are you looking for?" he asked, bits of cake falling down onto the front of his bloodstained shirt. He looked more like a butcher than a man of medicine and law.

"Mr. Mitchell's death is under my personal investigation. I merely wish to verify your earlier diagnosis as to the cause of death."

"Heart attack." Sheedy shoved the rest of the cruller into his mouth and proceeded to lick his fingers clean. "No signs of foul play. Tested him for poison in case that wife of his wanted to do him in. Nothing showed up."

Gray said nothing. He would have preferred to study the body alone but that would have required paying off Sheedy. Gray had plenty of money but he had no desire to line the man's pockets any further.

Mitchell had been, to the naked eye, in fine health. Tests showed that he was in the early stages of at least two different sexually transmitted diseases, however, and Gray was fairly confident that he had not acquired them during relations with his wife. He tilted the head to the side and noticed something on the dead man's neck. It looked like a hematoma of some kind, circular in shape with a number of red spots in the center. It had faded some as the blood had settled but the remnants were still there, indicating that it had been fresh at the time of death.

Sheedy leaned over the body, dropping crumbs onto the dead man's suit.

"Yeah, I saw that, too. Looks like he and the wife had gotten frisky a little bit. It's a love bite."

Gray stared at it. The mark had other names, as well. In America, it was often referred to as a hickey. In India, it was dubbed a Kamasutra bite. Gray was certain that Lorraine would deny that she had left this mark on her husband. Despite what she'd said about trying for children, it was apparent to Gray that she and her husband were estranged. She had the air about her of a long-suffering woman who was far more upset about the mummy's actions than she was over the recent death of her lover. So who had done this to him? Surely he hadn't found the time to meet with a mistress right before his heart attack... but the only other woman in the house besides Lorraine was Femi.

Gray suddenly had a clear image of Mitchell unwrapping the lower portion of Femi's face and running his hand over her dried skin. He'd leaned in, possibly even kissed her, and then placed his cheek against hers in a morbid parody of a lover's embrace. Imagine his horror when the mummy screamed and then closed her lips around his throat, sucking so hard that she ruptured the cells beneath the skin. He'd panicked and died, falling to the floor where Lorraine would later find him.

It was all conjecture, of course, but Gray felt certain now that Lorraine was telling the truth. Femi was alive, in some blasphemous manner. He stepped back, whipped off his mask and gloves, tossing both to Sheedy. "Thank you, Doctor. This has been most enlightening."

He stepped outside and found Samantha waiting for him. She looked so worried that he immediately sensed something was wrong. "What is it?" he asked.

"I made the call and got a lot more information. I went straight to the Mitchell place to warn Morgan and I found that they were gone: all three of them. And I don't think they left on their own."

Gray's mismatched eyes sparked with anger. He knew who the 'three' were: Morgan, Lorraine Mitchell, and Princess Femi. "We'll rendezvous with Eun at headquarters," he said.

"And then what are we going to do?"

Lazarus thought there was a surprising amount of concern in Samantha's voice, more than usual in these kinds of situations. Was it because Morgan was among the missing? "Then we will rescue our friend and client... and destroy the abomination that is Femi!"

Chapter III
The Undying

Morgan woke up with one of the worst headaches of his life. He blinked through blurry vision, trying to figure out where he was and as things slowly came into view, he realized that he was in a lot of trouble.

He was in a poorly lit room whose walls were composed of gray brick. Torches were mounted on brackets here and there, casting the room in flickering light. In the center of the room lay twin altars. Upon the first lay the cloth-wrapped body of Princess Femi. On the second lay the nude form of Lorraine Mitchell. She was bound hand and foot, stretched out as far as her body could stand. Morgan could see blood welling up around her bonds, which were cruelly tight. She writhed as much as she could, tears streaming down her face and terror mounting in her eyes.

Morgan himself was standing up against the wall, his arms raised over his head. His wrists were shackled together just below the ceiling and as he tested the strength of his bonds, he realized that he would never break through.

In the room with him and Lorraine were five men, all dressed in black robes with hoods. Around each of their necks was a large golden ankh necklace. Two of the men were laying out a set of ceremonial knives, placing them beside Femi on the altar. Two more stood guard at the single door that led into the room, keeping close eyes on the activities in front of them. The fifth man approached Morgan when it became clear that he was awake. The man reached up and drew back his hood, revealing a thin face and a hooked, hawkish nose. The man was obviously Egyptian from the coloring of his skin and the accented English he spoke.

"You've decided to join us at last, have you? Good. I am Achmed. And you are?"

"Going to knock your teeth out if you don't let me go."

Achmed laughed, displaying a set of yellowed teeth. "American bravado. It's always entertaining." The man's smile vanished quickly and he drove a painful punch into Morgan's midsection, making him cry out. "Now I will ask you again: what is your name?"

"Morgan Watts. I'm a member of Assistance Unlimited and if you know anything about this town, you'll realize what a terrible mistake you've made."

Achmed's expression did change a bit at the name of Morgan's employers. He covered it up quickly, however, turning back toward the struggling form of Lorraine Mitchell. "By the time Lazarus Gray could find this place, we will be long gone. And our Princess shall live again."

"You're madmen! All of you!" Lorraine spat out. "Let me go and I can pay you! I have enough money to make you all rich men!"

"We don't care for money." Achmed picked up a slender blade that gleamed in the firelight. "We care only for our sacred mission."

"And what's that?" Morgan asked. He had an awful feeling that nothing good was going to come of that knife and Lorraine's current position so if he could keep the man talking, that meant more time for Lazarus and the others to save the day.

"We are known as The Undying," Achmed answered, slowly running the point of the blade between Lorraine's breasts. The dagger's point was so sharp that its progress left a thin red line in its wake. "For centuries, we have pursued our beautiful Femi, always waiting for the proper time. She fell in with our cult during the final days of her life, renouncing the old gods. For her sins, she was put to death and strange spells put upon her. Some say the gods did these but we know better – it was the priesthood who put her into these undying slumbers, so that they could make an example of her. They feared that if the common man lost their faith, they would lose their power. And they were right. For her sacrifice, The Undying swore to do whatever it could to revive her. We have tracked her from owner to owner, always hoping to steal her away so that she could be revived. After all the failures of my predecessors, I shall at least succeed. Tonight, she awakens!"

Achmed turned to the men at the door, gesturing for them to open the aperture. They pushed the heavy doors until they slid noisily across the floor, scraping the stone. A chill wind blew in, carrying with it the salty stench of the harbor. Morgan knew where they were, now: they were in one of the storage bays located near the pier. There were dozens of them, each rented out to one or more of the ships that made stops in the harbor.

The Egyptians all gathered around the bodies of the two women, one living and the other trapped in an awful state of un-life. They began to chant and Achmed looked over with shining eyes at Morgan. For some reason, they wanted Morgan alive, so he could watch, but as to why that was, Morgan didn't have a clue.

Achmed raised his dagger high and brought it down with incredible suddenness, piercing Lorraine's heart and silencing her screams of terror. Blood sprayed into the air, splattering wetly on the Egyptian's face. He looked mad as he began tearing and rending at the poor girl's chest, not stopping until he'd carved out her heart. He raised the still beating organ into the air over Femi's cloth-covered body. He squeezed, reducing the heart to a bloody pulp, bits of which fell all over Femi's body.

Morgan felt his stomach lurch and anger blazed inside his chest. He'd seen murder before but rarely had it been done so callously and in such a cowardly fashion.

As the blood soaked through the rags and into Femi's dried skin, a startling transformation began to occur. Her breasts became fuller, her hair took on a lustrous quality and her skin returned to the pallor and shape of life. She sat up, tearing the bandages from her eyes and as she looked about her, the expression on her face was one of mixed emotions. She seemed elated and yet horrified, as if she was all too aware of how unholy her existence now was. She looked straight at Morgan and opened her full lips. "God is dead!" she hissed and the words carried with them such malice that Morgan winced. This was a woman who despised the religion that had surrounded her in life and which had trapped her for eternity in this horrid state.

"Princess! You have returned to us!" Achmed squealed. She turned quickly, regarding him with suspicion. When she answered him, it was in an ancient dialect that Morgan couldn't understand. He watched as Achmed and Femi conversed for several seconds and his blood froze as Femi slid from the altar, taking several steps toward him. Achmed switched back to English so Morgan could know what was about to happen. "Femi lives and breathes but she still retains the dark hungers that have been set upon her. She requires nourishment, Mr. Watts. And you, sir, are going to be her celebratory meal!"

Morgan recoiled in horror as Femi opened her mouth to reveal a mouth full of sharp teeth. The resurrected Egyptian princess lunged for him, wrapping her arms around his torso. Her tongue slithered like a snake across his throat and Morgan realized that he was about to die.

Miya Shimada was a Japanese-American and her beauty was the perfect mixture of the two races that made up her ethnic background: the slim features of the Japanese melded with the hips and breasts of a Western woman. Her jet-black hair fell in straight lines around her perfectly sculpted face and she wore a form-fitting black skirt and blouse, along with a small hat and veil. She looked like someone headed to a funeral but the cruel smile on her ruby red lips also made her look like the proverbial black widow, seeking fresh prey.

She stood in front of the shuttered windows of Benson Drugs, a pharmacy that had closed down in the days immediately following the great Stock Market Crash of '29. Now, the entire block was empty, save for the old hotel building across the street. It was now used as the headquarters of Assistance Unlimited, housing Lazarus Gray and his aides.

Miya stepped back into the shadows as Lazarus emerged from the building, followed closely by Samantha and Eun. The three of them moved with grim determination and Miya wondered what mission they were on. She found so much about Lazarus Gray fascinating and she yearned to know why he was doing these things.

Once, in another life, she and the man who now called himself Gray had been lovers. But that had been before he'd woken up here in Sovereign City, his past nothing more than tattered images and sounds.

Samantha slid quickly into the backseat of Gray's waiting car, while Eun took the passenger seat in the front. Gray was about to duck behind the wheel when Miya stepped into view. "Lazarus Gray?" she asked, raising her voice loud enough that he couldn't miss hearing her.

Lazarus paused and his mask of stoicism slipped. For a brief second, he looked like a confused and somewhat lost man. And then his resolve returned and he was once more the composed figure that had become so feared throughout the underworld. He turned his head to regard her, his heart hammering in his chest. Something about her voice was painfully familiar and he suddenly longed to feel her touch on his bare chest. "Yes?' he asked, valiantly maintaining his composure.

"It is you, isn't it?" Miya moved toward him, lifting the veil from her face. As soon as he saw her face, Lazarus gasped. Images flooded into his mind's eye, of her nude in his bed, of the two of them arguing horribly. He heard the word 'monster' very clearly but he couldn't be sure which of them had said it. "Do you remember me?" she asked, watching his reaction very closely.

Gray glanced back into his car, where both Eun and Samantha were waiting. He shut the door and gave a brief nod. "I think so, yes. But things aren't as clear as they should be. Can you tell me your name?"

Miya ran to him, wrapping her arms about his neck and hugging him so tightly that Lazarus thought he might choke. "I've missed you so much! I don't care what's happened to you, we're together again!"

Gray peeled her off of him and held her at arm's length, seeing the tears in her eyes. "Your name. Please."

"Miya." She reached out and touched his face. "You have no idea how long I've searched for you. Why aren't you using your real name?"

A muscle twitched in Gray's left cheek, a sign of his anticipation. "Miya," he said slowly, "can you tell me what my name is?"

"Of course I can! I can tell you everything."

"Chief?" Samantha was leaning her head out of the car window, her gaze flicking back and forth from Lazarus and this stranger woman. "Morgan needs us."

"Don't go," Miya pleaded. "Stay with me and I'll answer all your questions."

Though it only took the briefest of seconds, Samantha saw how much effort Lazarus had to exert to step away from Miya. "I can't. I have responsibilities.

Where can I reach you?"

Miya let her veil fall back over her eyes. "I'll be in touch, my love. Hurry back."

Lazarus turned without saying farewell. He ignored the pointed stares of his aides, driving off as quickly as possible.

As Gray's vehicle rounded the corner, Miya's emotional display came to an abrupt end. She adopted a cruel smile and quickly walked toward an alleyway that led to an adjoining street. Her partner in this affair, Walther Lunt, was waiting for her in a parked car. He had told her that Gray wouldn't fall for this, that he wouldn't come with her into so obvious a trap. Miya had disagreed, thinking that whatever lingering feelings Lazarus might possess for her – coupled with his desire to know the truth about himself – would propel him into her arms.

Next time, she mused, she would know better. Lazarus Gray was deeply entrenched in Sovereign City, with men and women he considered to be family. That would make her task a bit more difficult but not impossible.

Lazarus Gray would be hers again, one way or another.

———

"**C**hief? Who was that woman?" Eun broached the subject that Samantha couldn't bring herself to. The three of them had sat in silence for nearly five minutes, as Gray had skillfully navigated the crowded Sovereign streets. A slight drizzle was falling, making the pavement slick and deadly, especially at the speeds that Gray was approaching. But neither Eun nor Samantha was worried: they knew their employer was as skilled a driver as anyone in the world.

"A woman from my past. That's virtually all I can tell you. I recognized her immediately but the images that passed through my head weren't clear at all."

From the backseat, Samantha's voice sounded distant. "Was she your lover?"

"I believe so. But I'm not certain we were together when the end came."

Both Samantha and Eun knew what he meant. Something had left him unconscious on the shores of Sovereign, battered to the point of amnesia. He'd had only one thing in his possession that offered any clue as to who he was: a medallion upon which the image of a man with a lion's head was engraved with the words Lazarus Gray beside it. He'd adopted the name as his own in the hopes that it would lure into the open anyone who might know him. This was a dangerous gambit, since the first person he met after arriving in Sovereign City tried to kill him. So far, Lazarus had crossed paths with two people who knew him from before: a German named Walther Lunt, who had somehow managed to cheat death, and now this Miya woman.

Sensing that his employer was slipping into a brooding state, Eun switched topics. "Where are we going, Chief?"

"To the area of the pier where the storage areas are housed."

"You think that's where Morgan is?" Samantha asked, leaning forward so that her head appeared in-between Eun and Lazarus.

"I know it is. After the affair with The Devil's Bible, I asked all of you to drink a mixture of my creation."

"I remember," Samantha said, recalling the icy pink concoction that tasted a bit like chalk mixed with toothpaste. Lazarus hadn't explained his reasons for asking them to ingest the solution but that wasn't uncommon. Lazarus usually played his cards close to the vest and his aides trusted him implicitly, though there were certainly times when his secretive nature ate away at them.

"There were certain radioactive isotopes in there that have attached themselves to the lining of your intestines. I'm able to track it with a specialized device of my own design."

"So you know where we are at all times?" Eun asked.

"For precautionary measures, yes."

Lazarus swung his vehicle to the right, steering them toward the docks. In addition to the honest men and women who made their living in Sovereign City's harbor area, the place was also home to many unsavory types. These criminals ducked out of sight as Gray passed, recognizing one of the city's few crusaders for justice.

The car came to a stop in front of a set of storage units set into the side of a small hill. It was mostly beneath the main harbor area and was swathed in darkness. Rats, both human and animal, scurried away into the shadows. The three members of Assistance Unlimited were out of the vehicle in a flash. Lazarus held a Smith & Wesson Hand Ejector II in his right hand. The revolver was chambered with .45 caliber rounds and was his weapon of choice. Samantha held a smaller handgun, one that she normally carried strapped to her garter. Eun carried no weapon, preferring to use his hands and feet. Around his neck, he wore the seven-pointed star pendant.

Gray held his gun in front of him, slowly approaching one of the storage units. The heavy door was open, revealing a little of the stone floor within. There was flickering light that could be seen and Gray knew that it was from a mounted torch. He had been in similar places before, in his old lifetime. Places where men in robes conducted dark rituals, usually involving the defiling of virginal female flesh.

The three of them moved cautiously inside. Samantha gasped, being the first to spot Lorraine's bloodied body, still strapped to one of the two altars erected in the center of the room.

Gray's attention was fixed on the still form of Morgan Watts, who remained chained to the wall. "Samantha, please check on Mrs. Mitchell. Eun, remain in the door and make sure no one is watching us."

Gray lowered his weapon, moving quickly to stand beside Morgan. He felt for a pulse and found one, faint but steady. He lifted Morgan's head and noticed that his friend's throat was a bloody mess. It looked like a dog had attacked him, ripping away the skin until red meat was exposed. Gray peered through the blood and saw that while it was quite horrific, it shouldn't prove fatal and a full recovery was possible.

"How is he?" Samantha asked, standing just behind Gray.

"He'll live. Mrs. Mitchell?"

"She's dead. Her heart's been cut out."

Lazarus turned slightly, seeing how pale Samantha's face was. "Do you need to step outside?"

Samantha visibly composed herself. "Of course not. I'm just worried about Morgan, that's all."

Gray nodded, returning his attentions to Morgan. "Eun!" he said, raising his voice.

"Yes, Chief?"

"Start the car. We need to get Morgan to a hospital." Gray examined the cuffs that held Morgan's hands and he reached into the pockets of his coat to retrieve a set of lock picks. After only a moment of work, the cuffs snapped opened and Morgan sagged into his employer's arms.

To Gray's astonishment, Morgan began mumbling something. Given how much blood he had lost, Morgan was displaying incredible strength of will. Gray pressed his ear close to Morgan's mouth. "Tell me again," he whispered.

Morgan's words were so soft that Gray had to strain to hear them. "The Sovereign Museum. That's where she's leading them."

"Who?" Gray asked, though he knew the answer. He still had to hear it.

"Femi. She lives again."

———— ✖✖✖ ————

Chapter IV
Past Lives

The Sovereign Museum of Natural History was a sprawling structure, standing in the heart of downtown. Comprised of twelve interconnected buildings, the Museum housed well over a million specimens, only a relative few of which were on active display. With a scientific staff of over a hundred, the Museum funded nearly four-dozen scientific expeditions each year, sending explorers out all over the globe. The Museum was divided up into numerous displays but the most popular was the ever-present Start of Sovereign Hall, where the origins of the city were examined. To access this, visitors had to stride through the huge entranceway, where they could stare up at a full-size model of a Blue Whale which hung from the ceiling. It was an awesome view but none of The Undying cared for it, especially not their leader, the Princess Femi.

She led her followers past an old man in a security guard's uniform. He had been foolish enough to try and stop the group from entering the museum after hours.

Night had fallen in Sovereign and the streets were alive with activity: the frightened footfalls of the innocent and the stealthy movements of those for whom sin was second nature. No one had dared say a word to the beautiful woman encased in cloth rags or the mysterious hooded men who followed in her wake.

The group paused at the entrance to the Henry Jones Exhibition Hall. A sarcophagus stood in the doorway, next to a sign that read:

**NOW ON DISPLAY!
THE TREASURES OF ANCIENT EGYPT
MUMMIES, ARTIFACTS AND MORE
LIMITED TIME ONLY**

Femi traced the letters with her fingertips. The words slowly came into focus, just as the English language had done. She was no longer mortal and her brain was attuned to strange things. Language was not a true barrier any longer. She communicated with things on a primal level now: life and death were her constant companions.

"I need suitable clothing," Femi had said, which had inspired Achmed to lead her to this place. He'd visited the exhibit, feeling a sense of pride intermingled with disgust as he'd toured the museum. Here were the remnants of a great and mighty empire that he adored, put on display for the masses to gawk at.

They found the display room quite gaudy in its appearance. Artwork and styles of clothing from various ages of Egypt were lumped together into a mishmash of false history and the hieroglyphs on the wall were meaningless. Femi took note of the four mummies placed on display and sniffed disapprovingly. All were servants who had been buried with their masters so they could assist them in the afterlife.

A set of mannequins showed a Pharaoh and his bride in full regalia and it was to these that Femi strode. She smiled broadly, quickly divesting herself of the cloth rags that covered her ample beauty. When she was naked, she glanced over at Achmed, whose eyes were like burning coals. He drank her in and his frequent swallowing made it clear that he hungered for her.

"I will finally look like the Queen I always should have been," she purred.

"Nothing can improve upon the loveliness you already possess."

Femi laughed and began to remove the royal garments from the mannequin. She draped them across herself, noting that they fit perfectly, as if they had been meant for her. The dress featured a jeweled collar and it matched the elaborate nature of the rest of her attire. Rings, anklets and bracelets, along with a pair of glittering gold earrings, were all part of the mannequin's apparel and Femi felt like she were a goddess herself once she was finished donning them all.

She turned to face her followers and they fell to their knees, bowing before her. "You will be my priests and royal guard," she pronounced. "But you will not be enough. The men of this time are strong and their weapons are potent. If I am to rule, as I should, we will need assistance. Let our dead brothers rise again so that they may serve!"

Femi raised both hands and a strange silence filled the room. Not even the breathing of The Undying could be heard. And then, ever so faintly, came a stirring. It became louder until it sounded like a stuck door being forced open. A foul stench filled the air and Achmed wrinkled his nose. It was like being in a charnel house and his eyes began to water in response.

The four mummies in the room jerked to life, the sunken pits where their eyes had once been now glowing with a yellow light. With shambling feet and jerking movements, they pushed their way out of the caskets in which they had been propped, moving to stand before Femi. The Undying, stout men all, looked upon them fearfully, awed by the power of their resurrected Princess.

Femi looked around until she saw a replica of an Egyptian throne in the corner of the room. Mannequin slaves stood on either side of the throne, holding large fronds with which to fan the Pharaoh or his Queen. Femi marched toward it and sat down, enjoying the moment. After so long in her twilight sleep, she was breathing the air again and being doted upon by her followers. This was the ultimate proof of her victory over the old gods, as well. They had sought to punish her for heresy but here she sat, resplendent in victory.

With triumphant malice in her voice, Femi declared once more, "God is dead."

"**S**houldn't we call the police?" Eun asked, taking the museum steps two at a time in order to keep pace with Lazarus Gray. Samantha lagged slightly behind, though she herself was moving far quicker than most men could manage.

"All that would do is put more innocent lives at risk," Gray replied. Eun started to point out that with all the corruption in the ranks of the Sovereign PD, there probably wouldn't be all that many innocents involved. He held his tongue, however, and instead followed his employer into the cavernous entrance of the museum. They spotted the dead night watchmen immediately and after checking in the vain hope that he might still be alive, the three of them began to look about with caution.

Samantha Grace felt nervous as a cat on a hot tin roof. She'd hated to leave Morgan alone at the hospital but she also couldn't stand the thought of missing out on the showdown with Femi. When all this was done, she was planning on mending fences with Morgan. Perhaps she'd ask him out to coffee, assuming she could make it clear that she didn't think romance was – or should be – in the cards.

"We should have called ahead," Eun said. "We might have saved this man's life."

Gray impassively looked at the younger man. "I'm convinced that such a thing would have only led to more deaths. We came as quickly as we could. We can debate this later."

Eun nodded, knowing his employer was right. Gray allowed his aides to question his decisions to a certain extent but ultimately he was the man behind Assistance Unlimited.

"Chief," Samantha whispered. "Look at that."

Gray spotted it immediately: the sign that led into the Egyptian exhibit. It seemed too perfect that a resurrected mummy would seek out the familiar in a museum. "Single file," Gray commanded. "I'll be in the front, Samantha in the middle, Eun at the rear."

Down the corridor they crept, hearing voices up ahead. There was also a terrible stench that forced Samantha to pull a tissue from her pocket. She held it over her nose but it did little to help.

When they came round the corner, all three of them froze in place at the bizarre sight before them. Femi sat on her throne, looking like the Cheshire cat, with a grin that spread from ear to ear. The Undying cultists stood before her, talking softly to each other. The four mummies shuffled their feet, making hoarse groaning sounds in the back of their throats.

Femi spotted the newcomers and stood up, alerting The Undying in the process. Achmed clenched his hands into fists but remained silent, allowing Femi to determine how this should proceed.

"Who are you?" she demanded, using an imperious tone of voice.

Lazarus stepped forward, displaying no fear of the mummies who hovered nearby. "My name is Lazarus Gray and these are two of my assistants. Earlier this evening, you killed a woman who had hired us and left another of my aides near death. I've come seeking retribution."

"You address me as if you were an equal," Femi replied. "I do not like that."

"You might have been royalty at some point in the past," Gray countered. "But that was long ago. The world has changed."

"Then I shall change it back."

Gray took a deep breath before answering in the negative. "That won't happen. Surrender now and I'll see that your return to the grave will happen quickly and peacefully. Resist and I'll send you to hell with a scream on your lips."

Samantha blinked. Gray didn't usually use such strong language and very rarely did he go into a combat with death as his goal. She didn't know if it was something related to the woman from his past or just simply a recognition of the danger posed by Femi, but it was obvious that he wasn't playing around tonight.

Femi stared at Lazarus in evident disbelief. With a sneer, she raised her chin toward the four mummies who stood in the room, each of them smelling like an open grave. "My undead warriors… kill these intruders."

The mummies hissed, their bodies suddenly flooded by a devilish desire to murder. They shambled toward the three members of Assistance Unlimited while The Undying backed away, eager to watch the carnage. The first of the undead creatures reached Gray, who discharged three shells from his Hand Ejector II. The bullets ripped through the cloth and skin of the mummy but did nothing more than stagger it. It grabbed hold of Gray's wrist and bent it cruelly to the side, squeezing so hard that he was forced to drop his gun.

Eun sprang forward, attempting to distract two of the monsters before they could gang up on Samantha. He kicked one of them in the chest and sent it toppling backward, where it finally smacked into the wall. He then drove a karate chop into another's neck but the impact sent a shockwave of pain up his arm. Hitting the mummy felt like striking a sack of potatoes. The mummy shot out both hands and grabbed the young Korean around the neck, applying enough pressure that Eun quickly saw stars.

Having witnessed the futility of Gray's attempts at shooting his opponent, Samantha quickly hiked up her skirt and placed her own pistol back in her garter. She then allowed the fourth and final mummy to lunge for her. She grabbed hold of its arm and twisted, tossing it over her shoulder in a classic jujitsu maneuver. The mummy landed with a thud on the floor and Samantha drew back before diving down with knee extended. Her knee struck the mummy in the face, crushing its nose. The mummy made a wheezing sound as Samantha stood up again and began kicking its head, finally reducing its dried skull to a pile of dust.

The pretty blonde whirled about and realized that her two male companions were not faring nearly as well. Both Gray and Eun were grappling with their enemies, which left one mummy free. This creature was now lumbering toward her with malice in its glowing eyes. Samantha glanced up to see Femi had taken her place on the throne again and was watching the battle with obvious bloodlust.

Samantha knew that her same judo flip would probably not work on a second mummy so she elected to take the offensive. Now that she knew that the creatures might have tough flesh and be resistant to pain but that their insides were quiet brittle, she pulled her gun back out and rushed toward her foe. She jumped into the air, wrapping her legs around the mummy and jamming the barrel of her gun right down its gullet. She unloaded four rounds into the beast, completely blowing out the back of its head. It staggered before toppling over and Samantha rolled out of the way before she could be trapped beneath it.

Eun was close to passing out and his attempts at breaking the mummy's hold on his throat were growing feebler. He thought he saw the ghost of his father over the undead monster's shoulder, smiling to him. In Korean, his father seemed to be saying, "Do not give up. We will see you eventually... but now is not your time to die."

Drawing strength from the vision, Eun raised his hands to the mummy's face, digging his fingers into the toothless mouth. He focused all his strength on pulling the thing's maw open wider, hoping that the brittleness of the creature's bones would help him. The thing had dense flesh that felt like it was padded with some thick material but it was still an ancient thing and the bones had grown soft. Eun cried out as the mummy's skull cracked and the top half of its head gave way, splitting along the seam of its mouth. The top half of the skull flew into the air, smashing against a nearby wall and falling to the floor in shards of dust and bone.

By this point, Achmed was growing concerned. He looked desperately at Femi but the Princess merely held up a hand, obviously telling him to be patient. She was studying Lazarus Gray closely, her pink tongue darting out to moisten her lips. Achmed felt a surge of jealousy and turned his attentions back to the battle. He had hoped to become a consort to Femi – after all, it was he who had restored her to life. But now he recognized the signs of physical interest she had in Gray. If necessary, he swore that he'd kill Lazarus himself to ensure that no one came between him and his princess.

Lazarus and his opponent were still locked in a tight grapple but the founder of Assistance Unlimited was slowly gaining an advantage. Despite the undead's tremendous strength, Gray was possessed of an indomitable will that often allowed him to overpower seemingly superior foes. Lazarus gritted his teeth as he forced the mummy's arms out from his body and with tremendous effort, Gray suddenly brought them up and then down, cracking them at the elbows. Bone and dust flew from the wounds and Gray took one of the ruined limbs and used it to beat the mummy about the head, driving it to the floor. He continued his assault until the mummy's head was nothing more than powder.

The three heroes of Assistance Unlimited stood panting, wondering what would happen next. Femi was breathing just as hard and when she spoke, her words were not what any of them had been expecting.

"Lazarus Gray, you have impressed us with your display. All of you would be welcome additions to our ranks." Femi rose from her throne and crossed the room to where Gray stood. She placed a hand on his chest, a teasing smile on her full lips. "Become my mate and I will see that your friends are treated like royalty."

"No!" Achmed barked. He immediately looked chastened when Femi turned to glare at him and he softened his tone. "My princess, it would not be proper. He is not of Egyptian blood. He is a commoner."

"I think it is for me to decide such things, not for you," Femi replied coolly.

"Actually," Lazarus interrupted, "I have no interest in bedding you. In fact, my only reason for being here is to see that you and your allies are silenced forever."

Femi blinked as if slapped. It was quite clear that she had never considered that he might actually reject her proposal. "If you refuse me, then there is only one option left for you and your friends: death."

Gray leaned close enough to her that she could feel his breath on her face. "I'd advise you to reconsider. I meant my earlier offer. Surrender and I'll do what I can to ensure your passing is painless."

The look of rage that flew over Femi's face was incredible to behold. Her eyes shone with mystic fire. "Kill him," she hissed between clenched teeth. "Kill all of them!"

The Undying drew their weapons, a combination of guns and knives, but Gray had already delivered a backhanded blow to Femi that sent her flying. Normally, he would have felt qualms about hitting a woman but in this case, he had none. Femi was a monstrosity, doomed to un-life for heresy. Now that she had a second chance at existence, what had she done? Nearly killed Morgan and left a night watchman to bleed out. She had proven her unworthiness to live.

Femi landed on her back, scrambling into a crouch as The Undying rushed at Eun and Samantha. She saw the Korean leaping into the air, kicking one of her men so hard that his teeth were knocked from his mouth in a bloody spew. Samantha had dived behind a display of Egyptian art and pottery, exchanging gunfire with The Undying.

"You, Lazarus Gray, are going to regret this," Femi said. Her beautiful face twisted into something awful as her anger took hold. She stood up, looking resplendent in her Egyptian finery, and pointed both hands at Gray. Tendrils of foul energy shot forth from her fingers, wrapping around him. His skin began to shrivel and Lazarus felt as if the very life were being sucked from his lungs. "I'll show you what it was like for me," she stated. "I'll see how you like being a living mummy for the next few decades."

Gray bucked in agony, falling to his knees. His eyes seemed to shrink into their sockets and his mouth became as dry as sandpaper. As death seemed to swell up, ready to envelop him, he began to remember a similar event, another time when he had teetered on the brink of the abyss: Lazarus saw himself staggering through a burning building. The stench of burning flesh had made him retch and the wails of the dying filled had filled his ears. He'd been bleeding from a number of wounds, most notably from a massive hole in his neck. He'd held a blood-soaked rag against his neck as he stumbled from the building, out into the night air. It had been an autumn night in Mexico and as he had turned back to face the flames, he saw a young girl, no more than a child, trying in vain to escape the deathtrap. She'd howled like a banshee, her hands reached out to him beseechingly.

"I killed them," Lazarus hissed, even as Femi cast her dark spells on him. "All those people in the house – men, women and children. I killed them." He looked up at Femi and his mouth twisted into an expression of disdain. "I can't let you kill me. Not yet. Not until I know why I did those things."

Amazingly, Gray managed to force his way back to his feet. Even as his skin turned an unhealthy shade of white, Lazarus drew out one of his daggers. He took careful aim at Femi, who stared at him in disbelief. The knife flew through the air, embedding itself between her eyes. She gasped and fell back, her body beginning to decompose immediately. Her skin fell away in patches of dried earth and her skeleton disassembled, shattering as they hit the floor.

Achmed, who had been firing upon Samantha, howled in agony. He shouted for his men to cease their attacks and slowly they did as he asked, facing their adversaries warily. Lazarus was healing quickly, now that Femi's magic was no longer working on him, and he watched as Achmed crept over to the remains of Femi, kneeling at her side. He ran his fingers through the pile of dust and bone, tears shining on his cheeks.

"You monsters," Achmed whined. "You destroyed her. She was the last remnant of the great Egyptian dynasties and you killed her."

"She should have died long ago," Gray responded. He looked toward the hallway as a set of uniformed officers rushed into the room. Evidently, the sounds of gunfire had finally attracted the authorities.

"Chief? You okay?" Samantha asked, moving to stand at his side. He looked distracted and she was worried that his injuries were more severe than they looked.

"I killed children."

Samantha blinked. "Chief?" She looked around at the police officers, which were rounding up The Undying and taking a statement from Eun. "What are you talking about?"

"While Femi was attacking me, I had a vision of the past. I think I may have done some awful things, Samantha." He looked at her and his emerald-colored eye shimmered, even as his brown one seemed to darken. Samantha had always found it peculiar how they could do that. "It's time to stop playing around with the mystery of who I really am. The time's come for me to find out once and for all."

Samantha took his hand. "All that matters is who you are now, Chief. The old you... maybe he should stay dead and buried."

Gray looked down at the dusty remains of Princess Femi. "That's the problem, I'm afraid. Sometimes the dead don't stay in their graves."

⟡

Morgan Watts was sitting up in his hospital bed when Samantha slipped into his room. She had a brown paper bag with her, from which the smells of Morgan's favorite burger – a bacon & cheese concoction from Murray's Deli – rose up invitingly. "Mind some company?" she asked, holding up the bag.

Morgan smiled. "Not at all. Especially when you're bearing gifts!"

Samantha sat on the edge of his bed and offered him the bag. "How do you feel?"

"Rotten. But getting better. Sorry I missed all the fireworks."

"I think you saw plenty." Samantha waited until Morgan had pulled the hamburger out and taken the first bite before she began speaking again. "I'm sorry I slapped you. It wasn't fair. I had been leading you on a bit. It's not that I don't like you in that way – I think I could – but we're friends and coworkers and it's just not wise to get involved. So, how about we go out for coffee sometime and agree to keep it simple."

Morgan stared at her with wide eyes and a mouthful of hamburger. He swallowed hard and settled back. "I'd like that," he said slowly. "To be honest, I thought you might be harboring feelings for Lazarus and that's why you weren't interested in me."

With cheeks flaming red, Samantha laughed and looked away. "No! That'd be silly. The Chief doesn't have time for romance."

"If I were him, I'd make the time where you were concerned." Samantha looked pointedly at him and he shrugged his shoulders. "I'm saying that as a friend, of course."

A smirk appeared on Samantha's face. "Of course." She noticed a basket of flowers sitting nearby and stood up to look at them. "Who sent you flowers?"

"Dunno. They were there when I woke up. Haven't even looked at the card yet. I figured they were from Assistance Unlimited."

Samantha picked up the card and opened it. She knew that no one at the office had sent them and was curious who had. "Mind if I take a look?"

"Go ahead."

The words printed on the card made Samantha pause and, for some reason she couldn't fathom, they seemed to bode ill for all involved: *Get well soon. I look forward to getting to know you and your friends. Sincerely, Miya.*

Samantha stared at the card, picturing the attractive Asian woman who had so unsettled Lazarus. She crumpled up the card in her hand and tossed it into the trash.

"Who are they from?"

"Wrong room," she said cheerily. She picked up the flowers and headed for the door. "I'll make sure they get where they should have gone."

Morgan watched her go, taking another bite of his hamburger. Women, he mused. You just never knew about them.

THE BURNING SKULL

An Adventure of Lazarus Gray
Written by Barry Reese

—⊗⊗⊗—

Chapter I
Blood Red

"Who am I?"

Under normal circumstances, such a question would have seemed absurd. But where Lazarus Gray was concerned, it was a perfectly valid inquiry.

Just over eighteen months before, he had woken up near the Sovereign City Harbor, battered and weary. He'd had no memory of who he was or how he'd come to be there and the only clue to his identity had been a strange coin on his person. It had depicted a nude man with the head of a lion, the words 'Lazarus Gray' printed below the image.

Within minutes of coming to, Lazarus had found himself the target of an assassination attempt. That had set the tone for his time in Sovereign City, which had been filled with one dangerous threat after another. Along the way, he had formed Assistance Unlimited, a group dedicated to aiding those for whom there was nowhere else to turn. He had adopted the name he'd found on the coin, hoping that it would draw out anyone who might know the truth.

It had taken far too long for Gray's liking, but in the end, the strategy had

EUN JIWON
THIS TACITURN WARRIOR, BORN OF RAGE, FINDS
SOLACE AS A MEMBER OF ASSISTANCE UNLIMITED.

worked. Miya Shimada had arrived outside the Assistance Unlimited headquarters and her arrival had brought with it a flood of contradictory memories: he knew that he and Miya had been lovers but he also knew that they'd had an awful fight that had ended their relationship. Furthermore, he'd seen images of himself setting fire to a small building in Mexico, deliberately killing men, women and children.

Now Lazarus and Miya were dining together at Amici's, an upscale restaurant in the heart of the city. Normally, reservations had to be in place for weeks ahead of time but the maitre d' had once been nearly put to death by a bizarre and insidious form of poison. Assistance Unlimited had not only managed to find an antidote, they had also proven beyond a reasonable doubt that the person responsible for the attempted murder was the man's own brother.

Miya took a sip from her glass of wine and cast a glance outside. It was raining cats and dogs, as it always seemed to do in gloomy Sovereign. She saw men and women scampering about in vain attempts at staying dry, their feet splashing in the puddles that lined the streets. "Is this really how you want to spend the evening?" she asked. "I was hoping to renew our friendship before diving into all the mysteries surrounding you."

Gray's impassive face showed no trace of emotion. He was a handsome man, with hair that was more gray than brown, making him appear older than he was. His eyes were mismatched, with one being a dull brown, while the other glittered like an emerald. He wore a dark suit and driving gloves. "Miya, I've spent the past eighteen months not knowing if I was a monster or a saint, or something in-between. Do you realize that I don't even know my real name? I'd love to renew our friendship, as you put it, but the first step to doing that is you telling me all you know about my past."

Miya stared down at the pasta on her plate. "Can I at least eat while we talk?"
"Feel free."

Miya sighed, noticing that Lazarus didn't bother picking up his own silverware. He was obviously planning to wait until she'd explained things. She reached up and brushed a strand of raven black hair behind her ear and she caught him watching the motion. A tiny smile touched her lips. So he did still find her attractive. That was nice to know. She knew that her mixed heritage – she was a Japanese-American—gave her an exotic appearance and she'd accentuated it by wearing a Western style evening dress and Japanese-themed earrings and necklace. "We met nearly eight years ago, in Tokyo. You were there with a German named Walther Lunt and I was working in my father's shop. The two of you came in just before closing and Lunt told my father that he was there to purchase a small statue called The McGuinness Obeslisk."

"What sort of shop did your father run?"
"He collected and sold occult books and artwork."

Gray wasn't surprised. From his own spotty memories, he knew that his past was filled with mysticism. A prior encounter with the disfigured Lunt had made him wonder if he and the German had once been allies or enemies. Apparently, he now knew the answer. They had worked together in some capacity.

Miya paused while she savored the exquisite cuisine. "The Obelisk was supposedly capable of controlling the minds of any female within 100 feet of it. My father kept it under lock and key so it wouldn't affect myself or my mother." Miya smiled shyly, avoiding Gray's gaze. "I was enamored of you from the first moment I laid eyes upon you. When Lunt and my father could not agree on a price, I stole the Obelisk and took it to your hotel room, hoping to impress you."

"And did you?"

"Yes. You took me to your bed that very night."

Lazarus shifted uncomfortably. More and more, he was becoming convinced that he wasn't going to like the man he used to be but he couldn't find the strength to stop the hunt. He had to know the truth. "And after that?"

"I went back to Europe with the two of you. I was indoctrinated into The Cabal. That's just what I called it, of course. It has no real name, though people have attributed many to it over time: The Damnation Society, The Hellfire Club, The Illuminati, The Seekers. It's a group of occultists who seek forbidden knowledge and who aren't afraid to use it for their own ends."

"And I was a part of this?"

Miya hesitated and though Lazarus didn't know her very well, he was sure she was keeping something from him with her answer. "Oh, yes. You were a willing participant. In everything."

"Including burning children alive in Mexico?"

Miya blinked before suddenly leaning forward and taking Gray's hand. She squeezed it hard but he didn't reciprocate. "Oh, you poor dear! It must be so hard to remember only bits and pieces, without context! Those weren't innocents, my love. Those were vampires. A coven of them. They'd even turned children into the undead. It was horrible. You did them a favor by releasing their spirits."

"You still haven't told me my name."

Miya withdrew her touch and took a deep breath. "All right. We'll handle things your way. Your name is Rich—"

"Mr. Gray?"

Lazarus glanced up at the maitre d', who looked slightly chagrined. "Yes?"

"Please forgive me. I know that you said you didn't wish to be disturbed but... well, there's been an incident up front that might require your attention."

It was then that Gray noticed a murmuring amongst the other restaurant guests and even a few stifled cries. Normally, he was so sensitive to his environment that he would never have missed something amiss but Miya's recounting of his past had obviously obscured his awareness.

Gray stood up and spotted the source of the disturbance. A man had entered the restaurant and then collapsed, landing facedown in front of the maitre d' station. "Have you contacted the authorities?" Gray asked, hurrying toward the fallen man, the maitre d' in tow. Miya remained at the table, momentarily forgotten.

"Not yet. Should we?"

Lazarus understood the hesitance. The police force in Sovereign was little more than an extension of various criminal enterprises. There were good men who wore the badge but not enough of them to instill confidence in the city's populace.

"Go ahead and place the call," Gray ordered. The maitre d' nodded at another employee, who bolted toward the phone.

Kneeling at the man's side, Gray quickly rolled the fellow onto his back. Just by touch, Gray had surmised that it was too late to save the man's life. He was quite dead already. Several people who were standing about gasped at the sight that was presented to them and one of the waitresses let out a bloodcurdling scream. She fainted into the arms of a busboy.

The skin on the dead man's face had been burned away, as if by acid. As a result, all that was left was red muscle and white bone. The corpse now bore the horrific visage of a bloodied skull. Gray refrained from touching the ruined mess, for fear that some danger lingered on the raw flesh. There was a peculiar odor emanating from the dead man – something that smelled a bit like almonds. Gray checked to make sure his gloves were securely in place and began rifling through the man's pockets. He found his wallet easy enough, along with a small card identifying him as Wallace J. Newton, Private Eye.

A uniformed police officer burst in at that moment and Gray recognized the type immediately: a burly, blustery fellow who enjoyed showing off his power. It only took the briefest examination to spot the signs.

"Get away from him, fella," the police officer barked, directing his comments to Lazarus, who slowly complied. To the rest of the people standing around, the officer said, "Everybody take your seats or get out! We gotta leave room for the medics when they get here!"

Gray took note of the man's badge number. He had committed to memory every officer in the city, matching them up with their badge number. "Officer Mulvaney, there's precious little that a medic could do here. This man is dead. His demise is peculiar enough that I would like to take his body back to Assistance Unlimited for further analysis."

Mulvaney glowered at Gray and it was immediately apparent that he didn't think much of Assistance Unlimited and its mysterious founder. "How about you stay out of police business? You may have some special privileges but that doesn't mean you can tell me what to do."

Gray reached out and placed a hand on Mulvaney's shoulder. He gave it just a slight squeeze, though with the incredible strength he possessed, it was enough to bring a grimace to the officer's face. "I appreciate the difficulty you must face in doing your job, Officer Mulvaney. People don't show adequate respect for your uniform and badge. But in this case, I need you to be sensible. If you take this body to the morgue, they'll call me in eventually and we'll have wasted valuable time that could have been used to find Mr. Newton's killer. So let's work together on this."

Mulvaney withered under the intense gaze he received from Gray. With a shrug and a small shred of remaining defiance, he said, "Fine. Take it away. But you better share all your findings with the department. You're not a law unto yourself, you know."

Gray turned away, hoping to catch Miya's eye and offer an apology. When he looked back at their table, he saw that she had taken the opportunity to slip away. Gray frowned slightly, knowing that she hadn't left through the front door or else he would have seen her. That meant she'd vanished through the kitchen and out the back.

Forcing his thoughts away from the darkness that was his past, Gray bent down and gently lifted the corpse of Wallace J. Newton.

———— ∞∞ ————

Miya hurried down the alleyway, ignoring the rain that pelted her hair and soaked through her dress. Walther Lunt waited for her at the end of the street and he opened the car door so she could slip inside.

"You're alone," the German noted. "I suppose that means you failed to bring him over to our side. What a surprise." One side of his face had been disfigured years before and now it was nothing more than a twisted mass of scar tissue. It ruined what otherwise would have been a cruel but handsome face.

Miya resisted the urge to roll her eyes. "He was distracted by a dead man."

"Again, nothing we shouldn't have accounted for. Men and women are always dying in Sovereign and Lazarus Gray is always involved somehow."

"Are you just going to complain or are you going to drive?" Miya opened her purse and took out a handkerchief. She began to dab at her forehead and face, ensuring that her makeup didn't run.

"What did you tell him?" Lunt asked, starting the car. He slowly pulled out onto the rain-slicked streets.

"About how we met. And he was concerned about that group of vampires he killed in Mexico. I assured him that he wasn't a murderer."

"Not in that case, at least. Did you tell him about The Illuminati?"

"Some."

"Does he know that he turned against us?"

"I didn't mention that part." Miya looked out the window, staring at the grimy city that she'd called home these past few weeks. "I don't want to play into his notions of being a hero. He has just as much blood on his hands as any of us."

"This is too dangerous. I've asked the rest of our members to give us the option to simply kill him. The last thing we need is for him to become a thorn in our side again."

"We should wait. He's like clay right now... all it takes it is the right manipulations and I can sculpt him into whatever we want."

Lunt glared at her. "Don't let your lingering feelings for him get in the way of your common sense."

Miya laughed softly. "There's no chance of that happening, Walther. And I do agree with you, somewhat. If it becomes clear that he won't come back into the fold, then we'll have to take measures to prevent him from interfering."

"Even if that means killing him?" Lunt prodded.

"Yes," Miya sighed. "Even if that means killing him."

Chapter II
The Diabolical Mr. Skull

Garrison Montreux was French-Canadian by birth, though from his accent, people assumed he was from the American Midwest. This was because he had long ago divested himself of any native inflection his words might carry. He had grown up hating his home province, always yearning for the American dream. Originally a slight child, Garrison had begun lifting weights in his teens and he was now a barrel-chested brute with massive biceps and a mean streak. Preferring to dress in dark suits and ties, Garrison's body somehow suggested that he was a massive gorilla forced to wear a man's clothes.

But the most chilling aspect of his appearance was his head. Garrison no longer bore the visage of a normal man. There was no flesh on his skull, leaving it terrifyingly bare. Tiny flickers of yellow-orange flame danced around the exposed bone when he was angry and a pair of glowing orbs shone out of his eye sockets. As a result, he no longer answered to his birth name. He was Mr. Skull, a silly name that no one laughed at.

Mr. Skull sat behind a large desk, staring at the men who were his chief lieutenants. Since arriving in Sovereign, he'd made quite a few inroads in the underworld, building a small name for himself very quickly. It was rough going, however, and he'd already made an enemy of The Monster, who was Sovereign's current criminal kingpin. What no one knew was that Mr. Skull wasn't your standard gangster. He loved money and power as much as anyone but that wasn't his ultimate aim. He had darker desires than anyone realized.

"So the private dick is dead?" Skull asked, using the tough-talking gangster voice he preferred. It was nothing like the prim words used by his parents, nor was it anything resembling the way he had talked for most of his life.

Malone, a thin man with bad teeth, grinned in response. "We hit him right in the face just you like wanted. The Bone Dust worked like a charm. He ran off screaming into a nearby restaurant."

"Good. I want it mentioned on the streets that he was killed for poking his nose into our business. We need to use the Bone Dust again soon – let everybody know it's a weapon we've got and we aren't afraid to use it."

"Sure, boss, sure." Malone looked at the other men in the room and shifted his feet. They were all waiting expectantly for him to bring something up. He'd been tasked with the duty by drawing the short straw and he was none too happy about it. "Listen, there's something I have to bring up...."

Mr. Skull turned his full attention on Malone and a few flickers of flame appeared around his skull, a sure sign that Malone was treading on thin ice. "Go on."

"Some of the boys think we'd actually be getting a little bit further without the whole flaming skull bit. I mean, it's an incredible mask and it scares the living spit out of anybody who sees it but it works a little too good, y'know? A lot of guys don't wanna work for you because they're terrified."

Mr. Skull stood up and Malone took a step back. He instantly regretted having spoken up at all. "I'm sorry, boys. I'm too scary, is that it?"

"Well... that's what some folks say; people who aren't as tough as the rest of us. We don't think that."

"So you don't find me frightening, Malone?" Mr. Skull adjusted his tie and moved closer, towering over his employee.

"Uh," Malone stammered. He wasn't quite sure how to answer. If he said no, it might be construed that he was taunting his boss. If he said yes, then that might be seen as an insult as well. "I think you're gonna be running this town soon. And I'm glad to be on what's gonna be the winning side."

Mr. Skull patted Malone on the shoulder. "Good answer. But not quite quick enough on your feet." The flames around his head grew much brighter, dancing about like living things. He gripped Malone by the throat, lifting him off his feet with one hand. To the others, who were now watching with horror, he said, "Tell everyone. Make it clear so that they understand. Mr. Skull doesn't wear a mask. This. Is. My. Face!"

Malone whimpered as Mr. Face slammed him onto his back on the desktop.

Mr. Skull used his free hand to pull out a small silver vial. His thumb easily pushed off the top of the vial and a reddish powder began to spill out, falling onto Malone's face. Malone began thrashing wildly, recognizing the mixture dubbed Bone Dust.

The powder transformed into a corrosive liquid as soon as it touched Malone's skin. The chemical reaction left an almond odor in the air and Malone's screams were so awful that even the hardened criminals in the room looked away, with some of them retching.

When Malone ceased his fighting, his face was a ruined mess and his labored

THE BURNING SKULL

breathing slowly came to an end. Mr. Skull released his hold on him and turned to face the others. "Anybody else got anything smart to say?" he demanded. When no one said anything, he shoved Malone's corpse to the floor and took his seat behind the desk. "Get that mess out of here."

Two of the men jumped to the task and Mr. Skull turned his chair so he could look out the window. "Boys," he said to those who remained. "I think it's time to speed up my plans a little."

One of the men cleared his throat. "Whatcha wanna do, boss?"

Mr. Skull watched the rain that spattered against the window. In a very low voice, he said, "I want to kill some people, boys. A lot of them."

The former hotel that served as headquarters for Assistance Unlimited was a three-story affair. The first floor was for visitors and also contained several small apartments used by Gray's aides. Lazarus Gray lived alone on the third. The second floor had been gutted, leaving a massive meeting area for the group. It was here that Morgan Watts, Samantha Grace and Eun Jiwon had gathered.

Morgan stared at what they'd dubbed 'The Monster Board' and let out a whistle. It was an accounting of all the known crimes attributed to the city's most notorious criminal over the past six months, with pins stuck on a map of Sovereign. The crimes were numerous and spread out haphazardly all over the map. It seemed that The Monster had his evil fingers in virtually every criminal enterprise imaginable. "It's unbelievable. How can one man be involved in so many things?"

Samantha, a gorgeous blonde who was dressed today in khaki pants and a button-up white shirt, sat atop a nearby desk. Her knees were crossed in front of her and Morgan found himself admiring her calf-length boots and long legs. "Well, it's not like he'd personally be handling all these crimes. He has a network of goons to do the dirty work for him."

"Still. You'd always think there was more than one of him." Morgan played with his moustache as he stared at the board. The oldest member of Assistance Unlimited, Morgan was very fastidious about his appearance. His hair was always slicked down and he was never seen without a coat and tie.

Eun stepped forward and tapped one of the photographs attached to the side of the display board. "Why don't we ask for permission to question some of his men who've been busted?"

"Because too many of them are on the turnstile system. They get processed and are back on the street within 24 hours." Morgan shook his head. "The Monster's got way too many judges and lawyers on his payroll. He's virtually untouchable. Our best hope is to actually catch him in the act and take him down ourselves."

Samantha was about to suggest that one or more of them should go undercover when Gray's voice sounded over the building's intercom system. "All hands to the medical lab, please. We have a new case."

The three of them jumped to action. Morgan pushed the display board into a small closet while Eun summoned the building's elevator car. He held it open for his associates and pressed the button for the basement sub-level. It was there that Lazarus Gray did autopsies, as well as experiments that would be too dangerous for the upper levels.

"I didn't even realize the Chief was back," Eun said.

"He's like a cat," Samantha said with a smile. "Comes and goes as he pleases."

Morgan cleared his throat as the elevator came to a rest. "I figured he'd still be on his date."

"Date?" Samantha asked, arching an eyebrow.

"Didn't you know?" Morgan asked, knowing quite well that Samantha had been unaware of Gray's evening plans. Morgan had a growing attraction to Samantha but she'd put a halt to any romantic notions. Though she'd claimed it was simply because she didn't believe in workplace relationships, he suspected that she was actually harboring a crush on Lazarus Gray. "Lazarus and that Miya girl went out for dinner tonight. Given how crazy she seemed to be about him, I didn't expect him back so soon."

"Well, just because one person likes another, it doesn't mean that feeling is reciprocated," Samantha answered frostily.

"Don't I know it," Morgan muttered under his breath. He noticed that Eun was trying unsuccessfully to hide a smirk and he playfully swatted the younger man on the arm.

The three of them entered the medical lab and were immediately hit by the antiseptic smells that they associated with the room. Lazarus stood next to a body covered by a thin white sheet, wearing a medical smock and gloves. Without any preamble, Gray said, "This man was killed by a toxic formula that ate the skin off his face. It's a unique compound and I've already been in touch with the various chemists in the area. The ingredients that would be needed to make this were bought in bulk less than two weeks ago, with instructions to deliver them to an address on Ferguson Street."

Samantha looked down at the covered corpse and felt a sense of relief that Gray had not left it exposed. "Do you think Doc Pemberley might be involved?"

Gray nodded. "I believe he might be. We know he's been on the run for the past month or so[1] and this seems like the sort of thing we'd associate with his work. Eun, if you don't mind, please call the authorities and ask them to pick up this body. Samantha, I'd like you to visit the victim's office. He was a private investigator and I'd like to know what cases he was working on before he met his demise."

Gray began stripping off his medical gear, tossing the gloves into a trashcan

---

1) Since the events of "The Girl With the Phantom Eyes"

located nearby. "Morgan, you're with me. We're going to drop in and pay a visit to our old friend, Doctor Pemberley."

Morgan grinned broadly. "With pleasure, Chief. I owe that kooky old bird a good thrashing."

Chapter III
Deadly Clues

Melvin Pemberley was fifty years old, though he could pass for a man in his mid-thirties. He was handsome, with short-cut blond hair, blue eyes that resembled chipped polar ice and a coolly efficient manner of conducting himself. He tended to wear white lab coats and was rarely found without a pair of surgical gloves. It was a bit of irony that a man who so often dabbled in blood and guts was uncomfortable getting his hands dirty.

Doc Pemberley was completely amoral. Where the average person would cringe, Pemberley stared unabashed. When a normal man would rush in to save those in need, Pemberley was more apt to pick up a sheet of paper and begin recording the events occurring before him. He had run afoul of the law on numerous occasions since losing his license to practice medicine. Selling his services to anyone who could meet his fee meant that Pemberley not only stitched up gangsters, he also worked on creating chemical weapons. He had fled Sovereign more than once but always ended up returning home. Mr. Skull had come along at the perfect time for Pemberley, giving him steady employment after Assistance Unlimited had smashed his latest scheme.

Ferguson Street was far from being the sort of area where Pemberley preferred to reside. Violence was so routine in this part of the city that no one even looked out the window when screaming or shooting began. Before being discredited, Pemberley had lived in relative luxury but those days were long gone. Now his lab consisted of a converted kitchen and the experimental surgeries he carried out on neighborhood stray animals were far from hygienic in nature.

Pemberley was wiping bloody hands on a filthy smock when a pounding came at his front door. He froze in place, a frown settling on his handsome features. Mr. Skull's men were the only ones who knew about this hideout and all of them knocked with a special code: two hard and fast beats, followed by three shorter ones. The vile doctor threw a sheet over the suffering creature stretched across the dining room table. He was continuing his experiments related to the grafting of one dog's head onto a second one's body and had experienced limited success, with the grafted head living for up to three hours.

After grabbing a small pistol from under a counter, Pemberley cautiously approached the front door. He stepped over to a nearby window and pulled the shade slightly aside, peering outside. To his surprise, he didn't see anyone there. He was just about to turn back to the kitchen when he felt the cold barrel of a gun press against the back of his head.

"Put the gun down now," Morgan hissed. "Or I'm going to put a new hole in your head."

"Morgan Watts," Pemberley said. "I wish I could say it was a pleasure." The doctor held the gun out from his body and let it dangle from one finger before it fell to the floor. "How did you get inside? I paid for some very expensive locks."

"There's not a lock in the world that I can't break," Lazarus Gray said, entering the room. Morgan glanced at him and saw that his employer looked even more grave than usual. "I put down that poor animal in your kitchen, Pemberley. If there's such a thing as Hell, you've confirmed your place in it."

Pemberley quickly spun around, knocking Morgan's arm aside. He tried to follow it up with a quick punch to the man's stomach but Pemberley found his arm in Gray's iron grip. Lazarus applied enough pressure that Pemberley cried out like a child, falling to his knees. Gray maintained his hold on him.

"A man died tonight, the victim of an acid attack. The skin on his face was burned off. Do you know anything about that?"

Gritting his teeth, Pemberley nodded. He was enough of a realist to know when he was licked and in the face of more abuse, he was quite willing to betray anyone and everyone if it might help his own cause. "Mr. Skull paid me to make it for him. He calls it Bone Dust."

Morgan whistled. "I've heard of this Mr. Skull guy, Chief, but I figured he was just a story, a kind of urban bogeyman. They say he doesn't have any face at all – from the neck up, he's just bones."

"Is that true?" Gray asked, directing the question to Pemberley.

"Yes. Don't ask me how but it's the truth. He's a sadist. He didn't just want something that would kill, he wanted something horrible."

Most people who met Lazarus Gray thought that he was relatively emotionless but his closest friends knew the truth: Gray felt disgust and remorse just as strongly as they did, perhaps more so. At the moment, Morgan could see in his employer's eyes that he hated Pemberley with every fiber of his being. Gray raised his free hand and brought it crashing down on the doctor's head. The blow was enough to knock him out and Gray dropped his hold on him, allowing the villain to fall onto the floor.

"I'll truss him up," Morgan offered, taking out some extra-strength cord from his pocket. "Should we call Samantha and Eun – tell them to be on the lookout for this Mr. Skull character?"

"Yes. You take of that, if you don't mind. I'd like to look around this house and make sure that there aren't any more monstrosities lurking about."

"Did Miya tell you about your past?"

Gray paused, somewhat surprised by the question. But then he knew that his aides were also more than that – they were friends and they were concerned for his wellbeing. "She told me some things but not enough. I know that I was a part of an occult organization with Walther Lunt and that they did some terrible things. I also know that some memories I'd had about an event in Mexico were slightly misleading – which was a good thing. But I still don't know my name or how much blood might be on my hands. I'd like to think that my participation in the group might have been attributed to some naïveté on my part and that I left their number when I realized what they were up to… but that might not be the case."

"Well, whatever you did in the past, Chief, it doesn't define you now. You've been given a whole new life and you've done so much good since coming to Sovereign that I bet it balances the scales against anything you might have done before."

Lazarus smiled and the sight was so rare that it froze Morgan in the act of tying up Pemberley. "Thank you for that, Morgan. We might have some things in common. Both of us have turned over a new leaf."

Samantha was no stranger to breaking and entering. It was an odd thing, how proficient she had become at such a thing. Growing up in the midst of wealth and luxury, she had never seemed like the kind of girl likely to become adept at picking locks or shimmying in through windows.

Life was strange like that.

Wallace J. Newton's office had been near the wharf in a rather seedy-looking two-story building. There were three other nameplates on the door outside the building's entrance, with one of them offering private massage therapy and the other two offering income tax assistance. In all three cases, Samantha was sure that the legality of the services offered was questionable at best.

Newton had apparently never encountered a piece of paper that he deemed worthy of being thrown away. There were mounds of the stuff all over every available surface and Samantha couldn't be sure where the desk even was at first, though she soon reasoned that it must be located somewhere near the rolling chair that had been converted into a shelf.

Samantha regarded the mess with a stoicism that was reminiscent of her employer. She knew that delaying it wouldn't improve the situation any, so she simply dove into the task with gusto. In a surprisingly short amount of time, she'd uncovered a small folder filled with information about a man named Mr. Skull. As her eyes scanned the documents, she learned that the mysterious criminal was actually Garrison Montreux, a Canadian who had moved to Sovereign recently. From the looks of things, Newton had become curious about the man after learning that Doc Pemberley was working for him. Samantha couldn't help but admire Newton for doing this much digging when he wasn't being paid for it. It must have taken many hours of work: he'd compiled a list of men who worked for Skull, along with their usual haunts and what hours they were there.

A notepad shoved into the folder was filled with Newton's musings on the matter: again and again, it seemed, he was wrestling with what to do with the information. Like most people in Sovereign, he knew that going to the police was a risky endeavor since at least some of the cops were likely to be crooks themselves. Samantha's heart skipped a beat when she saw the words Assistance Unlimited followed by a question mark. The words were circled and in red underneath had been hastily scribbled 'Yes!' Apparently, Newton had been planning to turn over all this information to Gray at some point.

She heard heavy footsteps and the muted voices of men in the hallway. Quickly shoving the folder into the compact purse she carried, Samantha crawled under the desk as someone pushed open the door. From her vantage point, she could only see the feet of those who entered but it looked like three men. Two sets of legs were in ratty pants and soiled shoes. The man in the front, however, was wearing shoes so highly polished that Samantha was sure she'd be able to see the man's face in them, had her position been better. His pants, too, were of the highest quality.

"Search the place, boys," the well-dressed man said. "If that private dick had any information on me, I want it now."

"You got it, boss," one of the others answered. As the two men began rifling through boxes and papers, casually tossing them to the floor when they were done with them, Samantha felt a chill go down her back. So this was Mr. Skull... things were beginning to fall into place. Newton was tracking Pemberley, which led him to Skull, who didn't appreciate the attention. So Mr. Skull had Newton silenced, which inadvertently accomplished what Newton had wanted all along: to bring Skull to the attention of someone who could stop him.

Mr. Skull sauntered over to the window, peering outside. "When we're done here, we're headed over to the reservoir."

One of the men paused long enough to ask, "Uh, what for, boss?"

"We're going to dump some of the Bone Dust into the city's water supply. By this time tomorrow, we should have a few hundred, if not a thousand, dead. When the citizens of Sovereign see their husbands, wives, children all suffering before their eyes, they'll be ready to do anything in exchange for an end to it. I'll be able to name my price."

Samantha's eyes went wide. What sort of man would do such a thing? She shuddered to think of the horrors that would ensue. It was one thing to murder a grown man like Wallace Newton – but to disfigure and kill children? She bit her lip to keep from crying out in disgust.

Apparently, the acts under discussion gave even Skull's men reason to pause. The second man, the one who had asked about the reservoir, cleared his throat. "That's gonna attract all kinds of heat, boss. I mean, it's not just gonna be the law after us – I bet we'd be dealing with Doc Daye or Assistance Unlimited!"

"Then let them come!" Mr. Skull bellowed, turning to face his men. Something either in his words or demeanor made both men take a few steps away him and Samantha wrinkled her nose. It smelled like something was burning in the room and was she imagining it or did she hear the crackling of flames? "I'm not afraid of them," Mr. Skull continued, lowering his voice. "If they stick their noses in my business, they'll get their heads handed to 'em."

Samantha thought it strange that a French-Canadian should speak with a rough-and-tumble Gangster speech pattern. She slowly reached into her purse, hoping to find one of the small radio communicators that Lazarus had recently given to all members of the group. There were two settings on the device: one that functioned much like a standard walkie-talkie and the other where a silent signal was transmitted to all other devices, alerting them that there was someone in danger. As she grabbed hold of the device, she accidentally bumped her fingers up against a small makeup mirror, which slipped from her purse and fell to the floor. She quickly swiped her hand out to grab hold of it but it had rolled out from under the desk, bumping against the shoe of Mr. Skull.

Samantha quickly pressed the emergency button and sprang into action. She could hear Mr. Skull muttering something as he bent down to pick up the compact mirror and she knew that whatever he was saying, it wasn't going to be anything good. She rolled out from under the desk, bumping into the rolling chair and sending papers spilling to the floor. By the time Samantha was on her feet, she had already drawn her pistol and was aiming it directly at the closest of the thugs. Without giving him the chance to surrender, she pulled the trigger and a slug slammed itself into his left shoulder, sending him toppling backwards in shock.

It was when she whirled about, intending to threaten Mr. Skull, that she experienced the shock of her young life. Though she'd seen some strange things in recent weeks, the image of a man with a burning skull for a head had to be the most bizarre of all.

"Put the gun down, doll," Skull said. He gestured for his men to retreat out into the hallway. The one who had been shot in the shoulder glared daggers at Samantha as he backed out. "Whom do you work for? Nobody told me that Newton had a secretary."

Samantha refused to cower, even in the face of such horror. "You're one sick bastard," she hissed.

"Such language," Mr. Skull chided, taking a step toward her. "I bet your parents would be shocked, Miss Grace. That is your name, isn't it? Now that I get a better look at you, I'm pretty sure I recognize you from the society pages."

"Can't say that you have a familiar face," Samantha said, cocking her gun. "I can't even say you have a face at all. Don't come any closer or I'll shoot."

The flames danced higher around Skull's head and he laughed, a rumbling sound that rose up deep in his chest and emerged through his skeletal teeth. "Go ahead and try it." He lunged forward, gripping hold of the desk and tossing it aside. It slammed against the wall, sending papers and pencils flying.

Samantha was true to her word, pulling back on the trigger. The barrel spat out hot metal death, the bullets slamming repeatedly into Mr. Skull's midsection. He staggered back, grunting with each impact, but when Samantha was out of ammunition, he resumed his approach, backing her up against the wall.

"That wasn't nice," he whispered, leaning in so close that Samantha feared her hair would be singed from his flames. "Look at me," he demanded. Though she was terrified, she did as he asked, keeping her gaze as steady as possible. "There was a time when dames like you wouldn't have given me the time of day. But now... now I have girls like you jumping when I snap my fingers."

"It must be because of your rugged good looks," Samantha retorted, sarcasm twisting her words into something ugly.

Skull gripped her around her throat, applying enough pressure that she immediately began struggling to breathe. She raised the gun and slammed the butt of it down against his head, the flames burning her hand in the process. She did it again and again and the villain finally backed away when a crack appeared in his skull. He reached up and lightly touched the affected area, his fingers coming back with splintered bone on their tips. "You little bitch," he hissed. "I'm going to kill you for that."

Samantha's neck felt like someone had run it through a meat grinder but she could breathe again and that gave her renewed hope. She decided to turn the tables on her foe, rushing toward him and driving a hard kick into his chest. The blow was enough to knock him back and he fell over a stack of papers, landing on his back. She jumped over him and yanked open the door, planning to deal with Skull's two goons. To her surprise, she saw Eun standing there, the two men unconscious at his feet. He looked up at her and smiled but his grin vanished as Samantha grabbed hold of him and yanked him down the hallway. "Let's go!" she yelled.

"But what's going on?" he gasped, struggling to keep up with her. His head jerked around as the door to the office suddenly flew off its hinges and Mr. Skull emerged into the hall. He glared at them, the hollow orbs of his eyes moving from his fallen men to the fleeing members of Assistance Unlimited. "What is that?" Eun wondered aloud.

"Trouble," Samantha replied and Eun had no doubt that she was right about that. The two of them burst out onto the street and were inside one of the company cars within seconds. Samantha slid behind the wheel, starting the engine and slamming her foot down on the accelerator. She cast a quick glance behind them and saw Mr. Skull slowly walking down the building's front stairs. He and his men watched them go and then headed toward their own vehicle.

"Are they going to come after us?" Eun asked.

"No. They have much worse plans." Samantha smiled at her friend. "Thanks for coming after me."

"You're welcome. Glad I got there when I did. Your neck looks awful."

"Could have been worse. We need to get the Chief on the horn. That Mr. Skull character is one of the most dangerous we've ever faced."

<hr />

Walther Lunt stared at his reflection in the bathroom mirror. The right side of his face was a mangled mess of scar tissue, the result of an acid attack. There were some in The Illuminati who whispered that the acid had done more than simply scar Walther's face: they intimated that it had unhinged his mind, as well.

Those closest to the German, however, knew the truth: Walther had been quite insane even before that. His desire for power and his willingness to do anything to achieve it were traits that had made him a valuable member of his guild and he'd quickly risen through the ranks. His one mistake had been a costly one, however. It had been his decision to recruit the man who had become Lazarus Gray into the secret society, inadvertently creating a terrible enemy.

Lunt turned away from the mirror and strode into the living room of the apartment he was sharing with Miya. Not long ago, he'd been killed in combat with Gray but Miya had been sent by the Illuminati to revive him. Now given a second chance at life, Lunt was eager to make the most of it. He took a peek into the bedroom where Miya lay under the covers. She was nude but all he could see were her bare shoulders and her lustrous dark hair, as she lay facedown. He felt himself stirring with lust for her but he pulled the door closed and tried to forget about the pleasures her flesh could offer him. Like all women who weren't being paid to share his bed, she regarded his features with barely disguised disdain and that fact soured his lust, turning it into something violent and ugly.

The apartment's telephone sat on a small table located near a large couch and two adjoining chairs. Lunt sat down on the couch and lifted the receiver, quickly dialing in the phone number for 6196 Robeson Avenue. He wasn't sure if anyone would answer the phone or if he'd be connected to the automated answering service that Assistance Unlimited possessed but either way, he planned to leave quite a surprise for Lazarus Gray.

Miya's plan to slowly seduce Gray was a failure in Lunt's eyes. It was taking far too long and there was no guarantee of success. After all, The Illuminati had authorized her to sleep with him before in the hopes that it would tie Gray to their will, only to find that he was willing to toss aside their relationship in the name of his sickening morality. Lunt had decided that it was now time to roll the dice and take the offensive. Let Gray know the truth: either he would realize his mistake and come back into the fold or he would have made it clear that Lunt needed to kill him.

To his great astonishment, it was Gray himself who picked up on the other end. In grave tones, Lunt's former associate said, "You've reached Assistance Unlimited. How may I help you?"

"Your name is Richard Winthrop. You were born in San Francisco. Both of your parents died when you were in your early teens but they left behind a trust that enabled you to take care of yourself. You graduated with honors from Yale University. The night of your graduation, agents of The Illuminati, who were aware that you showed a curiosity for things of an occult nature, approached you. You were brought onboard with promises of access to hidden libraries scattered across the globe. Of particular interest to you were spells related to the binding and summoning of elder entities. I think you found it appealing to believe that man could harness the powers of the ancients.

There were attempts to subvert you to the ways of the Order but you resisted. In particular, you rebelled at the kinds of blood sacrifices that were required for us to maintain our status. You turned against us and became quite the thorn in our sides. In the end, you snuck onboard a boat headed here to Sovereign, intending to stop one of our operatives from stealing a rare tome from the museum. You were discovered not long after the boat docked in the harbor and suffered a concussion. You managed to escape but you passed out on the shore. One of our men went looking for you, disguised as a member of local law enforcement. That's the man that you killed, immediately after waking up. Our man on the boat apparently thought it best not to let anyone know that you'd escaped. He told us you were dead and that he'd dumped your body overboard. Imagine my surprise when I saw you here in Sovereign."

If Lunt was expecting Gray to react with shock, he was disappointed by the calm tone of voice that Lazarus used in response. "And the coin that I was holding?"

"The image of the man with the lion's head is our symbol – and the name that was engraved under the picture was the name of our founder. The real Lazarus Gray died centuries ago."

"I see."

Lunt was about to tease his old foe with more information but to his surprise, he heard the click of the line being disconnected. He stared at the phone for a moment in disbelief. Had Gray actually hung up on him?

He set the phone back into its cradle and looked over his shoulder at Miya, who was stepping from the bedroom. She took one look at the expression on his face and paused. She had only a sheet wrapped around her lithe form but Lunt seemed unaware of how close to being naked she really was.

"What's wrong?" she asked, her eyes narrowing.

Lunt looked away and for one of the few times in their relationship, Miya realized that he was genuinely afraid. "I think I may have made a terrible mistake."

Lazarus Gray was looking out the window when his aides entered the meeting room. All of them had met up again after their various adventures, exchanging information as they did so. They had warned the authorities to increase security around the water stations for fear of Mr. Skull making good on his earlier schemes.

"Chief?" Samantha asked. "We were waiting outside by the car but you were taking so long that we got worried. Who was it on the phone?"

Gray's face remained impassive but there was a flicker of emotion in his mismatched eyes. Samantha noticed it but wasn't sure if it was sadness, anger or excitement, or some combination of all three. When Gray looked at her, all traces of emotion had vanished, leaving his eyes looking as placid as usual. "It was no one important," he said at last. "We shouldn't waste any more time on that. Let's go. We have a criminal to catch."

Chapter IV
Death from the Skies!

Sovereign City was home to a fairly large airport but it also had a number of private airfields that catered to those rich enough to afford them. Mr. Skull was one of those lucky few and he owned two small planes, both little more than crop dusters but he treasured them both. He'd gotten a pilot's license before coming to Sovereign and enjoyed the opportunity to take to the skies, where all those below him looked like nothing more than ants.

As he strode into the private hangar where his two planes were housed, the guard who was paid to be on duty stood up quickly. He held a trash pulp magazine in his left hand and cup of coffee in the other. The expression on his face was so sheepish that Mr. Skull was reminded of a little boy caught with his hand in the cookie jar.

"Mr. Skull! I didn't expect you!"

"Obviously." He peeled off the coat he wore and tossed it to the guard. The act of catching the garment caused him to spill his coffee all over his pants and shoes. "I'm taking her up," Skull said, gesturing to the closer of the two identical planes.

The guard peered outside and noticed that Skull was alone. He had no way of knowing that his employer had dropped off his injured lackey at the hospital, leaving the other man to keep an eye on him. The guard did realize that it was strange to see Mr. Skull out and about without anyone with him.

Skull was already strapping himself in and beginning his pre-flight routine when the guard took a few steps forward. "Sir?" he asked, yelling over the sound of the engines roaring to life.

Skull glanced down at him. He didn't wear any goggles when flying, since they were rather pointless in his current state. The flickering flame that surrounded his skull usually vaporized any particles or insects that flew too close to his head. "What do you need?" he asked.

"Should I be expecting anyone else? Should I tell them where you've gone or when you'll be back?"

"If anyone comes looking for me, tell them nothing."

The guard backed away quickly as Skull began driving the plane toward the open hatch. He watched as the bizarre figure vanished into the sky, wondering not for the first time how Mr. Skull pulled it off. That was the most realistic mask he'd ever seen. If the guard hadn't known better, he'd have almost believed that was the man's actual face....

THREE YEARS BEFORE

Borys had sat in the darkest corner of the Vatican Library that he could find, pouring over the ancient records. He loved books, the feel of the ancient pages against his fingertips lulling him into a sense of security that he found nowhere else. Since the age of 13, when he'd made the decision to pledge his love only to God, he'd found an almost sensual pleasure in the written word. It was his little flirtation on the side, so to speak, giving him something to think about during the long, difficult years of celibacy.

And it was not as if women would have scorned his attentions, had he chosen to pursue them. He was handsome, with classic Polish features and dark hair. It was his eyes, though, that had drawn the most attention from others. Even as a little boy, they could captivate men and women alike. They were so dark that they were almost black, with an intelligence that seemed to be projected from far within.

He'd fled Russia over a decade ago, settling in Canada. He'd made his dream of becoming a priest into reality and it was after one of his services that he'd met a young man with a stout body and a desperate need for acceptance. The young man, along with a few other young ones, had moved under the wing of Borys, believing him when he'd told them of visions he'd had: of a world on the brink of destruction, with ethnic cleansing and the rise of an evil axis of power. The three of them had even followed him here on this trip to Rome, where Borys was convinced that he'd learn the secrets to averting disaster.

"Find anything useful?"

Borys didn't bother looking up from the yellowed papers. "There was a Christian seer in the 14th Century who recounts a vision he had with the Virgin Mary. She allegedly told him that there would come a time of great tribulation, prior to the Second Coming." He cleared his throat before continuing. He adopted the mock professorial style that so greatly annoyed his companion. "*The creatures of the pit will rise up and walk alongside the Holy; Men and women of little faith will follow the quick and easy paths, while the true son will face an uphill struggle.*"

"Typical religious double-talk."

Borys sighed. "Garrison... Why are you here if you don't want to learn?"

Garrison Montreux sat down beside his Borys, looking him square in the eye. Garrison was a much harsher figure than Borys, with a deep scar that lined his left cheek and the weathered appearance of a life-long fighter. It was obvious to everyone who met him that Garrison had to struggle for everything he'd ever gotten and this had hardened him.

"Because you asked me to come."

Borys didn't answer that one. It was true enough, though he would have gladly visited these sacred halls even without a mission at hand. "Where are the others?"

"Valerie and Michael are at the hotel, waiting for us. They're anxious to be gone from here and I don't blame them. This place is an anachronism. It doesn't have any place in the modern world."

That was too much for Borys to ignore. "Damn you, Garrison! Are you trying to provoke me? I know that you're an atheist but this is the holiest of places! It is home to God's chosen representative and in these books is the wisdom of the ages! There are dark days coming and it is here that we might find the source of inspiration!"

"You really believe that?" Garrison asked. "That the secret to avoiding another world war lies in one of these old books? That's a bit much, don't you think?"

"We've run out of other options, haven't we? Besides, my powers are derived from God himself... if he chooses to reveal the truth to us, this is as likely a place as any."

"Derived from God," Garrison snorted. "What makes you think that? Do you think Doc Daye gets his abilities from the King of the Jews, too?"

"That's not for me to judge." Borys looked down at his hands. He wore thick cloths tied around each palm, leaving the fingers free. Dark spots in the center of his palm were beginning to spread again. "The stigmata is proof that--"

A book flew off a shelf nearby, landing with a loud thud. Both men were on their feet at once, with Garrison's hand creeping down to the gun he kept holstered beneath his heavy coat.

"What the hell?" Garrison whispered. He looked about the library. "I thought we were alone here."

"We are," Borys replied. He walked over to where the book had fallen and picked it up, staring at its leather-bound cover. Stamped on the front were the words **Chaldean Magic**. "This is one of the forbidden books... What is it doing here, in the open?"

"Perhaps your God wanted us to find it." Garrison's voice, though full of sarcasm, also held a note of concern. Borys realized that he felt it too -- the sense that something momentous was occurring.

Borys felt along the edge of the book, finding one page that seemed to have been marked somehow with a tiny notch in the top of the vellum. With trembling hands, he opened the tome and began to read....

"Well?" Garrison prompted.

"It's here," Borys whispered, in a voice full of holy reverence. "God has shown us the way." He held the page up for Garrison to read.

There on the page, amongst various occult diagrams, was a spell entitled *The Bonding of Man and Demon*. Beneath the spell was a drawing of a demon rising out of the abyss... and the demon's skull was aflame.

The image shook Garrison to his core and in a moment of supernatural clarity he realized that in these words lay the power he'd always wanted. He'd built his body into something strong and deadly but he'd needed more, which had led him to follow Borys on this wild goose chase.

"Give me the book," Garrison whispered. He reached for it and tried to wrest it free from his mentor's grasp but Borys held it tight. There was a look of fear in the older man's eyes.

"No. I don't like the way your expression changed when you read that page. It's not healthy for you. Let me keep it."

Garrison snarled like a caged tiger and before he'd even realized what he was doing, he'd drawn back a fist and then slammed it hard into his friend's face. He repeated the attack several more times until Borys lay quietly on the floor, drops of his blood splattered on the pages of the book.

Garrison had stood there panting for a long minute before grabbing hold of the text and shoving it into his jacket. He had turned to flee, leaving the priest to slowly bleed out. In the book lay power... power that would be his and his alone.

❦

Mr. Skull knew that the reservoir was off-limits now but there had to be some way he could bring death to the citizens of Sovereign. He had finally decided to drop Bone Dust right over downtown. The wind would carry the dust far and wide, spreading it so thin that it might not kill all it touched.

But it would burn and it would scar.

After bonding with the demon that now resided inside him, Garrison had realized what a curse he'd accepted. He was terrifying to behold, which both pleased and repulsed him. He was also driven half-mad by the creature's voice in his head: it gave him great power and a long leash but it craved death and destruction, both of which Garrison found himself giving it in spades. That was the secret of it all: though he masqueraded as a mobster, Mr. Skull was as much a true killer as he was a criminal. Money was secondary in the end, a distant concern compared to the opportunity to sow terror amongst the innocent.

His plane banked to the west and down below lay the gambling ship known as The Heart of Fortune. It was a little over three miles off the Sovereign coast and the ship's lights showed that a large crowd of revelers were enjoying themselves. Mr. Skull thought about dropping the Bone Dust here, just a few handfuls, to see what effect it would have on the gamblers. He held off, however, preferring to save it all for the more heavily populated areas. He spurred his plane to greater speeds and within moments land was once more beneath him. He saw the courthouse and city hall up ahead, recognizing them by their distinctive shapes.

To his great surprise, however, something rose up from below, rocketing toward him with tremendous speed. It took him a moment to realize that it was a small rocket fired from a bazooka – Mr. Skull had read up on the devices and knew that they'd first appeared on the scene back in the Great War. Originally known as Rocket-Powered Recoilless Weapons, they were quite deadly – sometimes as much so for the one firing it as the one on the receiving end.

Mr. Skull tried to avoid the missile but it came at him too quickly, shearing off the plane's left wing and sending him hurtling toward the ground with smoke and fire trailing after him.

Skull unbuckled his seat restraint and began to crawl from his seat even as his plane hurtled to its destruction. He was going to come down on a large hill overlooking downtown, part of a district that mixed various small businesses with homes. Whether by divine providence or simple luck, the plane was on a direct course with a large playground and park that was currently empty.

Skull threw himself away from the plane, landing in a roll that carried him in the opposite direction from the crash. He felt the impact through the ground and felt the rush of heat as the gas tank exploded, but he was unharmed, aside from a few rips in his clothing. He patted his pockets and found that the vials of Bone Dust had not been shattered.

Standing up, he quickly looked around for the source of the attack. He didn't have to look far. The members of Assistance Unlimited were less than a hundred feet away and the man known as Lazarus Gray was dropping a bazooka to the ground. Morgan and Samantha both had handguns drawn, while Eun was standing relaxed but obviously ready for combat.

"Garrison Montreux," Lazarus said. "Surrender now or I cannot promise that your life will be spared."

Mr. Skull gestured around at the houses and businesses. "You're really going to do this here? What about all the people who might get hurt?"

"All evacuated." Gray's mismatched eyes glittered with cold humor. "Once Miss Grace had surmised who you really were and informed us of your plans to commit mass murder, I began to look into your business holdings. It didn't take much digging to find out that you owned two planes, housed at a private airfield."

"And you just happened to have a weapon like that?" Skull laughed hoarsely. "Gray, you're a real piece of work."

"Can't I shoot him, Chief?" Morgan grinned like a wolf. "He's not going to surrender, you can tell."

Mr. Skull's head was now fully ablaze and it was so bright that it nearly equaled that of the burning plane. "Bullets won't hurt me. The girl knows that." He cracked his knuckles and began moving toward them. "I'm going to enjoy this."

Eun rushed forward, moving with the speed of a panther. He caught Mr. Skull in the midsection with a flurry of punches, followed by a hard kick to the villain's knee. In an ordinary man, such an attack would have left him writhing in agony. But Mr. Skull was not like other men. He struck back quickly, backhanding Eun so hard that the young Korean was lifted off his feet. Eun cried out as he landed right atop Samantha, knocking them both on their backs.

Morgan knelt quickly at their sides, checking to make sure they weren't badly wounded. Eun was groggy and suffering from a mild concussion but Samantha looked merely stunned.

Gray had taken in all of that with a mere glance. He turned away from them, focusing all of his attention on Mr. Skull. The villain was laughing again, an eerie sound that combined with the horrific nature of his appearance, making the entire scene appear quite surreal.

Skull threw a powerful left-handed punch but Gray caught it, knocking it aside with the back of his hand. Before Skull could attack again, Gray had pushed both hands under the man's armpits and pushed, momentarily knocking the fiery killer off-balance. Gray danced around his foe, wrapping his powerful arms around Mr. Skull's midsection. He held on with all his strength as Skull began trying to free himself.

Keeping his head just out of the range of the villain's flickering flames, Gray lowered his voice and whispered, "You don't strike me as an occultist, Mr. Montreux. If I had the time, I'd love to know how you managed to turn yourself into this monstrosity… but in the end, it doesn't matter. You're a threat to everyone you come into contact with."

"I'm going to pour the Bone Dust right down your throat!" Mr. Skull bellowed.

"No. You're not. Enigha m'luktu omnarium. Varily'u fedda b'eginas!"

The strange words that Lazarus Gray said were delivered almost under his breath and yet all of his aides, even battle wounded Eun, reacted to them. They saw their employer's emerald colored eye glow brightly as he said those awful phrases. These were words that were part of a lost tongue, ancient even when Atlantis sank beneath the waves. They were a litany of power, spoken by men who had bartered their souls for the dark gifts. It terrified them to know that Lazarus Gray knew them.

The flames around Garrison's head began to die out and the light in his empty sockets dimmed. He began to cry out in alarm and pain but his words were gibberish, bundled up in shock and horror. When the final flame died out, he slumped in Gray's grasp, his soul having been driven from its mortal shell. To the nether realms the demon had been banished once more and to the dark, stygian depths of Hell went the soul of Garrison Montreux.

It was Morgan who found the courage to ask what they were all thinking. "Chief… What the heck were those things you were saying?"

Gray set down Mr. Skull's body with far more dignity than Eun thought it deserved. "It was a spell from a book entitled ***Chaldean Magic***. There are only a handful of copies in existence so I'm not quite sure where he would have found one. When I saw his physical appearance, I recognized what spell had been used." Gray noticed that his friends were watching him with shocked expressions and his normally emotionless face relaxed a bit, soothing their concerns. "I used to be a specialist in spells relating to the binding and summoning of demons. I'd forgotten that until earlier this evening. That phone call I received back at HQ sparked something in me."

Samantha, leaning against Morgan for support, asked, "So do you remember anything else?"

"Several things."

"Do you know your real name?"

Gray paused, his gaze shifting away from Samantha's. He appeared to be considering something quite important and when he spoke, his words carried great conviction. "Yes. I do. It's Lazarus Gray."

Epilogue

Miya was furious as she hurried down the stairs to the waiting taxi. The driver had been given instructions to take her directly to the airport, where she had plans to fly back to Europe. She was going to inform the rest of The Cabal that Walther had ruined her plans and betrayed valuable information to the man once known as Richard Winthrop.

She carried her heavy bags out to the car and set them down, expecting the driver to get out and help her. When he didn't, she moved around to look at him. He was lying unconscious behind the wheel, a nasty looking bruise on his left temple.

"Miya. Don't move."

The cool barrel of a gun pressed against the back of her head and Miya's shoulders slumped. "Lazarus. Or do you prefer Richard now?"

"Lazarus will do. Where's Walther?"

"Gone. Now that you know who you are, he believes we won't be able to recruit you. He's going to kill you. That's what he wanted to do all along."

"And you?"

Miya did turn now, staring past the gun into the eyes of the man she used to regard as a lover. "I'm loyal to The Illuminati but I do care for you. I want you to be with me. I know that you've always been uncomfortable with some of their methods but I think we can change them from within. This organization has been around for centuries. It can't be destroyed – the best we can do is try to mold it."

Gray's face betrayed no emotion whatsoever. "I don't remember everything, Miya, but I remember enough. That group is evil. They want to control the minds of men and women throughout the world. I can't let that happen."

"Are you willing to kill me?"

"I'd like to see you brought to justice."

"But there's no crime you can pin on me. If you turn me over to the authorities, I'll be free by the end of the night."

"I know that. And that's why I'm going to let you go."

Miya couldn't hide her surprise but she recovered quickly. "You do love me, don't you?"

Gray gave a curt shake of his head. "That's not why I'm allowing you to walk free. Like you said, there's only so much I can do to hold you legally. So this is what I want to do: I know you've bought tickets on a plane headed to London. I want you to go there and I want you to tell The Illuminati that I'm watching them. I plan to destroy their organization piece-by-piece and brick-by-brick. If they stay out of Sovereign, they might last a bit longer... but if they force my hand, I won't rest until every last one of you is dead. Do you understand?"

Miya saw nothing in his eyes to suggest that he didn't mean every word that he said. She shivered and wasn't sure if it was because a soft drizzle had begun to fall or if it was because she was staring at a man who had just sworn her eventual destruction. "I don't want us to be enemies, Lazarus."

"Then you need to turn against the people you work with."

"I can't do that. It's madness to fight them."

Lazarus took a step back, lowering his weapon. "Then get out of my sight. And never come back."

Miya looked like she wanted to say more but in the end, she merely returned to loading her bags into the car. When she was done, she turned to look at Lazarus one last time...

But he had vanished, as quietly and as quickly as a fading memory.

THE AXEMAN OF SOVEREIGN CITY

An Adventure of Lazarus Gray
Written by Barry Reese

———— ∞∞∞ ————

Chapter I
Terror in the City

It was nine o'clock in the evening and a man sat in his office, reading a newspaper.

There were several factors that made this simple-sounding scene remarkable: the location of his office, the headline on the newspaper's front page, and the man himself.

The man in question was tall and well sculpted. His hair was mostly gray though there were patches of brown interspersed. Despite the salt-and-pepper hair, he was in his late twenties and obviously quite vital and strong. His face was set in grim determination and his eyes were startling. One of his eyes was a dusky, dull brown in color while the other was emerald green.

He was Lazarus Gray, known and far wide as the founder of Assistance Unlimited. A mysterious stranger who had literally washed up on the shores of Sovereign City, Gray's memory was a series of patchwork images, providing him with only the barest knowledge of who he had once been. Having awakened with a bronze medallion in his possession, depicting the image of a nude man with the

CRIMINALS OF THE WORLD BEWARE,
FOR THOSE IN NEED ARE ABOUT TO RECEIVE...

ASSISTANCE UNLIMITED!

head of a lion and the words "Lazarus Gray" imprinted beneath it, he had chosen the name as his own.

The place in which Gray sat was a former hotel located on Robeson Avenue. Three stories tall, the building contained numerous offices, labs and meeting rooms, as well as living quarters for the four members of the squad.

Two of those members were in the room with Gray now: Eun Jiwon, a Korean youth with dark hair and angry eyes, stood with arms folded while Samantha Grace, a stunning blonde with peaches-and-cream skin, sat perched on the side of Gray's desk, long legs crossed in front of her.

"What do you think, Chief? Is this something we ought to look into?" Eun asked. Given the expression on his face and the tension in his slender body, it was obvious where his opinion on the matter lay.

Gray's eyes flicked to Eun, studying him before returning to the printed page. The headline of The Sovereign Gazette was printed in bold type and Gray knew that it was bound to sell quite a few copies:

THE AXEMAN STRIKES AGAIN!
THREE LOVELY LADIES TERRORIZED!
POLICE BAFFLED!

Accompanying the text was a pen and ink drawing of a shadowy figure menacing an attractive young woman in torn stockings and ripped blouse. Though the artist's name was not given, Gray assumed it was Howard Bloomberg, who usually handled the paper's political cartoons.

The article described, in typically lurid fashion, how three young girls had left a basketball game around 7:30 pm, intending to walk each other home. Less than a mile from the arena, the three women (who were described as "nubile" no less than four times over the course of the article) experienced a tremendous shock when a man wearing a thin mask over his face rushed them from a dark alleyway. The man was brandishing a bloodstained axe, which he used to attack the girls. There was no conversation on the part of the man and he didn't make any attempt to rob them. Two of the girls were left with wounds to their hands, torsos and faces but the third was killed via decapitation. As the paper made sure to point out, this was the sixth murder at the hands of the so-called Axeman in the last month. So far, the victims had included a wealthy banker and his wife, a nine-year old boy and an elderly woman.

Gray set aside the newspaper and stood up, pushing his hands into the front pockets of his slacks. He was wearing a white shirt, a red tie and black trousers. Leather gloves covered his hands, preventing him from leaving fingerprints on anything that might become evidence. "Business is slow otherwise, so I think we can spare the time to investigate these attacks."

Samantha arched an eyebrow, sensing that her employer was engaging in what – for him – was a rare feat. He was making a joke.

Assistance Unlimited did take on cases from the general public, charging only what their customers could afford. But they were all wealthy enough that they didn't really need the money. The group did its work because it was the right thing to do.

"I've found something interesting about the Axeman, Chief," Samantha said. She patted a small pile of papers that she'd brought with her to the meeting. "There's a lot of similarities to a series of attacks that took place in New Orleans from May 1918 through October 1919."

Lazarus picked up the papers and quickly looked through them. "Any chance that the same man is behind both sets of attacks?"

"Possible. Nobody ever caught the New Orleans killer. But maybe it's a copycat."

Gray devoured the information in the press clippings, dissecting the articles and filing the information into the steel trap that was his mind. The Axeman of New Orleans had terrorized the city for nearly 18 months but his identity was never uncovered and the attacks ended as mysteriously as they began. The savagery and utter randomness of the attacks understandably caused great panic. There were even comparisons of the killer to the notorious Jack the Ripper, as the Axeman (or something claiming to be him) wrote a series of taunting letters to the newspapers hinting at his future crimes and claiming to be a supernatural demon "from Hell."

"Curious," Gray murmured under his breath. "Good work, Samantha."

The pretty blonde blushed at the compliment and nodded. "So what's our next step?"

Gray turned his face toward a map of the city that took up a good portion of the wall. "There doesn't appear to be any rhyme or reason to the attacks and they've been scattered throughout the city. The first thing we need to do is speak to one of the survivors and find out all they can remember about the Axeman. I don't trust the police reports or the journalists to have done their jobs accurately." He looked back at his aides. "Samantha, please visit the hospital and speak to one, if not both, of the girls who was attacked last evening. Eun, you'll come with me. I have a few leads of my own to follow up on. When do we expect Morgan back?"

The corners of Samantha's mouth turned downward. It was one of the worst kept secrets in the world that she and Morgan Watts had a hot-and-cold relationship. Morgan had tried to steer their friendship toward a romantic one but Samantha had rejected his advances, straining things between them. Now they alternated between flirting and giving each other the cold shoulder. Morgan's decision to take out a young woman of Samantha's acquaintance on a date this evening hadn't helped matters but Eun was of the opinion that Morgan was simply trying to make Samantha jealous. "Who knows?" Samantha asked, trying a bit too hard to make it look like she didn't care. "Should I call him in?"

"Let him relax for now," Gray answered. The stoic leader of Assistance Unlimited reached over and turned off one of the lamps that illuminated the room. "Let's go find us a killer."

---

*T*he *Heart of Fortune* was anchored three and a half miles off the coast of Sovereign City. With a crew of 300 people and enough space to accommodate another 2,000 in guests, the ship was a masterpiece of gaudy elegance. Morgan Watts loved it and he could sense that his date for the occasion, Molly Sims, was equally entranced. The gambling ship was one of the most popular attractions in the city and catered to the high rollers. Morgan earned a nice living working for Assistance Unlimited and he didn't have many expenses since he lived at their headquarters, so splurging on a night like this was well within his means.

Morgan held Molly's hand as they exited the dance floor, which was packed with partiers who couldn't get enough of Joe 'Monarch' Redfern and his orchestra. Molly loved to dance but Morgan was eager to move on to other pleasures. The siren call of the grand casino was luring him in that direction but as he glanced at Molly, he caught sight of the fine sheen of sweat on her bare shoulders and he realized he might strike the jackpot in more ways than one tonight.

Molly was an attractive girl with red hair, green eyes and a fine spray of freckles that covered her cheeks. Her father was in real estate and was a good friend of Samantha's parents, which was how Morgan had ended up becoming acquainted with her. "This is fun," Molly said between gasps of air. She sat down heavily in her chair and grinned, looking far younger than her twenty-five years of age. "I can't believe you're not even breathing fast. How do you do it?"

"Lazarus keeps us all in tip-top shape," Morgan replied, sitting across from her and gesturing for a waiter to bring them both a drink. "I do more calisthenics than a fresh army recruit."

"Well, it certainly keeps you trim," she said admiringly.

Morgan accepted the compliment with a smile, reaching out to squeeze Molly's knee with his right hand. "Well, you make me feel a good ten years younger than I actually am."

Molly looked up as the waiter set a drink down in front of her. She took a sip, wincing a bit as the alcohol burned its way down her throat. "I'm not going to get you in trouble with Sam, am I?"

Morgan's hand drifted away from her knee. "What? Of course not. We're just friends."

"That's what both of you say but I'm not sure I believe it."

Morgan couldn't quite hide the eagerness in his voice. "Really? What's she said about me?"

Molly laughed gently. "Next to nothing. That's the point."

"I don't get it."

"You're a man," Molly pointed out. "You're all a bit clueless when it comes to these things."

Morgan replied with a grunt. He couldn't really argue what she was saying – when it came to understanding women, he was in the same boat as most men in the world: he couldn't fathom what went on in their pretty little heads. He was spared from having to admit such by a sudden murmuring amongst the crowd. He craned his head to see whose arrival was having such an effect. He saw two men pushing their way out of the casino. One of them wore a tattered top hat, a threadbare coat and vest and dark trousers. His skin was so dark that it made his eyes and teeth look gleaming white in comparison. He carried a gnarled walking stick in his left hand and muttering angrily under his breath. He looked to be in his early fifties though there was something about him that made Morgan wonder if he wasn't much older than that.

Trailing along behind was one of the most massive brutes that Morgan had ever seen. The man wore heavy work boots and overalls. A stained white shirt peeked out from beneath the overalls and the man's fingers were so filthy that Morgan wondered if he'd washed them any time in the current decade. The man had to be nearly seven feet tall, with shoulders so broad that even Morgan, who had spent a lifetime around heavy bruisers, was impressed. But it was the mask the man wore that caused such a ripple through the crowd. It was wrapped around his bald head with heavy leather straps, leaving a plastic covering over his face. It was shaped like a human face, with a nose, curved lips and gentle indentions around the two holes that allowed the man's eyes to peer out at the world.

"My gosh," Molly whispered. "Why is he dressed like that?"

"I don't know," Morgan answered. "Could be that he's disfigured and thinks that mask would disturb people less than seeing what's underneath."

Molly shivered. "I find that hard to believe."

The two men came to a stop not far from their table and the man in the top hat began to smile, his eyes widening at the sight of Morgan. "Mr. Watts?" he asked, speaking in an oily sort of voice. It reminded Morgan of a snake oil salesman, about to launch into a pitch for his newest product.

Morgan could feel Molly's gaze on him, wondering how he could possibly know these two men. He wondered that himself. "Yes. Can I help you?"

"Perhaps you can. Yes, perhaps you can, indeed." Without being asked, the man pulled out an empty chair at the table and sat down in it. The masked brute remained standing, though he came closer so that he stood directly behind his friend. Morgan sniffed delicately, aware that the big man stank to high heaven. The black man in the top hat didn't seem to notice. He swept the hat off his head and set it on the table between Molly and Morgan. "You can call me Mr. Dinkins. The big fella is named Muggsy."

"That's an unusual name," Molly whispered, sliding closer to Morgan. She seemed to be begging him with her eyes, pleading with him to ask Dinkins and his companion to leave. Morgan sympathized but his curiosity wouldn't allow it.

"Nobody knows his real name," Dinkins said. "He just showed up one day and we all took to calling him Muggsy. It's a joke, you see. Because his mug is so damned ugly we have to make him wear a mask."

Morgan was growing increasingly disturbed by the smell emanating from Muggsy. "I'm actually here on a date so if you want to talk business, you either need to make it fast or call Assistance Unlimited and make an appointment."

"I apologize for having interrupted," Dinkins said. "But I do think that my case might be the sort of thing that you'd taken an interest in. You see, my friend and I traveled all the way from New Orleans. We're looking for a young woman, little more than a girl really, named Monique. She took something that rightfully belongs to me and I don't take kindly to thieves, I can tell you that. In the weeks that Muggsy and I have been here, we've heard that she's been around but haven't been able to find her. So I said to Muggsy, let's hire Assistance Unlimited to help us. But I figured that your boss must be an expensive fella so we came here to try and win us enough money to make it worth his while."

"From the way you exited the casino, I gather your plan didn't work out?"

Dinkins drew an ugly face. "The games are rigged," he said in disgust.

Morgan doubted that. Everything he'd heard said that Fortune McCall ran as clean an establishment as any in the country. "We don't normally track down thieves. Maybe you'd be better off going to the police. They're bound to be cheaper anyway."

"Ah, but this is no ordinary theft." He began unbuttoning the vest that he wore under his threadbare coat. When Molly shifted uncomfortably, he offered a wan smile. "My apologies, my lady, but I have to show this so that your paramour will understand." Once the vest was pulled away, Morgan saw a bandage over the man's heart. Blood had seeped through the bandage and the medical tape used to hold it in place looked like it was about to give way.

Morgan narrowed his eyes. "I'm not following you. She attacked you when she stole this item?"

"It was a necessary part of the theft," Dinkins answered. He tore away the bandage and revealed a gaping hole in his chest. The sight was enough to cause Molly to scream out loud. She stood up so quickly that she knocked her chair to the floor and Morgan was upright just as fast, catching her and turning her face so that the girl could bury it in his neck. Dinkins' smile never wavered during all of this. "Look closely, mon ami. That clever girl cut my heart out and took it with her!"

∞∞∞

Chapter II
The Heartless Man

Samantha gently opened the hospital room door and peered inside. A young woman named Tracy Gethers lay in the bed, swathed in bandages. Her mother sat in a chair nearby, her eyes shining wetly with tears and a crumpled tissue in one hand. The mother looked up when Samantha stepped inside.

"Are you a friend of Tracy's?" the woman asked. Her voice sounded hoarse with emotion and Samantha felt out of place. She'd known why Lazarus had tasked her with this job, though: Eun was a foreigner and Morgan, if he had been available, was a bit too gruff for this kind of work.

"No, ma'am. My name is Samantha Grace and I work for Assistance Unlimited. Have you heard of us?"

"Of course I have. I've seen Mr. Gray in the papers. But we've already given a statement to the police and Tracy needs her rest. Besides, I don't have any money to pay you."

Samantha smoothed out her skirt and shook her head. "We don't want any money. Sometimes we take cases just because it's the right thing to do."

"Well," the mother said uncertainly, "I don't think Tracy could tell you anything she didn't already tell the police so I'm going to have to ask you to leave."

"Momma, let her stay. Please. I don't mind talking some more."

Samantha turned to look at Tracy, who was staring out her from beneath the bandages on her face. The girl was slight of build and, from what Samantha had been told, had possessed a fragile beauty. Unfortunately, the wounds to her face were going to rob her of that. "Thank you," Samantha said gratefully, coming to sit on the edge of Tracy's bed.

"Well… don't tucker yourself out." Tracy's mom stood up and moved toward the door. "I'm going to grab some fresh air but I'll be right back. Is that okay?"

"Sure, momma." When her mother was gone, Tracy lowered her voice conspiratorially. "She doesn't want to hear it all again. I think it's harder on her than it is on me."

Samantha smiled, realizing that she liked Tracy already. "Well, we can stop whenever you need to. I really don't want to interfere with your rest."

"You're sweet but don't worry about me. I may look a fright in this mummy makeup but I'm okay. I was pretty scared at the time but I'm bouncing back quick. I just feel terrible about Janice. She was a nice girl and her daddy sure did love her. I bet he's a wreck right now."

Samantha couldn't help but be impressed. Less than 24 hours after being brutally attacked, Tracy was more focused on the suffering of others than what she was going through herself. "The newspaper said the Axeman didn't try to steal anything from you. Is that true?"

"It is. He just came at us screaming those nonsense words and then started swinging that axe."

Samantha blinked in surprise. "He talked to you? The paper said he didn't say anything."

Tracy snorted in an unladylike way but it drew a laugh from Samantha. "They also said we were 'nubile beauties.' No, he did say some things to us but it didn't make any sense."

"Can you remember what it was?"

"Let me think… I believe it was something like 'Où est son coeur? Dites-moi donc je ne peux cesser de tuer!'"

"That's a lot better than I was expecting," Samantha admitted.

"I've always had a good memory for things like that. I suppose it might have been French but it was spoken with such a thick accent that I'm not sure. He sounded like one of those French people from the Bayou."

"A Cajun?"

"Yes! That's it!" Tracy sat up in bed, visibly excited. "Do you know what it means?"

Samantha nodded. She was fluent in five different languages and French was one of her strongest. "Roughly translated, it means 'Where is his heart? Tell me so I can stop killing.' Doesn't make any more sense now that you know what he was saying, does it?"

"No, it doesn't. I guess he's just a lunatic."

"Maybe so." Samantha patted Tracy's leg and stood up. "I think you helped me. Thanks for your time."

Tracy shook her head. "I don't know how. But I hope all of you catch him. He's too dangerous to stay on the loose."

Samantha paused at the door. "If there's anybody alive who can capture him, it's Lazarus Gray. When you're out of the hospital, give me a call at the office. If you're interested, we might find some work for you. You seem like you have the right kind of spirit for what we do."

Tracy nodded. "I just might do that. Thank you."

Samantha exited the room, running the Axeman's words through her head. What did it mean? She couldn't wait to get back to the office and compare notes with the others.

⸙

Monique DuChamp was a beautiful young woman. She had long curly black hair that fell around her shoulders and her skin was a rich caramel color that evoked both sides of her ancestry. Her father had been a black farmer in New Orleans while her mother had been a white woman who had fled an abusive husband up north. They'd raised Monique in a house filled with laughter and love but none of that had stopped their little girl from falling in with the wrong crowd. She'd always been sensual, even as a young child, and when she began turning into a woman, she attracted the attentions of many men, including Mr. Dinkins. He'd introduced her to drugs and sexual magic, using both to achieve their separate aims: Dinkins had gotten the chance to indulge his lusts with a ripe young girl and Monique had gotten a taste of true power.

It was a heady time for both, with each striving for more and more. Monique played with her sexuality, using it to lull Dinkins into a false sense of security. Then one night while he'd slept, she'd bound his hands to the bed and carved his heart right out from his chest. It had been bloody, disgusting work but Monique hoped it would propel her into a new level of existence.

Unfortunately, it hadn't been quite so simple. Monique had read in one of the old man's books that the heart of a sorcerer could be a potent thing: if ground into a powder, it could impart knowledge upon anyone who ingested it; if carried on your person, it could keep you young and vital; and if set aflame during a full moon, it could summon an ancient entity who would answer any three questions for you. Monique had decided to take the young and vital option for now – she could always ground it up or burn it later on.

But Dinkins was too powerful to be so easily killed. He still lived through magical means and he'd set Muggsy on her trail. They'd pursued her all the way to Sovereign and Monique was fearful that it was only a matter of time before they caught up to her.

Monique lay atop a soft bed now, her nude young body barely visible in the dim lighting that drifted in from the window. The man she'd picked up in the hotel bar was undressed in front of her, his eyes glued to her curves. He was a big man with a barrel chest and massive biceps. He had a vaguely Cro-Magnon look to him but Monique didn't mind that: intelligence wasn't high on the list of attributes she was seeking at the moment.

The man kicked off his pants and moved to the bed, crawling over her on all fours. "I've never been with a Negro before," he whispered and Monique felt her skin crawl. She accepted his passionate kiss, trying to pretend that the way his tongue plunged into her mouth excited her. She reached one hand under her pillow and slowly pulled out a large knife. She waited until her would-be lover was kissing her neck to raise the blade and plunge it into the side of his neck. He screamed and jerked away but Monique worked fast, slicing through his neck. Blood spurted over her breasts and his hands flew up to try and cover his wound. He thrashed a bit as she pushed him onto his back.

Monique slid off the bed and pulled on her underwear, letting him bleed out. Her purse was stuffed full of the things she would need but she felt a rush of nervousness, having never performed this ritual before. It was going to be necessary, though, she knew that.

If Dinkins had Muggsy, then Monique would need a champion of her own. She smiled at the dying man, her fear beginning to slowly turn into excitement.

"Time to get to work," she said aloud.

———

"**W**hat is this place?" Eun asked, standing uncomfortably in the front room of the privately owned building. There were chicken bones hanging from the ceiling, along with living birds stuffed into cages. The room was lit by candlelight and there was a peculiar odor in the air that reminded him of the one time he'd visited a Korean holy man before his family had moved to the United States. There were piles of trash in every corner of the room and Eun was positive that he saw rat droppings on the floor. "I'm surprised it hasn't been condemned."

"It is my home. Do not be rude." An old man entered the room and Eun noticed that he was blind, with a long beard that nearly reached the floor. He walked with a cane held in front of him, moving gently to and fro. His clothes were all black, save for a white button up shirt and white socks. If he'd held a tin cup in his free hand, Eun wouldn't have been surprised. He looked like the stereotypical blind peddler. "What do you want, Gray? I thought our business was finished."

"I'm afraid not," Gray replied, watching as the old man shoved a pile of garbage out of a chair and sat down heavily. "The young man with me is--"

"Eun Jiwon. I know." The old man smiled, revealing crooked teeth. "All your associates are known to me. Once I enter into business with someone, I take it upon myself to learn all that I can about them." He turned blind eyes toward Eun. "My name is Ebenezer Smith. I'm also known as The Information Broker."

Eun blinked in surprise. He'd heard of The Information Broker – a shadowy figure who knew everything, for a price. It was said that finding out how to contact him was only half the battle: the other was in convincing him that your money or your case was interesting enough to warrant his attention.

"Surprised that I'm a blind man, living in a hovel?"

"Yes, actually."

Ebenezer sniffed disdainfully. "Only one of us is truly blind. I am rich beyond your imaginings."

Eun looked around doubtfully but said nothing.

"So. The last time you were here you wanted me to verify certain things about your past." Ebenezer cleared his throat. "So what is it this time?"

Lazarus glanced at Eun. "The Broker was quite useful. He found quite a bit about Richard Winthrop's life, before and after he fell in with The Illuminati."

Eun once again bit his tongue. All of the aides had noticed Gray's new habit of referring to his old life in the third person. It was like he was regarding Richard Winthrop as a separate entity from himself.

Gray removed a small vial of what appeared to be blood, stepping forward to push it into Ebenezer's hand. The old man removed the stopper from the vial and raised it to his nostrils, sniffing it and nodding.

"This is more than enough for almost anything, I'd wager," Ebenezer said, replacing the stopper and setting it on a crowded table at his side. "What do you need to know?"

"There were a series of murders in New Orleans almost twenty years ago and now a similar set are occurring here in Sovereign City. I was wondering if you knew anything about them."

"Ah," Ebenezer said, his lips stretching wide. "You want to know about the Slashers."

"The Axeman," Eun corrected.

Ebenezer shrugged his bony shoulders. "Same thing."

Gray crouched in front of him, studying the blind man's features. "Tell me everything."

"For as long as there have been men who sought power through sorcery, there have been Slashers. They've been known by different names in different times but they're always men or women who have been transformed into killing machines, subject to the whims of their masters. They kill for two reasons: because someone tells them to and because they must. They no longer eat or drink as we do, they feed off the life essence of those they kill. Using them as foot soldiers is good because they won't stop moving after their target but it's also dangerous: they have to kill again and again, which can lead to unwanted attention. Jack the Ripper was a Slasher in service to a man named William Gull. And the Axeman of New Orleans was a Slasher, too."

"Is it the same one that's killing people here in Sovereign?"

"Could be. But it doesn't matter. They're a Slasher, which is all you need to know. The Slasher is dangerous, of course, but the one pulling the strings is even more so."

Eun could no longer maintain his silence. "So the one who wrote the papers as Jack the Ripper – was that the Slasher or the mastermind?"

Ebenezer turned blind eyes toward Eun. "Boy, it doesn't matter. Jack the Ripper isn't here, now is he? All that matters is there's a killer out there and he's going to be damned tough to defeat. Just like they don't eat or drink like we do, they don't die like we do. They're stronger and more resistant to pain."

Gray reached out and lightly touched Ebenezer's shoulder. "Is there anything else you can tell us? Is there a way to easily trace who's behind all this?"

"That shouldn't be too hard. Just look in your own home."

Chapter III
Death's Head

Morgan Watts led Mr. Dinkins and Muggsy into the headquarters of Assistance Unlimited. He'd hated to cut short his date with Molly but meeting a man with no heart took precedence over a night out and he hoped she'd understand that. If not, that was too bad for her. Morgan considered his job with Lazarus Gray to be one of the most important things in his life and any partner of his would simply have to understand that.

The group's headquarters was based in an old hotel and there were facets of its old purpose still on display. One such item was the clerk's desk, where once upon a time men and women stepped up to check on their reservations. Morgan stepped around this desk while Dinkins and Muggsy stared at their surroundings. Morgan checked a small magnetic board attached to the back of the desk. On the board were written the names of Assistance Unlimited's agents, with two columns drawn next to them: In and Out. Small black dots could be slid back and forth as necessary. Morgan wasn't surprised to see that all the dots were currently in the Out column. He slid his own to In and sighed.

"Lazarus and the others are out right now but you can wait in the next room. I'll bring you some coffee if you want."

"Thank you, Mr. Morgan." Dinkins took his hat off and held it with both hands. "I do appreciate you bringing us here. I know that you were involved with what promised to be an entertaining evening."

Morgan tried not to show his chagrin at the reminder. "Don't worry about it. Go on and have a seat." He gestured toward an open door that led into a small waiting area. There were several plush chairs set against the wall and a table in the center with magazines of all types arranged around a floral centerpiece. As with most things of an aesthetic nature in the building, it was Samantha's handiwork.

Eun and Morgan had no eye for such things and though Lazarus was incredibly well read and quite aware of appearances, he stepped aside and let Samantha use her skills whenever necessary.

Once Dinkins and his oversized companion was out of sight, Morgan activated the small handheld communications device that all members of the team carried these days. It had two settings: one for radio conversation and another that simply sent an emergency signal to the other devices. In this case, Morgan opted for the latter. He wasn't sure why he erred on the side of such caution but he didn't want Dinkins listening in to any conversation that he might have. He didn't trust either of his guests and it wasn't simply the fact that a shiver went down his spine every time he visualized the old man's wounded chest. There was something more at work here and he hadn't liked the way that Dinkins' eyes had lit up at the suggestion of coming here.

Still, Morgan felt better having them in a place he considered safer than Fort Knox. He moved into the small office behind the desk, preparing a fresh cup of coffee and was just beginning to wonder what Samantha was up to. She'd seemed unaffected by his news that he was going out on a date with Molly, which had both surprised and disappointed him. There was a big part of him that just wanted to give up on any chance of a love affair with her but he just couldn't bring himself to do it. He knew she was right: workplace romances were almost never a good idea. Besides that, there was the age difference. Morgan was in his forties and Samantha was barely past twenty. It might not cause problems right now but where could they go from here? What if wanted children? Could he really deal with fatherhood when turning fifty lay just around the bend for him?

He was so lost in thought that he almost didn't hear the sound of the waiting room door opening and closing. It was done quite quietly but all the members of Assistance Unlimited were trained to sense danger in all its forms. He stepped back out to the desk to see what was going on and quickly stopped in his tracks. Muggsy was standing with a large axe held in his right hand. The blood caked blade dangled against his leg and the big man's eyes shone out from behind his mask with murderous intent.

Mr. Dinkins stood just to the left of Muggsy, a peculiar look on his face. He sounded apologetic as he said, "I'm sorry about this, Mr. Watts. You've been quite good to us and I'd hoped that what happened last night would slake his thirst for the time being. But our Muggsy needs a lot of blood to keep his strength up. And, just between you and me, I think he simply likes the killing."

Morgan reached into his jacket and withdrew his pistol, which he quickly trained on the big man with the axe. "Take one step toward me, fella, and I'll kill you."

Muggsy stared at him. When he spoke, it was with a deep, almost ponderous voice. "Où est son coeur? Dites-moi donc je ne peux cesser de tuer!"

Morgan, who didn't know much of the French language, besides a few dishes he could order in restaurants and a handful of sexual slang terms, stared in confusion.

Dinkins laughed. "Sorry, mon ami. He's asking you where my heart is. He's a bit single-minded, this one. I know you won't believe me, but I really did hope to hire Mr. Gray to help me. He'd solve all this without nearly so much bloodshed." Dinkins gave Muggsy a playful shove. "Go on, then. Get it over with."

The Axeman of Sovereign City raised his killing blade and began to advance on Morgan.

—⁂—

Samantha's car was pulling into the garage located behind the Assistance Unlimited headquarters when Morgan's alarm began going off in her purse. She quickly parked the car and yanked out the communications device, seeing a flashing number on the tiny device's screen: "2." That meant that it was Morgan, since Lazarus was # 1, Samantha was # 3 and Eun was # 4. The address below the flashing number read '6196 Robeson Avenue," which indicated that Morgan was actually inside the building – and in some form of mortal danger!

Samantha was out of the car in a flash, a small handgun clutched tightly in her left hand. She moved around to a side door, one that was marked for deliveries. A small number pad was set into the wall next to the door and she quickly entered a private code that caused the door to open with a pop. She crept inside and moved stealthily through the darkness until she neared the front corridor. She jumped when she heard a gunshot, followed by the unmistakable sounds of Morgan engaging in physical combat.

Any lingering anger she felt toward her friend for his romantic pursuits was completely forgotten and she surged forward, whipping around the corner with her gun raised. What she saw was enough to stop her in her tracks for a moment. A large brute armed with an axe was towering over Morgan, who was bleeding from a deep gash in his right shoulder. Morgan's pistol lay on the floor, covered in blood. Standing just out of harm's way was a Negro wearing a top hat and a broad grin.

Samantha immediately knew that Morgan was too close to the man with the axe for her to get a clean shot off. She had to hope that Morgan could stay alive long enough for her to seize an opportunity. But the man in the hat… he was fair game.

Samantha dropped her gun into the purse she wore slung over one shoulder and rushed into the scene. Dinkins jerked his head to the side, eyes widening at the sight of her. Despite her dainty appearance, Samantha was as adept at the martial arts as any of her peers, if not more so. She drove one of her spiked heels into the side of the old man's head, knocking him off balance. He tumbled to the floor, blood seeping from a nasty looking scratch. He uttered a string of curses at her in a Cajun dialect and Samantha had her suspicions confirmed: these two were related to the Axeman crimes.

Morgan spotted his friend and was almost so distracted that he forgot to duck under another swipe of The Axeman's blade. "Samantha! Get out of here! Go get help!"

Samantha bristled at Morgan's words. She knew that he respected her too much to treat her like some fragile flower but in recent months he'd become more protective of her, in direct correlation to his desire for a relationship with her. She drove a hard kick into Dinkins' belly and he rolled onto his back, gasping for air.

Morgan, meanwhile, dove for his gun but it slid away from him and The Axeman caught him with a hard elbow to the back of the head. Morgan saw stars for a minute and his feet slipped in a puddle of his own blood. He landed awkwardly and The Axeman raised his blade high, intending to finish off his opponent with one further stroke.

It was then Samantha drove her shoulder hard into Muggsy's back. She was light as a feather compared to the big man but the impact was enough to take his attention off of Morgan. He turned slowly, gazing down at Samantha with a tilted head, as if he were gazing at something wholly new and unexpected. Samantha was rubbing her shoulder, wondering if she'd broken something. She fumbled with her purse, intending to draw her pistol but The Axeman batted it away from her with a beefy paw.

"Samantha," Morgan whispered, trying to find the strength to rise again. He stared hard at the beautiful girl, knowing that his heart would break if he saw her seriously hurt. He threw himself at The Axeman's feet, holding on tight to the man's ankles. The Axeman roared in anger, trying to dislodge Morgan's grip but failing. This gave Samantha the time to scurry after her purse. She pulled out her gun and whipped it around toward The Axeman.

Just as she was taking careful aim at the killer's skull, a blue-tinged powder flew into her face. Samantha coughed but it was too late. The substance was in her eyes and throat. It burned and itched but more than anything, it brought a terrible drowsiness that not even Samantha's incredible strength of will could resist. She looked through watery eyes at Dinkins, who was back on his feet, with another of powder clutched in one of his hands. Though she knew it might end up costing her life, Samantha slid into unconsciousness, falling heavily to the floor.

The Axeman, meanwhile, had managed to yank one of his legs free. He drove the heel of his boot into Morgan's face, crushing his nose. Blood gushed from the wound and Muggsy slammed the butt of his axe handle down onto Morgan's skull. He then walked around the prone man's form, hefting his axe once more.

"Leave him be," Dinkins warned.

The Axeman looked up sharply, his eyes burning like coals beneath his mask.

Dinkins stared him down. "You think it's coincidence that she showed up when she did? I bet he sent out an alarm of some kind. Might be one of those silent ones like they have in the fancier banks. That means Gray and his Korean man might be here any second and it's going to bad enough if they find their friends like this. Let them see Morgan there with his head cut off and they might go into a frenzy."

The Axeman panted like a dog and shook his head, as if to say that he didn't fear anyone or anything.

"I agree, mon ami. You could deal with them easy enough." Dinkins lowered his voice, soothing his ally. "But we need to go. No time to play, you hear? I don't want to take no risks. It's obvious now that this Gray fellow and his men aren't the mercenaries I thought they were. They're something else entirely and that makes them dangerous. So come with me now and we'll find the door this little lady came in through. I promise you'll get your fill of blood soon enough."

Muggsy looked at the carnage around him and finally relented, losing the tension in his body. Samantha looked gorgeous in repose but Morgan was a bloody mess.

When the villains were gone, the building fell quiet, save for the deep breathing of Samantha Grace and the quicker, shallower breaths of Morgan Watts.

———∞∞∞———

Lazarus and Eun received the summons from Morgan as well. They were just leaving Ebenezer's home when the signal came through and though they rushed back at far above the posted speed limit, they arrived too late to see The Axeman or Dinkins exiting the scene. They entered cautiously and came upon their fallen comrades within moments of arriving. Lazarus knelt to check on Morgan first, noting the large amount of blood surrounding the man. Of all his aides, it was Morgan who always seemed to get the worst of their adventures. The man had been shot multiple times, stabbed, nearly drowned and even set on fire in the past. Now it looked like another hospital visit lay in his future.

"Samantha's okay but I can't wake her up," Eun said, examining the girl with a practiced eye.

Gray stood and crossed to where the girl lay on the floor. "Go and summon Dr. Hancock at once. Morgan has lost a lot of blood." Eun hurriedly moved to follower his employer's command. Doctor Hancock was on call 24/7 for the exclusive use of Assistance Unlimited. He was paid so handsomely that he had been able to abandon his traditional practice, despite having had the reputation for being one of the top practitioners in Sovereign.

Lazarus opened one of Samantha's lids and noticed a small grain of blue powder in the corner of her eye. He carefully brushed it onto the tip of a finger and studied it with an attentive gaze. He'd seen something similar to this before, though it had been long before his life as Richard Winthrop had come to an end. During a trip to Africa, he and several other members of The Illuminati had found a witchdoctor who used this powder to induce a coma-like state in his enemies.

The substance wore off after several hours but a large enough dose could prove fatal.

"He's on his way," Eun said, stepping back in. "Should I apply pressure on Morgan's wounds?"

"Yes. And I'm going to need you to wait here until Samantha wakes up. If Dr. Hancock wants to take Morgan to the hospital – and I'd wager that he will – I still want you to remain with Samantha. Do you understand?"

"Of course. But where are you going to be?"

Lazarus stood and headed toward the door. "The person or persons who did this can't be far ahead of me. The scene is too fresh. I'm going to try and catch up to them. I'll be back."

<hr />

Monique and her companion walked through the streets, which became more and more deserted as they continued. A soft drizzle was falling and there was a nip to the air but neither of those were the reasons for the dearth of people on the streets. They were nearing Robeson Avenue, which was completely owned by Lazarus Gray. He had bought up all the other buildings to ensure that no one moved in next to his Assistance Unlimited headquarters. As such, there were no cars driving up and down these roads nor were there shoppers or business people about.

Monique looked at the man who trudged along in silence at her side. He wore a rust-colored potato sack over his head, with two holes cut in ragged slits over his eyes. His beefy fingers opened and closed repeatedly, the muscles in his arm clenching in time. He looked like he was strangling some invisible creature hanging at his sides. The sack was a necessity since the process that turned men into Slashers left them a horror to look at. It twisted their features into something inhuman and awful.

"Stop," Monique said, raising a hand to prevent her companion from walking forward. They were standing at the end of the block, looking directly at the Assistance Unlimited front entrance. She had come here after an attempt at turning the tables on Dinkins. She was hoping to catch him by surprise. He wouldn't expect her to become the hunter but now that she had her own Slasher, she thought it was time. She'd spilled the blood of a live chicken and then slit it open, yanking out the bones so that she could pick through its entrails and try to divine the movements of her enemy. She had been led here but there was no sign of Dinkins: he had obviously come and gone before Monique's arrival.

The big man suddenly cried out in pain, falling forward on to his knees. Monique's head whipped around to see Lazarus Gray standing over the big man, his right hand clenched into a fist. It boggled the mind to believe that the moderately built Gray could have felled the Slasher with one blow but that was apparently what had happened.

As if reading her mind, Lazarus said, "No matter how big your opponent is, he's just as vulnerable to certain nerve attacks as anyone else." Gray stared at Monique, his mismatched eyes catching hers and holding them like a steel trap. "Identify yourself."

"Stammering, Monique forced out the words, "My name is Monique. I came here looking for help."

Gray didn't seem to believe her lie. He raised a foot and drove it hard into the big man's kidneys, drawing another grunt of pain. "And this brute? Is he The Axeman?"

Monique paused, her eyes widening. "No! We're on the run from him! And from a man named Dinkins. They're the ones killing all those people, not us!"

Lazarus searched her face, looking for signs of honesty. What he saw did little to set him at ease. She was young and beautiful but there was a savagery in her eyes that led him to suspect she was capable of doing horrible things.

"Is this man a Slasher?" he asked, already knowing the answer but wanting to hear it from her lips.

A slight widening of the eyes made it clear that Monique hadn't expected him to be so knowledgeable. "Yes," she admitted after a moment, obviously having decided that it would do her no good to pretend otherwise. "I needed him to help protect me from Mr. Dinkins and his killer. They're the ones you really want."

"And did this man ask to have this procedure done to him?"

Monique's expression hardened. "He was not a nice man," she stated in a flat tone of voice. "I've given him purpose and strength."

"At the expense of a normal life." Gray quickly pulled a dagger from the interior lining of his coat. "I assume he's under your control. Tell him to restrain from violence of any kind or else I'll kill him. The same goes for you."

With surprising speed, Monique struck at Lazarus, raking his neck with the sharpened nails of her left hand. Gray threw himself away from her but she still managed to leave three crimson trails across his skin. Gray reached out and grabbed her wrist, applying enough pressure that she cried out in pain and sagged to her knees. The Slasher was beginning to rise but Gray raised a foot and drove it hard into a nerve cluster on the big man's spine.

"Let's try this again," Gray said, ignoring the rain that was now beginning to fall harder all around them. Because the city's drainage was in constant need of repair, large puddles of water had a tendency to form and several were already well on their way to becoming small lakes. "You said that Dinkins is the real threat. But why is he after you?"

Monique gritted her teeth but finally succumbed to the pain and whimpered. "I stole his heart."

"He was in love with you?"

"I didn't mean it like that. I cut his heart out. But he's still alive."

Gray considered this and nodded. During his old life, he'd become quite familiar with the occult and had heard of such things. Some men sold their souls to demonic forces, allowing them to continue existing long after a normal man would have died. But there was a cost to all things....

"So all of the madness that's been going on in this city... it's because Dinkins is looking for you?"

Monique looked down, her eyes filling with tears. "Yes. Please help me. I can pay you... money, sex, whatever you want. But don't let him catch me. The things he'll do to me...."

Gray yanked her to her feet, his eyes looking cold and impassive. "I hate to tell you this, but there's no way out for you. We're going to lay a trap for Dinkins and his Axeman. And you're going to be the bait."

Chapter IV
In Clawed Hands

Berlin, Germany

Walther Lunt strode through the marble corridors, ignoring the servants who offered pleasantries as he passed. The German was in a foul mood and he felt more than a bit uncertain about what was to come. He had recently returned from America, where he had discovered that his old associate Richard Winthrop still lived, now operating under a new identity as Lazarus Gray. Lunt had actually died during their reunion and his subsequent resurrection had not come without strings attached. He had to bathe no less than three times daily or else the foul odor of the grave seemed to rise from his pores. And though his sexual appetites had not waned, it was increasingly difficult for him to reach his peak, leading him to greater acts of depravity in the hopes of getting the pleasure he sought.

Lunt paused before two large white doors, knowing that on the other side waited the rest of The Illuminati's inner circle. By now they would have read his report and would know that Gray was once more in possession of the knowledge about their organization. Would Gray renew the war against them that had led to his supposed death? Or would he wisely stay in Sovereign City and out of their way?

He rather doubted the answer would be the latter.

After reaching up and lightly scratching the ruined flesh on the right side of his face, Lunt pushed open the doors and walked inside, hoping to portray a sense of utter confidence. He saw that there were four men and two women seated at the central table, all dressed in dark robes with hoods drawn. To his surprise, however, Miya was there, standing just behind the chair occupied by Mobius, the group's current chairman. The Japanese-American woman wore a skintight green dress that accentuated her Dragon Lady persona. She smiled at Lunt's distress and barely stifled a laugh.

"Walther," Mobius said, gesturing toward the one open seat at the table. "Please join us. It's been too long since we've all been together like this."

"I assume you've all seen my report," Walther said as he slid into his chair. "I'd like to point out that Miya made a strong attempt at seducing him but that it was an utter failure, prompting me to take drastic action."

Mobius smiled coolly. He was a gaunt man with a bald head and dark rings around his eyes. His teeth were yellow and he smelled like a pack of old cigarettes. "Walther, you don't have to explain yourself to us." Mobius said this in a tone of voice that suggested the very opposite was true. "Your description of events matches up very well with what Miya has said. While there were some of us who felt that it was a bit... unwise... to have sparked Winthrop's memory regarding us, what's done is done. Now we must make an appropriate response."

Walther glanced at Miya and saw that her expression had shifted slightly. Whatever Mobius was about to say was known to her already and she wasn't in total agreement with it.

Mobius sat back in his chair and steepled his fingers in front of him. "Richard Winthrop was a tenacious enemy. He knew our inner workings and was quite ready to do whatever it took to disrupt our plans. Now that he's reinvented himself as Lazarus Gray, I daresay he's even more dangerous. Before, he operated alone. Now he has three quite capable aides and the backing of some important people. We need to strike quickly and decisively. That's why I've contracted with someone that I think can bring our old enemy to his knees."

"We have assassins in our employ," Walther murmured but he knew immediately that Mobius had already discarded that notion.

"And they've failed against him in the past. Despite all our best efforts, Richard Winthrop is not dead."

"Actually," Miya said, momentarily ignoring the protocol that said guests held their tongues during Illuminati meetings, "I'd argue that point. Richard Winthrop *is* dead. Lazarus Gray has some of Richard's character traits but he's not quite the same as he used to be."

Mobius snorted derisively. "Nonsense. Changing one's name doesn't make them a different person."

"I knew Richard Winthrop," Miya argued. "And I think I know a little bit about Lazarus Gray. He's stronger now, inside and out. It's like the darkness we'd managed to put inside him has been burned away."

"You sound like you admire him," Mobius said.

Miya said nothing but there was no denying the spark of emotion in her eyes.

Walther cleared his throat, drawing all eyes back to him and his ruined face. "I wouldn't have couched it in those terms but I think Miya is correct. He is more dangerous than before. I hope you took that into account when it came to hiring an outsider to deal with him."

One of the faceless men around the table leaned forward, his voice carrying an edge to it. "The Illuminati has existed for centuries, Walther. We are capable of dealing with one lone enemy, even if you yourself have failed repeatedly to handle the situation."

Walther felt stung by the rebuke but he managed to keep it from showing on his features. "Of course. I meant no disrespect."

Mobius spoke loudly, obviously tired of the back-and-forth regarding the issue. "Enter please!"

A door opened and closed behind Walther's back and he turned to see who had entered the room. The sight that greeted him was enough to freeze the ice in his veins. Though at first glance the figure that moved toward him appeared human, it didn't take long to disprove that notion. The figure had yellow-green skin and pointed ears. His head was completely hairless but covered by a black skullcap while his mouth was a leering parody of a man's. The animal-like maw was filled with razor-sharp teeth. The creature's hands were held at its sides and the fingertips ended in long blades that looked like they could disembowel a man with ease. Walther had heard stories of such a creature, a monster that ruled over a tiny island in the Pacific named Ricca. It was said that he was known by many names but the ones that were most common were "The God of Hate" and "The Claw."

"You must be joking," Walther muttered, turning to look at Mobius. "You're going to pay good money to… that *thing*?"

"I'm surprised at you," Mobius replied. "You've seen demons that slithered up from the shadows and you're that disturbed by The Claw? I think you owe him an apology. I won't abide rudeness."

Walther started at Mobius with barely disguised loathing. Mobius had personally choked the life from children and now he was protesting a bit of rudeness? It was enough to drive Walther to near madness. Even so, he knew his place and didn't want to risk himself any further than he already had. With forced kindness, he addressed The Claw, trying to ignore the look of smug satisfaction on the hideous creature's face. "I hope that I didn't offend you. It wasn't my intent. I merely meant that we have so many resources of our own that it troubles me to go to an outsider."

When The Claw spoke, his voice was strangely high-pitched and disconcerting. "I know exactly what you meant, Mr. Lunt. You think me nothing more than a monster, capable of scaring children with the way I look. But I'm far more than that. Catch me when the moon is right and I'm capable of things that would boggle your mind."

Walther could no longer hide his disdain. It bubbled forth in the words, "I highly doubt that. Perhaps you have no idea who you're dealing with."

The Claw took several steps toward Walther and with each step he grew in height. By the time he reached the German, he was well over twelve feet tall, his head scraping against the ceiling. He looked down at a shaken Walther and grinned, baring all his fangs. "Have you ever seen anything like me?" he asked.

Walther swallowed and managed to find his voice. "No. I have to admit… I haven't."

The Claw's form seemed to shimmer as he once more assumed his normal size. He turned to Mobius, dismissing Walther as no longer a concern. "I will kill this Lazarus Gray but I want assurances that my payment will be delivered on time."

Mobius nodded. "Thirteen virgin girls, all aged 12 to 17, just as you requested. We'll make sure their ethnicities are mixed, as per your requirements. We'll deliver them to Ricca within six hours of Gray's confirmed death."

The Claw's tongue flicked out like a snake's, brushing across the tips of his teeth. "Then I will make arrangements to travel to Sovereign City. Do you have any problem with me causing massive destruction in the pursuit of my goal?"

Mobius laughed. "Burn the city to the ground if it suits you."

While Mobius and The Claw bargained, Walther caught Miya's eye. Though the two of them had no real love lost between them, both were thoroughly disgusted by The Claw. Still, while Miya had feelings for their enemy, Walther did not. If The Claw were able to rid them of Gray, then Walther would deem all this as worthwhile.

Mr. Dinkins studied the entrails spread out on the table before him, a pensive expression on his face. He ignored the steady back-and-forth pacing of Muggsy behind him, focusing all of his attention on understanding the future laid out in front of him. He saw signs that indicated that he'd finally find Monique… but there were other figures present as well, and Dinkins couldn't be sure who they were. He hoped that it wasn't Lazarus Gray and his aides. It had been a terrible mistake to approach Morgan Watts but, as he'd said, he'd heard much about the man's employer and thought he might be a kindred spirit. Everyone else in Sovereign was corrupt so why not Gray? Unfortunately, that hadn't proven to be the case.

Dinkins straightened up and rubbed his eyes. His chest ached where she'd stolen his heart and he'd found that his magical means for staying alive were beginning to take their toll. He looked around the shabby hotel room in which they were staying and felt a sudden yearning for New Orleans. "I'm going to die here," he said aloud and the words surprised him, for he hadn't realized he was going to say them.

The Axeman shifted, studying him from behind his mask.

Dinkins waved a hand at him. "Ignore me. I'm just thinking out loud."

The room's telephone rang and Dinkins crossed the floor to pluck it up with slender fingers. "Yes?"

The hotel clerk came on briefly, letting him know that he was connecting an outside call. After a brief pause, the voice of Monique came through the line, surprising Dinkins. "I want to see you," she said breathlessly.

"You've led us on a merry little chase," Dinkins answered. "I thought Muggsy was going to have to carve up most of the city's young girls before we found you."

"I know. I saw the papers. Listen, I'm sorry about what happened. I thought I could get by without you, but I don't know enough to really use your heart. I'm willing to submit to you in any way you want if you'll just take me back."

Dinkins was glad she couldn't see his face because he knew his expression was an ugly one. "Why would I take you back and train you any more? You'd just turn on me again later on."

"I wouldn't! I swear! I've learned my lesson."

"This wouldn't be a trap, would it?"

Monique paused. When she continued, her voice had taken on a chastened tone. "I deserve that. I tried to kill you after you'd done so much for me. I was a bitch for that and you'd be right to hate me forever. But I think we were good together before that... and I know what you like. I can do those things for you again."

Dinkins felt some of his anger subside. He didn't want to admit it but his desire for her body made him a very weak man. It had led him to lower his defenses, allowing her to strike at him in the first place. Even now, when he'd sought her punishment for so long, he couldn't stop thinking of the things he could now demand of her... all the depravities he could imagine could be his. She could refuse him nothing!

Monique seemed to sense that his silence meant that he was considering her offer. "Could we get together tonight? I could show you how obedient I can be."

Dinkins exhaled, feeling tightness in his chest. "Where?"

Monique gave him the address to a hotel located on the outskirts of the harbor region. Dinkins scribbled it down on a piece of paper, his hand shaking with lust. "Don't disappoint me," he warned.

"I won't, my love. Never again." Monique hung up the phone, leaving Dinkins with a hungry smile on his face.

———— ∞ ————

Eun tried to keep from pacing but it was difficult. He was a young man of boundless energy and it was sometimes hard to channel all of that into being stealthy. It simply wasn't his nature. He was crouched on the rooftop of the Reich Hotel, a German-owned establishment that catered to sailors and sea captains.

Christopher Reich was the man behind the hotel and he was an ardent admirer of Lazarus Gray. Reich had run afoul of a blackmail scheme a few months back and Assistance Unlimited had managed to capture the villains behind it all, earning Reich's eternal trust. The blackmail had been linked to Reich's sexual tastes, which ran toward athletically built young men. The entire incident had been somewhat embarrassing for Eun, since it skirted very close to his own-closeted secret.

When he'd first joined Assistance Unlimited, Eun had gone carousing with Morgan in an attempt at bonding. It had gone well enough and Eun had even forced himself to engage in some harmless flirting with Samantha… but he still suspected that the others knew that he was a homosexual. If they did, they weren't ones to let it affect how they viewed him and he respected that. Eun hadn't told his parents before they'd died, knowing how they would have reacted. It was the way most people in the world would have, with disgust and worry. But Eun couldn't change who he was… and truth be told, he didn't want to. He'd been quietly dating a dockworker named Edward Lee for about six weeks now and they were very happy together. Combine that with the pleasure he derived from working with Assistance Unlimited and Eun was relatively happy, despite the anger that often drove him to acts of impetuousness. Even so, it was hard sometimes, facing prejudice both because of his race and his sexual orientation.

A yellow cab that pulled up in the front of the hotel drew Eun's attention. He leaned over the rooftop's edge, pulling out a small spyglass that allowed him to study the two men who emerged from the rear of the vehicle. One of them was a Negro dressed in ratty clothes and a top hat, matching the description given by both Monique and Morgan, who had finally awakened just before being taken to the hospital. The other fellow was a monstrous brute who wore a mask to cover his face. The big man held an axe in his left hand and even without the spyglass, Eun would have recognized the gore that caked the blade.

Turning quickly away from the rooftop's edge, Eun sprinted back inside the building. He entered the hotel room they'd set aside for their trap, only slightly out of breath thanks to his incredible physical conditioning. "They're on the way up. The Axeman has his blade with him."

Samantha and Lazarus were the only ones in the room. Monique and her Slasher were both being held in containment cells back at headquarters, though Eun wasn't sure what would happen to them later. So far, neither of them had committed any kind of crime that would hold up in court: It was true that Monique had attacked the man who had become her Slasher but the sheer weirdness of the crime would confuse most judges.

Samantha, dressed in jodhpurs and a cream-colored blouse, looked at Lazarus with surprise on her pretty face. "I can't believe he's just carrying his weapon like that."

Gray nodded. "It's a good thing we evacuated the hotel. Reich is manning the front desk and will be the only person who has to see them before they make it up here."

"Should I go downstairs and make sure he's okay?" Eun asked.

"No. I installed a panic button behind the clerk's counter. At the first sign of danger, Reich can summon us. He's quick enough on his feet to be able to make it to the office behind him and lock the door if he needs to."

Eun nodded and moved to take his spot behind the door. The plan was simple: lure Dinkins and Muggsy into the room and then take them down. The Assistance Unlimited crew had them outnumbered three to two and all three of them were well trained in personal combat. Gray and Samantha also had pistols on them but the hope was to avoid a firefight in these close quarters.

Heavy footsteps in the hall made them all tense and Samantha moved to take up a position in the small doorway that led into the washroom. Gray remained where he was, in plain view of anyone who entered the room. The first to do so was The Axeman, who stopped in confusion at the sight of someone besides Monique. Eun reached out and gave the big man a hearty shove, pushing him further into the room. He then spun into the hallway, where he came face to face with Dinkins. A hard punch to the old man's throat sent him to his knees and Eun finished him off with a hard driven knee to the forehead.

Muggsy, however, was not going to be so easily beaten. He raised his axe and swung it at Gray's head. The team's leader ducked under the blade even as Samantha moved from her hiding place. She expertly swung one of her long legs between The Axeman's and, by timing her motion with the big man's lumbering, caused him to lose his balance. He crashed down atop a small table, shattering it.

Gray drove the heel of his shoe against the back of The Axeman's head but Muggsy managed to swing his axe out and the blade caught the back of Gray's leg, drawing blood.

"Chief!" Samantha cried out as a small river of red flowed out from her employer's pants.

"I'm fine," Gray answered, moving away from the axe-wielding brute. Gray knew that Muggsy was more resistant to pain in his current state and that there was no way to undo the mental and physical damages that had been done to him. Gray waited until The Axeman was facing him, the killer's back toward the large window that overlooked the harbor. Gray lowered his shoulder and sprinted toward the big man, ignoring both Eun and Samantha, who uttered expressions of disbelief. Lazarus barreled into The Axeman and grunted in pain. It felt like slamming into a tree trunk. Still, his momentum was enough to force the big man backward and they slammed into the window, which shattered under their combined weight. The two men toppled out of the fifth story room, vanishing from the sight of Gray's employees.

Eun jumped over the shattered table and arrived at the windowsill a millisecond before Samantha. Their shoes crunched on broken glass and Eun leaned out of the window, heart thudding at the possibility of seeing Lazarus broken and dead on the ground below. To his tremendous relief, that wasn't what he laid eyes on.

The Axeman lay shattered and broken on the city street but Gray himself was hanging for dear life onto a large flag pole that jutted out from the hotel's façade.

"Hang on, Chief!" Eun bellowed. "We're gonna get you down from there!"

Lazarus said nothing, trusting that his aide would be as good as his word. He cast a downward glance at Muggsy's dead body. He detested killing any living thing but The Axeman was barely human at this point. In the end, Muggsy lived for murder and could never be rehabilitated. Thus, Lazarus had done both Muggsy and society a tremendous favor by ending his existence.

It was a hard thing, being a self-appointed judge and jury. But Gray was prepared to take on the responsibility – especially given that he lived in a city where the men and women appointed to do such things could no longer be trusted.

A hard rain began to fall.

Epilogue

Morgan was back at his desk within three days' time, much to the chagrin of Samantha, who fussed over him like she was a mama bird and he was her baby chick. Though it embarrassed him, he didn't put up much of a complaint.

Eun was mostly out of the office during this time, as he was helping Edward move into a new apartment.

With his three aides thus engaged, Lazarus Gray busied himself by executing Monique's Slasher and scouring the girl's personal belongings until he found that she was in possession of several controlled substances. Thus armed, he was able to see that she was entered into the legal system appropriately. Dinkins was a far easier case – the man was wanted on a litany of crimes both great and small back in Louisiana. Gray personally transferred him over to the law enforcement agents who came from the Bayou to collect him.

When the cleanup from the Axeman case had been settled, Lazarus returned to his third floor apartment in the Assistance Unlimited headquarters. It was there that he spread out a series of papers he'd been accumulating as of late. There were photographs of men and women from around the world, as well as a detailed tracking of their movements. He was the only man alive who had been at the center of The Illuminati and had survived breaking ties with it. It was only a matter of time before they came for him again and he intended to be ready.

In fact, Lazarus intended to strike first.

THE GOD OF HATE

An Adventure of Lazarus Gray
Written by Barry Reese

———— ✕ ————

Chapter I
Cry Vengeance!

The rain fell steadily over Sovereign City, drenching man and beast. It had stormed for six days in a row, prompting some to joke that it was well past time to start work on an ark. The figure that strode through the puddles, his body hidden beneath a wide-brimmed fedora and a thick jacket cinched at the waist, cared nothing for the bitter cold or the freezing rain. He was known as The God of Hate to those brave enough to follow him and he ruled over an island nation with an iron fist. He was The Claw and he had come to Sovereign City on dark business.

His inhuman features were quickly turned away from any pedestrian who happened to wander too close. Though he was of the general shape and height of a man, his ears were pointed, his mouth was a gaping maw filled with razor-sharp teeth and his fingers ended in the claws from which he took his name.

The Claw came to a stop before a large structure. His eyes ran across the lettering on the brick sign that rested on a grassy knoll in front of the building: Doc Daye's Home for Forgotten Children. The orphanage was home to nearly six-dozen little tykes, as well as the women who cared for them. It was one of the

"YOU'RE A STRANGE ONE, MR. GRAY. EVER GET THAT MEMORY OF YOURS STRAIGHTENED OUT?"

city's most beloved institutions and Daye himself was frequently sighted at the facility.

At this hour of night, all the children were nestled tight in their warm beds, dreaming of potential new families. Unfortunately, those dreams were never going to come true.

The Claw stared at the building for a few seconds before glancing up at the full moon that hung bloated in the sky. His power waxed and waned in conjunction with the phases of the moon and tonight he was going to be near his strongest. He knew that he should be expending this energy in pursuit of Lazarus Gray but an old, bloody debt was calling to him.

"Tempus, my old friend, I only wish that you were sleeping alongside these innocents, so that their fate could be your own. The vengeance I owe your father can only be satisfied by your death." The Claw's voice sounded oddly high-pitched for such a frightening entity. He raised both arms, exposing his sharpened nails to the light. He whispered dark words under his breath, speaking in a tongue long forgotten by civilized man. The storm clouds overhead seemed to thicken and swell, bolts of lightning tearing from their midst.

In reaction to The Claw's commands, the lightning strikes grew ever closer to the orphanage until with stunning ferocity no less than three dozen bursts of electrical power honed in on the building, striking with all the force of a thousand pounds of TNT. The building exploded in a fireball, some of the bricks flying with such force that they knocked out windows on buildings across the street. The smell of burning flesh filled the air as dozens of young boys and girls were ripped from the world at far too early an age.

The Claw turned away from the scene, a bubble of laughter emanating from deep in his throat. This visit to Sovereign was meant to be one of business, for he was being richly paid for his work. But that didn't mean that he couldn't enjoy himself along the way....

Paris, France

Morgan Watts tried to ignore the nagging pain on his left side but the condition was so persistent that he finally put a hand on the affected area and grunted in annoyance. Over the past few months, he'd had the misfortune to suffer one injury after another. As a result, his body now carried with it more aches and pains than most normal men could have withstood.

That was part of the reason why he'd volunteered for this mission. He wanted to get out of Sovereign in the hopes of breaking his run of bad luck. When Lazarus had announced that he wanted one of the team to travel to Paris and have a little "talk" with a member of the Illuminati that lived there, he quickly snatched up the opportunity.

Morgan sat in a small café, bundled up against the wintry chill. A cup of coffee sat on the table before him but it had remained untouched since the waiter had brought it to him. Morgan's attention was fixed on the hotel across the street and he sat up straight when his target finally emerged.

Joseph "Jack" Conrad was an American by birth but he'd moved to Europe at the age of six and had spent the last twenty years of his life here in Paris. He served on the Board of Directors for one of the most prominent museums in France and was regarded as one of the most eligible bachelors on the continent. Thin but well-defined, Conrad had white-blond hair that came to a widow's peak, dark eyes and a somewhat distant persona. He always dressed to the nines and was rarely seen with out a cigarette balanced between the fingers of his right hand. Indeed, as Morgan watched, Conrad stopped on the hotel steps, pausing long enough to shake a cigarette out from a case and then light it. He took several long drags on it, exhaled slowly, and then began heading down the street at a leisurely pace. Morgan exited the café, dropping a few coins on the table as a tip.

Morgan followed, staying far enough behind that Conrad wouldn't notice that he was being tailed. From what Morgan had been told, Conrad had joined The Illuminati in his late teens, having been invited to join mainly because of his family's money. Whereas many members of the organization possessed some measure of skill in the areas of the occult, Conrad was an exception. The son of a wealthy banker, Conrad helped provide needed capital and connections but was otherwise kept out of the loop when it came to the full extent of their supernatural affairs.

But he still knew enough to be useful.

Morgan recognized the area they were entering, having meticulously studied maps of the city. He ducked down an alleyway, confident that he knew where he could cut off Conrad's progress. Indeed, he found himself waiting at a point, just ahead of the other man within moments and as Conrad passed, he reached out and grabbed him, yanking him off the street. He kept one hand over Conrad's mouth while the other held the barrel of a gun against the man's forehead.

"Don't move. Understand?"

Conrad's eyes were wide and frightened. He nodded quickly, wetting his lips when Morgan released his hold on him. "I have money," he said, starting to reach into his coat pocket.

"Keep your hands where I can see them." Morgan cocked the gun and Conrad quickly raised his hands, showing the palms to Morgan. "I don't want your money. I want information."

"What do you mean?" Conrad seemed both relieved and guarded. "If you're looking to pull some sort of art heist, you'll find that there's only so much I can help you with. The museum's inner workings aren't known to me."

"Do I look like an art thief?" Morgan reached into his coat and pulled out a photograph of Walther Lunt. The German had one side of his face ruined by an acid attack years before and the assault had left him with a glint of madness in his eye. The photo showed that quite clearly. "You know this man?"

Conrad hesitated, wetting his lips once more. "Yes."

"I understand you're both part of the same group. Am I right?"

"We're in a gentleman's club together, yes."

"Nice name for it. Your father is in banking and I bet that Lunt and some of the others use you to help keep their money hidden. Am I on the right track?"

Conrad said nothing for a moment and when he did speak, his voice had dropped an octave. "You're playing a dangerous game, my friend. You don't want to mess with these people. They'll hurt you in ways that you can't even imagine."

Morgan narrowed his eyes, his grip on the pistol never wavering. He was pretty sure that one reason why Lazarus agreed to let him go on this mission was because of his past. Morgan had once run with the toughest thugs in Sovereign. He'd done lots of bad things and on a few occasions, he'd had to kill to save his own skin. Unlike Samantha or Eun – and maybe even Lazarus – Morgan was quite capable of pulling the trigger if need be. "I'll take that risk. Now answer the question: do Lunt and the others use your father's bank?"

"I'm pretty sure that you already know that they do. That's why you're here, isn't it?"

"Smart boy." Morgan reached out and grabbed Conrad by the arm, yanking him close. He shoved the gun hard into the younger man's ribs, keeping it out of sight as he walked Conrad back out onto the city streets.

"Where are we going?"

"To the bank. It's after hours but you can get us in, can't you?"

Conrad's jaw worked in helpless frustration. "And then what?'

"You're going to give me addresses, phone numbers and anything else I can think of for those people Lunt works with."

"And when you're done, do you think I'm not going to warn them?" Conrad's eyes widened as the words left his mouth and he visibly realized that he should have kept his lips shut. "Oh good lord, you're going to kill me, aren't you?"

Morgan just smiled coldly, letting Conrad fill in the details. He actually had no desire to commit murder, even though he was capable of it. He'd brought along a small drug cocktail that Lazarus had perfected. It would wipe Conrad's memory of the last 24 hours and leave him a very confused man. "I won't shoot you unless you make me. That's a promise."

Conrad stared into Morgan's eyes, not sure if he believed the older man's words. In the end, he knew that he had no choice: even a faint hope of survival was better than none. "I'll get you the information you need... but I think you're making an awful mistake. Lunt alone is a lunatic. If you go after the other members of the cabal, too, you're a guaranteed dead man."

"I'll roll the dice on that one. Now let's go." Morgan gestured for Conrad to lead the way and the two of went off in pursuit of the information that would, hopefully, lead to a critical strike against The Illuminati.

—∞∞∞—

"**. . . C**ity continues to mourn the loss of 57 innocent lives in last night's terrible fire at Doc Daye's Home for Forgotten Children. Sovereign Fire Chief Gabriel Sanders says that the tragedy is like nothing he's ever seen before...."

Lazarus Gray turned off the radio, well aware of the somber mood in the room. With him in the meeting area of Assistance Unlimited's headquarters were Samantha Grace and Eun Jiwon. Both of them stood in silent contemplation, eyes downcast.

"It's so awful," Samantha said at last, wrapping her arms tightly around herself. The daughter of socialite parents, Samantha had never been one of the city's 'forgotten children,' but her kind heart allowed her to easily empathize with those who had perished. It was horrible enough to be alone in the world, with no family to speak of... but to have that life cut so cruelly short was almost too much to bear.

Eun glanced up, finding Gray's eyes upon him. "What are we going to do, Chief?"

The man who now called himself Lazarus Gray bore an unusually grim expression, even for him. "As both of you know, this was not a random act of God. No matter what the authorities might wish to believe, this was an attack. A warning, if you will."

Eun nodded, his gaze moving toward the crumpled letter that lay on the meeting room table. Eun had been the first to discover it, dropped in their mail slot sometime overnight. Its surface was scrawled with horrible handwriting that somehow seemed to transcend mere ugliness: this was the mad doodling of a demon, straining to muster an attempt at English.

The note read: **THOSE CHILDREN ARE JUST THE BEGINNING. I WILL BURN THIS CITY TO THE GROUND UNLESS YOU GIVE YOURSELF TO ME. FALL UPON YOUR KNEES BEFORE THE GOD OF HATE.**

"The first thing we need to do," Lazarus answered, "is find out who sent this letter."

Samantha pulled a chair out from the table and sat down. She was a beautiful girl with a peaches and cream complexion, but at the moment she looked deathly pale. "Are we going to go to the police? Or let Doc Daye know what's going on?"

Lazarus considered the questions before shaking his head. "Going to the authorities would do no good. They could place the citizenry on a general alert but we have no idea where this killer might strike next. A panic would do no one any good. As for Doc Daye, I will forward a copy of the letter to him and ask him to share with us any clues that he might come upon."

Eun nodded in agreement. "Okay. I'll start looking through the archives to see if I can find any reference to The God of Hate." Assistance Unlimited had one of the top newspaper clipping collections in the world, as well as many priceless bound volumes that would have set any bibliophile's heart aflutter.

Lazarus fixed his gaze upon Samantha, who straightened immediately. "While Eun is doing that, I want you to come with me. We should see the crime scene firsthand."

The three members of Assistance Unlimited sprang into action but while Samantha and Eun's expressions were brimming with excitement, Gray's remained impassive. There was something eating away at the edges of his frayed memory, some past association that the words 'God of Hate' almost brought to the fore.

There were dark days ahead, he knew. And he prayed that his friends were strong enough to stand up to the test before them.

———⁂———

Chapter II
Horrors Laid Bare

The God of Hate reclined on a bed of soft pillows, the smell of opium thick in the air. Three whores lay scattered about the bed and the floor, their clothes lying in an unruly pile next to the door. The girls had been drugged and then thoroughly violated in ways that would leave emotional scars for years. Thankfully, the opium would most likely prevent any of them from having a clear memory of what had occurred.

The room in which The Claw lay was rented and paid for by The Illuminati, who had hired him to deal with Lazarus Gray. In return, he would receive several young virgins that he could sacrifice for even greater power. Such was the world in which The Claw moved: humans were nothing more than bags of meat, to be eaten, screwed or traded.

A bedside radio had alternated between horrified reporting of the orphanage tragedy and the popular music of the day, which sounded like the bleating of animals to The Claw's ears: *Cheek to Cheek* by Fred Astaire and Ginger Rogers; *Lullaby of Broadway* by The Dorsey Brothers; and *You're The Top* by Cole Porter. The Claw found he preferred the shocked tones of the reporters to the wailing of the singers, so he reached over with a sharpened nail to turn the radio off.

He rose from the pillows, stepping over a naked girl whose nose had been shattered. Her beauty would never fully return but The God of Hate felt no sympathy for her. She had served her purpose and been discarded, like a used tissue.

The Claw dressed slowly and methodically, putting his skullcap on last. He looked at himself in the mirror, smiling so that his razor-sharp teeth could be seen. There were bits of bloody flesh caught up near his gums and his tongue flicked up to work at them, savoring the flavor.

The origins of The God of Hate were unknown to all but a few on this planet and The Claw saw no reason to reveal his true nature to his enemies. But he was not birthed of this world and he would be alive long after its sun had grown cold. Immortality could be a curse, with eons of boredom. But The Claw refused to allow himself to stand still. He was always moving, always expanding his power base… and this attracted opposition, which The Claw secretly enjoyed. By pitting himself against so-called 'heroes,' he found a way to keep himself amused.

And this Sovereign City was certainly full of challenges. There was Doc Daye, Lazarus Gray and Fortune McCall, all living in this one troubled locale. It was almost enough to make him consider moving his base of operations away from Ricca….

But no, Ricca was too perfect a home. He would destroy Gray as he'd promised, and perhaps take his revenge upon the Daye family… and then he would leave.

Behind him, one of the girls was beginning to stir, a low, pained moan escaping her cracked lips. The Claw felt a renewed stirring within his loins and considered playing with her a bit more, but in the end he simply walked to the door and exited the hotel room. He had wasted enough time and he was here on business, after all.

He harbored no doubts about how Lazarus Gray would respond to the letter he had sent him. Gray would never surrender.

Which was just how The Claw wanted it.

∞∞∞

Morgan Watts sat in the back of a cab, a heavy folder on his lap. He'd actually managed to get a lot more information than he'd ever dared hope and he couldn't wait to get back to America so he could share it with the rest of Assistance Unlimited. When Gray had first told them of the scope of The Illuminati's activities, Morgan had felt overwhelmed. How could Assistance Unlimited, four people strong, topple an international cartel that had their fingers in every level of finance, industry and the occult? But now, he was beginning to feel differently. Today had gone very well and the information could be used to badly hurt Lunt and his friends.

Morgan glanced out the window just in time to see the cab miss the turn that would have taken them to the airport. He leaned forward, tapping the driver on the shoulder. "Monsieur, you should have turned left back there."

The driver pushed harder on the accelerator and the car sped along faster than ever. Morgan now realized that he was in tremendous danger and reached for the door. He cursed under his breath when it refused to open. He was fumbling to pull out his gun, intending to force the driver to stop, when the vehicle abruptly braked. Morgan looked out the window to see that the cab was now parked near an open field, where five large men stood smoking cigarettes. One of them held a pistol in his left hand. The gunman was bald with a hook-shaped scar that ran from the corner of his mouth up to just under his right eye.

The driver got out of the car and stepped around to open Morgan's door. "Your stop, Mr. Watts," the driver said, a faint smile on his lips.

Morgan stuffed the folder into the lining of his jacket. Gray had altered all of his aides' clothing to allow for hidden pockets. He stepped out of the car with gun in hand and quickly backhanded the driver, shattering the man's jaw and knocking him to the ground. The other men reached into their own coats but stopped at a motion from the bald man. The movements confirmed Morgan's worst fears: he was facing not one armed foe, but five.

Addressing the bald man, Morgan said, "I bet you know all about me and I know nothing about you. Seems a bit unfair. What's your name? And who do you work for?"

"I suspect you know the answer to that last question," the bald man answered. "But my name is Louis. I don't suppose you knew that all members of The Illuminati, especially those who safeguard valuable information, are subject to observation. We saw your kidnapping of Mr. Conrad. Now I'd like you to give us all the information you gathered. If you cooperate, we may not hurt you too badly."

Morgan bit his tongue before he voiced his doubts about that. They were going to kill him regardless of what he did. As casually as possible, he reached into his pocket, pretending to comply with Louis' request. He pulled out a small slip of paper on which he'd written Conrad's address and usual schedule. As he was doing so, his fingers brushed against a small radio device that was used by all the aides to keep in contact with one another. One of its settings was a simple distress signal that would alert all the others that the user was in danger. Of course, its range was somewhat limited but Gray had managed to find a way to piggyback its signal over international wires. There would be probably be no way for anyone at Assistance Unlimited to actually help him but Morgan wanted to warn them, nonetheless.

"Here you go," Morgan said, folding the paper in half and then handing it over. "I didn't take much information, actually. I just wanted to know how to reach a man named Walther Lunt."

Louis obviously recognized the name. His back stiffened and a terrible sneer touched his lips. "That bastard… if it were up to me, I'd let you have him."

Morgan sensed an opening and leapt for it. He gestured with his free hand toward the scar on the man's face. "Is he responsible for that?"

"Among other things, yes." Louis shook his head, obviously trying to clear it of bad memories. "Down on your knees. "

"Aren't you going to look at the paper? That's everything, I swear."

Louis hesitated and then began to unfold the paper. When his eyes dropped,

Morgan sprang into action. He knew he was a dead man but he wasn't going to risk going down without a fight. He threw himself into Louis, knocking the man off his feet. Morgan made sure to shove the bald man into one of his henchmen.

Using instincts honed as a member of Assistance Unlimited, Morgan was a blur of action. He drew his gun and had blown off the head of the nearest thug before the remaining two men had even reached for their own weapons.

Morgan ducked and rolled, evading gunshots from the two men who were still on their feet. When he came back to his knees, he fired twice more, each bullet ripping through the throats of his targets.

In just a few seconds, Morgan had killed three men, which left him facing only two more: the odds had improved immensely. With any luck, he might get out of this in one piece, after all.

Louis gestured for his remaining ally to hang back. He held his hands up, his gun still clutched tightly. Morgan held his weapon aimed at the bald man's head but didn't pull the trigger. He was curious what Louis was up to.

"We can talk about this," Louis said. "We both hate Lunt."

"I thought you said it wasn't up to you, though. You've got your orders, right? Take the information I've gathered and kill me. That's the basics, right?"

"That's what I was told to do, yes. But that doesn't mean we can't change things."

Morgan stood up, his eyes flicking over to the cab that had brought him here. The driver was sitting in the front seat, watching intently. Given the blood that freely trickled from his ruined jaw, the driver's hatred for Morgan was obvious. No way was that guy going to sit by and let Morgan negotiate his way to freedom. "I don't think that's going to happen and we all know it."

Louis swallowed hard and then spun about. He shot the man standing behind him, blowing a hole directly between the man's eyes. He then turned toward the car and fired three times before one of the bullets ended the driver's life. He then tossed the gun aside and turned back to Morgan. "Now can we talk?"

Morgan took a deep breath and nodded. He lowered his weapon, wondering about the wisdom of this. A part of him said he should simply kill Louis on the spot and flee back to the States... but what if he could gather more information this way? What if Louis knew something that would allow Assistance Unlimited to drive a stake through The Illuminati's heart?

"Make it good," Morgan said at last.

And Louis began to speak.

———

The crime scene was abuzz with activity but Samantha found it hard to concentrate on the men and women around them. She kept focusing on all the tiny bodies that had been laid out to the side, sheets carefully placed over the ruined remains. The smell was awful and she knew that at least part of that came from the burned flesh of children.

"Samantha? Are you going to be all right?"

Samantha glanced over at Lazarus, noting the look of concern in his eyes. His face remained stoic but for those who knew him well, it was obvious when he was troubled. "I'm fine," she lied. "Really."

After a moment's consideration, Lazarus nodded and resumed walking through the debris. Samantha followed right behind him, primly watching her step on the treacherous terrain.

The various officers in charge of the investigation were watching Gray with a mixture of hopefulness and disdain. Though most of the police force was in the back pockets of gangsters like The Monster or Big Tony, some of them were legitimate enough to appreciate the assistance that Gray provided. But they still felt some jealousy when the man stepped onto the scene and found something that they'd missed.

Gray brushed aside some charred pieces of wood with the toe of his shoe. He spotted something amidst the ash and knelt to take a closer examination of the object, lifting it up between two fingers. He blew on it to clear off some of the dirt and held it up for Samantha to see. "What do you think this is?"

Samantha bent at the waist, placing her hands on her knees. She was aware of – but tried to ignore – the stares of the cops nearby. She knew she was attractive but there were so few men who were her intellectual equal that she found it hard to enjoy all the attention. The object that Gray was holding appeared to be shaped out of stone and resembled a crescent moon, though there were three deep scratches across its center, as if a cat had marked it with its claws. "I've never seen anything like it. What kind of rock is that?"

"Not one from this world," Gray answered. He stood up and dropped it into the pocket of his coat. "I've seen stones like that before. It's from the moon."

Samantha's gaze drifted upward, toward the hazy morning sky. "But... how?"

"Sometimes they're brought to earth on the backs of meteors. But I'd wager that this one came the old fashioned way: I think someone went to the moon and picked it up."

"That's impossible," Samantha responded.

"Not really. Think about all the bizarre things we've seen in the course of our adventures. Is it really so shocking that men might be traveling back and forth to the moon?"

"Yes," Samantha said with a smile. "It's still pretty damned shocking."

"Such language from a young lady. It's disgraceful."

Samantha straightened and looked over at Inspector Cord of the Sovereign PD. He was a whippet-thin man who had one eye that seemed to be perpetually narrowed.

"Sorry if I offended you, Inspector."

"I'll recover but thank you." Cord gestured toward Lazarus. "Did I see you pick something up and put it in your pocket? I sincerely hope not, since you don't have leave to remove evidence from a crime scene."

"Is that what this is?" Samantha asked sweetly. "A crime scene? I thought it was just a freak accident."

Cord grimaced. "Well, yes, of course it is… Still, seems a bit ghoulish to have you lot coming in here and removing souvenirs'."

While Samantha and Inspector Cord were exchanging words, Lazarus had moved away. He knew that Samantha would keep the man occupied long enough to allow him to finish his business. The reference to 'The God of Hate' in that letter, coupled with the presence of a moonstone, was sparking his memory again. He wanted to check with Eun to see what the young man had come up with, but he was beyond positive that all of this was related to something quite evil. Lazarus was sure that during his previous existence, he'd never crossed paths with The God of Hate but he'd heard of him and the stories had been quite terrifying.

It was at that moment when Lazarus spotted one last clue: it was a sheet of paper, the sort used by schoolchildren the world over. Someone had drawn a crude image of a monster on it and Gray felt a chill go down his spine as he lifted the paper from the ground. Evidently, a child had been awake at the time of the stranger's visit and had drawn this image of him while looking out his window. Gray saw a human figure staring back at him but the face was filled with razor sharp teeth and elongated ears. The monster's hands looked like each finger was topped by claws.

"I see you," he whispered aloud, as if the figure on the page could hear him. "I see you."

⁊⁊⁊

Eun Jiwon turned the yellowed pages of the manuscript, his mouth feeling increasingly dry. It hadn't taken long to find references to The God of Hate in the library but the things that he'd uncovered had boggled the mind. The God of Hate, also known as The Claw and by half a dozen other terrifying identities, was practically a demonic force unto himself.

According to the dozens of sources he'd found, The Claw was an inhuman figure that had lurked along the outskirts of humanity for centuries. There were unconfirmed stories that he'd once been a human who had either bargained away his soul for power or a scientist whose pursuit of dark answers had led him astray. But most of the tales simply said he was a monster who had emerged full-force into an unsuspecting world.

Eun paused at a charcoal depiction of The Claw and he wondered how accurate it truly was. Surely, he mused, this was an exaggeration of the figure's actual appearance. With the oversized teeth and claws, along with the elongated ears, it looked like a distant cousin to Max Schreck's Nosferatu.

The young man was so lost in thought that he failed to hear the soft footsteps behind him. It wasn't until a cold, dry hand closed around his mouth and another grabbed his arms that he realized he was no longer alone. Being a man of action, Eun struck back quickly, driving an elbow back into the midsection of the person who had grabbed him but he cried out in shock. It felt like he'd struck a brick wall and from the pain in his elbow, Eun wondered if he'd broken it.

"Shh," a slightly high-pitched voice whispered into Eun's ear. The man's voice was as cold as the grave and Eun involuntarily shivered. "I won't harm you, Eun Jiwon. Not now. My war lies not with you but with the man you serve. If I release my grip upon you, will you listen to what I have to say?"

Eun nodded, forcing himself to relax. When he felt the hands leave him, he spun about quickly, his eyes widening. Standing there before him was the living proof that the charcoal artist had been right: The Claw was just as hideous as the book had promised.

The Claw smiled coolly and his sharp teeth glistened wetly. "Your master is off in search of me? He got the letter I sent?"

Eun tried to keep the horror from his voice but he failed to do so, which shamed him. "Yes. He's going to stop you before you kill again."

"He will try," The Claw agreed. "But as you can see, the impressive defenses he has put around his home failed to stop my entrance. I have no doubt that in personal combat, I would be able to best him." The God of Hate stepped closer and the foul odor that came from him caused Eun to back away, until his rear bumped against the table covered by books. "I wish to be done with this business between us. Tell him that. Tell him that I will hold his lover in my grasp until he comes for her. He should come alone and unarmed. Then we will see which of us is the deadlier. You will tell him this?"

Eun nodded, wondering at the creature's words. Gray's lover? Who was he referring to? He'd bet his last dollar that Lazarus and Samantha weren't carrying on a secret affair and the girl from Gray's past – Miya Shimada – had fled Sovereign. Nevertheless, Eun knew what he needed to do. "I will make it clear to him that you mean business."

The Claw laughed. "Good. Then I will let you live, so that you might pass on this message. I have shown him my cruelty and now I show him how easily I could take away what means most to him."

Eun watched as The Claw spun about and exited the room. After waiting a few seconds, Eun bolted after him, hoping to see how the villain had pierced the base's defenses. But all he saw in the hallway was a still and quiet emptiness.

Chapter III
Loves Lost Forever

Samantha had developed the bad habit of chewing her nails. She wasn't sure when it had begun but she'd first noticed it during Morgan's last stint in the hospital. She was engaging in the habit now as she sat in the passenger seat of a black sedan, parked across the street from The Sovereign Museum of Natural History. If Eun, who was seated beside her, noticed her actions, he didn't comment upon them. In fact, they'd been sitting in total silence since Lazarus had left them, wandering alone into the museum.

The Sovereign Museum of Natural History was a sprawling structure standing in the heart of downtown. Comprised of twelve interconnected buildings, the Museum housed well over a million specimens, only a relative few of which were on active display. With a scientific staff of over a hundred, the Museum funded nearly four-dozen scientific expeditions each year, sending explorers out all over the globe. The Museum was divided up into numerous displays but the most popular was the ever-present Start of Sovereign Hall, where the origins of the city were examined. To access this, visitors had to stride through the huge entranceway, where they could stare up at a full-size model of a Blue Whale which hung from the ceiling. It was an awesome view and one that Samantha had enjoyed on many visits. But at the moment she couldn't bring herself to think about anything but Lazarus and his secrets.

"I can't believe he's never mentioned this," she said at last, tearing a thin piece of nail off with her teeth.

"Why would he? It was before he'd met most of us. It's not like we share all the details of our personal lives with each other."

Samantha glanced over at Eun, a look of disbelief on her face. "What are you talking about? Every time one of us goes out on a date, everybody knows it.

I guarantee you that Morgan knows all the men I've ever so much as held hands with."

"Yes, but that's because Morgan is romantically interested in you. I don't parade my romantic entanglements for all to see."

Samantha paused, realizing that Eun was right about that. Early on, he'd made a few perfunctory passes at her but even then she'd thought his heart hadn't been in it. And since then… she'd never seen him with any girl at all. Apparently, he was more private than she'd realized. "Okay," she finally admitted. "But if Lazarus had been sleeping with the daughter of the Museum's curator, I think we'd have heard some mention of it."

Eun sighed, knowing that Samantha carried a torch for Lazarus Gray nearly the size of the one borne aloft by the Statue of Liberty. But she also had feelings for Morgan, which led to all kinds of stress within Assistance Unlimited. Gray seemed unaware of Samantha's desires, which only made things tenser.

Only Eun stayed out of the group's romantic entanglements, preferring to keep his homosexuality quiet. "Lazarus says that he had a brief fling with her a few months after coming to Sovereign. It didn't last, partially because his amnesia put a wall between them. That's all we need to know."

Samantha pursed her pretty lips. "You said that The Claw called her his lover. Present-tense."

"I don't think they're still together." Eun's tone became a bit harsher now, as his temper gave way. "And what difference does it make anyway? He has the right to live his own life. All of us do!"

Samantha blinked in surprise, realizing she'd hit some sort of nerve. "Sorry, Eun. I didn't mean anything, really. I was just jealous, that's all."

Eun looked out the window and took a deep breath. "No. I'm the one who needs to apologize. It's just… I've been keeping a relationship from the rest of you, too."

Samantha relaxed, feeling more at ease now. She reached out and patted Eun on the shoulder. "That's wonderful, Eun. When can I meet her?"

"Him."

"What?"

Eun turned his head slightly, so that he could see her face. "Him. Not her."

Samantha's mouth parted in surprise. "Oh." A second later, she recovered her usual sense of decorum. "Well, then. Him. When I do get to meet him?"

A faint smile played across Eun's lips. "You don't mind, do you?"

"Did you think that I would?"

"Not really. It's just hard to share sometimes. You understand?"

Samantha paused and then nodded slowly. She knew what Eun was really saying: that there were things everyone kept hidden. Maybe this was one of those sorts of things for Lazarus.

Though Samantha had thought of Kelly Emerson as merely "the curator's daughter," she was in fact much more. A graduate of Sovereign University, Kelly held doctorates in archaeology and anthropology. Standing nearly six feet tall and possessed of flowing red hair, she looked like a modern Amazon, with enough curves to unsettle even the most ardent of playboys. Her glittering green eyes and full lips had warmed Gray's heart when he'd first met her and their love affair was still recent enough that both of them found it slightly uncomfortable to be in the same room.

Lazarus stood facing her cluttered desk, his eyes traveling over the familiar walls. Several tribal masks from Africa were placed above a crowded bookcase, while a mummified cat sat perched watchfully on a nearby table.

Kelly wore a long white dress that buttoned down the front. She normally hated to wear dresses or skirts but found that it eased dealings with men when she was at the museum. Given her druthers, she would have traipsed around in hiking boots, khaki shorts and a sensible shirt. Alas, it was still a man's world, even in the modern era of 1935.

"You can sit down, you know," she said, opening a slim cigarette case. "You still don't smoke?"

"No, I don't." Gray picked up a stack of papers and set them on the floor, freeing up a chair for him sit down in. "You don't seem to be taking this very seriously."

Kelly took a drag on her cigarette and leaned back in her chair. She crossed her legs, somewhat disappointed that Gray's eyes didn't take the bait. "Let me get this straight. The person who burned down the orphanage is actually a demon known as The God of Hate. This monster has threatened to take your lover hostage and so that's why you're here?" Kelly shrugged her shoulders. "We haven't been lovers for a long time, Lazarus. You don't think he meant anyone else?"

"I haven't been with another woman."

Kelly dropped her gaze and sighed. "You're a strange one, Mr. Gray. Ever get that memory of yours straightened out?"

"Somewhat. I know what my name used to be and I know a few details about my past. But most of it still seems like a dream; like it happened to someone else."

"What's your real name?"

"Lazarus Gray."

Kelly laughed. "Okay. So the old you is dead and gone, then?"

"For all intents and purposes. There's still an organization out there that I used to have ties to... but I hope to take care of that soon."

"Well, I'm happy for you." Kelly blew out a long stream of smoke, her lips pursed. "So what do you want me to do? Lock myself in my office until the danger's passed?"

"No. I'd like to keep you at Assistance Unlimited headquarters."

"But you said The God of Hate managed to waltz right in there. What makes you think I'd be any safer there?"

"I'd feel better if you were closer to me."

The silence that followed was uncomfortable for them both. When Kelly decided to speak, her voice was much softer and the confidence she generally exuded seemed shaken. "Do you really think he's going to come after me?"

"I'm positive of it."

Kelly ground out her cigarette in a small tray on her desk and stood up. "Okay. Let me go tell Daddy that I'm going to be going away for a few days. Then I'd like to go by my home and get some spare clothing and toiletries."

"I can drive you there," Gray said, getting to his feet.

"Okay." Kelly opened the door and offered him a brief smile. "Daddy's office is just down the hall. Wait for me?"

Gray nodded quickly, watching her go. He moved to the door and kept his eyes on her as she moved to a nearby office and stepped inside. After hearing Eun's description of The Claw's visit, he'd become more unnerved than before. Threats to his friends and loved ones were the worst sort: they made him feel helpless and desperate.

A small chirruping sound emanated from the pocket of his coat and he reached inside, pulling out one of the small radio devices he used to keep in contact with his aides. To his surprise, the device was showing the numbered code that belonged to Morgan, along with the extension code for danger. Since Morgan was overseas, that meant his call had been relayed through a number of different circuits before finally arriving in the States. How long ago it had been sent was impossible to determine.

Lazarus was about to call Samantha and Eun when a loud crash came from the office of Kelly's father, followed by a scream of terror that could only have belonged to Kelly herself.

Before anyone else on the floor had even poked their heads out of their own offices, Lazarus had reached the scene. When pressed, he was as fast as a cheetah and nearly as graceful.

Unfortunately, no human alive would have been fast enough to stop what was occurring. By the time he flung open the door, gun drawn, it was too late. The Claw had somehow walked straight through the walls, just as he had back at Gray's Robeson Avenue home. He had kidnapped Kelly and left her father lying on the floor, a deep gash in his neck.

Gray crouched down at the man's side, immediately applying pressure to the wound. He looked up as another museum employee looked inside. "Get an ambulance! Now!" Gray barked and the man jumped to follow the orders.

Even as he assured Mr. Emerson that everything was going to be all right, Gray was mentally berating himself for allowing her out of his sight.

The Claw was keeping his word so far and Gray knew that he had no choice but to play along if he wanted to ensure Kelly's safety. His eyes caught sight of a paper hanging off the edge of the desk and, without losing the pressure he was applying to the man's neck, he snatched it up with his other hand. The scrawled words matched those from the earlier letter he'd received: **COME TO THE OLD ABANDONED CHURCH ON EISNER WAY ALONE AT NINE O CLOCK TONIGHT. DO NOT IGNORE MY INSTRUCTIONS OR THE GIRL WILL SUFFER!**

Lazarus tossed the paper aside and fished out his communication device. He began speaking at once, transmitting to Eun's radio, knowing that Samantha would hear every word as well. "The Claw's taken her. I'm going to take care of him but I need the two of you to board a plane and head to Paris right away. Morgan needs help."

"But what about you, Chief?" The tone in Eun's voice made it clear that he didn't like abandoning his employer.

"The Claw wants me to come alone, so I'm not going to be able to use you two. Morgan's overseas, facing The Illuminati. Without more details, we have to assume the worst. Sending one of you might not be enough to save him."

Morgan had long since forgotten about the distress signal he'd sent. Things had proceeded to a point where his thoughts were entirely shifted away from where they had been. Louis had told him that he could take him to a hidden location, a vault of artifacts where Morgan could not only find out more about The Illuminati but also personal details related to Walther Lunt.

It had crossed Morgan's mind that this might be another trap but he'd seen something in the other man's eyes that made him trust the fellow. Louis hated Lunt and was willing to risk his own life if it meant striking back at his enemy.

And so they had come to a small chateau just outside the city. The grasses were high and the entire property looked abandoned. Louis had told him that this was one of Lunt's safe houses, one of nearly two dozen scattered throughout Europe. It was here that he stored many of his treasures and personal papers. Louis had been inside only once before, having accepted an invitation from Lunt himself several years before the incident that had severed their relations.

Morgan had wandered around the house before rejoining Louis at the front door. Assured that there seemed to be no ambush waiting to happen, Morgan consented to follow the other man inside. The house had been quite nice, with several paintings that were probably worth more than Morgan would have made in a lifetime, even at the generous wages provided by Lazarus.

But it was what lay in the cellar that had driven all thoughts about his friends from Morgan's mind. Louis had shown him a small metal box about the size of a footrest. There was a knocking from within the box, a thrashing about that intensified as the men approached. It sounded like someone had locked a small dog or cat inside.

"What's in there?" Morgan asked, staring at the container, a sense of dread rising up from the pit of his stomach. His bowels suddenly felt loose and threatening.

"The truth about The Illuminati and how it's managed to become all that it is."

Morgan frowned, not liking the overly dramatic presentation. Even so, he sensed that Louis truly meant these words and was not using them in an attempt to scare him.

Morgan knelt in front of the box and slowly unlatched its lid, opening it a few inches at a time. When he finally saw what lay within, looking dried up and emaciated, he let out an audible gasp and backed away, letting the box lid drop shut. Though he'd only gazed upon the unholy creature for a matter of seconds, he knew the image would be burned into his mind forever: though the beast had looked half-mummified, it still lived and the drooping folds of its skin indicated that in full health, it would have possessed a bloated corpulence. The creature's head was pulpy and tentacled, surmounting a grotesquely scaled body with rudimentary wings. The monster was vaguely anthropoid with an octopus-like head. Sharp claws on the hind and forefeet made it quite clear that this was a dangerous beast but most awful of all was its fearsome and unnatural malignancy. This was something that **should not exist**. And yet, it did… and it fought against its own death even now, thrashing about in the box that was its prison.

"What in God's name was that?" Morgan asked, once his strength of will had returned.

"Cthulhi," Louis answered. "The Star-Spawn of a great and powerful creature. They arrived on Earth with their unholy master and most of them are trapped beneath the waves now, all locked away in the basalt city of R'lyeh. The Illuminati are the human servants of these ancient beasts. They hope to be amongst the few to survive the terrors that will come when R'lyeh rises from beneath the sea."

Morgan turned away from the horrible box and the horror it contained. He wished that he could talk to Lazarus right now. His employer knew a lot about these sorts of things and how to deal with them… but Morgan was simply an old con man who had gone straight. He wasn't really suited to dealing with fallen gods. "I'm not sure how you think this is going to help," he said at last, turning his head toward Louis.

"Because once you understand why a man does what he does, you have a chance of beating him. Walther Lunt and all the rest of them, they're looking to accomplish two things: the first is that they're accumulating all the occult knowledge in the world so that they can find the key to unlocking R'lyeh's prison.

They want to raise it again, awakening all the monsters that slumber within. But before they do that, they want to make sure that they're in positions of power the world over. When the Old Ones return, The Illuminati hope to be overseers for the human slaves who will be like cattle for the monsters. In return, they'll be granted favors and – hopefully – be spared the full brunt of the terrors that await humanity."

"And that's why you work with them?"

Louis laughed hoarsely. "No. I work for them because they pay very, very well. It's a gamble, you see… I'm not high enough up the food chain to look forward to the raising of R'lyeh. I'd end up dead or worse in the New World Order. But The Illuminati hasn't raised that city in all the centuries they've been around so I'm taking the chance they won't do it during my lifetime, either."

"You know all this… What they're really about… and you still take their money? You still work to help them?"

The cultist shrugged his shoulders. "The world's never done much for me. Why should I care what happens to it?"

Morgan had holstered his gun before unlatching the box but he drew it now, making Louis tense. "Thank you for showing me this," he said. "It does solidify something for me."

Louis watched him warily. "And what's that?"

Morgan walked quickly toward the box, kicking the lid open with the toe of his shoe. He pointed his pistol at the awful thing within and pulled the trigger three quick times in succession, the bullets reducing the sickly monster to a splatter of blood and goo. When the deed was done, Morgan turned the gun on Louis, who quickly raised his hands in submission. "Monsters need to die."

Morgan pulled the trigger twice more.

Ten minutes later, Morgan was outside the chateau, having busied himself by pouring gasoline around the exterior of the property. He struck a match and tossed it onto the ground, moving away as the flame sent the gasoline into a sudden frenzy. He knew that Lazarus didn't really approve of murder – and that's what this had been, no doubt about it. But Morgan had realized something while listening to Louis: this wasn't some gang lord they were trying to take down or a criminal enterprise, even a worldwide one. This was a war, one that would hold the continued existence of the human race in the balance. As far as Morgan was concerned, there was no murder in war, at least not so far as it concerned two combatants.

And the sooner the rest of Assistance Unlimited realized the same thing, the better off they'd all be.

Chapter IV
The Beast

Eisner Way had once been a nice residential area and the O'Reilly Church had been one of the beating hearts of the community. But like so much else in Sovereign City, it had gradually become grimier until all the beauty was hidden beneath several layers of sludge. When the economy crashed back in '29, Eisner had slowly become a veritable graveyard as families moved to less expensive parts of the city. The church had finally shut its doors in '32.

Lazarus Gray stood outside the church and tried to imagine it in better times. This city was so much like him in that both had held such promise. He had been a brilliant student, for whom the whole world seemed to beckon. Sovereign had been a port city that could have become the very best of America.

But then Lazarus had fallen prey to The Illuminati and corruption had threatened to overwhelm him, just as Sovereign had become a breeding ground for those who would use their power for abuse.

It had taken death and resurrection for the man known as Richard Winthrop to become Lazarus Gray. What would it take for Sovereign to rise phoenix-like into a new and better form?

Lazarus looked up at the sky and a drop of water struck him in the forehead. It felt as if the city herself was about to cry. Gray hurried toward the doors of the church and was unsurprised when they opened of their own accord at his approach. He had kept his end of the bargain, arriving alone but he was far from unarmed. Beneath his jacket he wore two guns holstered over each breast, a knife at his hip and a police baton strapped to his right calf. He wasn't sure any of those things would help against The Claw but he was willing to give them all a try.

Nearly two-dozen candles, arranged throughout, illuminated the interior of the church. Many pews remained though almost all had been turned over or shattered. The smells of mildew, urine and rotten wood filled Gray's nostrils but he ignored everything except the sight above the pulpit. Kelly Emerson hung upside down, her arms and legs tied securely to an inverted cross. A gag was clenched tightly in her open mouth and her face was crimson, from the strain of her position and from the fear she obviously felt. There were no bruises or marks on her, though her shirt had been torn during the affair, revealing her white brassiere and heaving bosom. Her eyes widened when she saw her former lover and Gray could sense sudden hope springing forth from her.

Addressing her, Lazarus said, "I'm going to get you down from there, Kelly. Trust me."

The girl nodded quickly, indicating that she did.

"Enticing you here proved ludicrously easy."

Gray jerked his head around at the sudden intrusion. The Claw was stepping from the shadows to his left, looking monstrous. The villain held his arms in front of him, his hands clasped within voluminous robes. "If you wanted to face me, you could have at any point," Gray said. "You proved that when you broke into my home. So why kidnap Kelly? Why kill all those innocent children?"

"You know the answer to that," The Claw responded. "I did those things because I enjoyed them."

Gray took a deep breath, not enjoying this confrontation at all. He was on someone else's home field with a loved one in danger. And the creature behind it all was insane enough that he was capable of anything. "Let her go and we can settle this."

The God of Hate laughed and in that bubbling sound there was no mirth, only promises of pain and death. "I think not. Don't you want her to see your heroism as you seek to stop me? I'm sure it will warm the embers of romance within her breast."

Lazarus had heard enough. He reached into his jacket and pulled out one of his pistols, firing it in the same motion. He snapped off four quick shots and all of the bullets hit home, striking The Claw between his neck and stomach. The villain jerked wildly before toppling backwards, his body vanishing as it fell over a church pew.

Gray did not pretend to think that this was the end of his opponent. Even as Kelly began to scream into her gag, wanting him to cut her down, he slowly began to approach the spot where he'd last seen The Claw. As he moved within a few feet, he caught a brief glimpse of the monster's robe on the floor. He sprang forward, leaping over the pew. He landed directly atop the robe but found that it was empty, having obviously been discarded. A sudden flurry of movement from behind him was coupled by another scream from Kelly. He realized that she was trying to warn him but in truth, she was doing more harm than good: with her making so much noise, he was unable to hear The Claw with any effectiveness.

Still, he managed to turn his body just in time to see the villain rushing toward him, claws extended. Gray ducked under one swipe of the deadly knives but the second caught him on the left shoulder, slicing through fabric and skin easily enough. Gray dropped his gun deliberately at this point, the weapon clattering at his feet. He used both hands to grab hold of The Claw's arm and yanked him forward. The motion took The God of Hate by surprise and he nearly lost his footing. Gray drove a hard punch into The Claw's chin and the villain's sharp teeth bit through a section of his own bottom lip, causing blood to flow freely.

The Claw jerked away, anger clouding his eyes. He roared like a trapped lion and swiped out with his claws again, narrowly missing taking off Gray's head.

Gray bent to retrieve his pistol and charged forward, lowering his shoulder and slamming it hard into The Claw's midsection, lifting the villain off his feet. Gray drove him back into the wall and plaster rained down on them both. Lazarus began pummeling the villain's body with punches, slamming them home with all the strength of a desperate man.

The Claw seemed shocked by the way the combat was going and he angrily shoved Gray away from him, giving him just enough time to indulge in one of his most useful spells: before Gray's shocked eyes, The Claw began to grow in size, his entire body expanding until he was so tall that his head scraped against the high vaulted ceiling. He looked down at Gray and laughed at the man's expression. "Do you see now? Do you now grasp what it is you face? I am no mere goon for you to batter with your fists! I am a force of nature! I am Hate personified!"

Before Gray could respond, The Claw reached out with one of his hands and swiped at Kelly's back like he was swatting a fly. The inverted cross that held her aloft snapped in two and she was sent hurtling to the floor. Lazarus burst into action, throwing himself toward her. He made it just in time, slowing the woman's impact by literally placing his body between her and the floor. Gray screamed in pain as a shard of the cross buried itself in his midsection, pinning him to the floor. His hands were free and, despite the pain, he quickly undid Kelly's bonds as The Claw stomped toward them.

"Get out of here," he wheezed.

Kelly looked indecisive. Her eyes kept flitting back to the mammoth horror that was now towering over them but she was obviously hesitant to leave Lazarus. "Maybe I can get you free," she said.

"No." Lazarus gripped her arm painfully hard. "If you stay here, you'll get hurt. I need you to get out of here."

"The argument is moot," The Claw stated. "Because there is no freedom to be had for either of you." The villain raised his foot, obviously intending to grind both Kelly and Gray into paste. Before he could do so, however, a powerful spear-like object passed through his chest, entering from the back and exiting in the front. The object, which upon closer inspection Kelly recognized as a harpoon, imbedded itself in the wall. Blood spurted from The Claw's wound and he whirled about to see where the attack had come from.

Eun Jiwon stood in the doorway of the church, quickly pushing another slender harpoon into a handheld variant of the device so common on whaling vessels. It was one of the group's many emergency weapons and upon first seeing it, Eun had wondered when they would have ever have cause to use it. Now, he knew. "It's a good thing Lazarus has friends, huh?" he taunted.

Gray wasn't sure whether he should be pleased or angry. "What are you doing here?" he shouted.

"Ignoring your orders," Eun answered, pointing the weapon back toward The Claw. "Samantha and I figured that you'd need the help so we decided to split up." Eun pulled the trigger and another harpoon shot forth, this one catching The Claw in the throat. It hung there and the monster began to shrink almost immediately, using most of his energy to try and heal his wounds.

Eun tossed aside the harpoon gun – it was a powerful weapon but the weight of it and the ammunition made it impractical to use for very long. As the young Korean dropped into a fighting stance, The Claw hissed at him in fury.

Kelly, meanwhile, was using every ounce of strength to yank the shrapnel out of Gray's belly. The normally placid features of her former lover were now twisted into a mask of pain but he stood up despite the fact he was losing blood at a prodigious rate. "Thank you, Kelly. Now please – get to safety."

"You're in no shape for fighting," she began but Gray was already on the move.

The Claw was struggling to move – the harpoon was now much larger in relation to his shrunken body and it was almost impossible for him to remain upright.

Lazarus grabbed hold of the point of the harpoon and used it drive The Claw to his knees. "Surrender," he hissed between clenched teeth.

The Claw turned baleful yellow eyes upon him. "Never."

Lazarus stared at the God of Hate and felt bile rise up in his throat. He suddenly knew why the monster was here and why innocents had died along the way. "They sent you here, didn't they? They wanted you to kill me."

"You frighten them," The Claw whispered. "They hate you with every fiber of their being."

"Then let's give them reason to do so." Gray motioned for Eun to come over and take over for him. The young man grabbed hold of the harpoon, twisting it painfully every time The Claw looked like he was starting to resist.

Gray removed his second handgun and swapped out the clip that it held. Part of his arsenal consisted of explosive shells that looked like ordinary bullets. But they carried enormous power that could blow a hole in an elephant. He held the barrel against The Claw's head now and his mismatched eyes – one emerald green, the other a dull brown – seemed to shine with an inner fire. "Go back to Hell."

"This will not be the end of me," The Claw gasped, each word punctuated by a flow of blood from his neck.

"Let's test that, shall we?"

———

Several days later, the entire Assistance Unlimited group sat together in one of the expansive meeting rooms of their headquarters. Morgan and Samantha had returned from Paris the night before and the story that Morgan had revealed had left the entire room feeling somewhat despairing.

"So we're not just dealing with a worldwide conspiracy... we're trying to prevent the return of The Old Ones?" Samantha looked pretty in a peach-colored dress but the look on her face was so grave that not even Morgan felt like flirting with her.

"We already knew it was going to be tough," Eun countered. "This doesn't change anything."

"That thing I saw," Morgan whispered, "It was... **wrong**. I don't know how else to describe it. I can still see it when I close my eyes, can still hear the noises it made. We have to not just stop them... we have to destroy them."

"That's not going to be easy," Eun said. "I was there when Lazarus blew the head off The Claw. And do you know what happened? The thing's body turned to smoke. He's not dead. He's still out there."

Morgan nodded. "Maybe so. But I killed that little bastard that was in the box. They **can** die. Maybe we've just got to get them so weak first that they can't perform their magic...."

Gray cleared his throat and all eyes turned to him. He was dressed in a somber black suit and tie, his handsome face looking as still as the grave. "Morgan got us some useful information while in Paris and our defeat of The Claw will let The Illuminati know that we're not to be trifled with. We have to consider this a victory."

"Won't they just send The Claw back after you? Or somebody even worse?" Samantha asked.

"In time, yes. But for now I think we've given them enough to think about that Sovereign should be free of their influence for the time being." Gray stood up, smoothing down his suit. "And now I'd like to take all of you out to dinner."

Morgan blinked in surprise. The group often ate together in the dining room but they'd never gone out en masse before. "What's the occasion, Chief?"

"As I said, we've won some hard-earned victories lately. And I want to show my appreciation to all of you. Though it's not always easy for me to admit it, we're more than coworkers. We're friends."

Eun cleared his throat, exchanging a glance with Samantha. "Mind if I invite somebody along?"

"Not at all. I think we'd all like to meet this mystery person you've been dating. I imagine he'll fit right in."

Eun smiled, relaxing a bit. He instinctively knew that Samantha hadn't told his secrets: Lazarus simply saw the truth, as he always did. "Thank you."

Lazarus nodded. "So. Where shall we go?"

"Italian."

"A steak house."

"That deli on 8th Street."

The group looked around at each other and everyone abruptly began to laugh. It was a good sound, Lazarus decided. He hoped to hear more of it as the days went by.

DARKNESS, SPREADING ITS WINGS OF BLACK

An Adventure Starring
Lazarus Gray & The Rook

Written by Barry Reese

———— ∞∞∞ ————

Chapter I
Birds of a Feather

Maurice Chapman opened a small white container and pushed a rubber-gloved finger into the white material it contained. He then smeared the grease under his nose, wincing slightly. He offered the container to the two people who were in the autopsy room with him: the dainty, beautiful Samantha Grace and her employer, the tall and thin Lazarus Gray. "You'll want some of this," Maurice said when neither of his guests took the container.

"We'll be fine," Gray answered, his mismatched eyes focused on the body that was hidden beneath a white sheet. The corpse's feet extended past the sheet and he could see that her toes had been painted red, probably a week or so before the murder. The paint was chipped in places and in need of a touch-up. The scent of medicinal products and cleansers was almost overwhelming, but it didn't come close to matching the odor of putrification that arose from the dead body.

Chapman resisted the urge to press the matter. He was sixty-two years old, born and raised in the cesspool that was Sovereign City. He'd seen burly cops enter his lab and turn away vomiting at the things he showed them. He knew false bravado when he saw it – and neither of these two were displaying it. Lazarus

Gray looked like a man who had seen enough death to no longer be disturbed by it. Chapman studied him for a moment, having read about the man in the newspapers but never having met him before. The head of Assistance Unlimited's hair was more gray than brown, making him look older than he was, though a close examination of his features revealed that he was in his late twenties. He was tall and slender, though with a rangy musculature that indicated he could more than hold himself in a fight.

The girl was another matter entirely and it was only because Chapman had known the girl during her youth that he knew she was more than she appeared. A stunning blonde whose parents were wealthy philanthropists, Samantha had grown up with every opportunity possible. She could speak five languages fluently, was a champion swimmer, and was a veritable encyclopedia on topics as varied as fashion, European history, and the socio-political climate of the Orient. Chapman would normally have balked at having a female in his lab, especially when he was about to show off a corpse in this state – but Samantha Grace was no mere slip of a girl, despite how she might look at first glance.

Chapman set the container aside and pulled the sheet away, revealing a body that had been horribly mutilated. The nude form was neatly bisected at the waist and the face had been slashed from the corners of the mouth to the ears, giving her a macabre parody of a smile. The dead woman's black hair was matted and still bore traces of leaves and insect casings. Her body was that of a fit young woman and was admirably formed, but the unhealthy condition of the body was consistent with being exposed to the elements for several days before discovery.

"The victim was 24 years of age," Chapman began. "Her body was found in a vacant lot on the west side of South Page Avenue midway between West 42nd Street and Robeson Avenue."

Samantha exchanged a quick glance with Lazarus. "That's not far from our headquarters." She was obviously troubled to think that a woman could have been brutally assaulted so close to where she and her friends slept every night.

Gray nodded silently, urging Chapman to continue with a quick motion of his hand.

"The body was discovered by a local resident named Betty King who was walking with her four year old son earlier this morning. If you'll notice, the wounds are very clean. They were done with surgical instruments and the body was drained of blood. There are signs that the corpse was washed, probably in an attempt to remove traces of evidence. Furthermore, the body was posed with the left arm draped across the breasts and the right hand covering the pubis region."

"As if she were covering her nudity," Samantha observed and Chapman murmured an agreement. "So she wasn't killed at the scene? Someone dumped her there?"

Chapman spread his hands. "I'm no detective but in my opinion, that would be the case."

"Who was she?" Lazarus asked. Chapman found himself staring at the man's eyes: one was a dull brown and the other a glittering emerald.

"Her name was Claudia Schuller. A packet was sewn to the skin between her shoulder blades and it contained the items you see over there." Chapman gestured toward a nearby table upon which a number of papers had been arranged.

Gray moved toward them, slowly touching each one. Claudia's birth certificate was the first thing he lifted, but he also brushed his fingers across business cards, photographs, names written on pieces of paper, and an address book with the name Max Davies embossed on the cover.

"Has anyone contacted Mr. Davies?"

"Of course we have. We don't just sit around waiting on you to solve all the crimes for us."

Lazarus turned his head to see that Inspector Cord of the Sovereign PD had entered the room. He was a whippet-thin man who had one eye that seemed to be perpetually narrowed. His disdain for Assistance Unlimited – and its founder, in particular – was well known. "Inspector. Just the man I was hoping to see."

"I doubt that." Cord reached up and removed his hat, bowing slightly to Samantha. "Afternoon, Miss."

Samantha gave him a cool smile in reply.

"You were saying that your men had contacted Mr. Davies?" Lazarus prompted.

"Oh, yes." Cord took out a cigarette and lit it, though he knew that Gray hated the smell. He moved closer to Gray, blowing out a long cloud of smoke that enveloped the taller man. "He's here in Sovereign, on business he says. Apparently, his father – Warren Davies, now dead – was a newspaperman back in Boston. One of the papers he owned at one time was The Sovereign Gazette. The younger Davies still has some stock in the paper, though he's a minority holder. Says he met Miss Schuller for the first time about a week ago at a dinner party thrown by the Gazette's current majority owner, Theodore Groseclose. Supposedly, they went out together for drinks two nights later and that was the last time he saw her. Coincidentally, it's the last time anybody's reported seeing her."

Samantha looked at Chapman. "How long ago did she die?"

"I'd estimate it was about five days ago, given the rate of decomposition."

Lazarus knew what his aide was getting at and so did Inspector Cord. Five days ago would have been the same night she'd had dinner with Max Davies. "Where is Mr. Davies now?" Gray asked, confident he already knew the answer.

"He's coming in for questioning right now. I think we've got him dead to rights." Cord took a long drag on his cigarette, a look of confidence on his face. "Last man seen with her and there's his address book right there."

"Then who sewed this packet onto her back?" Gray asked, his words carefully neutral but his eyes betraying his dislike for the other man.

"What do you mean? He did, of course. Davies."

"Why would he include his own address book? And these business cards: Robert Phillips, Chairman of the city's Building Association; Merle Hansome,

Attorney; Theodore Groseclose… all of them should be questioned but I don't think any of them are the killer." Lazarus looked back at the corpse of Claudia Schuller. He tried to imagine her in life, young and beautiful. It was difficult with her reduced to a bisected piece of meat. "Whoever did this horrible act wanted us to know these men's names. The question is: why?"

Cord looked like he'd bitten into something sour. "You're over thinking things, Gray. In order to kill like this, a man has to be insane. Once you establish that, none of his actions should be taken as a surprise. I've seen killers throw themselves into our grasp, explaining every gruesome detail of their acts. That's probably what happened here. Davies wants to be caught." Cord lowered his voice, doing a stage whisper that was easily overheard by Samantha. "Besides, this isn't the first time that Davies has come to the attention of the law."

Gray looked at him steadily, waiting for Cord to continue. When it became obvious that Gray wasn't going to say anything, Cord took several more puffs on his cigarette before uttering a sigh.

"Back in Boston, there were accusations that he might be related to a murderous vigilante known as The Rook. Nothing could ever be proven but get this: he's put his home up for sale. Rumor has it he's planning to head out west or maybe down south. Why would an innocent man flee the town he'd grown up in? Maybe because he's not so innocent?"

Gray turned away from Cord and caught Samantha's eye. Without a word to Cord and just a brief thanks to Chapman, the duo exited the room.

"Where to, Chief?" Samantha asked, the clicking of her heels on the tiled floor seeming very loud. Gray noticed she was wearing a new scent today and he found the perfume to be quite pleasing. He wasn't blind to her interest in him but for many reasons, he didn't think it wise to encourage it.

"We're going to speak to Max Davies."

Samantha smiled softly. "You're planning to get to him before Cord does, aren't you?"

A rare grin seemed to dance upon Gray's lips, but it vanished so quickly that Samantha wasn't sure if she had actually seen it. "No sense in allowing the Inspector to ruin a perfectly good investigation."

———

Max Davies was thirty-five years old, though he could have passed for a man ten years younger. He was stunningly handsome with wavy black hair and a slightly Olive complexion, which made Samantha think that he had Mediterranean ancestry. He wore a black suit, white shirt and red tie, looking like he'd stepped off the cover of a European fashion magazine.

Having booked the penthouse at Sovereign City's most expensive hotel, Davies was reclining in relative luxury when Lazarus and Samantha arrived to speak with him. The room looked barely lived in, despite the fact he'd been staying there for over a week.

Davies was sitting now, his legs crossed before him. He held a small glass of scotch in one hand though Gray was positive the man was merely swirling it about in his glass for effect. Twice he'd brought it to his lips without actually taking a sip.

"You two just caught me," Davies was saying, gesturing for both of his guests to take a seat. "I was just walking out the door."

"We appreciate you taking the time to speak to us," Samantha said, smoothing her skirt over her long legs. She noticed that Max's eyes dipped down to watch the gesture and she smiled. Though she was the equal of any man when it came to a fight, she wasn't above using her beauty to her advantage. After all, it was one more weapon in her arsenal.

"How could I refuse an invitation from someone so attractive?" Max smoothly replied. With a twinkle in his eye, he added, "And might I say, Miss Grace, that you're quite a looker as well."

Samantha stared at him for a moment before the joke hit her. She looked over at Lazarus and saw that he wasn't quite as charmed as she was.

"Mr. Davies, perhaps you don't understand the severity of this situation," Lazarus said, his voice betraying absolutely no emotion. "You're the last person known to have seen Claudia Schuller alive. And an address book bearing your name was found on her person."

"Along with the business cards of other men, isn't that right?"

"How did you know that?" Lazarus asked, his eyes narrowing.

"Inspector Cord told me when he phoned earlier."

Samantha could see Lazarus visibly composing himself. He didn't care much for Cord's methods, which bordered on the incompetent at times. "You're still considered the prime suspect. Could you tell us the nature of your relationship with Miss Schuller?"

"She was at a party I attended. Apparently, she works in the newspaper secretarial pool. She was alone at the soiree and so was I. We struck up a conversation and I invited her to have dinner with me. She agreed to do and a couple of nights later, we went out and ate at O'Malley's. Afterward, we came back here."

"And then?"

Max glanced quickly at Samantha, who was the very picture of decorum. "Miss Schuller remained here for several hours and left my residence just past midnight."

"Did the two of you have sexual relations?" Lazarus asked.

"No. Not if you mean intercourse, anyway."

Samantha felt a flush rise to her cheeks and she smoothed out her skirt once more.

"And everything that happened here was consensual?" Lazarus didn't seem shocked by Max's intimations and Samantha remembered that in his old life, the one he'd had before arriving in Sovereign City, Lazarus had lived in Europe and traveled a great deal. He'd been exposed to things that weren't openly discussed in polite company.

As Max answered in the affirmative, Samantha found herself studying her employer. Not quite two years ago, Lazarus Gray had literally washed up on the shores of the city with no memory of who he really was. In his possession had been a small medallion depicting a nude male figure with the head of a lion. The words 'Lazarus Gray' had been printed below the image and he'd taken the name as his own. It wasn't until after founding Assistance Unlimited, a group dedicated to helping those in need, regardless of their ability to pay, that Lazarus had learned the truth: that once he'd been Richard Davenport, a member of a ruthless International organization known as The Illuminati. He'd turned against them and had nearly lost his life in the process. Now, he fought against his old allies, standing up to the forces of darkness with only his three aides at his side: Samantha, the young Korean Eun Jiwon, and former confidence man Morgan Watts.

Max set down his glass and leaned forward, clasping his hands between his knees. "I assure you, Mr. Gray, that I'm not the kind of man who would have done those things to a woman. To anyone, really." Something passed over the man's face that caught Samantha's attention – it was like a veil had fallen over his eyes. "I saw my father gunned down by criminals when I was eight years old. He was a good man and he taught me to stand up for those in need. I've tried to do that all my life. The kind of killer who did this… that's the kind of man who should be brought to justice."

Lazarus said nothing in response for a long moment, though it was obvious that his mind was running through everything that Max had just said. "I believe you, Mr. Davies. But it doesn't change the fact that a young woman is dead and that someone, for whatever reason, wanted your name thrown into the mix. Do you have any idea how your address book came to be with her body?"

"No. Someone obviously broke into my hotel room at some point but I never saw any sign of it and when I asked the clerk downstairs, he assured me that no one other than the cleaning staff had been here in my absence."

Samantha spoke up, voicing a thought that had come to her repeatedly since they'd left the morgue. "Maybe they just wanted to waste everyone's time, forcing the police down fruitless paths, while the real killer escapes town."

"That's possible," said Max, standing up and quickly crossing to a small briefcase that lay on a nearby table. He opened it as he continued to talk. "But unlikely. The killer's still here in Sovereign."

Gray watched as Max returned with several newspaper clippings in his grasp. Gray took them and his eyes quickly scanned the words, drinking in their meaning. "This wasn't the first murder," Gray murmured.

Max nodded, noting the look of surprise on Samantha's face. "Three years ago, a prostitute was found with her hands and feet removed. The body had been bled dry and washed. Six months later, a fourteen year old runaway girl was found, beheaded and with one leg missing. Again – surgical cuts, the body was dry and had been washed. Last fall, a third one was found: a Chinese immigrant who made a living washing clothes for others. Her breasts had been surgically removed but the other aspects matched perfectly: the body had not a drop of blood left in it and the murder occurred elsewhere with the body having been cleaned afterward."

Samantha shook her head in amazement. "That doesn't make sense. Why didn't Cord mention that?"

"Because he doesn't know," Lazarus answered. "Miss Schuller is the first victim who would be considered of any importance. Prostitutes and immigrants aren't high priorities. There aren't many family members to press for an investigation. They're simply forgotten."

Max nodded. "That's right. It's actually the real reason why I'm here. I sometimes comb through old crime reports, looking for story ideas that I can feed to the editors of the papers I still have a stake in. I came here to talk to Mr. Groseclose about these murders and to see if the Gazette could look into them."

Lazarus took a deep breath before speaking. "May I take these clippings with me?"

"Feel free."

Lazarus collected them and nodded to Samantha. She understood the gesture and stood up. They were leaving, as Lazarus had evidently gotten everything he thought he needed from Max Davies.

Lazarus placed a hand on Max's shoulder. "I'm sorry to say that you'll still be expected to visit the police station and file a formal statement. I think you should heed my advice: don't mention these clippings or the other murders. To a man like Cord, your knowledge of such things might only increase the likelihood of your involvement."

"You believe me, though?"

"Yes. I do. You're much more than you appear to be, I'm sure of that… but you're not the man we're looking for."

Samantha wondered at those words, but said nothing until they were outside in the car. "I'm not sure I believe all that," she said at last.

Lazarus started the car and began smoothly gliding it down the perpetually rain-slicked streets of the city. "You mean that he came here in response to the murders?"

"Well, yes. I mean, it seems terribly convenient, doesn't it? He comes here because he knows women are being murdered. They're all vagabonds or street people so nobody cares about them. Then he meets a girl who doesn't fit that pattern – but sure enough, the killer takes an interest in her anyway."

Lazarus glanced toward her and that faint hint of a smile that he sometimes got reasserted itself before vanishing, like a thin wisp of smoke. "I'd wager that we only saw the real Max Davies at the end of that conversation. The moment he shared with us the details about those other murders, his demeanor changed. Before that, the bored playboy routine, the overly flirtatious act — it was just that. An act."

"So you think he might be the killer?"

"Oh, no. I don't think that at all. I think he's someone with genuine concern about these women but for some reason, he doesn't want the world to know it. I'll look into his background when I get the chance but for now, I don't think we should waste our time focusing on him."

"What about the other men whose names were found with her body?"

"As we were leaving the station, I stopped to call the Assistance Unlimited HQ. Eun and Morgan have been looking into the other men who have been implicated in this."

Samantha nodded, looking out the passenger side window. She saw one gray-colored building after another. It looked like the entire city was slowly falling under a haze of decay. "That poor girl. No one should die like that. And to think that more women have died over the years, with no one missing them... It makes me wonder if we can ever really save this place. My grandparents used to tell me that Sovereign wasn't always like this but nowadays it's hard to believe that. There's something rotten at the core of the city, Lazarus. It's breeding murder, corruption and despair."

Samantha felt her employer's hand settle on hers. He gave it a firm squeeze and when he spoke, there was unusual emotion in his words. "You're right. The heart of Sovereign is spoiled. That's why we've got to find the source of the evil and carve it out."

Chapter II
Men of Power

The death of Claudia Schuller was front-page news on every paper in the city. The Gazette ran two photos, one depicting Claudia on the day of her high school graduation and the other a grainy crime scene image with a body draped by a police blanket. The grisly details were listed in explicit detail, bringing fresh pain to the victim's family and friends.

Speculation was rife. Though the names of the men implicated were not revealed in the papers, rumors linked virtually every prominent businessman in the city with the young woman. Stories circulated that she had been of loose morals and had traded her beauty for monetary gifts from the men.

"Read about de slain beauty! Police officials baffled as investigation continues! All de details included here! Will the killer strike again?"

A newsboy's cry caught the attention of two men who were riding down Main Street in a taxi. One of the men – an elderly, gray-haired gentleman in a tweed suit – turned to his young companion and asked, "What's this about a murder, Smithson? I didn't hear anything about such a thing when we were coming in on the train yesterday."

"Young Miss Claudia Schuller was brutally murdered a few days ago," Smithson answered. He was a handsome man with dark hair and eyes. "The papers are abuzz with the news. It was quite awful, from what I've heard."

"I haven't read any of today's papers," remarked the elderly man. "Such a violent city," he added with a shake of his head.

Smithson waited for the question that he knew was inevitably going to come.

"Schuller, you say? Didn't we meet her at the party thrown by Groseclose? Attractive young thing from his secretarial pool?"

Smithson nodded, his face drawn grave with concern. "We did, Mr. Melvin. She was quite generous in her praise of your revitalization efforts in the city's East

Side."

Donald Melvin bit his lower lip, his eyes taking on a faraway state. "Awful. To be cut down in the prime of life like that. She could have made some man very happy, you know."

Smithson said nothing, hoping that this turn of conversation wouldn't ruin his employer's mood. The meeting they were going to was an important one and Melvin sometimes lapsed into gloomy periods that impacted his decisions. Amalgamated Industries was Melvin's pride and joy and it was currently involved in the removal of dozens of unsightly tenement buildings, replacing them with tremendous structures that towered over the landscape. In decades to come, people would point to Melvin's work as a key part in the revitalization of Sovereign City.

———

Smithson and Melvin stepped from their cab and entered the lobby of The Amici Hotel, a massive building that occupied an entire block. One of the few new hotels to have opened since the Stock Market Crash of '29, The Amici prided itself on an aristocratic atmosphere.

Within the gorgeous lobby, Smithson made an inquiry at the front desk and then informed Melvin that their meeting was being held on the twenty-fourth floor.

After traveling upward in an elevator, the two men stepped into a conference room where a small group was waiting for them. One by one, Smithson introduced Melvin to the men, even though in most cases, introductions were not truly necessary. It was a formality and one that the older men seemed to enjoy, as if it confirmed their importance in things.

Theodore Groseclose, publisher and chief editor of the Sovereign Gazette, was the first to shake Melvin's hand. Groseclose was a tall, gray-haired man in a dark suit. He looked a bit unnerved and Melvin rightly assumed it was because of the death of the man's secretary.

Also present was Robert Phillips, Chairman of the city's Building Association. He was a bear-like man with a thick, bristled beard and piercing eyes.

The final man to whom Melvin was introduced was Merle Hansome, a wiry fellow with thinning hair and a nervous habit of licking his upper lip. One of the most prominent attorneys in the city, Hansome was very good at his job, despite not having the demeanor to put anyone at ease.

Phillips cleared his throat as everyone took a seat. He had a commanding presence and was obviously used to being in charge. "Let's get this under way, shall we? You've looked over the papers we sent your way?"

Melvin nodded, waiting for Smithson to take out a pad and paper before continuing. "I have. Fifty million dollars is quite an investment. If I'm going to do as you ask, I have to receive certain assurances."

Groseclose leaned forward, clasping his hands together on top of the table. "You know I'll do what I can for you, Mr. Melvin. I've kept all the news stories about what you're doing in a positive light. It's going to be a little bit tougher with this new deal, but I can swing it."

Smithson dutifully took notes while the men conversed. He was skilled enough in his craft that he could let his mind wander while his pencil spun across the page, distilling the conversation into shorthand. The three other men had approached Melvin with the idea of spearheading a plan to purchase the grounds on which a hospital for the poor now resided. The sick people who currently received treatment for their infirmities were going to be kicked to the curb if the plan bore fruit, but none of these men considered that worthy of stopping their plans. The men, women, and children who frequented the place were too poor to afford treatment at standard facilities, probably resulting in dozens of deaths.

But if things went to plan, a high-rise apartment building would pop up in its place. The bottom floors would contain expensive offices while the upper rooms were rented or sold to the lucky few who could afford them. It was all part of a long-term revitalization project and one that had sparked grumbling amongst those who had been displaced. Thankfully, Hansome had made sure that all the legalities were covered, while Phillips took care of all the required permits. Groseclose then handled the media side of things, ensuring that the general populace didn't focus too much on the negative.

Hansome stood up and began pacing, bringing the discussion to an abrupt halt.

"What the devil's the matter with you?" Phillips demanded.

"Aren't we going to talk about the murder?" the lawyer asked, his pink tongue darting out to wet his upper lip. "I mean, it's the elephant in the room, if you ask me."

Melvin blinked in surprise. "What are you talking about?"

"Schuller!" Hansome ejaculated. "Are you so dense that you don't realize what danger we're all in? That girl was cut to pieces and all of our names are associated with her! I heard from a source at the police department that Assistance Unlimited is working on the case, too!"

"I barely knew the girl," Melvin said, shrugging his shoulders. "I don't fear an inquiry and neither should any of you. None of you killed her, did you?"

"Of course not," Hansome muttered, though he cast a wary glance around the room. "But this could still derail our plans... the scandal!"

"There won't be any scandal," Groseclose said reassuringly. "Didn't you notice that I made sure none of our names ended up in the paper today? I have enough favors owed to me by the other publishers in this town to make sure we're not linked in any rival accounts, either."

"Word will still get around," Hansome protested.

Melvin loudly exhaled. "I don't see what all the fuss is about. So what if we all knew her? And so what if there are questions to be asked? The law will prove us innocent, mark my words."

Smithson cleared his throat and all eyes fell upon him. The handsome secretary rarely said anything during these meetings, preferring to share his views with his employer in private. "Miss Schuller was an attractive young woman but she was rather promiscuous. The rumors about that are already circulating, I believe. I think it goes without saying that several of the men in this room may have had… delicate relations… with her?" The silence that fell was answer enough - only Melvin seemed shocked by the suggestion and he was obviously about to say so when Smithson continued. "I think that Mr. Melvin is correct in saying that none of you have anything to fear. But just in case, perhaps Mr. Groseclose could have one of his journalists look into her background. Throw a bit of doubt upon her character, as it were."

Groseclose looked uncomfortable. "She wasn't a bad person. Not at all. I'd hate to make it appear that she was."

"It was just a suggestion. I think that if people assumed that she was a bit of a tart, then they'd be less likely to focus their attentions on all of you."

"Could be just the opposite," Phillips muttered. "A pretty young girl, illicit sex, and a grisly murder… no, the more details they get, the more the people will chatter away. But I'm not worried about the police or the press – I have an alibi for the night she was murdered."

Smithson looked around the room. "Who here doesn't have an alibi, if I might ask?"

Groseclose lit a cigar. "Of course, I saw all of you at the party earlier in the evening. After that, I retired to my bed. My butler brought me some warm milk at half past midnight."

"So it would have been possible for you to have left and done the deed," Smithson pointed out.

Groseclose looked offended at the suggestion but said nothing. He'd already heard that same accusation from the Korean who worked for Assistance Unlimited. The young immigrant had pushed Groseclose hard on the matter, but the newspaperman didn't plan to share that with anyone in this room. They were business partners but certainly not friends.

Hansome licked his lip again, a nervous habit that left his mouth perpetually chapped. "I don't have one. I went to a movie and then to a bar for a drink. I didn't return home until very late. I'm not sure I could find any of the men who might have seen me."

Smithson tried not to smile. Hansome's homosexuality was a poorly kept secret amongst the group. It made sense that he wouldn't want to call upon any of his male companions to verify his story. Plus, given the fact that Schuller apparently wasn't sexually assaulted might make Hansome all the more suspect if his secret came to light. Some would say that he would have struck at Schuller out of some deep-seated resentment of women.

"I think it's all a lot of poppycock," Melvin said. "We're all good men. To think that any one of us could ever assault a woman… it's preposterous!"

Phillips nodded in agreement. "To get us back on track here… Are you in for more money or not, Melvin? This new project could become the centerpiece for the revitalization effort and make us all very rich men in the process." Phillips chuckled. "Or, in Melvin's case, richer."

Melvin smiled in reply. "I am very excited about this, gentlemen. Very excited, indeed."

⸺⸙⸺

Night fell quickly in Sovereign City and the few residents who might be called innocents hurried for the relative safety of their homes, leaving the streets to those with darker intent.

A moving patch of darkness passed along the sidewalk beneath the glare of a street lamp. The long streak of darkness ended in a perfect silhouette. The man who cast this shadow was tall and well-built with an olive-complexion and wavy dark hair. He wore a long overcoat, a suit and tie but it was the adornment on his face that set him apart from every other man in the city: he wore a tiny domino-style mask over his eyes and on the bridge of his nose rested a tiny beak-like protrusion. This was The Rook, a being whom the underworld had come to greatly fear in recent years. Having left bullet-ridden bodies in his wake throughout the Northeast, The Rook was like a one-man police force, bringing the guilty to their final judgment, even when the Law could not touch them.

Just up ahead lay the private residence of Merle Hansome. It was a modest home, but it was light-years beyond the residences that were being torn down to make way for Melvin's new high-rises. The Rook calmly approached the wrought-iron fence that surrounded the property and expertly scaled the barrier, dropping easily down to the grass on the other side. He approached the front door and lightly tried the knob. It was locked, which drove him around back. The rear entrance opened easily and The Rook felt a small smile form on his lips. Even in a roach's den like Sovereign, there were men who felt themselves safe and sound in their own home. It was all like a fallacy, of course, but it made The Rook's job that much easier.

Very few people in the world knew that Max Davies led a double life and even fewer still understood why he did it. An armchair psychiatrist would have zeroed in on the events that occurred when Max was eight years old and while those would have helped filled in the gaps, they would not have told the entire tale. Max's father, Warren Davies, had run a newspaper campaign against mobsters who threatened to take over the city. When he refused to knuckle under the pressure they were putting on him, Warren found himself the target of a hired assassin. He was gunned down in front of his son and Max had the memory of his father's final bloodstained memories imprinted into his memory.

But it was what happened later that truly set Max Davies down the path of vigilantism. A series of painful visions began to plague him, ones of crimes yet to be committed. He discovered that if he took steps to prevent them or to bring their perpetrators to justice, the painful visions would recede. Compelled by the knowledge that he would continue to suffer unless he found a way to help others, Max embarked on a years-long trek around the globe in his teens. He learned every form of martial arts known to man, studied philosophy in the Mountains of Tibet, and mastered most known sciences. On the day he first created the identity of The Rook, Max Davies felt a sense of liberation take hold. It was as if he were a bird taking flight for the first time.

And those who slithered in darkness found a new enemy, one who would never stop until every innocent could sleep safely in their own bed.

⸺ ✸ ⸺

Hansome sat on the edge of his bed, dressed in a white dressing gown and slippers. His hands were shaking badly enough that the cup of warm milk he was holding threatened to spill. His tongue darted out, wetting his upper lip. He didn't understand why the others weren't taking this more seriously – even though he hadn't done the horrible deed, he had more than enough secrets that could be exposed by an investigation.

Even more troubling was the nagging question that resided in the back of Hansome's mind: What if one of the others **was** the murderer? He didn't think that Groseclose would do such a thing and Melvin was too old and feeble to have overpowered a healthy young girl… but what about Phillips? The man was brawny and had a temper. Maybe Phillips had tried to force himself on the girl and, when she refused, he'd gotten so angry that he'd cut her to pieces. Phillips had claimed to have an alibi, but Hansome knew those could be faked. Lots of things could be faked, which was something that both Hansome and Phillips knew well.

The lawyer drank the last of the milk and stood up, preparing to set the empty container on the nightstand and crawl into bed. He froze in place as the door to his bedroom unexpectedly open and a masked figure stepped into the room, a handgun held in his right hand. Hansome dropped the glass, jumping when it shattered on the floor.

"Merle Hansome," The Rook said, taking several steps closer to the nervous attorney. "Men call me The Rook. Have you heard of me?"

"Yes," Hansome answered, his voice barely above a whisper. "You're that vigilante who kills people."

"I kill bad people. Are you a bad person, Mr. Hansome?"

"No."

"Then you have nothing to fear from me." The Rook made a show of lowering his weapon and placing it inside a holster under his right arm. "I want to talk to you about the death of Claudia Schuller."

"I have sex with men." Hansome's hands flew up over his mouth and his eyes opened wide. He wasn't sure why he'd said that. It was like his nervousness had somehow caused him to admit his deepest secret in the hopes that it would somehow protect him.

The Rook seemed unfazed by the comment. "I know. And I know that you're not the killer. I'm not here to investigate **you**. I want you to help me investigate **them**."

Hansome relaxed somewhat though it wasn't in his nature to completely be at ease. "Are you talking about my business partners? Because if you are, the man you need to be looking at is Robert Phillips. I'd bet my last dollar that it's him."

"I don't think it is – at the very least, if he is involved, he wasn't involved in all the murders. He didn't move to the city until after the first girl was killed."

Hansome looked confused. "First girl? Are you saying that Schuller wasn't the first to die?" As he asked these questions, Hansome seemed to grow even more nervous. He seemed on the verge of sharing something with The Rook but was obviously hesitant to do so.

The Rook nodded. "That's exactly what I'm saying. What I want from you is access to their personal information – you handle all of them as clients, don't you?"

"Well, Mr. Melvin has his own lawyers so I only assist with the Sovereign affairs that he has. But for the others, yes." Hansome's tongue darted out, touching his upper lip. "But there's a matter of confidentiality. I can't just open their records to you."

"Not even if innocent women are dying?" Hansome hesitated and the Rook continued, "And what about if a prolonged investigation ends up revealing a lot of your dirty laundry? We wouldn't want that, would we?"

Hansome exhaled. "All right. What do you need to know?"

The Rook was about to provide a list of files that he wanted to see when the distinctive sound of footsteps moving stealthily up the stairs gave him pause. The Rook knew from the look on Hansome's face that the man wasn't expecting any company. He held a finger to his lips, indicating that Hansome should remain quiet, and drew his pistol once more.

The gun looked like a common automatic but it was actually proof of The Rook's remarkable scientific acumen. The chamber had been specially modified so that it could hold dozens of miniaturized bullets. It was whispered in the Underworld that The Rook's guns never ran out of bullets but that wasn't quite true – it was simply that each gun held so many shells that few ever saw him reload. The small size of the bullets said nothing about their power, however. Each one packed enough punch to send a large man tumbling backward, meaning that he rarely needed to hit a target more than once.

The Rook crept to the bedroom door and grasped the handle with his free hand. He yanked it open and came face-to-face with a man dressed all in black, save for a crimson mask. The mask was carved of wood and painted with vibrant red. It was a devil's leering face, a tongue jutting forth in a mockery of laughter. In the man's right hand was a long, curving dagger that gleamed in the light. The terrible sight was made all the more terrifying because of the man's great size: he was a veritable bear.

The Rook squeezed the trigger of his automatic, but the first blast went awry as the devil-faced man swung out with his knife, forcing The Rook to back away from the blow. The Rook was well versed in fighting but the man he was now facing was quick and quite skilled in the use of a blade. The Rook found himself ducking under another swipe of the blade and then hurrying to throw up an arm to prevent another. The sharp edge of the knife dug through flesh on the underside of The Rook's arm and blood began to drip onto the floor.

The Rook responded with a karate chop to the stranger's throat, causing the other man to squawk in pain and stagger back. The Rook then grabbed hold of the arm that held the dagger, applying enough pressure to the wrist that the masked man dropped the knife.

"Who are you?" The Rook demanded, driving an elbow into the side of the man's head.

"Call me Devil Face," the man answered, using a peculiar high-pitched voice that was obviously disguised. "And I'm not here for you. I just want the faggoty man. Give him to me and I'll let you live."

The Rook slammed a knee into Devil Face's midsection and for a moment, he thought he'd won the day. The masked man appeared to nearly lose his footing and The Rook made the mistake of letting up on his assault. It was then that Devil Face reached down to his right ankle and freed a second blade that he'd hidden in his sock. Devil Face sprang upward, stabbing The Rook in the left shoulder. Devil Face pushed on, using all his strength to slam the vigilante against the wall. The back of The Rook's head cracked against the wall and his vision began to swim. He slid to the floor, his eyes fluttering. Over the throbbing in his head, he heard the sounds of a scuffle, followed by a piercing cry. The Rook struggled to rise but he found himself unable to find his footing. He lost consciousness, the last sight he saw being that of Devil Face dragging Hansome's limp form out of the room.

Chapter III
Assistance Unlimited

Morgan Watts was a former confidence man, a lackey for more crime bosses than he cared to remember. But his life had taken a change for the better when he'd met Lazarus Gray. He'd realized that the emptiness he'd carried inside him for so long was his sense of morality. It was an empty cup, waiting to be filled. And Lazarus Gray soaked it to overflowing.

Morgan was seated in the briefing room of Assistance Unlimited's expansive headquarters. It was an old hotel that had been retrofitted to their purposes but some of the rooms retained the feeling of impermanence, as if no one was truly meant to call this place home. It was a building designed for fleeting visits.

Lazarus was standing in front of a flannel board upon which photos of the various suspects, along with the known victims of the killer, had been hung. "Morgan, you said that Phillips was at home at the time of the killing?"

"Apparently so. He returned home after the party at Groseclose's and found a car in front of his house with a flat tire. He helped get them patched up – he even produced the name and address of the man he helped."

"And you checked into that?"

"I did. Mr. Thomas Murphy of 1455 Hancock Street. Verifies everything Phillips said. Maybe a little too perfectly, to be honest. They both remember every detail in a way that doesn't usually happen."

Eun Jiwon, the young Korean member of the team, was seated between Morgan and Samantha. He leaned forward, staring hard at his employer's impassive face. "I know Mr. Phillips, Chief. He's a Grade A goon, just dressed up in a business suit. I don't know if he could kill a woman, but I know he's got a temper."

"You mean you knew him before all this began?" Samantha asked.

Eun nodded. He was a handsome young man but after an awkward initial series of flirtations, Samantha had realized they weren't really attracted to each other. In fact, Eun didn't care for women sexually at all, though it took some time before he trusted everyone enough to confirm that. "When I first moved to Sovereign with my parents, they had to jump through hoops to get Phillips to sign off on the permits they needed to build their store. It was pretty obvious that he didn't care for immigrants."

Lazarus turned to the board, staring at the images of the men there: Groseclose, Davies, Melvin, Phillips, and Hansome were all men highly respected in their fields. He knew that sometimes respectability was just a veneer that hid a sociopath's true nature, but he found it hard to believe any of these men were capable enough to have pulled off a series of murders like this. In the case of Phillips, he hadn't even moved to the city when the first of them began.

"Whoever did this is skilled with a blade," he said aloud, tapping his chin. "They also know enough about police work to know how to cover their tracks, washing away all the evidence that might implicate them."

"I don't think it's Hansome," Morgan stated. "The guy's way too nervous to have pulled this off. The guy folds under the least bit of pressure."

"Funny thing to say about a lawyer," Eun said. "They lie for a living, don't they?"

"Not the good ones," Lazarus replied. "But I agree with Morgan. I think we can cross Hansome off our list, at least in terms of being the killer. Nothing in his background suggests that he would be capable of this. Having said that, he might be still be involved as an accomplice somehow."

"Well," Samantha said, leaning forward with interest, "if it's not Hansome and it's not Phillips – since he wasn't in town when the murders began – that only leaves a couple of them as suspects, especially if you still believe that Max Davies isn't one of them. We're just left with Melvin and Groseclose."

"That's not quite true."

All eyes turned to the doorway, where The Rook stood, his body outlined in silhouette. He moved into view, his blood splattered form drawing a gasp from Samantha.

Eun moved around the table, intending to attack this intruder, but Morgan caught him by the sleeve. "Hold off," the older man warned. "I think I've heard of this guy."

The Rook nodded at Morgan before fixing his eyes on Lazarus. "Sorry for not knocking on my way in."

"How did you get past our locks and security devices?"

"What can I say? I'm amazing." The Rook flashed a crooked grin. "But I wanted to let you know that Hansome is missing. He was just kidnapped out from under my nose by a masked man calling himself Devil Face. I'm willing to bet that Devil Face is our killer… and he was far too fit and youthful seeming to be either Groseclose or Melvin."

"Then we're back to square one," Samantha said with an air of disappointment.

"You're forgetting about Smithson," The Rook answered, sliding his weary form into one of the spare seats at the table. "Young and fit, if I recall correctly. Maybe he's doing the dirty work on his employer's behalf. Or maybe he's flying solo on this."

"Do you have any proof that it's Smithson?" Samantha inquired.

"No. He's just the only one not on that list." The Rook noticed that Eun remained tense and he gave what he hoped would be a reassuring smile. "I'm not your enemy. I'm here for the same reasons you are: to help the innocent."

Eun sneered. "Only you choose to do it while hiding behind a mask."

"I have reasons for hiding my identity."

"All I know," Eun continued, "is that you're wanted on charges of murder, assault, and resisting arrest." The young Korean glanced at Lazarus, his entire body tense. "Tell me why we aren't arresting him, Lazarus. Please."

The Rook struck quickly, spinning the legs of his chair so that his body was now turned toward Eun. He drove the heel of one shoe hard into the younger man's stomach but Eun recovered quickly, having been trained in the martial arts since childhood. He grabbed hold of The Rook's ankle and drove an elbow down hard against it, nearly shattering the delicate bones.

The Rook gritted his teeth but continued with his planned moves. He had anticipated Eun's reaction and knew that it was a gamble to expose his ankle to such an attack, but it left Eun completely exposed up top. The Rook reached into an inner pocket sewn into his jacket and produced a small capsule that snapped open between his fingers. A fine brown mist exploded into the air and The Rook leaned forward, blowing the mist straight into Eun's face. The Korean dropped his hold on the vigilante's foot and began coughing, his eyes watering so badly that he was virtually blind.

By now, Morgan and Samantha were on their feet. Morgan was reaching for his gun when The Rook held up a hand. "I didn't come here to fight. I can give Eun an antidote for the dust I just sprayed him with – or he can wait an hour for it to clear up on its own. I just wanted to show you that there are multiple reasons for not trying to bring me in."

Lazarus spoke up, having made no move to interfere during this entire exchange. Though the battle had taken only a few seconds, Lazarus was fast enough that he could have intervened. "I assume reason number one is that you're innocent of all charges."

"I only kill people who deserve it and who leave me no other choice." The Rook retrieved a second capsule and shoved it into Eun's hand. "Crack this open and wave it under your eyes and nose," he directed.

Morgan, still glaring daggers at The Rook, released his hold on his pistol, leaving it holstered at his waist. "And what's reason number two?"

"I would have thought that would have been obvious," The Rook stated, a bit of arrogance creeping into his voice. "None of you are capable of taking me down."

Samantha crossed her arms over her chest. "If you're so high-and-mighty, why do you need us at all, then? Is this Devil Face really so tough that you can't handle him yourself?"

The Rook hesitated before lowering his shoulders. "I'm sorry. None of this is coming out the way I'd intended. I really do try to help people: that's why I'm here in Sovereign and that's why I went to visit Hansome earlier tonight. I wanted access to the private files he held on his clients. Like all of you, I assumed that one of the men whose names were in that packet was the murderer. But I don't think that's the case any longer. I can't guarantee that it's Smithson, but I think it bears looking into."

Eun was blinking away tears now, having regained the ability to see after using the second capsule. "In a fair fight, I think I could take you," he muttered.

"Maybe," The Rook said, trying to make a peace offering. "But I'd rather not find out."

Lazarus stepped around the table, his eyes flicking toward the clock mounted on the wall. It was late, nearing midnight, but he didn't feel they had any time to waste. "Morgan, I want you and Eun to pay a visit to Mr. Melvin. I'm fairly certain that he'll keep his secretary close to him at all times so they should be in adjoining rooms at their hotel. Samantha, please remain here to coordinate our efforts."

The Rook caught a nod from Lazarus, who was heading toward the door. Falling into step alongside the enigmatic founder of Assistance Unlimited, The Rook lowered his voice and asked, "Where are **we** going?"

Lazarus led the masked man toward an elevator at the end of the hall. "Our first stop will be the medical lab downstairs. I don't think your wounds warrant calling in a physician but you need some patching up. It should take no more than five minutes. I hate to waste even that amount of time, but we may need to be at full strength."

"And then?"

"Then we're going to look for Mr. Hansome."

"I don't have any clue where Devil Face has taken him!" The Rook muttered. "What are you proposing? That we drive around town in hopes of spotting them somewhere?"

"Not quite," Lazarus answered. "All of my aides regularly ingest a radioactive isotope that allows me to easily trace them should they vanish while performing their duties. It's quite harmless. Earlier today, I took action to ensure that all of the men on our list of suspects ingested those same isotopes."

The Rook stopped just inside the fully stocked medical lab. "Including me?"

"Including you."

"How in the world--?"

"It was different for each of you – but for you, I slipped it into the scotch you poured back at your hotel room. You barely sipped any of it, but you still managed to swallow enough for me to trace you."

The Rook's lips spread into a grin. "I just realized you just tricked me into revealing my identity."

"It wasn't hard to figure out," Lazarus said in all honesty, leading The Rook toward a chair. After the vigilante was seated and Lazarus had begun treating his injuries, he continued, "The authorities in Boston have nearly uncovered your dual identities on several occasions. You've been so sloppy that it almost seems like you want to be caught."

The Rook winced as Lazarus dabbed antiseptic into his knife wound. "Yeah, I've been told that before. It's just so hard to balance a personal life with my private war… Considering how my father was killed because his enemies knew who he was, I thought it was important to keep my own identity secret. But when push has come to shove, I've erred on the side of catching bad guys, even when it meant that my identity might be compromised."

"I understand about the nature of dual lives," Lazarus admitted. He was normally a taciturn individual, but he sensed that Max Davies was someone who could fully understand the difficulties he faced. "Not long ago, I was a man named Richard Winthrop. I was a member of an international cartel with their fingers in every occult conspiracy you can think of. When I turned against them, I was killed… but here in Sovereign City, I was reborn. Now I find elements of my old life encroaching upon the new with disturbing regularity."

The Rook seemed to sense that he was being honored with this show of familiarity. He reached out and squeezed the other man's arm. "Maybe we can help each other. You can give me advice when it looks like I'm skating on thin ice with my secret identity… and I can offer you assistance in dealing with those old friends of yours."

Lazarus pulled away, reaching under a counter where he retrieved a gauze bandage. "I just might take you up on that."

"I don't like him," Eun said for about the fifteenth time. He glanced over at Morgan, who was leading the way down the hotel lobby. They had used their status as members of Assistance Unlimited to convince the desk clerk downstairs to tell them what rooms belonged to Mr. Melvin and his secretary. To Morgan's surprise, Melvin wasn't in the penthouse – rather, he was in one of the rooms on the fourth floor. Smithson, as Lazarus had surmised, was in an adjoining suite.

Morgan reached up and rubbed his fingertips over the slicked pencil-thin moustache that covered his upper lip. "Eun, give it a rest. The Rook is on our side."

"He's wanted for murder."

"I've killed more men than I care to remember," Morgan pointed out. "Most of them were back in my criminal days but it doesn't change the fact that I'm a murderer. At least The Rook supposedly hasn't offed anyone who didn't deserve it."

Eun didn't bother responding but from the sour look on his face, there was no need to. Morgan knew he was smarting more from his hurt pride than anything else. Hoping that the younger man would get past his distrust of The Rook, Morgan stopped outside Melvin's door and gave it a hard rap.

There was movement from within and the door opened and revealed Melvin, dressed in a smoking jacket and slippers. He seemed alert, despite the hour. "Yes?" he asked.

"My name's Morgan Watts. I work for Assistance Unlimited. You've heard of us?"

"Of course. Who hasn't?" Understanding seemed to dawn in the old man's eyes and he stepped back, allowing them entrance. "This is about that horrible murder, isn't it? The Schuller girl?"

Morgan stepped inside but Eun hung back. "My friend's going to speak to your secretary. He's next door?"

"Yes. But I can access his room with our adjoining door."

"We'd rather speak to each of you separately." Morgan nodded at Eun, who moved toward Smithson's room. Morgan took the door from Melvin and shut it. "You're right about us being here about the murder. I wanted to ask you how well you know Mr. Smithson."

"I'd trust him with my life. If you're going to accuse him of some wrongdoing, you're just going to end up with egg on your face. He's morally upstanding." Melvin took several steps toward a table where a half empty bottle of vodka sat next to an empty glass. Morgan had thought he'd detected the smell of alcohol on Melvin's breath and now he knew his senses had been correct. "Can I get you a drink?" Melvin asked, sitting down with creaking knees.

"Normally, I'd like nothing better, but I can't afford that right now. I'm working." Morgan sat down across from Melvin, his eyes flicking toward the door that led into the adjoining room. If The Rook was correct and Smithson was the murderer, Eun might be in grave danger. At the first sign of danger, Morgan would burst into that room, guns blazing.

"What makes you think that Smithson is the murderer?" Melvin asked, pouring himself a glass. He tilted the bottle until the liquid reached the lip of the glass, threatening to overflow.

"We're not accusing anyone," Morgan said. "As a matter of fact, Smithson's name wasn't one of those found on the dead girl's body. But most of the others either have alibis or have other elements to their lives that preclude them from being part of the killings."

"Killings?" Melvin asked, his eyes shining. "There's been more than one?"

"Yes. The press and the local police don't seem to have noticed, but Schuller wasn't the first girl to be killed. There have been several over the past few years, mostly prostitutes and the like. We think we're dealing with a modern day Jack the Ripper."

"Oh, my," Melvin whispered, the color draining from his face.

"What's wrong?"

Melvin suddenly seemed very fragile. "I think I might know something about all of this, after all…"

Morgan leaned forward with interest. It was at that moment that the sounds of gunfire rang out from Smithson's apartment.

Eun knew that he was being wrongheaded but he couldn't bring himself to change his opinion with regards to The Rook. The man was trouble with a capital T as far as Eun was concerned. He was still pondering this as Morgan shut the door to Melvin's room and Eun began to knock on Smithson's. There was no answer and Eun repeated the procedure, applying a bit more force to the knocking this time.

When Smithson still did not appear, Eun reached down and tried the doorknob. It was locked and Eun pondered for a moment what to do. He could enter Melvin's room and try to cross over through the adjoining door, but he didn't want to expose the old man to any danger if Smithson was the killer.

According to the clerk, both Smithson and Melvin were supposedly in their rooms but only one of them was answering – and while it would have made sense for the elderly Melvin to be hard of hearing, it defied logic for Smithson to be the same.

Eun took a step back and raised his right foot. He drove it hard against the door, repeating the blow twice more before the barrier cracked and swung open. Eun heard movement from within and he hurried inside, saying, "Mr. Smithson? Don't be alarmed."

The first thing that Eun noticed was that the room was illuminated by a single lamp, which sat next to the bed. Lying on top of the sheets was Smithson, but any hopes that he might shed some light on the murders was smashed when Eun spotted the pool of crimson that lay beneath him. A bullet hole over his heart was the source from which the blood had flowed and Eun knew immediately that Smithson was dead and had been for at least an hour.

A rustle of fabric drew Eun's attention away from the body. Standing in front of the open sliding glass door that led to the balcony was a dark figure. Eun remembered The Rook's description of Devil Face and quickly realized that this man did not match that look at all. This man wore a white shirt covered by a gray vest, black tie, and an ebony jacket. Over all of this was slung a dark opera-style cape that was clasped about his neck. With black slacks and shoes, as well as leather gloves and a top hat, the figure looked like he might be on his way to a fancy ball. But the presence of an automatic in his right hand and a large domino-style mask made it quite clear to Eun that the man's presence was a sinister one.

"I know how this looks," the man began, "but it's not quite what you think."

Eun grinned and sprang toward the man, eager to redeem his earlier defeat against The Rook. He moved so quickly that the well-dressed man was unprepared for the first blow that came: Eun caught him flat on the side of the skull with a closed fist. The younger Korean followed with a knee to the man's midsection that knocked the air from the man's lungs.

Eun felt a sense of elation, realizing that he might be about to singlehandedly solve the entire case. If this man was the killer, then perhaps he was working with Devil Face – or, just as likely, The Rook had made up the whole thing and was working with this man.

The well-dressed man recovered faster than Eun would have thought possible. He raised his pistol and squeezed off two quick shots. The first whistled past the Korean's ear and passed through the sheet rock behind him. The second stuck Eun in the left thigh and caused him to grit his teeth in pain.

Eun had taken bullets before and refused to give in. He was about to strike back when the masked man pistol-whipped him, cracking Eun's lip and sending a spray of blood against the wall.

"I'm not the killer," the masked man said. "I came here for the same reasons you did: to talk to that man. I found him like that just minutes before you showed up."

"I don't believe you," Eun hissed. "I've had it up to here with masked men telling me lies."

"Not sure what you're talking about, friend, but I'm called The Dark Gentleman. And I'm working to clean up the cesspool that Sovereign City's become."

At that moment, the adjoining door to Melvin's room burst open. Morgan sprinted through, throwing himself into a rolling ball. He popped up next to the bed and, with barely a glance at the corpse in the bed, opened fire at The Dark Gentleman.

The masked man cried out in surprise, hurling himself backwards. He landed against the balcony railing and quickly twisted so that his legs were up and over it. He dropped out of sight, leaving Eun and Morgan to rush forward in hopes of catching a glimpse of his fate.

Down below, the city streets were empty. It was a three-story drop but there was no sign of The Dark Gentleman.

Morgan took note of his friend's bleeding shoulder and mouth. "What the hell happened?"

"That guy in the mask that you just shot at – he calls himself The Dark Gentleman. I'm starting to think that those names on that girl's body weren't suspects… they were targets. Hansome missing, Melvin's secretary killed… maybe these men know something and that's why they're being bumped off now."

"Something that's tied to the murders of all those girls?"

Eun shrugged. He turned back toward the bed, where Melvin was now standing. The old man was staring at the body of his confidante. Melvin looked horrified and one liver-spotted hand came up to cover his own mouth, as if he wanted to stifle a scream.

"Mr. Melvin, we're going to summon the police," Eun said. "Can you remain here and wait for them?"

Numbly, Melvin nodded. He turned away from the corpse and seemed to regain some of his strength now that he wasn't faced with his secretary's body. "He was a good man, almost like a son to me."

Morgan caught Eun by the sleeve. "How about making that call and then staying here with Melvin? I can go looking for that guy without you."

"No," Eun answered firmly. "I'm not being left behind."

"You're hurt."

"I'm fine."

Morgan sighed and nodded. He was pretty sure that The Dark Gentleman hadn't left them any kind of trail worth mentioning, but they had to make sure. He was about to step out into the hall with Eun when he remembered that Melvin had been about to say something to him before the shooting began. He hesitated a moment, gesturing for Eun to go on without him.

"Mr. Melvin... You were about to tell me that you might know something about these murders?"

Melvin didn't bother looking at Morgan. He simply shook his head and whispered, "Nothing. I have nothing to say."

———— ∞∞∞ ————

Chapter IV
Angels & Demons

"So that's how he did it!" Samantha sat back with a satisfied grin on her face. Ever since The Rook had interrupted their meeting, she'd wondered how he'd managed to bypass the security at Assistance Unlimited headquarters. It had taken a bit of digging through the archival footage to figure out what security flaw the masked man had uncovered but now she had it: he'd broken into one of the abandoned storefronts facing the old hotel that Assistance Unlimited used as their base. From there, he'd managed to travel through one of the underground tunnels that linked every building on the street. Everyone knew that Lazarus Gray had bought the entire block for purposes of secrecy but very few knew that they were all linked together, essentially transforming it into one giant headquarters.

Samantha still wasn't sure how The Rook had known about the underground tunnels, but at least she knew how he'd accessed the main building: he'd come in through the basement.

She was still marveling over the panache needed to break into their headquarters when Morgan and Eun entered the room. Eun looked pale, his shirtless body covered by bandages.

Samantha moved to fuss over his wounds but Eun waved her away and sat down heavily in a chair. "There's another masked man in town," he said. "Calls himself The Dark Gentleman."

Samantha straightened up. "That's odd. Sovereign's had its share of vigilantes in recent years, but most of them don't bother hiding their identities."

"Now we have two," Eun muttered, obviously still smarting from his wounded pride.

Morgan allowed the two younger members of the team to continue the discussion while he stepped into an adjacent room. He picked through some of the papers they'd accumulated on the various suspects. Something was bothering him, but he wasn't sure what... Obviously Melvin had thought about sharing something with them and then changed his mind. Was there some connection between Smithson and Hansome that they hadn't picked up on? And if so, how did it all play into the horrific murders of those girls?

He tapped a photo of Hansome and whispered, "I hope Lazarus can find you, shyster. I'm betting you have the answers we need."

⟋⟍

The duo of Lazarus Gray and The Rook had traced the radioactive isotopes in Hansome's bloodstream, following the trail to a small rental property on the outskirts of town. A sign in the front yard indicated that the A-frame house was for rent by the owner and Lazarus noted that the painted phone number on the sign had peeled away, leaving only the first couple of digits.

"This is a front," The Rook said, standing outside the front door. There were no streetlights around and the interior of the house was dark, so both men held sterling silver penlights.

"What do you mean?"

"Nobody's really trying to rent this property. If they were, they would have repaired that sign. And the house itself is filthy... smells like something's died here. Recently."

Lazarus knew what his friend was implying and he moved forward, taking up position to the right of the door. The Rook took the left and they nodded at each other before Lazarus took a few steps back and lowered his shoulder. He crashed against the door, using all his impressive strength to shatter the barrier.

The interior was cloaked in an almost stygian darkness and the odor of death was far thicker than before. The Rook followed Lazarus into the house, using his penlight to locate a small lamp. He turned it on, bathing the living room in a dull yellow glow. What they saw was stomach churning and, even for men as used to the unusual as these two were, shocking.

There were human, dog, and cat skeletons nailed to the blood-red wallpaper, many of them arranged in obscene positions. In between the bones, the wallpaper had been covered with odd drawings of horned demons, acts of bestiality, and crying faces.

The skeleton of a human male, its bones held together by twine, dangled from the center of the ceiling. Large wings forged of leather and wood had been attached to the skeleton's back and goat horns had been glued to the top of the skull.

A long table was set against the back wall. It was waist-high and carved from some form of shiny blood-colored wood. Its bowed legs were carved to resemble great serpents, their fanged mouths reached upward. At each of the four corners was a black candle resting in bronze holder. The holders were shaped like skulls, the lower the jaw of each protruding out to hold the candle in place. A stone basin lay in the center of the table and as Lazarus approached it, he recognized the presence of human bones and dried blood.

The scene was disturbingly familiar to Lazarus. In his old life, he'd witnessed things like this as a member of The Illuminati. It had been horrors like this that had led him to turn against his friends, eventually bringing about his death and resurrection in Sovereign City.

The Rook allowed Lazarus to investigate the strange table and its horrible contents. He opened the other doors, finding a bedroom that looked like it had never been touched; a kitchen that was so filthy that it nearly caused him to retch; and a bathroom that contained a very nasty surprise.

"Lazarus," The Rook said, placing the back of a gloved hand over his nose and mouth. "I found Hansome."

Lazarus appeared almost instantly, looking past the masked man at the lumps of flesh that lay in the tub. The soapy water was filled with bleach, cleaning away much-needed evidence. Hansome's body had been neatly cut up into six pieces: his head, his torso, his arms, and his legs. Several large buckets filled with the man's blood lay outside the tub and plastic tubing rested on the counter top next to the sink.

"There goes any doubts about Hansome's kidnapper being related to the girls' killer," The Rook murmured. "Guess he's branching out to the other gender."

Lazarus knelt beside the tub, holding a handkerchief over his nose. His eyes watered from the strong bleach fumes that hung in the air, but he wanted to check on a suspicion he had. He grabbed hold of Hansome's head and lifted it from the bath, carrying it out of the room and setting it gently atop the bloodstained table in the living room. While The Rook watched in mounting curiosity, Lazarus pulled up a chair and sat facing the dead man's terror-stricken face. After pulling out a magnifying glass, he leaned so close to the decapitated head that their noses were almost touching.

"What are you doing?" The Rook asked, no longer able to contain himself.

"Are you familiar with the work of Willy Kühne, professor of physiology at Heidelberg?"

The Rook searched his memory and slowly nodded, beginning to see where his companion was going with this. "He studied retinal chemistry, didn't he?"

"Yes. He theorized that the retina behaves not only like a photographic plate but like an entire photographic workshop, in which the artist continually renews the plate by laying on new light-sensitive material, while simultaneously erasing the old image. By using the pigment epithelium, which bleaches in the light, he set out to prove that it might be possible to take a picture with the living eye. He called the process optography and its resulting products optograms."

The Rook found himself getting wrapped up in the science behind the matter. "And the rabbit's eyes held an image of the bars," he whispered to himself.

Kühne had created a famous optogram by using an albino rabbit, whose head had been fastened so that it faced a barred window. From this position the rabbit could only see out onto a cloudy sky. The rabbit's head had been alternately covered with a cloth, to allow its eyes to acclimate to the dark, and then exposed to bright light. After this, the rabbit was decapitated, with its eye removed and cut open along the equator. The rear half of the eyeball, containing the retina, was laid in a solution of alum to set. The next day, Kühne had seen printed upon the retina a picture of the window with the clear pattern of its bars. This had been repeated in other experiments, leading Kühne to state that the final image viewed before death would be fixed forever, like a photo. If death were to occur at a moment when the pupils of the eyes were hugely dilated – because of fear, anger, surprise, or some other strong emotion – the retinal optograms of the deceased would be even more detailed.

"Do you see anything," The Rook asked.

Lazarus nodded, his eyes staring into those of the dead man. Reflected there, as clear as day, was the face of the devil.

Theodore Groseclose couldn't sleep. He was sitting in his study, a glass of warm milk in his hand, unable to stop thinking about the events of the past few days. He'd liked Claudia. She was smart and pretty, the sort of combination he always enjoyed having around the office. It was hard for him to visualize her body having been violated in the ways he'd heard. What sort of monster could do that? Who could snuff out a beautiful girl's light like that?

Groseclose looked up as he heard the unmistakable sound of the front door being unlocked. He set down his milk and moved to the foyer, his eyes widening as his 24-year old son Michael entered the house, looking disheveled. Michael was blessed with his mother's good looks and his father's intellect... but there were whispers that he was squandering both since dropping out of college two years before. Since then, he'd lurked in the shadows, vanishing for days on end with no explanation.

"What the hell are you doing?" his father demanded, all the frustrations of the past few days finding a new target. "I swear to heaven, I don't think you care what the community thinks, do you?"

Michael's jaw clenched, as if he were barely able to hold back his own anger. "I was out on business."

"At this hour of the night? I don't believe you. I believe you were out drinking and whoring, that's what I think!"

Michael shook his head and stepped around his father. "I'm going to bed."

"The hell you are!" Theodore bellowed, grabbing hold of his son's arm and clenching it tight. "I've had enough of you. You're my son! And that means people are going to look at you differently than if you were some ragamuffin off the street!"

Michael whirled around, bringing his face close to his father's. Had Theodore not been so wrapped up in his anger, he would have realized that there was not a trace of alcohol on his son's breath. "You know what, Dad? I've had enough of you, too. You sit in your office and you print your stories but what do you really know about life in this city? Have you walked its streets? Have you seen all the joy and happiness sucked out of its people because they can't believe in the system anymore? Do you know that there are dozens of mobs out there, all vying for power? And that the men in charge turn a blind eye to it because they're too scared or to crooked to do what's right?" Michael yanked his arm free. "Oh, but you would know about that last part, wouldn't you? You're the one helping make sure good people are being put out on the street so your buddies can build their high-rises."

Theodore's mouth moved silently for a moment before his anger gave him new voice. "How dare you?"

"I know a lot more about this town than you give me credit for. And I'm actually doing something about it." Michael spun on his heels and jogged upstairs, regretting the anger he'd shown his father, but refusing to back down. He slammed the door to his room shut and then sagged down onto his bed. He needed to get his own place if he wanted to really make a difference. Sneaking in and out of his own house was just one more headache that he didn't need.

Michael had trained for months, preparing to take to the streets as The Dark Gentleman… but what had happened on his first night out? He'd run into not one, but two members of Assistance Unlimited, both of whom now thought he was a murderer. He'd meant to question Smithson about the men whose names were linked to Claudia's death… but whoever had killed him had come and gone before Michael had arrived.

Claudia had been a lovely girl and one that would have normally attracted Michael's intense interest. But he'd been so single-minded as of late that he'd never bothered approaching her.

Michael stood up quickly and began pacing. He wanted to do something, wanted to prove that the past few weeks hadn't been some pointless lark. He could help Sovereign City, he was sure of it.

He suddenly realized that he needed to clear the air with Assistance Unlimited. Right now, they were probably wasting valuable time hunting him down when they could be going after the real killer.

Michael forced himself to stop. He had to get some rest. In the morning, he could go down to Robeson Avenue and make peace with them. Maybe they'd even agree to let him assist them in the case.

A smile suddenly blossomed on his lips. Michael realized he was beginning to feel like a kid hoping to fall in with the popular crowd at school. He needed to rest before he did anything reckless – more reckless than putting on a top hat and mask.

Devil Face stared in the mirror, marveling at the beauty of his visage. This was the true expression of his inner self, come to life in the form of a wooden depiction of Satan himself. The leering mouth, the jutting tongue, the crimson tint… They were everything that he so desperately wanted to be. They were far truer than the face he wore every day to the office, where he pretended to be so much less than he truly was.

It had been years since he'd moved to Sovereign City, this cesspool of immorality. The place had called to him and he'd recognized it as home. He had felt it in his blood and in the dark little corner of his mind where the Devil resided. At first, he'd tried to be good, tried to silence the voices that screamed for bloody murder… and he'd almost succeeded. But then he'd seen those whores, all made up like pretty dollies – they'd forced him to do what he'd done. He'd punished them for their sins, for using their breasts and their buttocks to tantalize and tease. Who knew how many boys they'd corrupted with their offers of love? He'd killed them and washed them, not to remove traces of his identity as the police had assumed: but to cleanse them of their filth.

Claudia had been different than the rest and she was the cause of all of Devil Face's current problems. She'd been so sweet and desirable, nothing like those tarts he'd killed in the past. Claudia was a good girl. She'd sobbed to him in the end, begging him to spare her. She claimed she was a virgin and Devil Face almost believed her – he'd wanted so badly to believe her. But he knew she'd gone to Max's apartment and they'd done *things*… dirty things that caused butterflies to swim about in his stomach when he imagined them. This made him realize that even if she wasn't a whore yet, she was well on her way. So he'd punished her for the sins she'd yet to commit.

And then had come the guilt, so quick that it had surprised him. He'd borrowed Max's address book during a brief visit to the other man's hotel room. At the time, he'd merely wanted to find out more about Davies, who had seemed to be more than he claimed to be. Davies had this way of looking at everyone as if he could see through him or her. It was almost as if he was looking at Devil's Face's real features, which had been both exciting and infuriating.

After Claudia's death, though, the idea of leaving the address book on her body had seemed the proper way to assuage his guilt. A part of him wanted the world to know who he really was and this dangerous game of leaving clues to his identity served his need for self-punishment.

But after her body had been discovered, the Devil had taken hold and a sense of self-preservation had emerged. Hansome knew his real identity, which meant he'd had to die. Hansome's sexual interests had forced Devil Face to give him the same treatment he usually reserved for the whores: after all, Hansome probably would have offered his body if he'd thought it would have saved him. It was sickening, what Hansome would have done if given the chance....

Smithson was another problem. Too smart for his own good, Smithson had discovered Devil Face's secret and actually sought to blackmail him. Devil Face didn't think that Melvin knew the truth, but he couldn't be sure. Smithson and the old man were very close. Since Smithson wasn't a sex fiend like Hansome or the girls, Devil Face had killed him like an animal. It was the first time he'd ever killed without using the precious ritual – the ceremonial cutting, the washing of the flesh, reducing the body to chunks of flesh.

Devil Face turned away from the mirror, reaching up to peel away his mask. He hated to look at the face he showed the world on a regular basis. It was so ugly, with every crease and line containing a litany of sins. It was only when his true face was on display that he felt truly confident.

After placing the devil mask in a box under his bed, he headed downstairs to have a drink. Killing those men hadn't left him as ecstatic as cleansing the whores usually did. Normally he would have been humming a song to himself and feeling like he was on top of the world: instead, he felt tense and paranoid. How long before Smithson's body was discovered? Would they find the gun he'd discarded in the trash bin outside the hotel? Could it be linked back to him? And what about Hansome? His body was still in one of Devil Face's many safe houses but with Assistance Unlimited on the prowl, who could say that it wouldn't be discovered?

He paused as the phone in the study began to ring. He looked up at the clock and realized that it was nearly dawn. Where had the night gone?

Walking quickly to pluck up the receiver, the killer took a moment to make sure he used the proper voice. His day-to-day voice was deeper than the one he used when wearing the Devil Face mask. "Hello?"

Theodore Groseclose sounded on edge. "You need to come over to my house. Immediately."

"What's wrong?" he asked, though he knew what the answer would be. How could he not?

"Smithson and Hansome... they're both dead. Melvin's already here and I'm about to call Max. We could all be in danger – what if the killer's planning to kill everyone associated with Schuller?"

"Calm down," he soothed. He caught a glimpse of himself in the mirror and paused. His hair and beard looked unkempt and his eyes were wild. He didn't look much like Robert Phillips at the moment: he'd have to clean himself up before he went over to Groseclose's. "I'll be there soon."

Devil Face hung up the phone and reached up to smooth his hair. Had Smithson told Melvin about what he'd learned? If he had, then the old man would have to die, too... and then there was Groseclose. The man was a journalist and he might start digging on his own. If he found out that Phillips had moved to

Sovereign and adopted a new identity for himself with Hansome's help, then all the dirty secrets might come out.

Phillips hurriedly bathed and dressed in fresh clothing, creeping down the stairs to the locked basement door before leaving for Groseclose's. He entered the finished basement, the coppery smell of blood filling his nostrils as he opened the door. Inside were 13 canisters filled with the blood of the women he'd killed over the years, dating back to before he'd come to Sovereign and adopted his current identity. He needed to kill only one more and then he'd be ready to leave this prison of flesh behind.

"Something troubles you, my love?"

The soft, purring voice of Lady Death echoed in his head. The temperature seemed to drop twenty degrees or more and his breath suddenly became visible in tiny cloudbursts that escaped his mouth. He turned to face the woman of his dreams, the only one who was pure in all things. He was the only one who could see her, the only one who heard her voice.

She was a few inches over five feet in height, her lush curves shifting beneath a hooded black robe. Her skin was a milky white that always reminded him of moonlight on water. Her ruby red lips and the lower half of her face was all that could be seen beneath the darkness of her hood, but he had seen her naked beauty before. The upper half of her skull was exposed, her eyes nothing more than two deep sockets of shadow that seemed to suck him right into their depths.

"My enemies are closing in on us," Devil Face answered, using the higher-pitched voice he normally saved for when he was masked. "I'm worried that they might stop me before I've accomplished my goal."

Lady Death reached out and touched his face, her icy grip making him shiver. "I am proud of you. You have done so much in my name... and now you only have to find one more whore, one more woman who needs to have her sins washed away. And then you'll be mine, in body and soul."

Devil Face leaned into her hand, his face lighting up like an excited puppy's. "I can go find another girl tonight!"

"No. You'll know her when you see her. There are only certain ones who fit our needs."

Lady Death pulled away, vanishing into the dark shadows of the basement. Devil Face reached after her, desperate to touch her skin once more but there was nothing there any longer.

Chapter V
But For the Grace of God

Max Davies woke up at six in the morning and immediately indulged in his daily ritual. He had a cup of warm tea followed by an hour-long session of yoga and Tai chi chuan. When he was done with his exercises, he dressed in a casual suit and placed the beak-like mask of The Rook over the bridge of his nose. He'd spent the night in the headquarters of Assistance Unlimited, enjoying the comforts that the former hotel offered. He felt a bit silly continuing to hide his identity – Lazarus knew who he was and he trusted the man implicitly. The fact that Lazarus in turn trusted his aides should have meant that Max did as well… but it wasn't quite that simple. The dark stares The Rook continued to receive from Eun were evidence that he wasn't fully accepted by all.

The Rook wandered downstairs to the team's meeting room and found that everyone else was already there. Morgan and Samantha were seated beside each other, their voices lowered to mere whispers. Morgan said something that Samantha found funny and she coyly covered her mouth as she laughed. Eun was leaning against the wall, looking as surly as ever. Lazarus himself was standing with his hands clasped behind his mask. His impassive face was pointed toward the window and the ray of sunlight that fell upon it accentuated his strong chin.

"Any breaks in the case?" The Rook asked, ignoring the way Eun muttered under his breath in response.

Lazarus looked toward him and gave a brief nod. "Perhaps. Groseclose is holding a private meeting at this hour with Phillips and Melvin. I understand they attempted to get in contact with Max Davies, but he's not at his hotel."

The Rook paused, a smile on his lips. "I might be able to reach Max and convince him to go to this little party. It would help us to know what was going on."

"That would be quite useful," Lazarus admitted. "We'll be waiting to hear back from you."

———— ∞ ————

Michael Groseclose was pulling out of the driveway just as the taxicab carrying Max Davies was coming to a stop in front of the house. Michael and Max locked eyes for a brief second before their travels carried them away from each other and Max was struck once more by how intelligent the young man seemed. They'd only met briefly at the party thrown by the elder Groseclose, but Max had felt a kinship to the youth.

Max was led into the house by a taciturn butler who looked almost as harried as Max felt. He wore on his lapel a miniscule listening device that would allow Lazarus to overhear every word that was said. Max was more impressed with Assistance Unlimited at every turn. The various skills of the aides were impressive enough, but combined with the various inventions and designs of their leader, they had become one of the most formidable organizations on earth.

Max found Groseclose in the sitting room, seated with his head hanging between his knees. Phillips, looking like an angry bear that had been roused from his winter's nap, was pacing in front of the fireplace. Melvin, looking older and frailer than Max could ever remember, sat pensively on a small couch, his eyes staring off into unfocused space.

Phillips stopped and stared, his mouth clamped into a thin line beneath his beard. "Davies. We were beginning to wonder if Devil Face had gotten to you."

"Devil Face?" Max asked, allowing a smile to appear on his face. He looked over at Groseclose, who had leaned back in his chair.

"According to a statement released by Assistance Unlimited, that's the name of the lunatic who's committing the murders," Groseclose said.

Max noticed that Melvin looked up sharply, his gaze shifting from Max to Phillips and back again. "You know about Smithson, don't you?" he asked. "They say Devil Face killed him, too, but he didn't mutilate him like he did the others."

Max knelt in front of Melvin and took the old man's hands. "I did hear and I'm sorry. I know he was like a son to you."

"He was. I don't know how I'm going to continue on without him. I'm not as young as I used to be."

Phillips growled like the animal he resembled. "I'm surprised the police don't have us all under protection. Two of the men whose names were on that dead girl's body have been murdered! We're important people, damn it!"

"Smithson's name wasn't in the packet," Max pointed out, drawing another dangerous stare from Phillips.

"I imagine they're planning to put us under protection," Groseclose said. "But I'm not sure that's going to be enough. Any man who could have evaded detection for as many years as this Devil Face has… I'm not sure he's human."

Melvin looked at him in surprise. "What do you mean?"

"Just that there are a lot of awful things in this world and not all of them can be explained by men. I haven't run half the rumors I've heard about Assistance Unlimited and the kinds of jobs they take on: demons, devil-worshipping cults, women who can kill men just by looking at them."

"Poppycock!" Phillips bellowed, though Max thought he saw a shadow of doubt pass over the big man's face. "Sounds to me like you've been paying too much attention to Gray's own rumor mongering. It's all an attempt to stir up an air of mystery around the man so he can charge more for his services!"

Max stood up and adjusted the sleeves of his coat. "Do we have any sort of plan here? Or is this meeting simply to share our concerns?"

Melvin struggled to his feet. "I'm leaving town. I only came to finalize our plans for the project and I daresay that they're on hold for now. I need to return home and inform Smithson's family about what's happened. I'm sure they've heard the news, but I want to tell them what the papers may not have."

"You can't leave town," Groseclose said sadly. "The police want us all to stay in Sovereign. We're persons of interest in the investigation."

Phillips stormed over to the table that sat in front of Groseclose's chair. He plucked up the morning newspaper and stared at the front page. It showed an old photograph of Lazarus Gray and his aides, under the headline **ASSISTANCE UNLIMITED HUNTS 'DEVIL FACE' KILLER!**

"Glory hounds," Phillips whispered, his eyes lingering on the pretty face of Samantha Grace. His lips moved a few more times, as if he were continuing to mouth words, but none of the other men could hear what he said. He abruptly threw the paper back on the table and stepped back, his eyes wide. "I hope for the best for you gentlemen. I don't plan to wait for either you or the police to come up with a scheme to protect me, however. I'll handle that quite well on my own!"

Max put a hand on the big man's arm, preventing him from walking toward the door. "Don't go off half-cocked, Phillips. The last thing any of us need to do is go out and get ourselves into trouble."

Phillips glared at Max, pulling his arm free as he did so. "You will be well advised to never touch me again," he said in a menacing tone.

"I'm just trying to help," Max answered, refusing to wilt before the bigger man's gaze. As they stared each other down, Max felt a tremor of recognition pass through him. He'd been face-to-face with Phillips before and never realized it. He'd be willing to bet his last dollar that it had been Phillips behind the Devil Face mask when they'd squared off in Hansome's bedroom. At the same moment that Max realized whom his enemy truly was, Phillips narrowed his own eyes, having come to the same realization.

"I don't need your help," Phillips hissed. "Just stay out of my way."

Max stared at the man's back as he exited the room. A moment later and they all heard the loud slam of the front door.

"Just let him be," Groseclose said wearily. "He's always been an aggressive sort and I imagine all this just makes him feel helpless. Lord knows that's how I feel."

Max looked over at Melvin, who was still standing in place. "Do you still want to leave?"

Melvin shrugged, looking pained with every breath. "I'd love to but I don't think it's very wise, do you? I can't leave the city and I don't want to stay at the hotel. Smithson was killed there so I wouldn't feel safe." He chewed his bottom lip for a moment before saying, "Smithson didn't like Phillips. Said he was dangerous. He warned me not to be alone with him. But he said something very strange to me just a few hours before he died. I thought about mentioning it to that fellow from Assistance Unlimited but then thought better of it. It sounds so foolish."

"What was it?" Max did his best to avoid looking overeager.

"Smithson said that Phillips was the same kind of man as Jack the Ripper: that he looked at other people, particularly at women, as slabs of meat. Mr. Watts of Assistance Unlimited compared the killer to Jack the Ripper, too. It reminded me of what Smithson had said." Melvin looked at Max and shook his head with a sad smile. "But Phillips is a respected businessman, just like I am. We don't do such things. Do we?"

⤜∞⤛

Michael Groseclose checked his appearance for the tenth time, ensuring that his top hat was perched just so atop his head and that his gloves were tugged on to a tight fit over his hands. He tried to ignore the feeling that he was a kid playing dress up as he strode toward the front door of Assistance Unlimited. He'd never worn the mask during the daytime hours before and it all felt a little silly in the light of day.

Before he'd reached the door, Eun Jiwon and Morgan Watts were waiting to greet him. Eun stood with fists clenched at his sides and Morgan's hand drifted close to the interior of his coat, where a gun obviously lay in wait.

The Dark Gentleman raised both hands and came to a halt. "Like I said last night, I'm on your side."

Eun raised his chin. "Then tell us why you're wearing that mask, Mr. Groseclose."

The Dark Gentleman flinched as if struck. His hands lowered immediately and he didn't even bother trying to hide his dismay. "You know who I am?"

"We have cameras mounted all over this entire block," Eun explained, triumph in his voice. "While you parked down the street and started changing into your getup, I was looking to see who those licensed plates belonged to. If you're getting into the vigilante game, you need to learn the ropes."

"Damn." The Dark Gentleman shook his head, unsure how to continue past this point. He was saved the trouble when Morgan relaxed his stance and pulled the door open.

"Come on in, kid. Let's hear your story."

———— ∞ ————

Samantha Grace had been charged with the task of watching the exterior of the Groseclose home during Max's meeting with the others. She had sat in a dark sedan across the street, listening in as the others back at Assistance Unlimited were doing. When Phillips had stormed out, she'd been forced to make a decision: should she wait where she was or should she follow the bearlike man who obviously had a temper? In the end, her female intuition told her to stick with Phillips, so she followed him at a distance as he drove back to his house. She drove past as she pulled into his driveway, circling back around the block and finally parking a few hundred feet from the front door. To her surprise, she saw that the entrance was standing wide open and that one of the potted plants just outside the steps had been overturned.

Never one to shy away from danger, Samantha was out of the car in a flash. Given the fact that both Smithson and Hansome were dead, it stood to reason that Phillips might be another target.

The petite blond hurried across the street, a small handgun clutched in her right hand. Her heels clicked on the asphalt and she was glad that she'd worn slacks today. She enjoyed the feeling of femininity that came with skirts and dresses, but they were difficult to fight in.

Samantha crept up the stairs toward the open door. "Mr. Phillips? Are you in there? I'm with Assistance Unlimited."

Stepping inside, Samantha noticed no signs of a struggle. She was about to raise her voice and identify herself again when she heard the creak of the door behind her. She whirled around to see Devil Face lunging for her, blade in hand. That it was Phillips was undeniable – the build and the fact that he still wore the same clothing made that quite clear. But the mask, with its distorted demon's features, was disconcerting.

Samantha pulled the trigger but her shot went wild, passing harmlessly over Devil Face's shoulder. Well versed in jujitsu, Samantha was able to quickly evade a swipe of the blade, but her position in the foyer didn't allow her much room to work with and Devil Face was so large that she was immediately pressed up against the wall.

"I'm going to help you," the killer said, speaking in a voice that was much higher-pitched than the one she had heard Phillips use earlier. "Don't be afraid."

If the situation hadn't been so terrifying, Samantha would have laughed. Was he really telling her not to be afraid, even as he was stabbing wildly at her with a sharpened blade? Men were always confusing to her but killers were the worst: the natural inclinations men had toward being dense were amplified by madness.

Samantha jammed her knee into the big man's crotch and she was rewarded with a squeal of pain from him. She drew up her pistol, pressing the barrel directly against the forehead of the mask but before she could fire, a white-hot pain sliced through her midsection. She felt rapidly spreading warmth spiral out from her stomach and she didn't have to look down to realize that the killer's knife was deep inside her.

If I die, I'm taking you with me, she thought, pulling hard on the trigger. Devil Face's head jerked back as the bullet struck his mask and he staggered back in shock. Samantha reached down and gripped the hilt of the knife, growing dizzy as she began to extract the blade from her stomach. She tossed the weapon down and blinked away the stars that were obscuring her vision. As she sagged to her knees, she realized that Devil Face had recovered and was standing over her. His mask had protected him from the full impact but it had split in two and the pieces now lay on the floor. Phillips was staring at her, a tiny dot of blood between his eyes. His hands continually opened and closed and he was breathing heavily, as if he were teetering on the verge of anger or tears.

"You bitch," he hissed. "You broke my face."

Samantha struggled to lift her gun again, but her strength was fading nearly as quickly as the blood was gushing from her midsection. She heard the sound of Devil Face's fist rushing through the air toward her head but she never saw it. The blow slammed her skull against the wall and rushed her into blessed darkness.

Phillips watched her for a moment before bending down and almost reverently picking up the broken pieces of his mask. "You have a lot of sins that are going to be washed away," he said, casting his gaze over Samantha's bloody form. "Just remember: pain is the crucible that will forge the perfect you."

The Dark Gentleman tried to maintain his composure but it was hard to, seated as he was in the headquarters of the famous Assistance Unlimited, with no less than Lazarus Gray himself facing him across the table. Morgan and Eun stood behind their employer, wearing very different expressions. Morgan looked bemused while Eun seemed to grow more annoyed by the minute. The face of Lazarus was so impassive that the Dark Gentleman had no idea what the man was thinking.

"So I'm here because I want to help. I'm not looking to join Assistance Unlimited, but I thought that we could pool our resources."

Eun barked out a laugh. "What resources do you have that we don't?"

"Enough," Lazarus said and Eun fell silent. "Michael, I admire your desire to help this city. It takes a special kind of man to put his life on the line for strangers. Nevertheless, it's foolhardy to go into situations like this without proper training and know-how."

"I've done the best I could," Michael retorted. "It's not like there's a vigilante school where I could enroll."

"Understandable," Lazarus admitted. "But you're just as likely to get yourself killed or get an innocent killed… if you'll permit me, I'd be willing to tutor you in various skills."

Michael couldn't hide the pleasure he felt. "I'd be honored."

Just then, a phone rang in the next room and Morgan went to answer it. He returned in less than a minute. "That was Davies. He says that the meeting's broken up at Groseclose's. But get this: Samantha's gone, car and all. He thinks she went off after Phillips."

Eun glanced up at the clock. "She should have reported in by now."

All of them had overheard Melvin's words at the meeting and understood what they meant. But the arrival of The Dark Gentleman had prevented them from going off in pursuit of Phillips for questioning.

Now Gray was in motion and it was a terrible thing to behold. His emerald-colored eye shone like a gem while the brown one seemed to smolder. His normally impassive face was now set in grim determination and from the way his jaw continually clenched and released, it was obvious that a cauldron of emotion was now at play. He stood up and began barking orders that were impossible to ignore.

"Morgan, bring the car around. Eun, tell Max to meet us at Phillips' house. Michael, you're with us."

The Dark Gentleman tried -- and failed -- to keep from grinning. "I'm ready."

"We'll see if you are," Gray responded.

⊶⊷

The Rook didn't need to be told where to go. He was already in flight before Eun ever made it to the telephone. He borrowed Groseclose's car without asking and burned rubber through the rain-slicked city streets. Before arriving in Sovereign, Max had heard the jokes about how often it rained here, but he'd quickly learned that it wasn't hyperbole. It was as if God himself were constantly shedding tears for what had become of Sovereign.

The Rook tried to ignore the pounding in his head, but it was strong enough to force him to grit his teeth. His vision was swimming as the world around him intermingled with possible futures. The visions of future crimes that he often saw were far more of a curse than a boon and he'd prayed numerous times to be rid of them. He was forced to pull over to the curb, knowing that he had to ride it out before he could safely continue on his way.

The vision became clearer, obliterating everything else. The Rook saw a dark basement, the walls stained with gore. There were barrels or canisters of some kind, filled with the blood of Devil Face's victims. Samantha was there, her nude body dangling from the ceiling, her arms stretched above her head. Devil Face was preparing his blades but he wasn't alone, there was another in the shadows, nearly invisible. The Rook, who routinely walked along the dark and narrow passage that lay between the sane world and the supernatural, felt like he recognized this figure: he knew she was female and that her stench had been a constant companion to him over the years.

With a shiver that rocked his spine, The Rook realized that Lady Death herself was there in that room. She was no simple manifestation of Phillips' madness, this was the dark lady herself, the one who kissed all men at the end of their days.

Lady Death stepped into view, her body hidden by her robes. She moved forward until she dominated The Rook's vision and he could see the curve of her jaw beneath her hood. She opened her mouth and spoke, her voice sounding so seductive that Max nearly forgot what an awful thing she was: he had spent his whole life fighting to avoid her and to save others from her embrace but now, he realized how easy it would be to fall into her arms. "Max," she whispered, "come to me. It's time."

A rapping on the driver's side window of his car snapped The Rook out of his reverie. He turned his head to see a police officer standing there, obviously having come to check on him. When the officer saw that The Rook wore a mask, his eyes widened. Before anything else could happen, The Rook floored the accelerator and left a trail of burning rubber in his wake. There was no time to waste now: Samantha Grace was in the presence of Death herself.

—⟨∞⟩—

Chapter VI
Darkness

Samantha woke up to a world of pain. The joints in her shoulders felt like they were on fire and as her mind cleared, she realized that she was shackled by her wrists to the ceiling of Phillips' basement. Her clothing was gone and her nude body was covered by a fine sheen of sweat. The back of her head throbbed and her mouth felt abnormally dry and tasted tinny. She realized that she had bitten her tongue before falling unconscious and swallowed a good bit of blood.

Devil Face was about ten feet away from her, humming a song to himself as he polished a series of sharp knives and bone saws. His mask had been crudely repaired with glue and even in the dim lighting, Samantha could see that it hadn't fully dried yet - bubbles of glue glistened in the candlelight. Even as she tested the strength of her bonds, Samantha recognized the tune that Devil Face was humming: *Smoke Gets In Your Eyes* by Paul Whiteman. She suddenly realized she was never going to like that song ever again.

Devil Face heard the rattling of the chains and glanced over at her. His eyes traveled up her toned legs, past the mound of Venus between her legs, over the flat stomach and pert breasts. He caught his breath, hating the way she made him feel. It was the way of women: to tantalize men with their bodies until the spirit was made weak. He would very much enjoy purifying her. He would cut away all the pieces that teased him and then he would drain her of blood, lovingly washing every bit of her until she was as pure as the driven snow.

"I was worried you weren't going to wake up," Devil Face purred, moving toward her with a scalpel in his right hand. His foot brushed a bucket filled with tubing and Samantha swallowed hard, not wanting to imagine what it was for. "You're going to be my thirteenth. That's a sacred number."

Samantha grimly regarded the killer, refusing to show even the tiniest bit of fear. She trusted that Lazarus and the others would find their way there – and if they didn't, she'd just have to free herself. "Should I feel honored?"

"Yes. You should."

"Let me go, Phillips. You're in enough trouble as it is. Hurt me and I can't promise that they'll even let the police take you in. Lazarus might just skin you alive."

"I doubt that. I've read all about your employer. He's committed to bringing criminals to justice. He'd actually blame himself if anything happened to me."

"Morgan won't beat himself up for putting a bullet in your brain," Samantha said with a smile. That, at least, wasn't a lie. Morgan carried quite a torch for her and she knew that he'd stop at nothing to avenge her.

Devil Face brought the scalpel up to Samantha's cheek and drew it slowly across the skin, leaving a thin trail of blood. "You're so beautiful," he whispered. "I wish you weren't such a whore… but if you weren't we couldn't share this moment together, could we? So maybe I'm secretly glad."

Samantha flinched at the onset of new pain, but she said nothing. Her eyes caught the flicker of movement over Devil Face's shoulder and she gasped. "Is someone else here with us?" she asked, unable to maintain her silence any longer.

Devil Face stepped back, his eyes wide with surprise beneath his mask. "You can see her?"

Samantha peered into the shadows but saw nothing at all. "I thought," she began, but then fell quiet again with a shake of her head. "It was nothing."

Devil Face smiled, momentarily taken aback but now once more in control. No one else had ever seen Lady Death, not even the girls who had rested on the precipice between the world of the living and of the dead. "Well, it's time we began in earnest. You're the last one."

"What does that mean?" Samantha asked, as Devil Face turned away from her. He moved over to the tray of sharp implements and set down his scalpel, plucking up one of the bone saws and examining the teeth on the blade.

"Thirteen girls have to die," he said, not caring if she knew his secrets. It was too late for her and he was too close to achieving ultimate power. What could it hurt? "And then Lady Death will cross over onto this plane and she'll make me her consort."

Samantha heard the dreamy nature of his voice and couldn't help but think he was absolutely insane. But she'd seen some very strange things as a member of Assistance Unlimited, so she wasn't prepared to discount it completely.

"I'm not sure why being Death's lover would be a good thing," she said, hoping to keep Devil Face talking long enough to allow her friends to find them.

"You haven't felt her touch," Devil Face replied. He turned toward her with the bone saw in hand. As he approached, he bent down and grabbed the bucket filled with tubing and carried it in his other hand. He set the bucket down next to her dangling feet. "But you will soon enough."

Samantha slammed her foot against Devil Face in an attempt to hurt him, but her position didn't allow her to put any real strength behind the blow and it elicited nothing more than a chuckle from the madman.

"Don't fight," Devil Face warned. "It will only make things harder for you."

The next moment was one that Samantha would long remember. Devil Face placed the sharp blade against her shoulder, obviously intending to remove her right arm with no anesthetic whatsoever. Just before he began his grisly task, a figure descended the stairs and threw himself at Devil Face's back. The impact knocked the villain aside, though the blade drug painfully across Samantha's arm, taking a long stretch of flesh with it.

Devil Face whirled about to see Lazarus Gray facing him, hands balled into fists. Rapidly moving into the room were Morgan, The Dark Gentleman and Eun, all of whom looked at Samantha with concern. Normally, she would have felt embarrassed by her nudity but at the moment she didn't care – her only desire was to be freed so she could help bring this killer to justice.

It was Morgan who reached her first, steadfastly keeping his eyes off her nakedness. He fumbled with the locks around her wrists, concern for her making him sloppy. "We'll get that cut sewn up," he said, as if her bleeding arm was important to her.

Eun saw that Morgan was busy with Samantha so he moved to assist his employer, The Dark Gentleman in tow. Devil Face was swinging his blade with great skill, forcing Lazarus to keep his distance.

"There's too many of them," Devil Face hissed. "Please – help me!"

The Dark Gentleman glanced around, wondering whom it was that Devil Face was talking to.

"He's talking to the woman over there," Lazarus explained, nodding his head in the direction of Lady Death.

"I don't see anyone!"

"She's there. Trust me." Lazarus knew that the woman before them was not human. His past experiences as a member of the Illuminati had included many forays into the supernatural. As such, his mind was open to perceiving things that most people could simply not accept. He could see Lady Death as clearly as Devil Face could – and, truthfully, so could all of his aides, but because of the unreality of the situation, their minds refused to accept what their eyes beheld. Thus, they could not acknowledge it.

Lazarus ducked under a swipe of Devil Face's blade and struck out with a karate chop that knocked the air from the man's lungs. Devil Face recovered quickly, however, driving the bone saw against Gray's neck an instant later. Blood spilled freely, but Lazarus knew that it would look worse than it really was: nothing vital had been struck.

Eun smelled something awful, like an ancient tomb had been thrown open. He gagged and backed away, his eyes widening as half a dozen figures emerged from the shadows, shambling toward them with open sores dotting their skins and portions of white bone protruding. These were the undead, summoned forth by Lady Death and their presence was a sign of just how close Devil Face was to completing his awful ritual. He had loosened the barriers between Death's realm and those of mortal man… and now her warriors were spilling through.

The first of the zombies uttered a long, guttural moan and reached for Eun. The young Korean batted the hand aside and unleashed a series of kick punches and kicks, most of which had no obvious effect. To Eun, it felt like he was attacking a side of beef. It wasn't until one of his fists crashed through the thing's ribs and was momentarily stuck that he realized the full danger he was in: these creatures were not alive and were thus immune to all forms of pain.

Eun looked about and saw that the monsters, all of which were grabbing at his clothes and hair, now surrounded him. One of them dug its claws into the meat of Eun's arm, tearing into the flesh and spilling blood.

The Dark Gentleman shared Eun's horror. Unlike the members of Assistance Unlimited, this was his first contact with the supernatural and it was almost enough to shake his sanity. But his sense of self-preservation was strong enough to propel him into combat, shooting several bullets into the torso of the nearest zombie. The impacts caused the undead creature to pause but didn't deter it from coming onward.

Lazarus knew that things were quickly spiraling out of control and made an effort to end his battle with Devil Face all the faster. He lowered his shoulder and charged like a maddened bull, slamming his bulk into the big man's chest. They tumbled back until the basement wall halted Devil Face's progress. Devil Face grunted hard and struck wildly with the bone saw. He repeatedly cut Gray's face and shoulders, but the leader of Assistance Unlimited ignored the pain and continued pummeling his enemy, breaking ribs, smashing a nose and finally fracturing Devil Face's hip.

The man who had lived as Robert Phillips these past few years, coasting on a fabricated past until he had achieved a position of power, now knew that his plans were swiftly coming to an end. He sagged to his knees, pain blotting out all rational thought. He saw The Rook entering the basement and he wanted to curse the unfairness of it all, but he knew that it was his own fault. He had stuck to a plan for years, killing only those girls who wouldn't be missed. But Schuller had been an impulse murder and it had led to his downfall.

"Don't give up hope just yet," Lady Death purred and her voice seeped directly into her follower's mind. "We may yet have our victory…."

The Rook stared about him in amazement. He saw the lovely young Samantha Grace being freed from her chains by Morgan Watts; Eun Jiwon was in danger of being ripped to shreds by a half dozen undead; Lady Death herself stood on the edge of it all, a haunting smile visible from beneath her hood; Devil Face was on the floor, flecks of blood on his lips; and – most

BARRY REESE

surprisingly of all – a villain from his past.

Turning to face him was Doctor York, a madman who had tried to open a portal to Hell back in '33. The Rook had defeated him then but the incident had haunted him ever since, mostly because he knew how close he'd come to losing the battle.

The Rook drew one of his pistols and took careful aim. If York was involved in all this, then things were even more dangerous than he'd assumed.

Lazarus Gray could scarcely believe what he was seeing. Coming down the stairs in all his arrogant glory was Walther Lunt. Lunt was the German mastermind who had recruited Richard Winthrop into the Illuminati and he had eventually become Winthrop's greatest foe, overseeing the plot that led to Winthrop's "death" and "rebirth" as Lazarus Gray. Since then, the two had clashed repeatedly and Gray had come to know Lunt's ruined visage almost as well as he knew his own. Badly scarred by an acid attack years ago, the right side of Lunt's face was a mass of burned tissue and the ugliness had seeped into the man's very soul.

Suddenly things began to fall into place: no doubt Lunt was somehow the puppet master behind all of this, pulling Devil Face's strings in some elaborate plot to destroy Gray and his allies.

After casting one quick glance at Devil Face to ensure that he was in no shape to re-enter the fray, Lazarus threw himself toward his old enemy. He managed to drive Lunt against the wall but the other man responded with more skill than Lazarus remembered him possessing, slipping an arm under Gray's and using the bigger man's momentum to toss him to the ground.

Lunt slammed a foot down, narrowly missing Gray's skull when Lazarus rolled out of the way. Lazarus reached out and grabbed Lunt's leg, driving a fist just above the German's kneecap. A loud cracking sound indicated that Lazarus had successfully broken the man's leg and Lunt quickly joined Lazarus on the floor. They grappled now, hands wrapped around each other's throat. There was no letting up now and it was obvious to each that this would be their final battle.

The Rook was in the fight of his life. In their last meeting, Doctor York had shown none of the skills that he was now displaying. The made scientist had just broken one of The Rook's legs and he was now choking the life from him. The Rook had to exert all his will to remain conscious as he fought to take York down. Somewhere in all of this, The Rook's pistol had been knocked from his grip, but the vigilante had more pressing concerns at the moment.

Stars were beginning to appear before The Rook's eyes and he knew that he was literally seconds away from blacking out. He drew his head back and then slammed it forward, smashing his forehead directly into York's nose. Blood spurted from York's nostrils and his grip weakened enough for The Rook to pull free, gasping for air.

The Rook scrambled to his feet, his shoe bumping against something hard on the floor. Looking down, he spotted his pistol and he quickly snatched it up. His broken leg ached horribly and he was unable to put much weight on it but with one good shot, the battle would be over.

York was on his feet again and The Rook realized that he had a perfect shot: one bullet to the villain's head and the city would be safe.

Just as he was about to pull the trigger, he caught a glimpse of Lady Death. The hooded figure was watching the battle with obvious interest and The Rook momentarily assumed that it was because she was concerned for York's survival. But then something occurred to him: where was Lazarus Gray? His aides were here, actively battling the zombies – even poor Samantha, naked as the day she was born. But their erstwhile leader was nowhere to be seen.

The Rook suddenly realized that he'd been duped. He twisted, turning the barrel of the gun on Lady Death.

⚬⚬⚬

Lazarus had tensed, preparing for a potentially fatal shot to come from Lunt's gun. Blood was flowing freely from his nose, but Lazarus was ignoring it. If he didn't time his movements just so, he was about to die... and all that he'd accomplished with Assistance Unlimited was going to come to an end.

Lazarus caught Lunt's eyes shift to something over his shoulder and he risked a glance, wanting to make sure that Devil Face wasn't back in the fray. What he saw gave him pause: it was Lady Death, standing half in the shadows. Seeing her brought a bit of clarity to his mind – something about this situation did not feel right. The last time he'd checked on Lunt's whereabouts, he'd been in Europe... how had he managed to spearhead this plan involving Devil Face? Especially since the murders began before Lunt ever came to Sovereign in pursuit of Lazarus? Had he just taken over a pre-existing plot of some kind? Or was all of this just a bizarre illusion perpetrated by Lady Death?

Narrowing his eyes and focusing all of his amazing willpower allowed Lazarus to suddenly see the truth: the man before him was not Wilhelm Lunt at all. He had been battling The Rook for the past several minutes, while his aides fought for their survival.

Just as The Rook turned his gun on Lady Death, Lazarus turned and jumped into the middle of the scene involving the zombies and the other members of

Assistance Unlimited. Samantha's body was covered with scratches and bruises. She was fighting bravely, but was unarmed and had been backed into a corner by two of the undead. They tugged at her hair and opened their mouths in an attempt to catch her tender flesh between their teeth. Lazarus unsheathed the dagger he kept on the calf of his left leg and drove the blade through the head of one of the monsters, freeing Samantha to dispatch the other by gripping its skull in her hands and repeatedly driving it into the wall. When the thing's head had been reduced to a liquid pool of gore, Samantha shoved it away from her.

"Glad to have you back with us," she said with a smile. "I was wondering what was up with you and The Rook."

Lazarus removed his jacket and draped it around her shoulders. "A momentary lapse of rationality," he explained.

A gunshot rang out, sounding abnormally loud in the basement. All heads, even those of the remaining zombies, turned to see Lady Death stagger back. The bullet couldn't really destroy her, but it was enough to ruin her tenuous hold on this plane. Her body shimmered, turning to thin trails of smoky vapor that eventually dissipated. Devil Face cried out, a mournful sound that spoke of dashed hopes and lost love.

The four remaining zombies seemed uncertain now, their hungers no longer enough to drive them forward. They became easy prey for Morgan, The Dark Gentleman, and Eun, the three men using differing means to dispose of the beasts: Morgan and The Dark Gentleman put bullets through their brains while Eun preferred bashing their skulls in.

In the aftermath, the heroes stood silently for a moment, lost in their own thoughts. When enough time had passed for everyone to feel like they'd regained their footing in the real world, it was Lazarus who spoke first. "We should tie up Phillips and call the authorities."

The Rook cleared his throat, gun still in hand. "I think we should kill him. He's dangerous – and the police won't believe half of the truth, even if we decide to tell them. With his money and clout, he might pay somebody off in this town and get off scot-free. The best way to deal with a rabid dog is to put him down."

"That's not how I do things," Lazarus retorted. "I know that the justice system in Sovereign is corrupt, but we have to give it a chance to do the right thing."

The Rook's fingers shifted on the gun he held and he knew that no one would be able to stop him if he chose to end Devil Face's life here and now. But he liked Lazarus and didn't want to test their friendship in that way. He holstered his weapon and nodded toward The Dark Gentleman. "Decided to add a masked man to your team, Lazarus?"

The Dark Gentleman smiled. "I'm just helping out."

The Rook watched as Lazarus used a thin, almost invisible cord to wrap up Devil Face's hands. The killer was sobbing softly and put up no resistance. The cord was obviously of Gray's own design and The Rook knew there was no chance of the villain escaping, even if he came to his senses and tried.

The members of Assistance Unlimited crowded around one another now, sharing their experiences. The men were anxious to know that Samantha was mostly unharmed and she was grateful that none of them mentioned the fact that they'd seen her naked.

The Rook slowly ascended the stairs, preferring not to say goodbye. He had forged some friendships here, but he had other places to be and he had never been good with partings. He noticed that The Dark Gentleman had the same idea. The young man was making his way to the stairs when The Rook stepped out onto the first floor and hurried out into the Sovereign City streets.

To The Rook's surprise, the sun had come through the clouds. The darkness still clung to the edges of the sky, but it looked like they were being driven back by the rays of the sun. For a moment, The Rook thought he saw the face of Lady Death in one of the clouds but then it was gone, replaced by a beam of light that shot forth, like a spotlight.

For one day at least, the forces of good had won – and in a place like Sovereign, that was something to be proud of.

A TIMELINE AS IT PERTAINS TO LAZARUS GRAY
AND OTHER CHARACTERS CREATED BY BARRY REESE

Major Events specific to certain stories and novels are included in brackets. Some of this information contains **SPOILERS** *for The Rook, Lazarus Gray, Eobard Grace and other stories.*

———

1748 - Johann Adam Weishaupt is born.

1776 - Johann Adam Weishaupt forms The Illuminati. He adopts the guise of the original Lazarus Gray in group meetings, reflecting his "rebirth" and the "moral ambiguity" of the group.

1865 - Eobard Grace returns home from his actions in the American Civil War. Takes possession of the Book of Shadows from his uncle Frederick. [*"The World of Shadow," The Family Grace: An Extraordinary History*]

1877 - Eobard Grace is summoned to the World of Shadows, where he battles Uris-Kor and fathers a son, Korben. [*"The World of Shadow," The Family Grace: An Extraordinary History*]

1885 - Along with his niece Miriam and her paramour Ian Sinclair, Eobard returns to the World of Shadows to halt the merging of that world with Earth. [*"The Flesh Wheel," The Family Grace: An Extraordinary History*]

1890 - Eobard fathers a second son, Leopold.

1895 - Felix Cole (the Bookbinder) is born.

1900 - Max Davies is born to publisher Warren Davies and his wife, heiress Margaret Davies.

1901 - Leonid Kaslov is born.

1905 - Richard Winthrop is born in San Francisco.

1908 - Warren Davies is murdered by Ted Grossett, a killer nicknamed "Death's Head". [*"Lucifer's Cage", the Rook Volume One, more details shown in "Origins," the Rook Volume Two*] Hans Merkel kills his own father. [*"Blitzkrieg," the Rook Volume Two*]

1910 - Evelyn Gould is born.

1913 - Felix Cole meets the Cockroach Man and becomes part of The Great Work. [*"The Great Work," Startling Stories # 5*]

1914 - Margaret Davies passes away in her sleep. Max is adopted by his uncle Reginald.

1915 - Felix Cole marries Charlotte Grace, Eobard Grace's cousin.

1916 - Leonid Kaslov's father Nikolai becomes involved in the plot to assassinate Rasputin.

1917 - Betsy Cole is born to Felix and Charlotte Grace Cole. Nikolai Kaslov is murdered.

1918 - Max Davies begins wandering the world. Richard Winthrop's parents die in an accident.

1922 - Warlike Manchu tutors Max Davies in Kyoto.

1925 - Max Davies becomes the Rook, operating throughout Europe.

1926 - Charlotte Grace dies. Richard Winthrop has a brief romance with exchange student Sarah Dumas.

1927 - Richard Winthrop graduates from Yale. On the night of his graduation, he is recruited into The Illuminati. Max and Leopold Grace battle the Red Lord in Paris. Richard Winthrop meets Miya Shimada in Japan, where he purchases The McGuinness Obelisk for The Illuminati.

1928 - The Rook returns to Boston.

1929 - Richard Winthrop destroys a coven of vampires in Mexico.

1932 - The Rook hunts down his father's killer [*"Origins," the Rook Volume Two*]

1933 - Jacob Trench uncovers Lucifer's Cage. [*"Lucifer's Cage", the Rook Volume One*] The Rook battles Doctor York [*All-Star Pulp Comics # 1*] After a failed attempt at betraying The Illuminati, Richard Winthrop wakes up on the shores of Sovereign City with no memory of his name or past. He has only one clue to his past in his possession: a small medallion adorned with the words Lazarus Gray and the image of a naked man with the head of a lion. [*"The Girl With the Phantom Eyes," The Adventures of Lazarus Gray Volume One*]

1934 - Now calling himself Lazarus Gray, Richard Winthrop forms Assistance Unlimited in Sovereign City. He recruits Samantha Grace, Morgan Watts and Eun Jiwon [*"The Girl With the Phantom Eyes," The Adventures of Lazarus Gray Volume One*] Walther Lunt aids German scientists in unleashing the power Die Glocke, which in turn frees the demonic forces of Satan's Circus [*"Die Glocke," The Adventures of Lazarus Gray Volume Two*]. The entity who will become known as The

Black Terror is created [*"The Making of a Hero,"* The Adventures of *Lazarus Gray Volume Three*].

1935 - Felix Cole and his daughter Betsy seek out the Book of Eibon. [*"The Great Work," The Family Grace: An Extraordinary History*] Assistance Unlimited undertakes a number of missions, defeating the likes of Walther Lunt, Doc Pemberley, Malcolm Goodwill & Black Heart, Princess Femi & The Undying, Mr. Skull, The Axeman and The Yellow Claw [*"The Girl With the Phantom Eyes," "The Devil's Bible," "The Corpse Screams at Midnight," "The Burning Skull," "The Axeman of Sovereign City," and "The God of Hate," The Adventures of Lazarus Gray Volume One*] The Rook journeys to Sovereign City and teams up with Assistance Unlimited to battle Devil Face [*"Darkness, Spreading Its Wings of Black," the Rook Volume Six*]. Lazarus Gray and Assistance Unlimited become embroiled in the search for Die Glocke [*"Die Glocke," The Adventures of Lazarus Gray Volume Two*]

1936 - Assistance Unlimited completes their hunt for Die Glocke and confronts the threat of Jack-In-Irons. Abigail Cross and Jakob Sporrenberg join Assistance Unlimited [*"Die Glocke," The Adventures of Lazarus Gray Volume Two*]. The Rook moves to Atlanta and recovers the Dagger of Elohim from Felix Darkholme. The Rook meets Evelyn Gould. The Rook battles Jacob Trench. [*"Lucifer's Cage", the Rook Volume One*]. Reed Barrows revives Camilla. [*"Kingdom of Blood," The Rook Volume One*]. Kevin Atwill is abandoned in the Amazonian jungle by his friends, a victim of the Gorgon legacy. [*"The Gorgon Conspiracy," The Rook Volume Two*]. Nathaniel Caine's lover is killed by Tweedledum while Dan Daring looks on [*"Catalyst," The Rook Volume Three*] Assistance Unlimited teams up with The Black Terror to battle Promethus and The Titan in South America [*"The Making of a Hero," The Adventures of Lazarus Gray Volume Three*]

1937 - Max and Evelyn marry. Camilla attempts to create Kingdom of Blood. World's ancient vampires awaken and the Rook is 'marked' by Nyarlathotep. Gerhard Klempt's experiments are halted. William McKenzie becomes Chief of Police in Atlanta. The Rook meets Benson, who clears his record with the police. [*"Kingdom of Blood," the Rook Volume One*]. Hank Wilbon is murdered, leading to his eventual resurrection as the Reaper. [*"Kaslov's Fire," The Rook Volume Two*]. The Rook and Evelyn become unwelcome guests of Baron Werner Prescott, eventually foiling his attempts to create an artificial island and a weather-controlling weapon for the Nazis [*The Rook: The Killing Games*]

1938 - The Rook travels to Great City to aid the Moon Man in battling Lycos and his Gasping Death. The Rook destroys the physical shell of Nyarlathotep and gains his trademark signet ring. [*"The Gasping Death," The Rook Volume One*]. The jungle hero known as the Revenant is killed [*"Death from the Jungle," The Rook Volume Four*]

1939 - Ibis and the Warlike Manchu revive the Abomination. Evelyn becomes pregnant and gives birth to their first child, a boy named William. [*"Abominations," The Rook Volume One*]. The Rook allies himself with Leonid Kaslov to stop the Reaper's attacks and to foil the plans of Rasputin. [*"Kaslov's Fire," the Rook Volume Two*] Violet Cambridge and Will McKenzie become embroiled in the hunt for a mystical item known as The Damned Thing [*The Damned Thing*]

1940 - The Warlike Manchu returns with a new pupil -- Hans Merkel, aka Shinigami. The Warlike Manchu kidnaps William Davies but the Rook and Leonid Kaslov manage to rescue the boy. [*"Blitzkrieg," the Rook Volume Two*] The Rook journeys to Germany alongside the Domino Lady and Will McKenzie to combat the demonic organization known as Bloodwerks. [*"Bloodwerks," the Rook Volume Two*] Kevin Atwill seeks revenge against his former friends, bringing him into conflict with the Rook [*"The Gorgon Conspiracy," The Rook Volume Two*]. The Rook takes a young vampire under his care, protecting him from a cult that worships a race of beings known as The Shambling Ones. With the aid of Leonid Kazlov, the cult is destroyed [*"The Shambling Ones," The Rook Volume Two*]

1941 - Philip Gallagher, a journalist, uncovers the Rook's secret identity but chooses to become an ally of the vigilante rather than reveal it to the world [*"Origins," the Rook Volume Two*]. The Rook teams with the Black Bat and Ascott Keane, as well as a reluctant Doctor Satan, in defeating the plans of the sorcerer Arias [*"The Bleeding Hells"*]. The Rook rescues McKenzie from the Iron Maiden [*"The Iron Maiden," The Rook Volume Three*]

1942 - The Rook battles a Nazi super agent known as the Grim Reaper, who is attempting to gather the Crystal Skulls [*"The Three Skulls," The Rook Volume Three*]. The Rook teams with Ascott Keane and the Green Lama to defeat a monster that has escaped from The World of Shadows [*"The Gilded Beast," The Family Grace: An Extraordinary History*]. The Rook becomes embroiled in a plot by Sun Koh and a group of Axis killers known as The Furies. The Rook and Sun Koh end up in deadly battle on the banks of the Potomac River. [*"The Scorched God," The Rook Volume Six*]. In London, the Rook and Evelyn meet Nathaniel Caine (aka the Catalyst) and Rachel Winters, who are involved in stopping the Nazis from creating the Un-Earth. They battle Doctor Satan and the Black Zeppelin [*"Catalyst," The Rook Volume Three*]. Evelyn learns she's pregnant with a second child. The Rook solves the mystery of the Roanoke Colony [*"The Lost Colony," The Rook Volume Three*] The Warlike Manchu is revived and embarks upon a search for the Philosopher's Stone [*"The Resurrection Gambit," The Rook Volume Three*]

1943 - The Rook is confronted by the twin threats of Fernando Pasarin and the undead pirate Hendrik van der Decken [*"The Phantom Vessel," The Rook Volume Four*]. Evelyn and Max become the parents of a second child, Emma Davies. The Rook teams with the daughter of the Revenant to battle Hermann Krupp and the Golden Goblin [*"Death from the Jungle," The Rook Volume Four*] The Rook battles Doctor Satan over possession of an ancient Mayan tablet [*"The Four Rooks," The Rook Volume Four*]. The Rook travels to Peru to battle an undead magician called The Spook [*"Spook," The Rook Volume Four*]. Baron Rudolph Gustav gains possession of the Rod of Aaron and kidnaps Evelyn, forcing the Rook into an uneasy alliance with the Warlike Manchu [*"Dead of Night," The Rook Volume Four*]. Doctor Satan flees to the hidden land of Vorium, where the Rook allies with Frankenstein's Monster to bring him to justice [*"Satan's Trial," The Rook Volume Four*]. Tim Roland is recruited by The Flame and Miss Masque [*"The Ivory Machine," The Rook Volume Five*]. The Black Terror investigates a German attempt to replicate his powers and becomes friends with a scientist named Clarke [*"Terrors"*]

1944 - The Rook organizes a strike force composed of Revenant, Frankenstein's Monster, Catalyst and Esper. The group is known as The Claws of the Rook and they take part in two notable adventures in this year: against the diabolical Mr. Dee and then later against an alliance between

Doctor Satan and the Warlike Manchu [*"The Diabolical Mr. Dee" and "A Plague of Wicked Men", The Rook Volume Five*].

1946 - The Rook discovers that Adolph Hitler is still alive and has become a vampire in service to Dracula. In an attempt to stop the villains from using the Holy Lance to take over the world, the Rook allies with the Claws of the Rook, a time traveler named Jenny Everywhere, a thief called Belladonna and Leonid Kaslov. The villains are defeated and Max's future is revealed to still be in doubt. Events shown from 2006 on are just a possible future. The Rook also has several encounters with a demonically powered killer known as Stickman. [*"The Devil's Spear," The Rook Volume Five*]. The Rook encounters a madman named Samuel Garibaldi (aka Rainman) and his ally, Dr. Gottlieb Hochmuller. The Rook and his Claws team defeat the villainous duo and several new heroes join the ranks of the Claws team -- Miss Masque, Black Terror & Tim and The Flame. [*"The Ivory Machine," The Rook Volume Five*]

1953 - The Rook acquires the Looking Glass from Lu Chang. [*"Black Mass," The Rook Volume One*]

1961 - Max's son William becomes the second Rook. [*"The Four Rooks," The Rook Volume Four*]

1967 - The second Rook battles and defeats the Warlike Manchu, who is in possession of the Mayan Tablet that Doctor Satan coveted in '43. Evelyn Davies dies. [*"The Four Rooks," The Rook Volume Four*]

1970 - William Davies (the second Rook) commits suicide by jumping from a Manhattan rooftop. Emma Davies (Max's daughter and William's brother) becomes the Rook one week later, in February. [*"The Four Rooks," The Rook Volume Four*]

1973 - The third Rook is accompanied by Kayla Kaslov (daughter of Leonid Kaslov) on a trip to Brazil, where the two women defeat the Black Annis and claim the Mayan Tablet that's popped up over the course of three decades. Emma gives it to her father, who in turn passes it on to Catalyst (Nathaniel Caine) [*"The Four Rooks," The Rook Volume Four*]

~1985 - Max resumes operating as the Rook, adventuring sporadically. Due to various magical events, he remains far more active than most men his age. The reasons for Emma giving up the role are unknown at this time.

Events depicted in the years 2006 forward occur in one of many possible futures for The Rook. As revealed in Volume Five of The Rook Chronicles, the events of 2006 onward may -- or may not -- be the ultimate future of Max Davies.

2006 - The Black Mass Barrier rises, enveloping the world in a magical field. The World of Shadows merges with Earth. Fiona Grace (descended from Eobard) becomes a worldwide celebrity, partially due to her failure to stop the Black Mass Barrier. [*"Black Mass," The Rook Volume One*]

2009 - Ian Morris meets Max Davies and becomes the new Rook. He meets Fiona Grace. Max dies at some point immediately following this. [*"Black Mass," The Rook Volume One*]

2012 - The fourth Rook (Ian Morris) receives the Mayan Tablet from Catalyst, who tells him that the world will end on December 21, 2012 unless something is done. Using the tablet, Ian attempts to take control of the magic spell that will end the world. Aided by the spirits of the three previous Rooks, he succeeds, though it costs him his life. He is survived by his lover (Fiona Grace) and their unborn child. Max Davies is reborn as a man in his late twenties and becomes the Rook again. ["The Four Rooks," The Rook Volume Four]

ABOUT THE AUTHOR

Barry Reese has spent the last decade writing for publishers as diverse as Marvel Comics, West End Games, Wild Cat Books and Moonstone Books. Known primarily for his pulp adventure works like The Rook Chronicles, The Adventures of Lazarus Gray and Savage Tales of Ki-Gor, Barry has also delved into slasher horror (Rabbit Heart) and even the fantasy pirate genre (Guan-Yin and the Horrors of Skull Island). His favorite classic pulp heroes are The Avenger, Doc Savage, John Carter, Conan and Seekay. More information about him can be found at http://www.barryreese.net

Made in the USA
Charleston, SC
25 September 2011